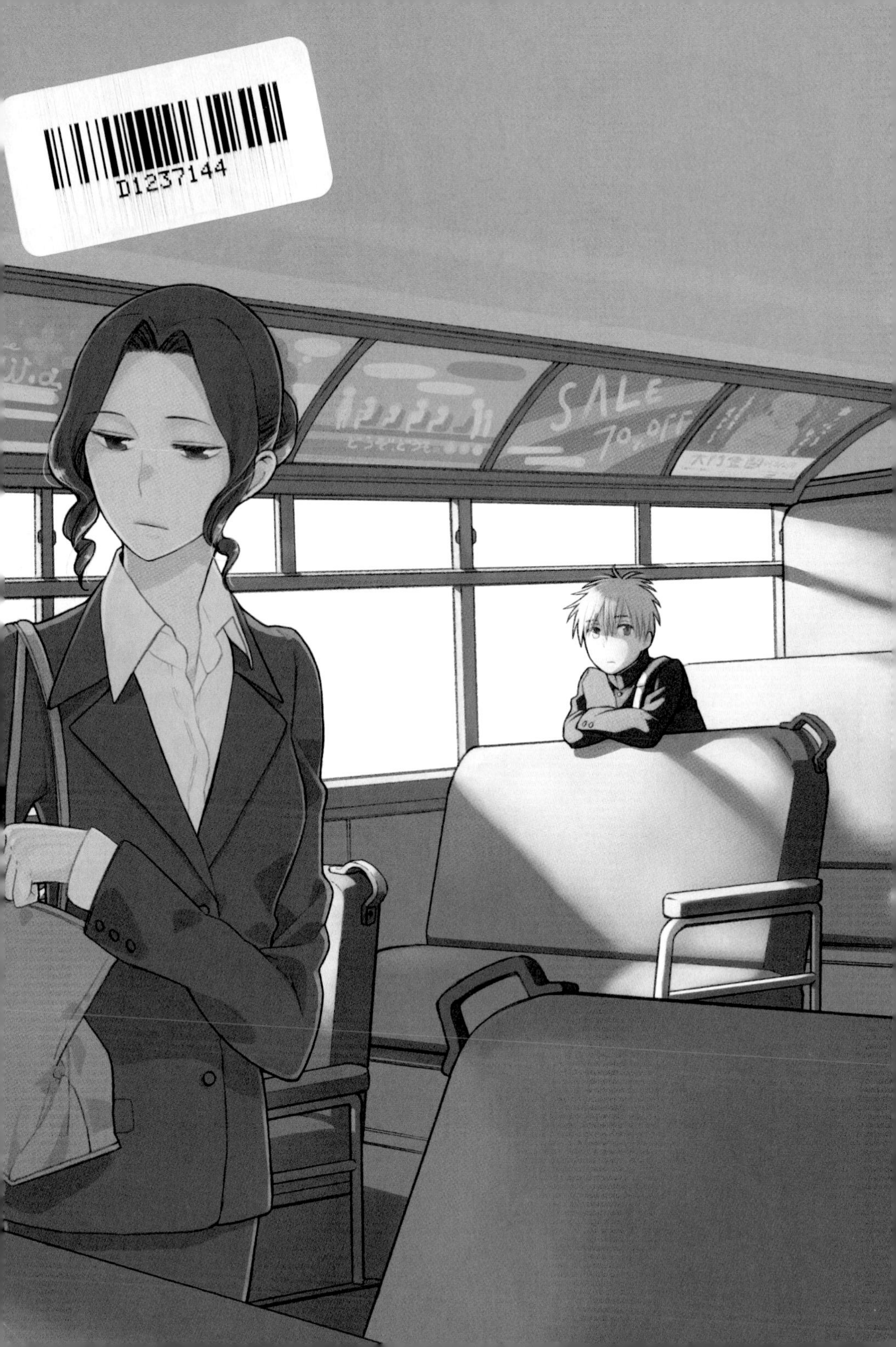
SALE

Contents

SYNOPSIS BY SASAKI-SENSEI, CLASS 2-B'S HOMEROOM TEACHER

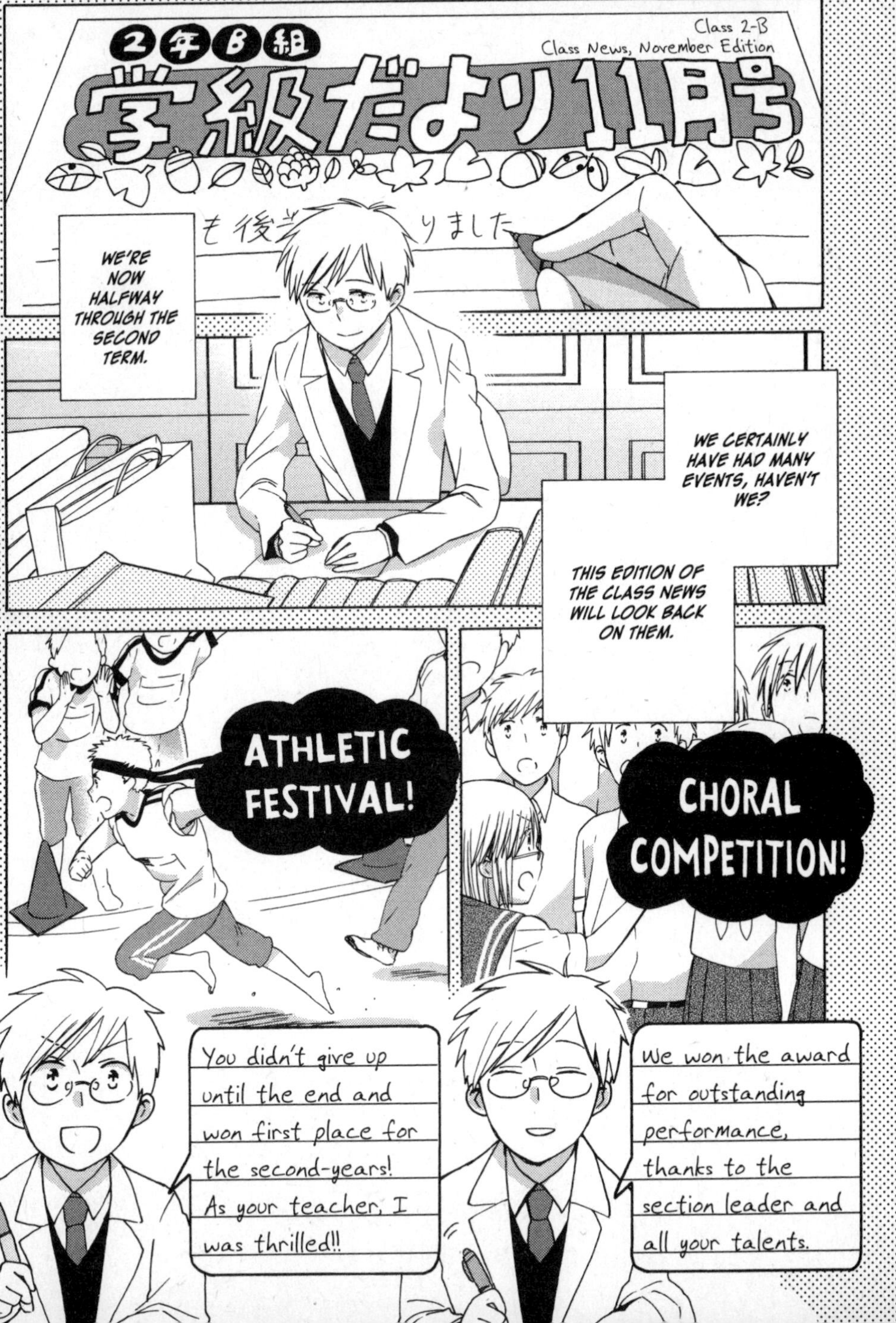
2年B組
学級だより11月号
Class 2-B
Class News, November Edition
WE'RE NOW HALFWAY THROUGH THE SECOND TERM.
WE CERTAINLY HAVE HAD MANY EVENTS, HAVEN'T WE?
THIS EDITION OF THE CLASS NEWS WILL LOOK BACK ON THEM.
CHORAL COMPETITION!
ATHLETIC FESTIVAL!
We won the award for outstanding performance, thanks to the section leader and all your talents.
You didn't give up until the end and won first place for the second-years! As your teacher, I was thrilled!!

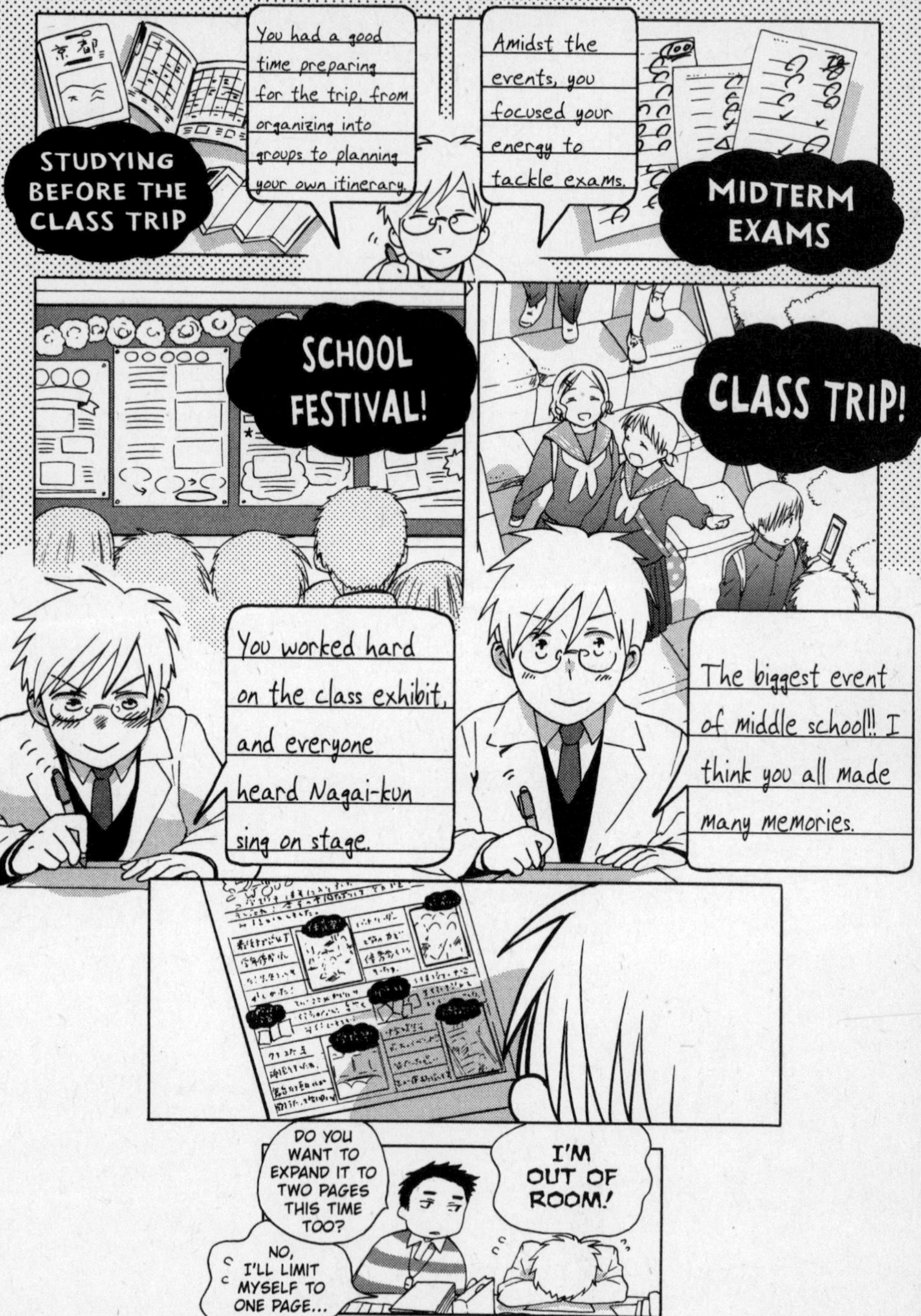
MIDTERM EXAMS
Amidst the events, you focused your energy to tackle exams.
STUDYING BEFORE THE CLASS TRIP
You had a good time preparing for the trip, from organizing into groups to planning your own itinerary.
CLASS TRIP!
The biggest event of middle school!! I think you all made many memories.
SCHOOL FESTIVAL!
You worked hard on the class exhibit, and everyone heard Nagai-kun sing on stage.
I'M OUT OF ROOM!
DO YOU WANT TO EXPAND IT TO TWO PAGES THIS TIME TOO?
NO, I'LL LIMIT MYSELF TO ONE PAGE...

Fin.

Love at Fourteen

[Intermission 36]

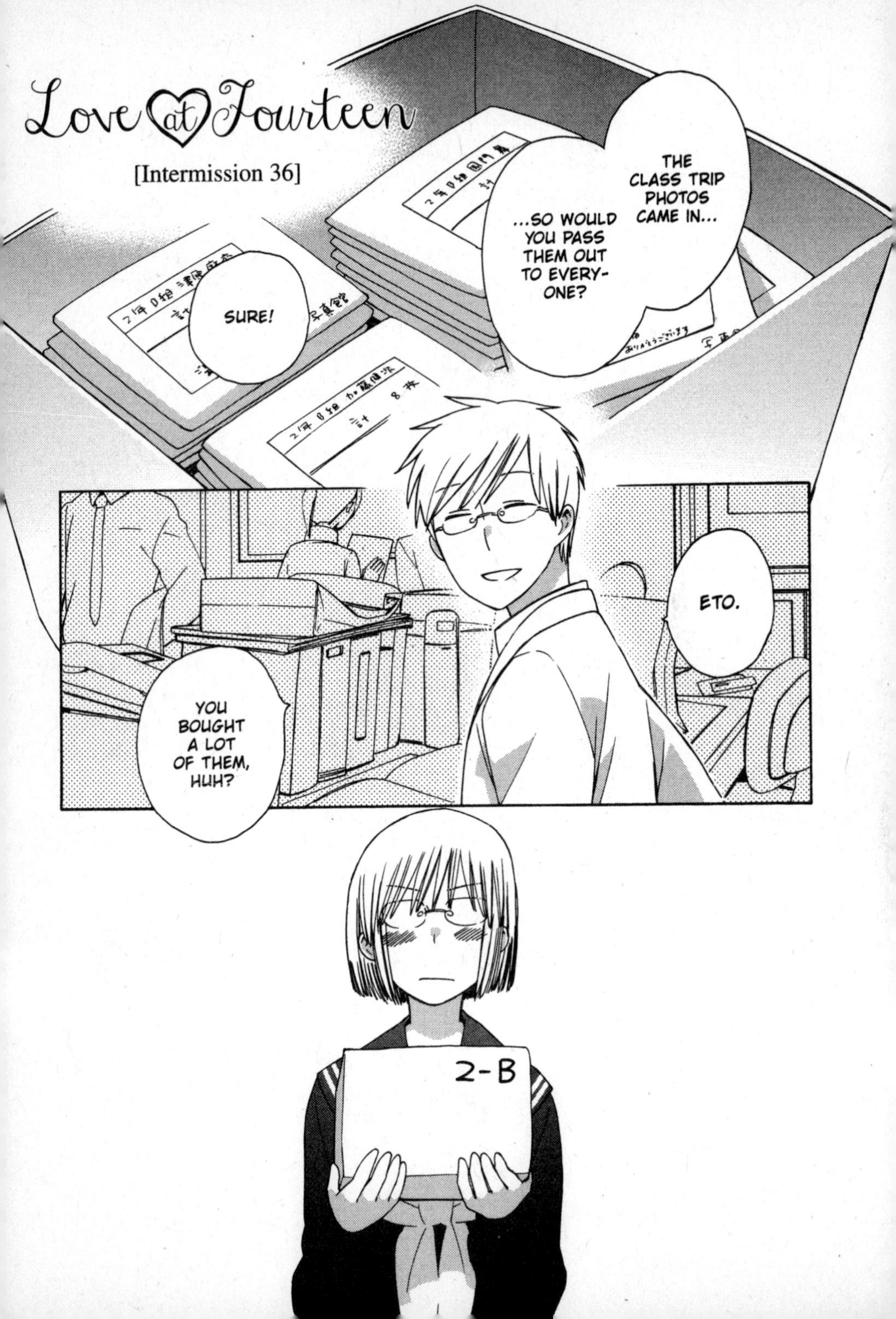
THE CLASS TRIP PHOTOS CAME IN...
...SO WOULD YOU PASS THEM OUT TO EVERY-ONE?
SURE!
ETO.
YOU BOUGHT A LOT OF THEM, HUH?
2-B

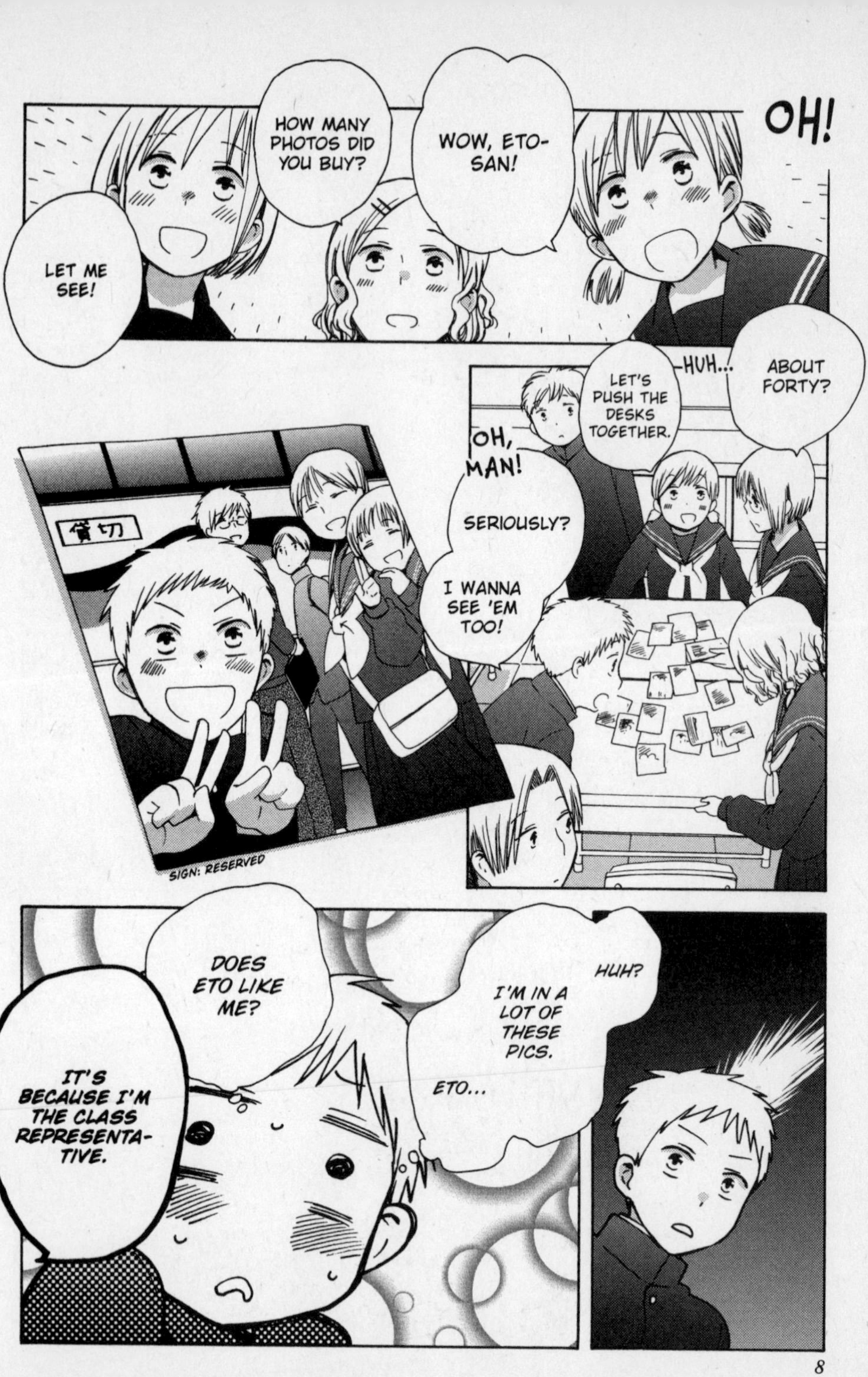
OH!
WOW, ETO-SAN!
HOW MANY PHOTOS DID YOU BUY?
LET ME SEE!
ABOUT FORTY?
HUH...
LET'S PUSH THE DESKS TOGETHER.
OH, MAN!
SERIOUSLY?
I WANNA SEE 'EM TOO!
貸切
SIGN: RESERVED
HUH?
I'M IN A LOT OF THESE PICS.
ETO...
DOES ETO LIKE ME?
IT'S BECAUSE I'M THE CLASS REPRESENTATIVE.

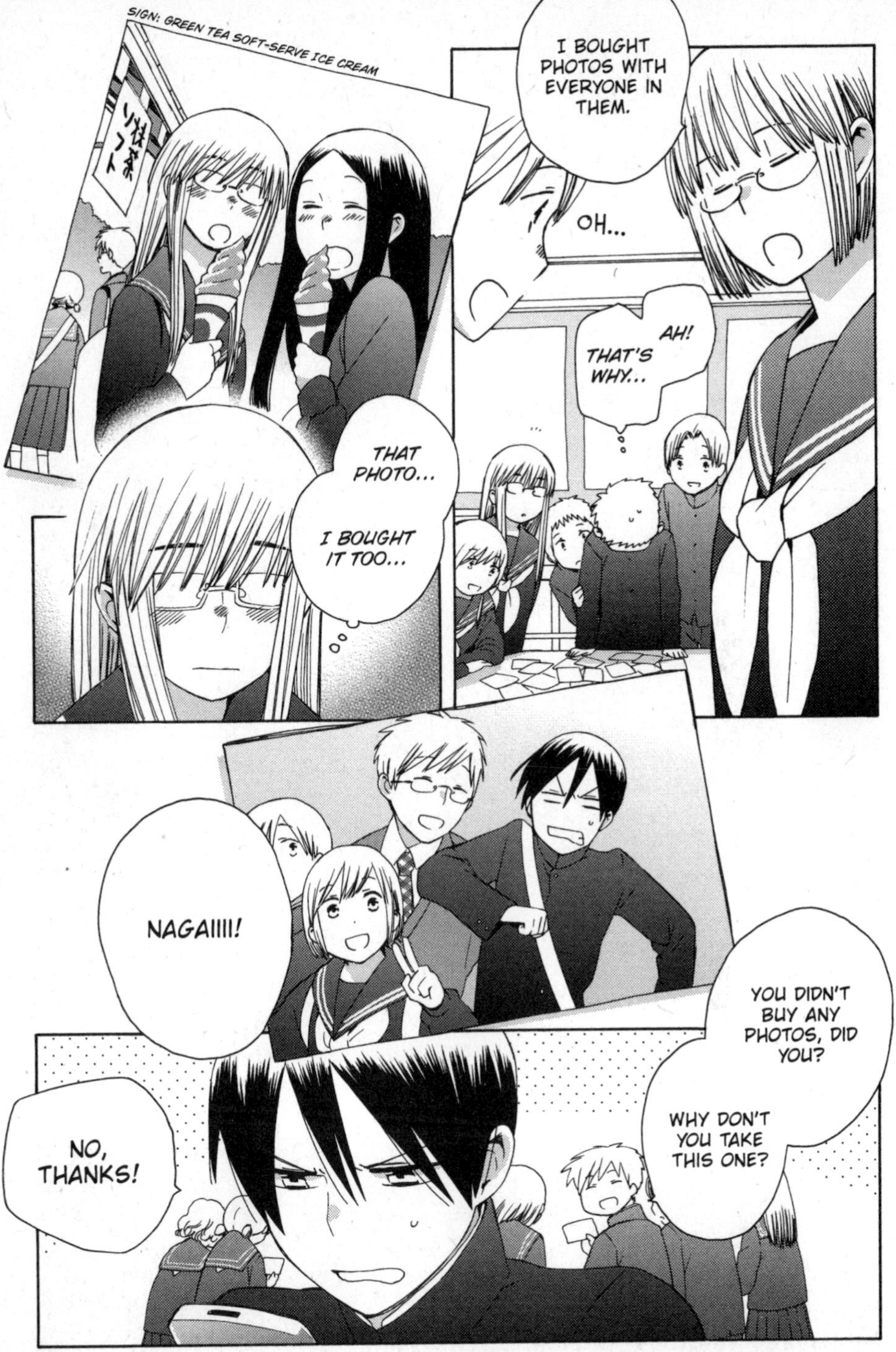
I BOUGHT PHOTOS WITH EVERYONE IN THEM.
OH...
AH! THAT'S WHY...
SIGN: GREEN TEA SOFT-SERVE ICE CREAM
抹茶ソフト
THAT PHOTO...
I BOUGHT IT TOO...
NAGAIIII!
YOU DIDN'T BUY ANY PHOTOS, DID YOU?
WHY DON'T YOU TAKE THIS ONE?
NO, THANKS!

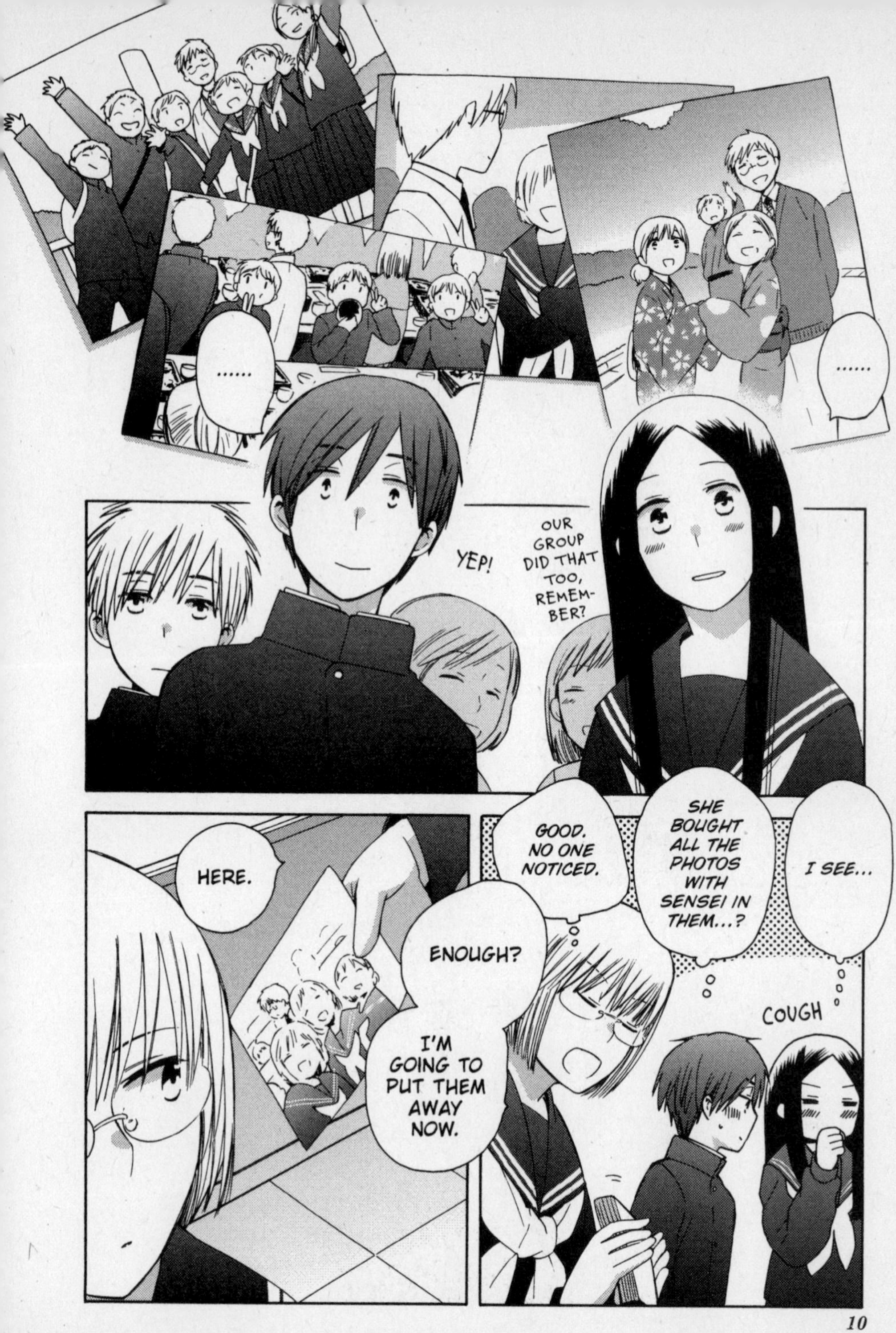
......
......
OUR GROUP DID THAT TOO, REMEMBER?
YEP!
I SEE...
SHE BOUGHT ALL THE PHOTOS WITH SENSEI IN THEM...?
GOOD. NO ONE NOTICED.
COUGH
HERE.
ENOUGH?
I'M GOING TO PUT THEM AWAY NOW.

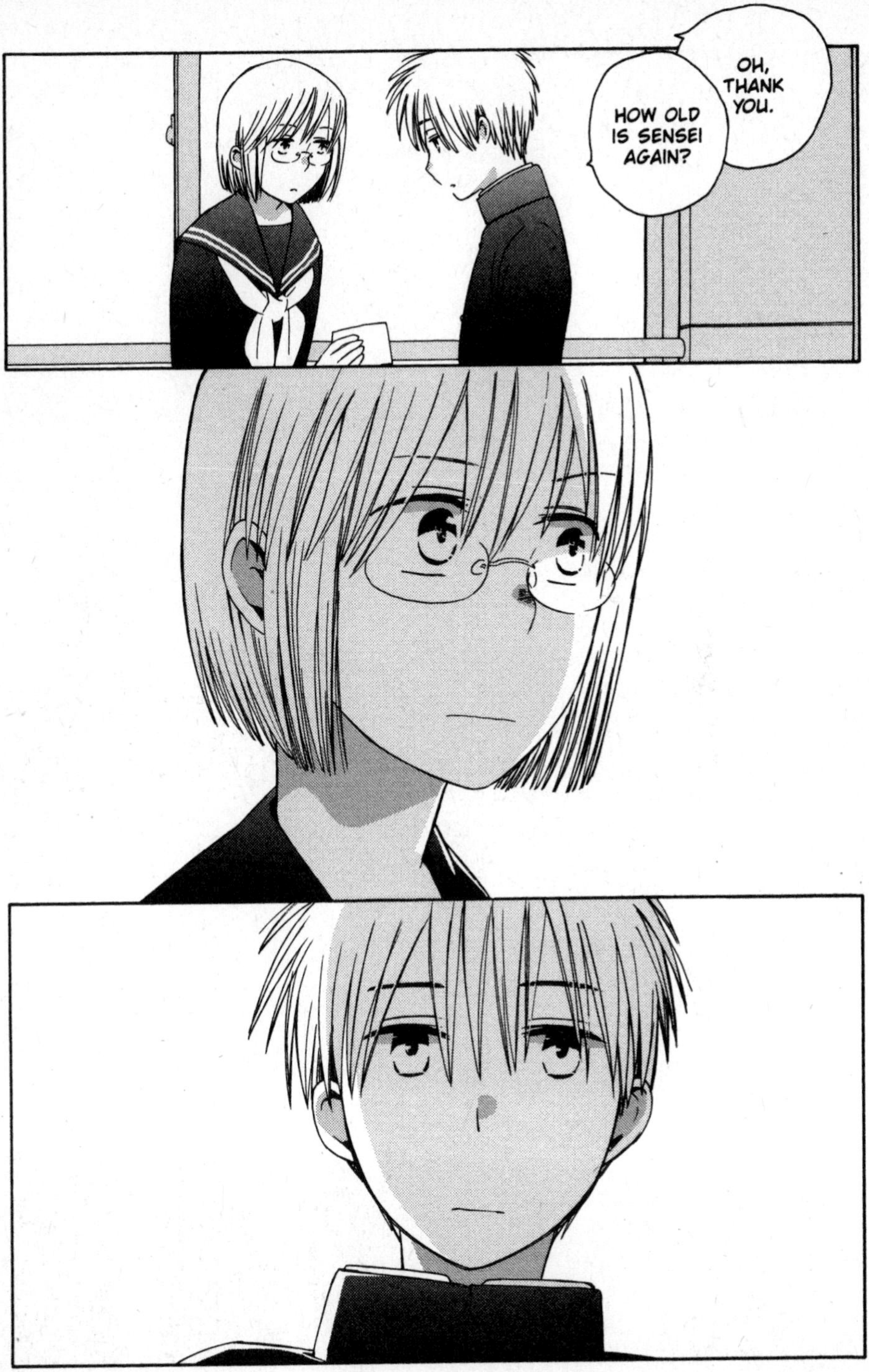
OH, THANK YOU.
HOW OLD IS SENSEI AGAIN?

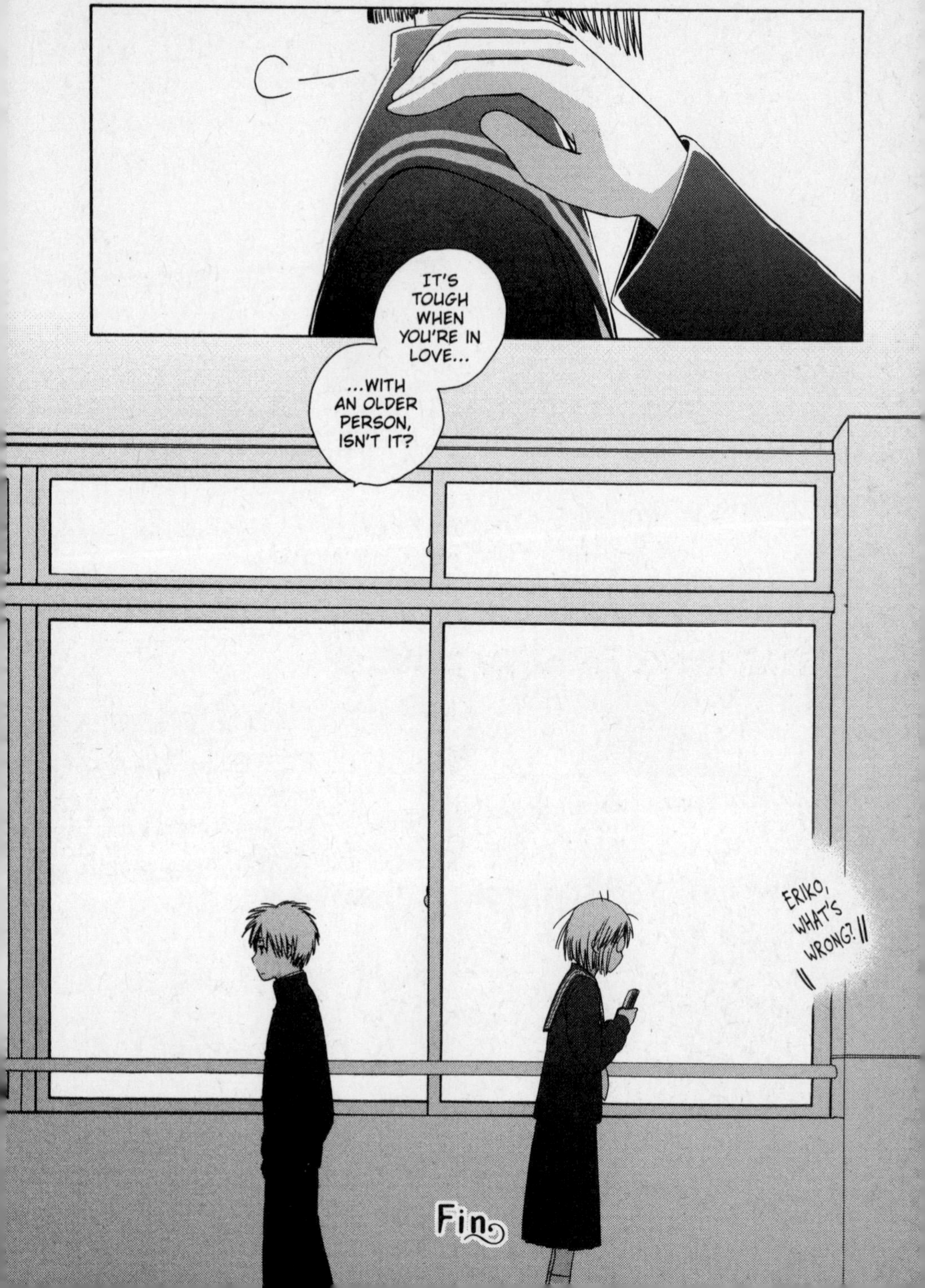
C—
IT'S TOUGH WHEN YOU'RE IN LOVE...
...WITH AN OLDER PERSON, ISN'T IT?
ERIKO, WHAT'S WRONG?
Fin

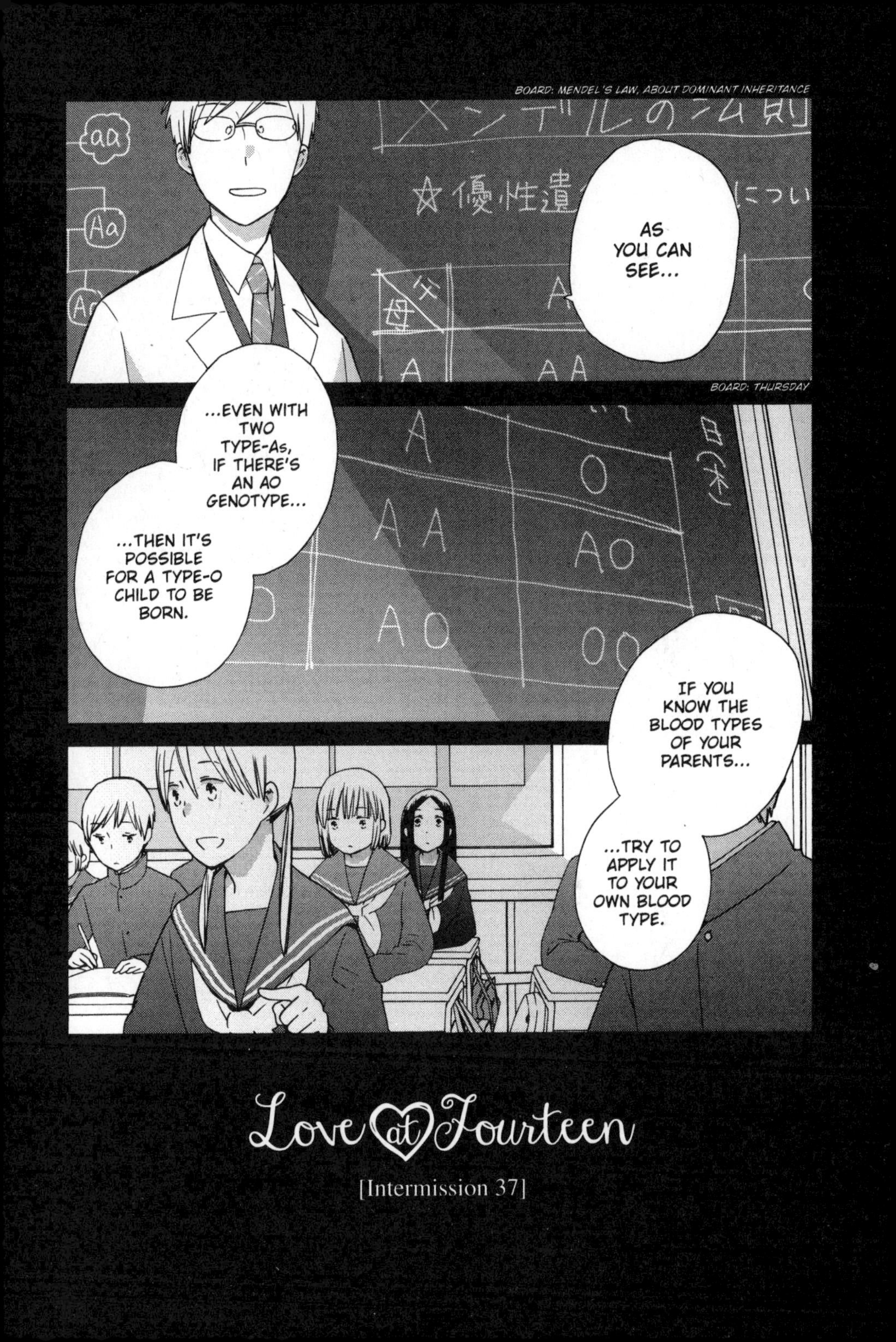
BOARD: MENDEL'S LAW, ABOUT DOMINANT INHERITANCE
AS YOU CAN SEE...
BOARD: THURSDAY
...EVEN WITH TWO TYPE-As, IF THERE'S AN AO GENOTYPE...
...THEN IT'S POSSIBLE FOR A TYPE-O CHILD TO BE BORN.
IF YOU KNOW THE BLOOD TYPES OF YOUR PARENTS...
...TRY TO APPLY IT TO YOUR OWN BLOOD TYPE.

Love at Fourteen

[Intermission 37]

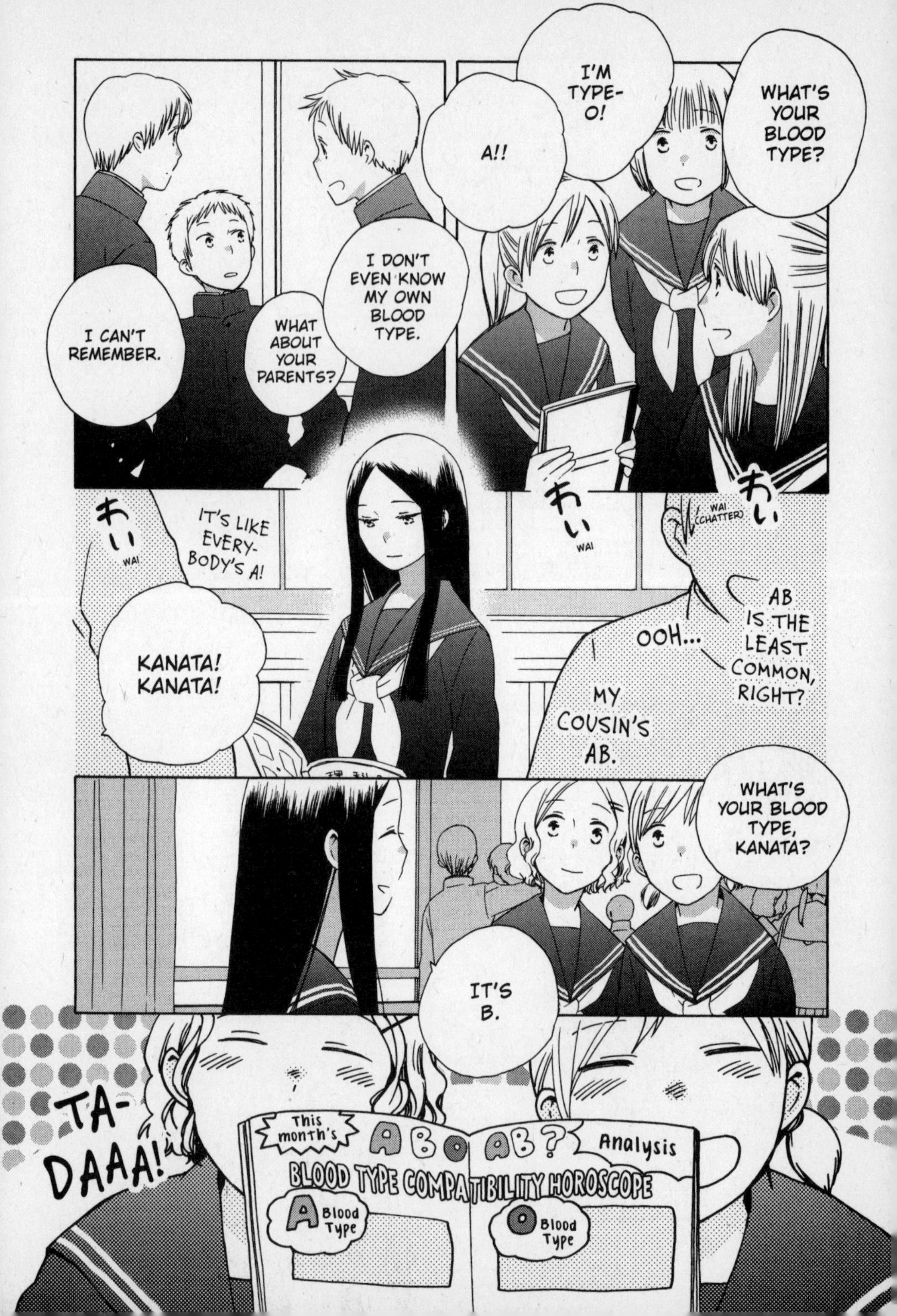
WHAT'S YOUR BLOOD TYPE?
I'M TYPE-O!
A!!
I DON'T EVEN KNOW MY OWN BLOOD TYPE.
WHAT ABOUT YOUR PARENTS?
I CAN'T REMEMBER.
わい WAI (CHATTER)
わい WAI
AB IS THE LEAST COMMON, RIGHT?
OOH...
MY COUSIN'S AB.
わい WAI
IT'S LIKE EVERYBODY'S A!
KANATA! KANATA!
WHAT'S YOUR BLOOD TYPE, KANATA?
IT'S B.
TA-DAAA!
This month's A B O AB? Analysis
BLOOD TYPE COMPATIBILITY HOROSCOPE
A Blood Type
O Blood Type

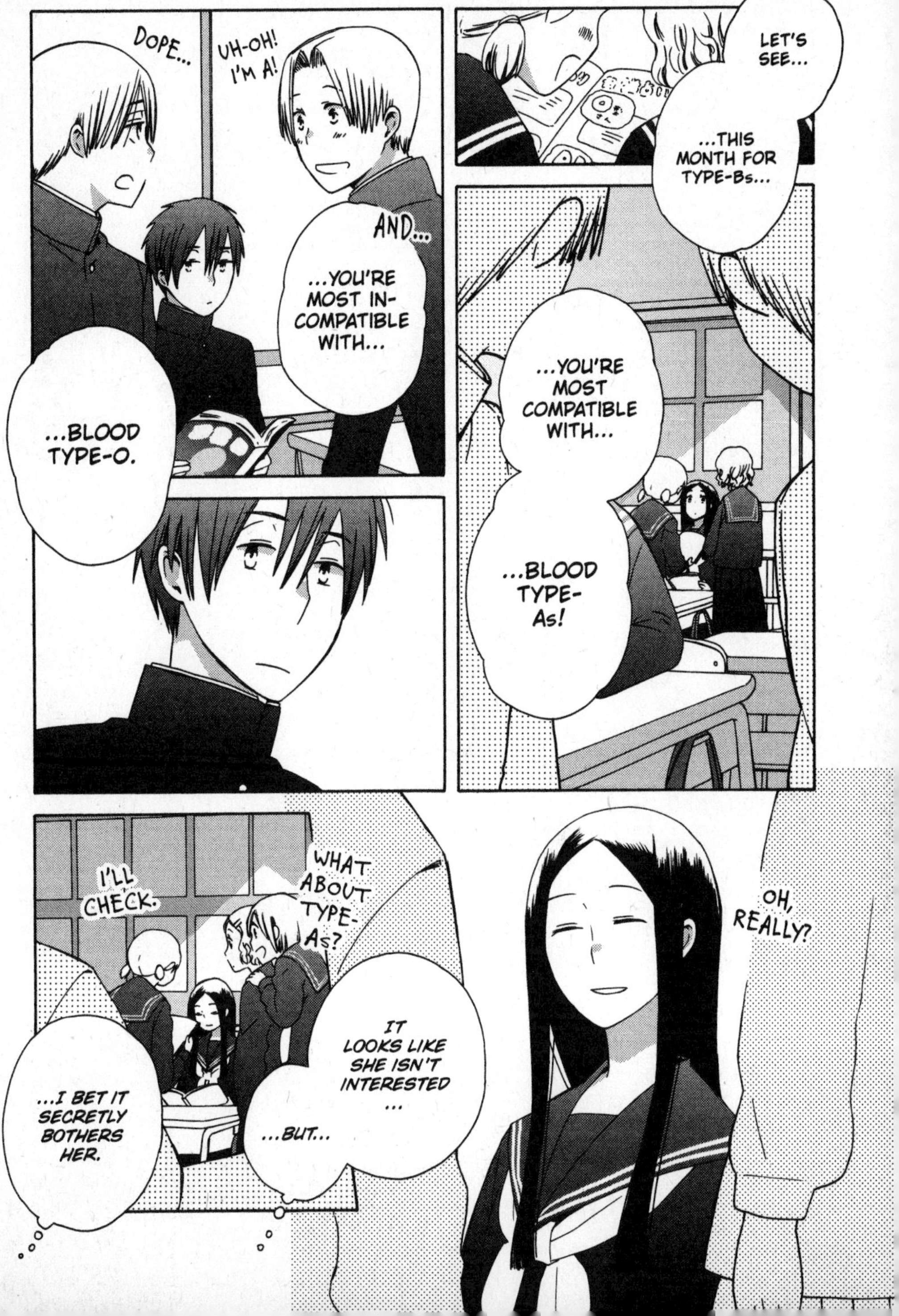
LET'S SEE...
...THIS MONTH FOR TYPE-Bs...
...YOU'RE MOST COMPATIBLE WITH...
...BLOOD TYPE-As!
UH-OH! I'M A!
DOPE...
AND...
...YOU'RE MOST IN-COMPATIBLE WITH...
...BLOOD TYPE-O.
OH, REALLY?
WHAT ABOUT TYPE-As?
I'LL CHECK.
IT LOOKS LIKE SHE ISN'T INTERESTED ...
...BUT...
...I BET IT SECRETLY BOTHERS HER.

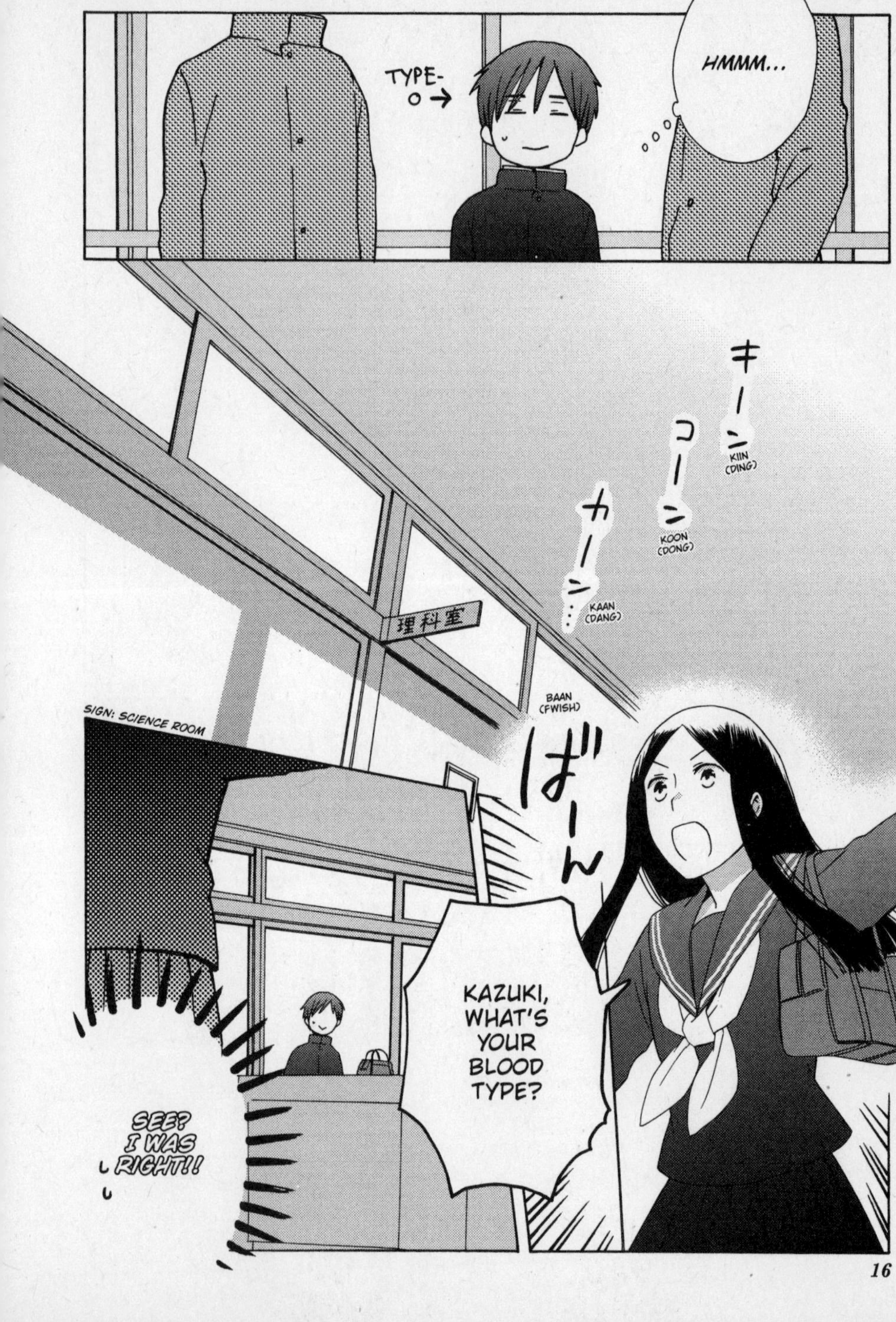
HMMM...
TYPE-O →
キーン
KIIN (DING)
コーン
KOON (DONG)
カーン…
KAAN (DANG)
理科室
SIGN: SCIENCE ROOM
BAAN (FWISH)
ばーん
KAZUKI, WHAT'S YOUR BLOOD TYPE?
SEE? I WAS RIGHT!!

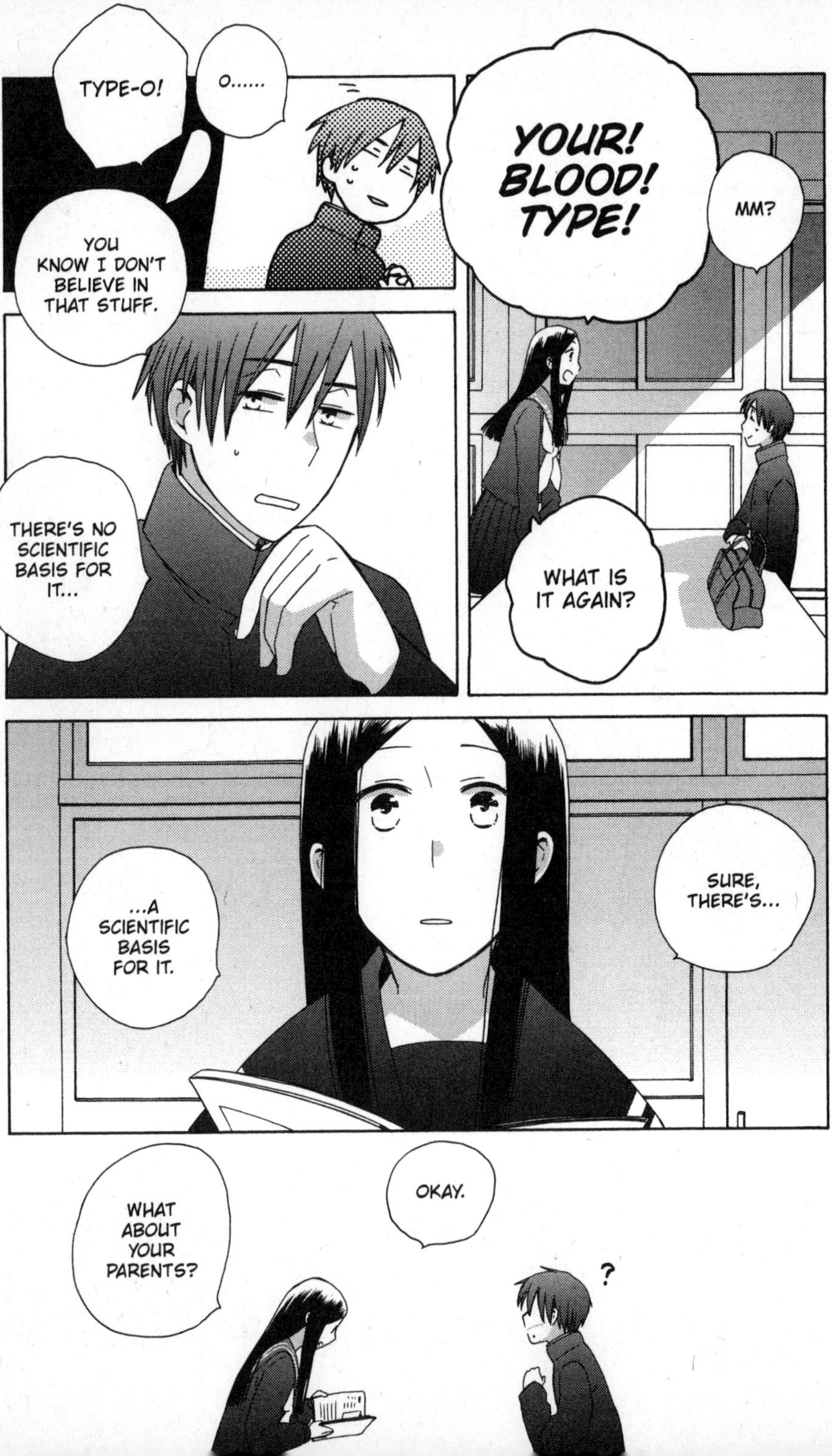
YOUR! BLOOD! TYPE!
MM?
WHAT IS IT AGAIN?
O......
TYPE-O!
YOU KNOW I DON'T BELIEVE IN THAT STUFF.
THERE'S NO SCIENTIFIC BASIS FOR IT...
SURE, THERE'S...
...A SCIENTIFIC BASIS FOR IT.
OKAY.
WHAT ABOUT YOUR PARENTS?
?

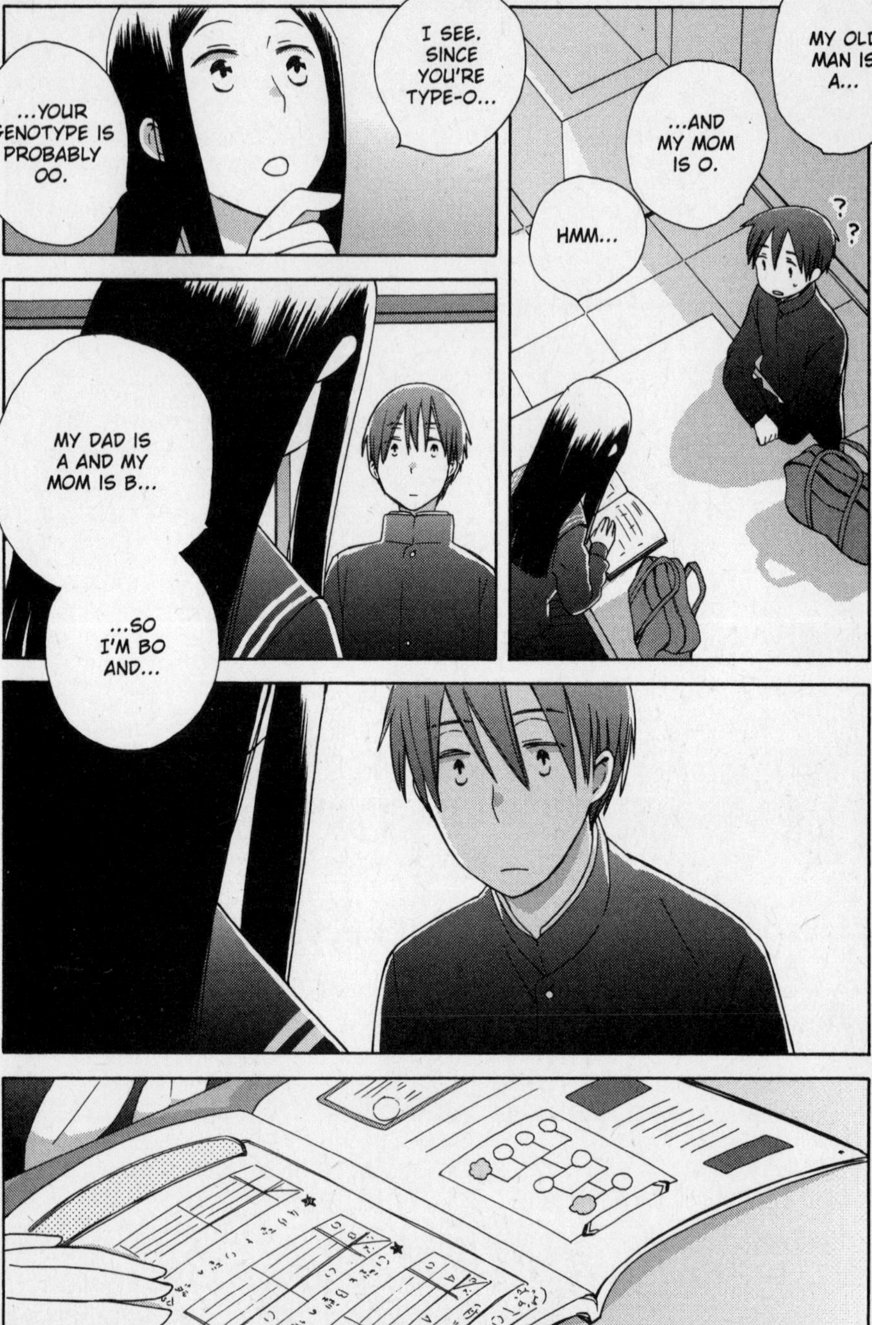
MY OLD MAN IS A...
...AND MY MOM IS O.
HMM...
I SEE. SINCE YOU'RE TYPE-O...
...YOUR GENOTYPE IS PROBABLY OO.
MY DAD IS A AND MY MOM IS B...
...SO I'M BO AND...

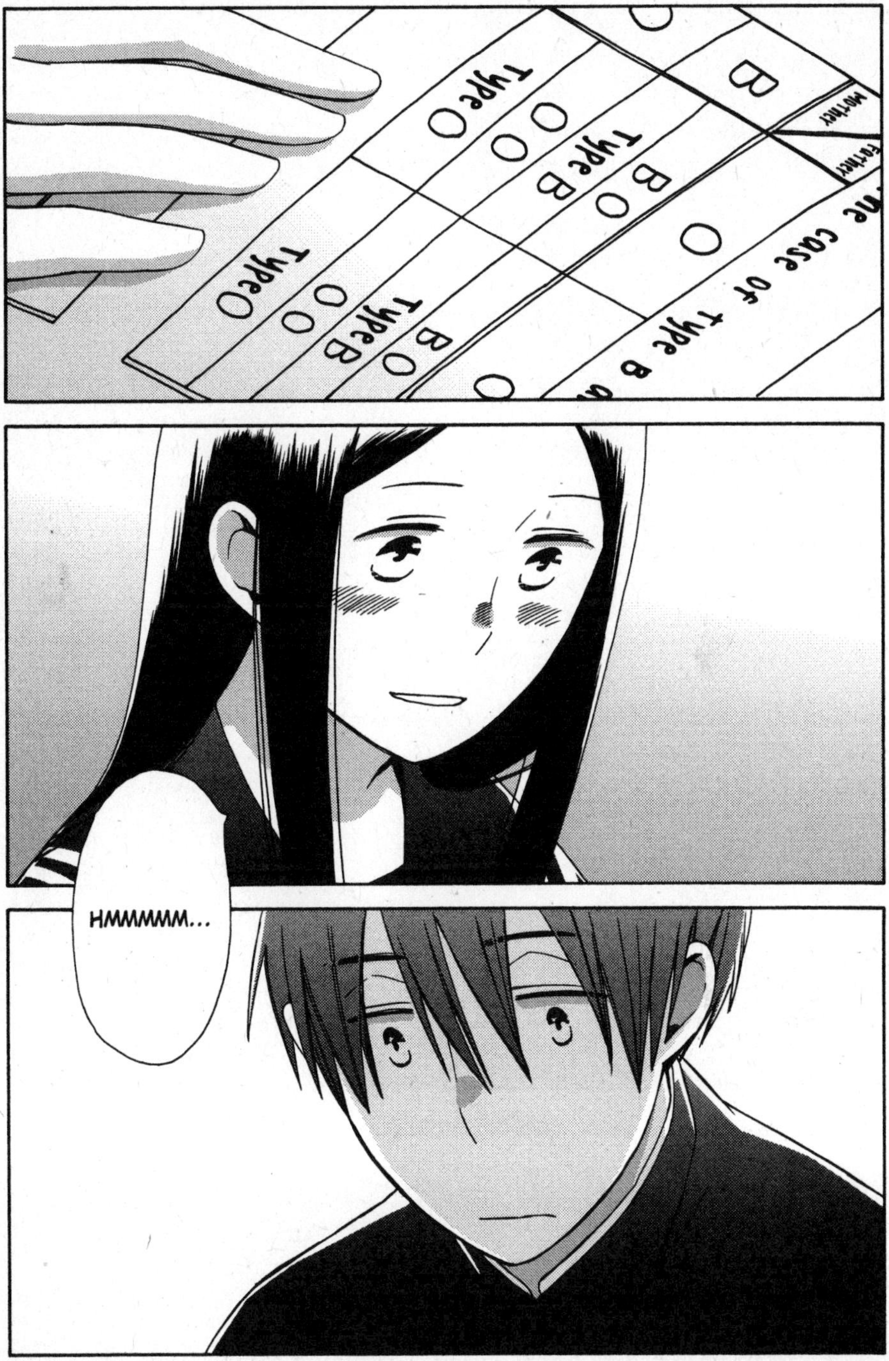
The case of type B a
Father
Mother
B
O
BO
Type B
OO
TypeO
O
BO
Type B
OO
TypeO
HMMMMM...

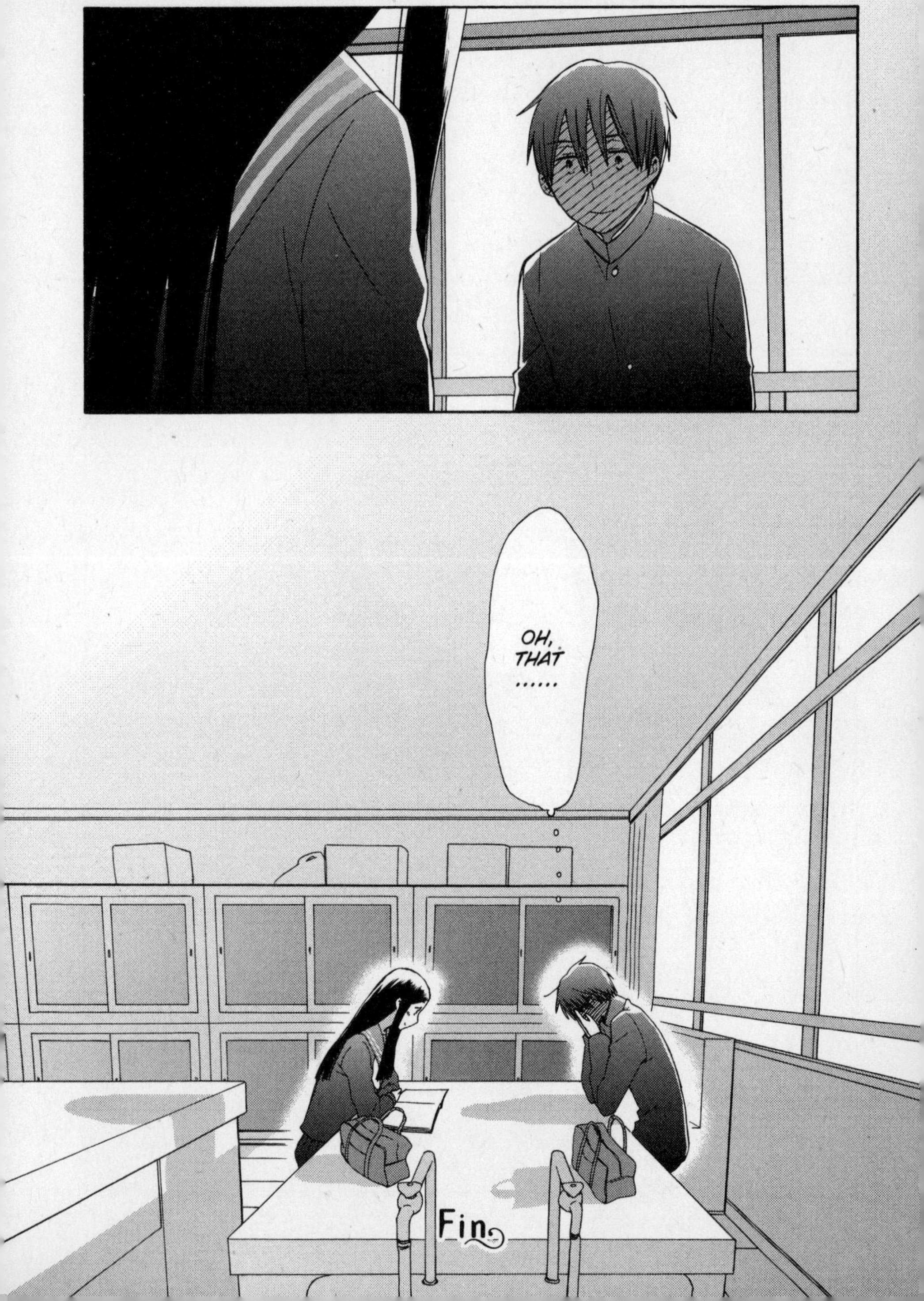
OH, THAT ......
Fin.

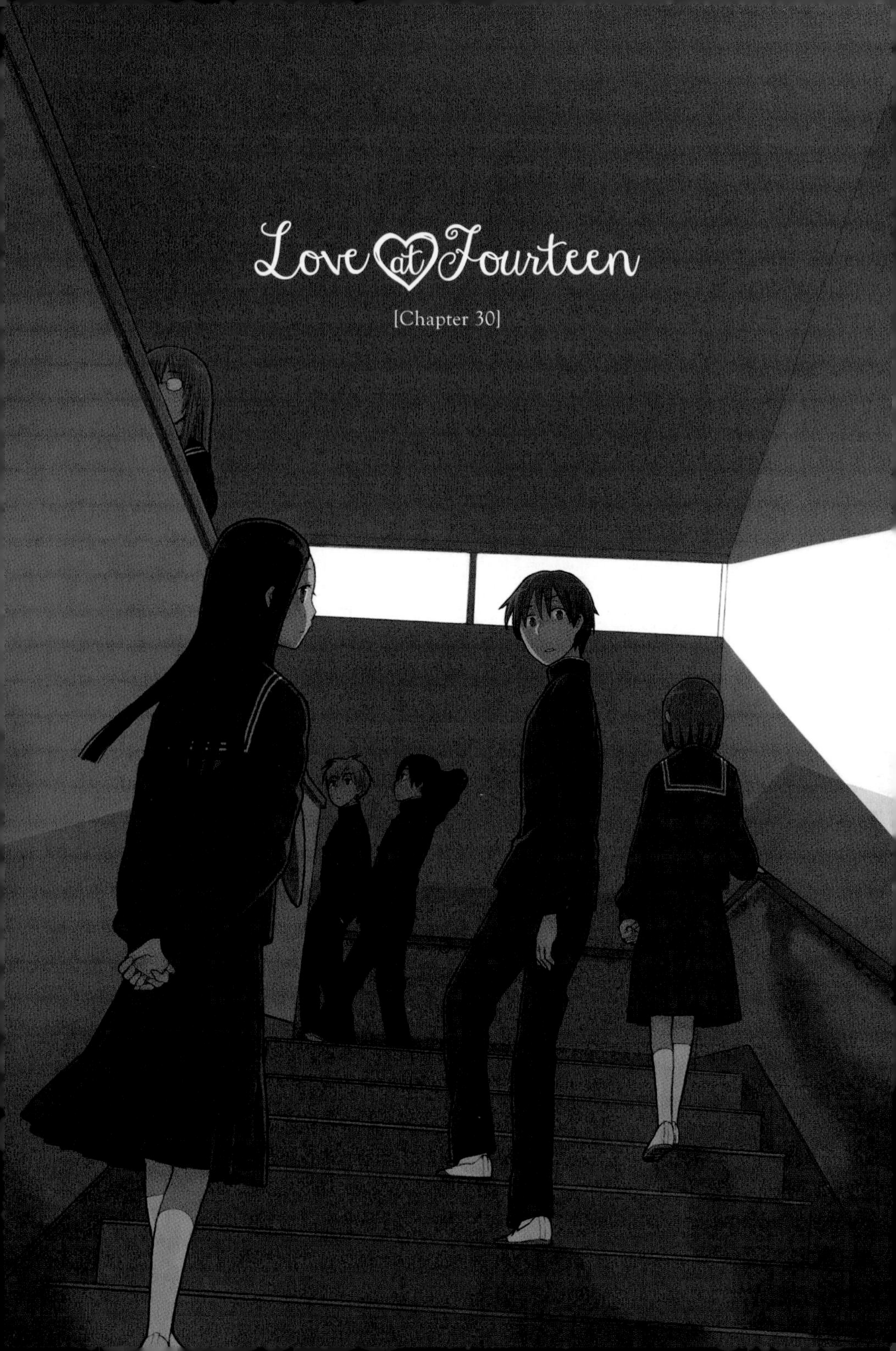
Love at Fourteen
[Chapter 30]

CLASS 2-B'S...

...KANATA TANAKA AND KAZUKI YOSHIKAWA ARE RATHER MATURE.

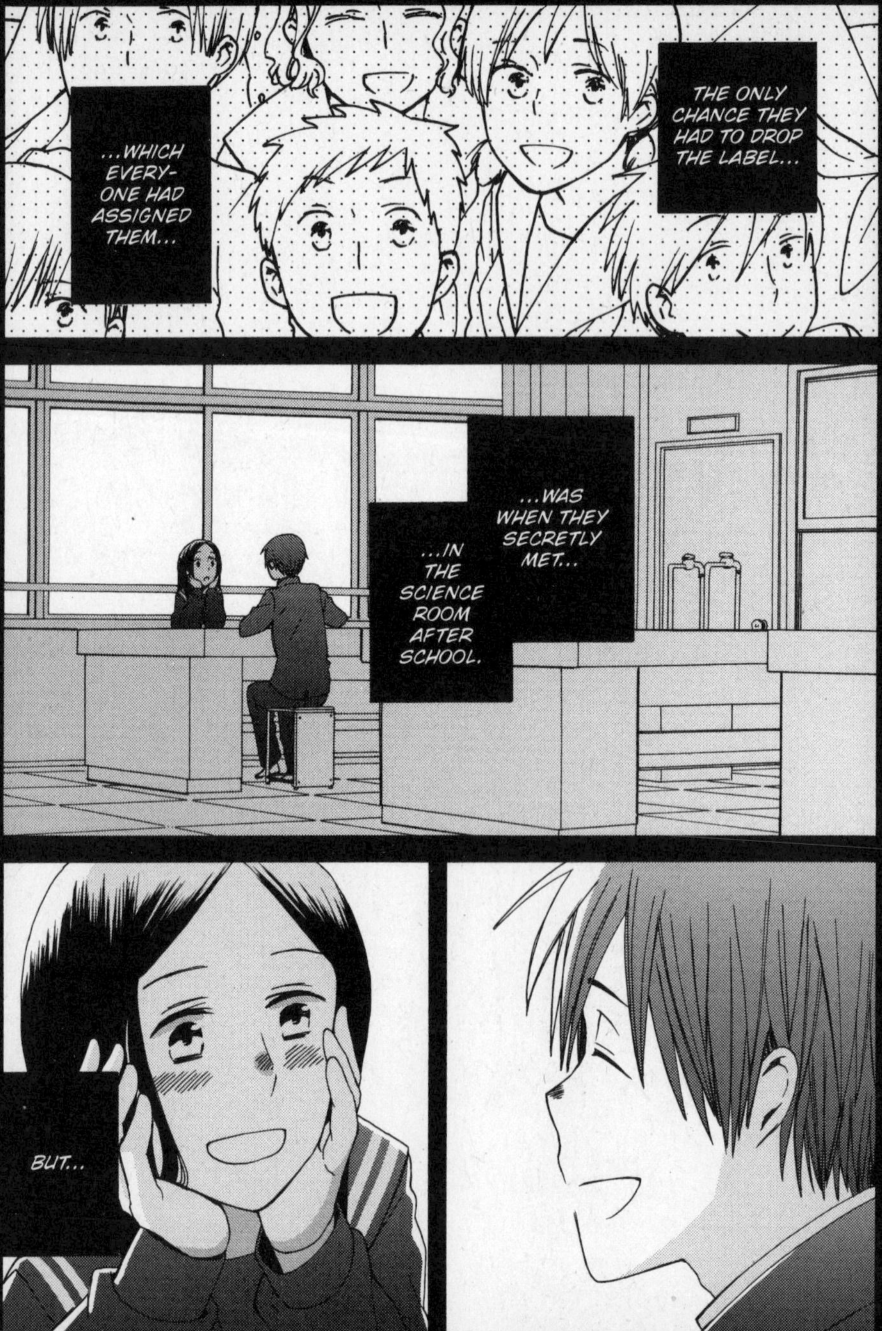
THE ONLY CHANCE THEY HAD TO DROP THE LABEL...
...WHICH EVERY-ONE HAD ASSIGNED THEM...
...WAS WHEN THEY SECRETLY MET...
...IN THE SCIENCE ROOM AFTER SCHOOL.
BUT...

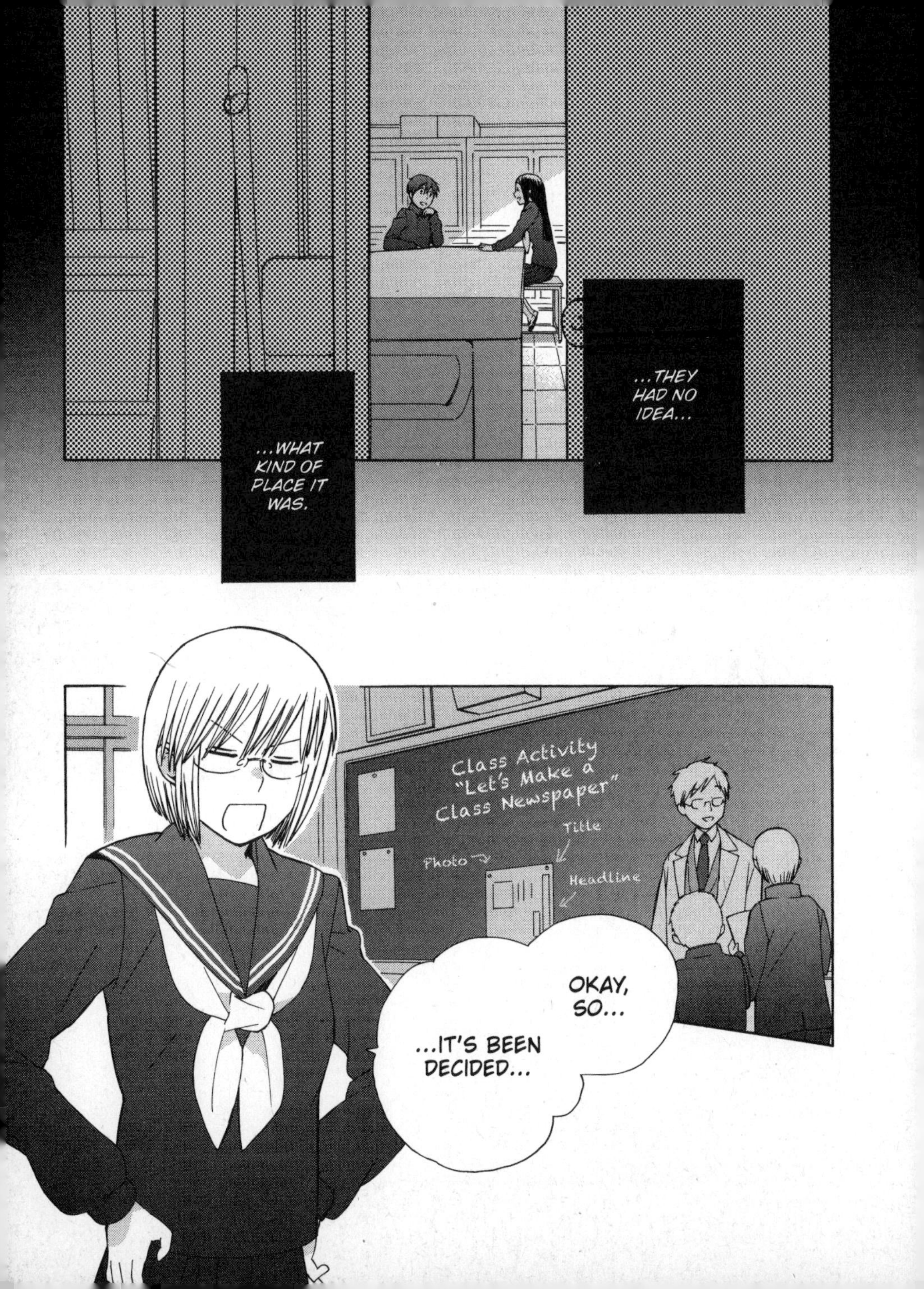
...THEY HAD NO IDEA...
...WHAT KIND OF PLACE IT WAS.
Class Activity "Let's Make a Class Newspaper"
Title
Photo
Headline
OKAY, SO...
...IT'S BEEN DECIDED...

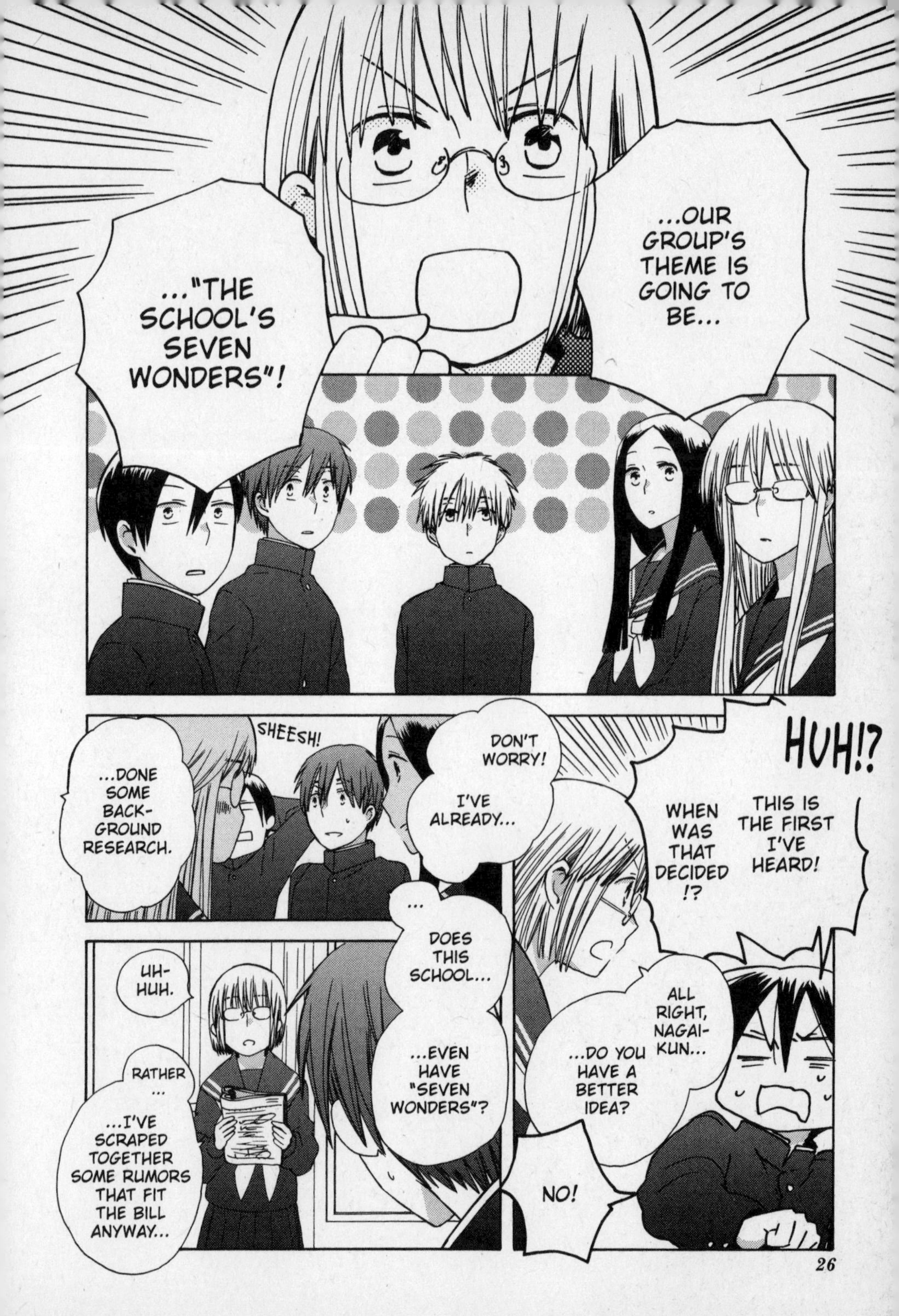
...OUR GROUP'S THEME IS GOING TO BE...
..."THE SCHOOL'S SEVEN WONDERS"!
HUH!?
THIS IS THE FIRST I'VE HEARD!
WHEN WAS THAT DECIDED!?
DON'T WORRY!
I'VE ALREADY...
SHEESH!
...DONE SOME BACK-GROUND RESEARCH.
ALL RIGHT, NAGAI-KUN...
...DO YOU HAVE A BETTER IDEA?
NO!
...
DOES THIS SCHOOL...
...EVEN HAVE "SEVEN WONDERS"?
UH-HUH.
RATHER...
...I'VE SCRAPED TOGETHER SOME RUMORS THAT FIT THE BILL ANYWAY...

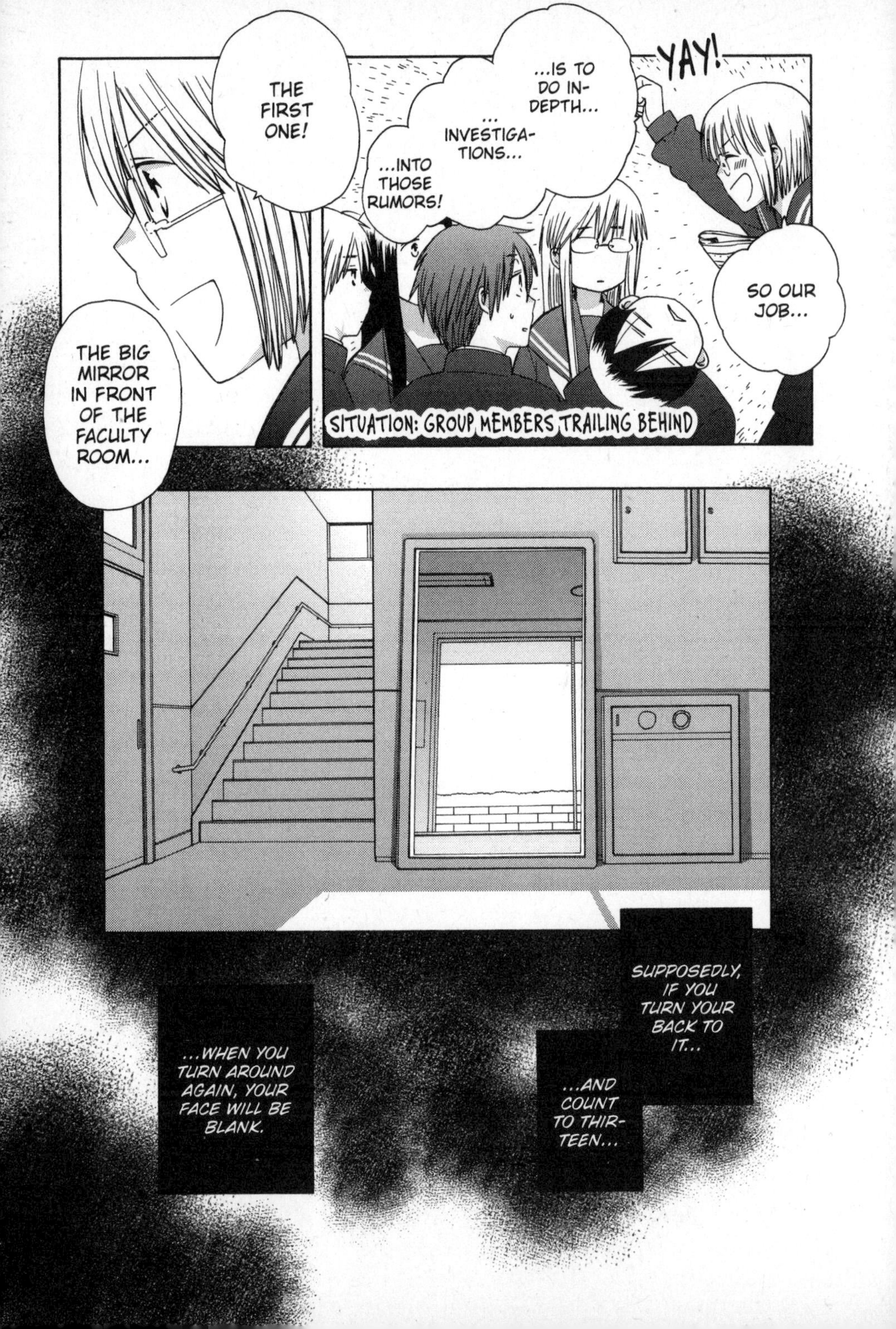
YAY!
SO OUR JOB...
...IS TO DO IN-DEPTH...
...INVESTIGATIONS...
...INTO THOSE RUMORS!
SITUATION: GROUP MEMBERS TRAILING BEHIND
THE FIRST ONE!
THE BIG MIRROR IN FRONT OF THE FACULTY ROOM...
SUPPOSEDLY, IF YOU TURN YOUR BACK TO IT...
...AND COUNT TO THIRTEEN...
...WHEN YOU TURN AROUND AGAIN, YOUR FACE WILL BE BLANK.

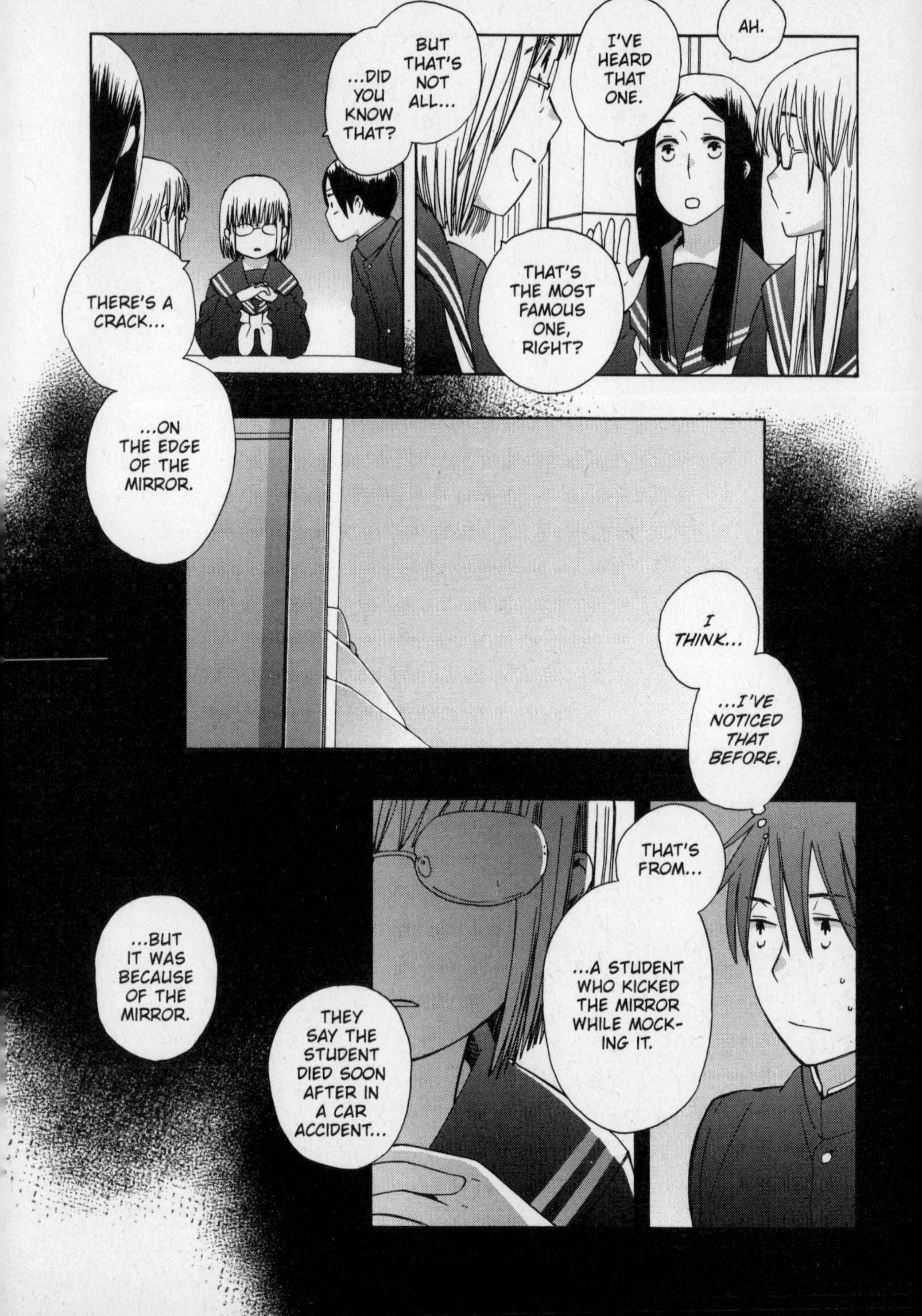
AH.
I'VE HEARD THAT ONE.
THAT'S THE MOST FAMOUS ONE, RIGHT?
BUT THAT'S NOT ALL...
...DID YOU KNOW THAT?
THERE'S A CRACK...
...ON THE EDGE OF THE MIRROR.
I THINK...
...I'VE NOTICED THAT BEFORE.
THAT'S FROM...
...A STUDENT WHO KICKED THE MIRROR WHILE MOCK-ING IT.
THEY SAY THE STUDENT DIED SOON AFTER IN A CAR ACCIDENT...
...BUT IT WAS BECAUSE OF THE MIRROR.

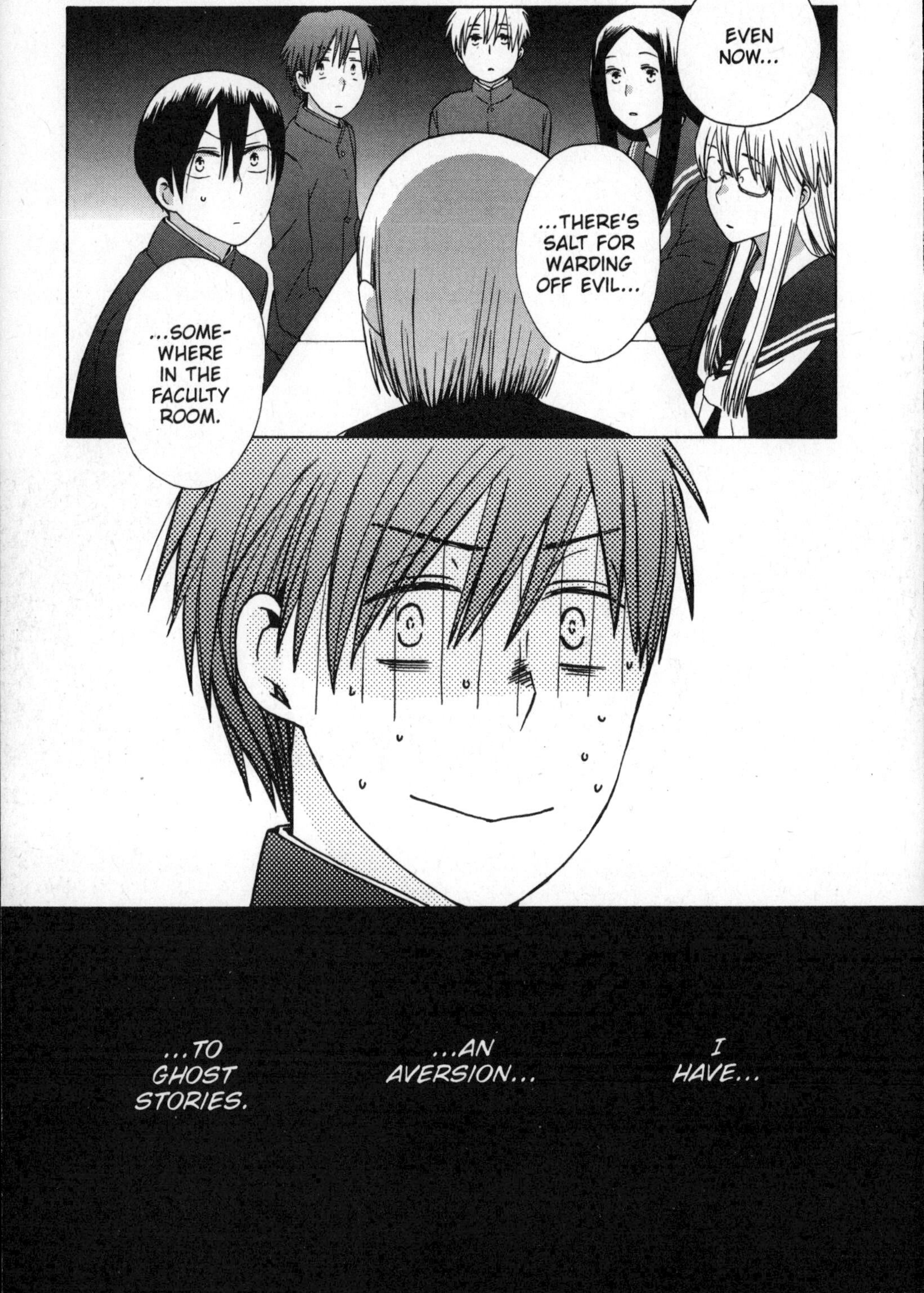
EVEN NOW...
...THERE'S SALT FOR WARDING OFF EVIL...
...SOME-WHERE IN THE FACULTY ROOM.
I HAVE...
...AN AVERSION...
...TO GHOST STORIES.

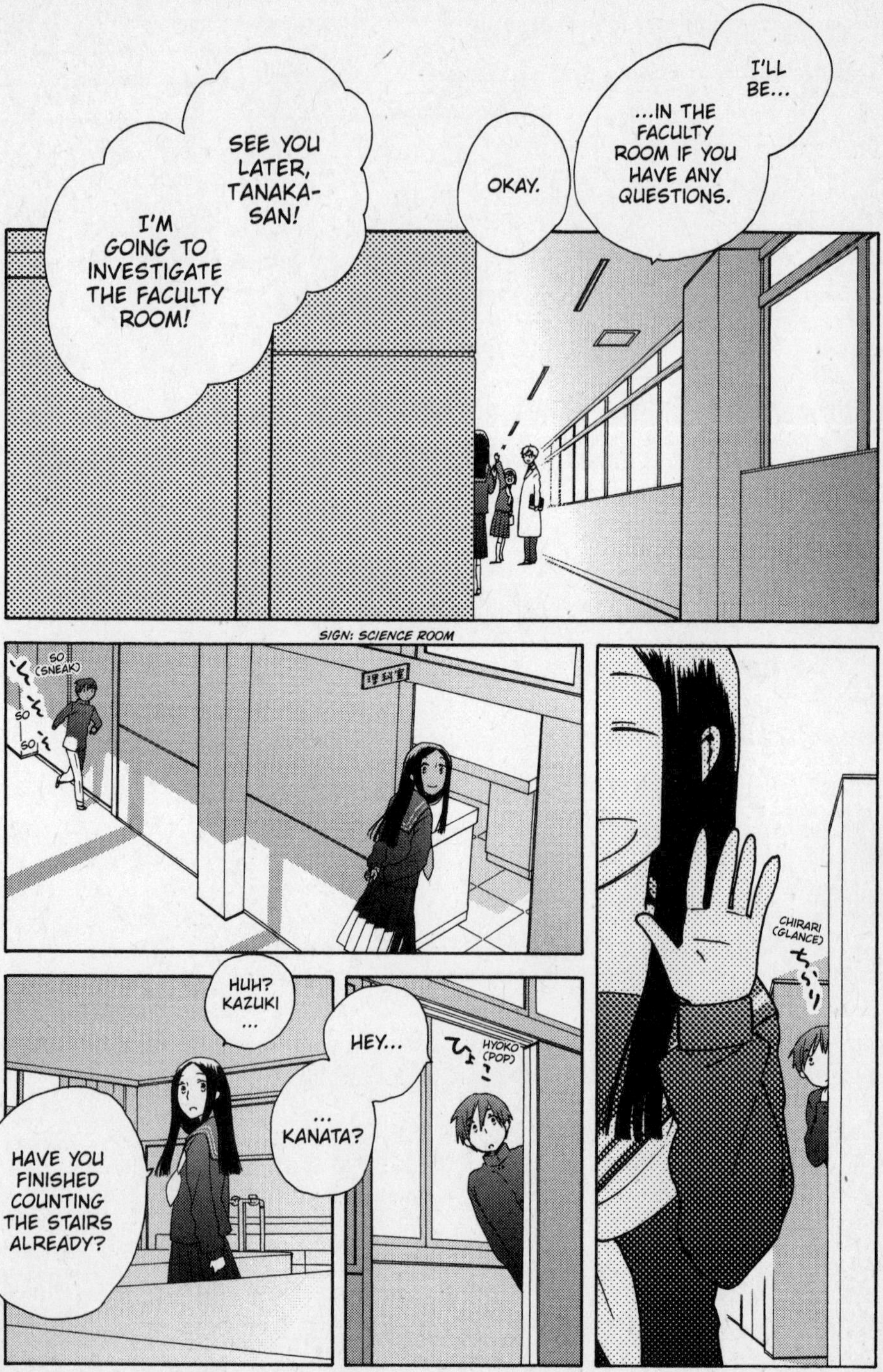
I'LL BE...
...IN THE FACULTY ROOM IF YOU HAVE ANY QUESTIONS.
OKAY.
SEE YOU LATER, TANAKA-SAN!
I'M GOING TO INVESTIGATE THE FACULTY ROOM!
CHIRARI (GLANCE)
ちらり
SIGN: SCIENCE ROOM
理科室
SO (SNEAK)
SO
SO
HYOKO (POP)
ひょこ
HEY...
...KANATA?
HUH? KAZUKI...
HAVE YOU FINISHED COUNTING THE STAIRS ALREADY?

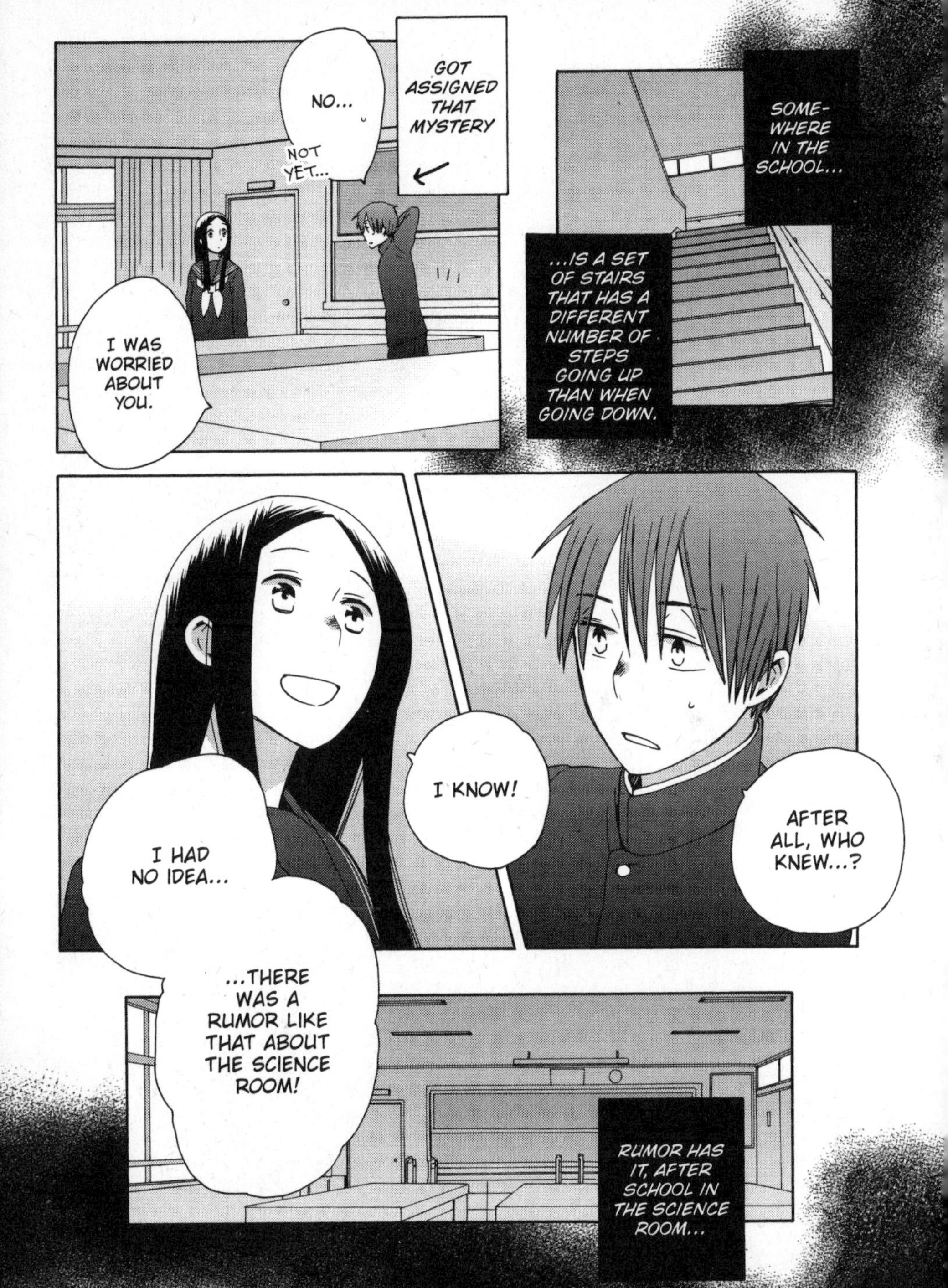
SOME-WHERE IN THE SCHOOL...
...IS A SET OF STAIRS THAT HAS A DIFFERENT NUMBER OF STEPS GOING UP THAN WHEN GOING DOWN.
GOT ASSIGNED THAT MYSTERY
NO...
NOT YET...
I WAS WORRIED ABOUT YOU.
AFTER ALL, WHO KNEW...?
I KNOW!
I HAD NO IDEA...
...THERE WAS A RUMOR LIKE THAT ABOUT THE SCIENCE ROOM!
RUMOR HAS IT, AFTER SCHOOL IN THE SCIENCE ROOM...

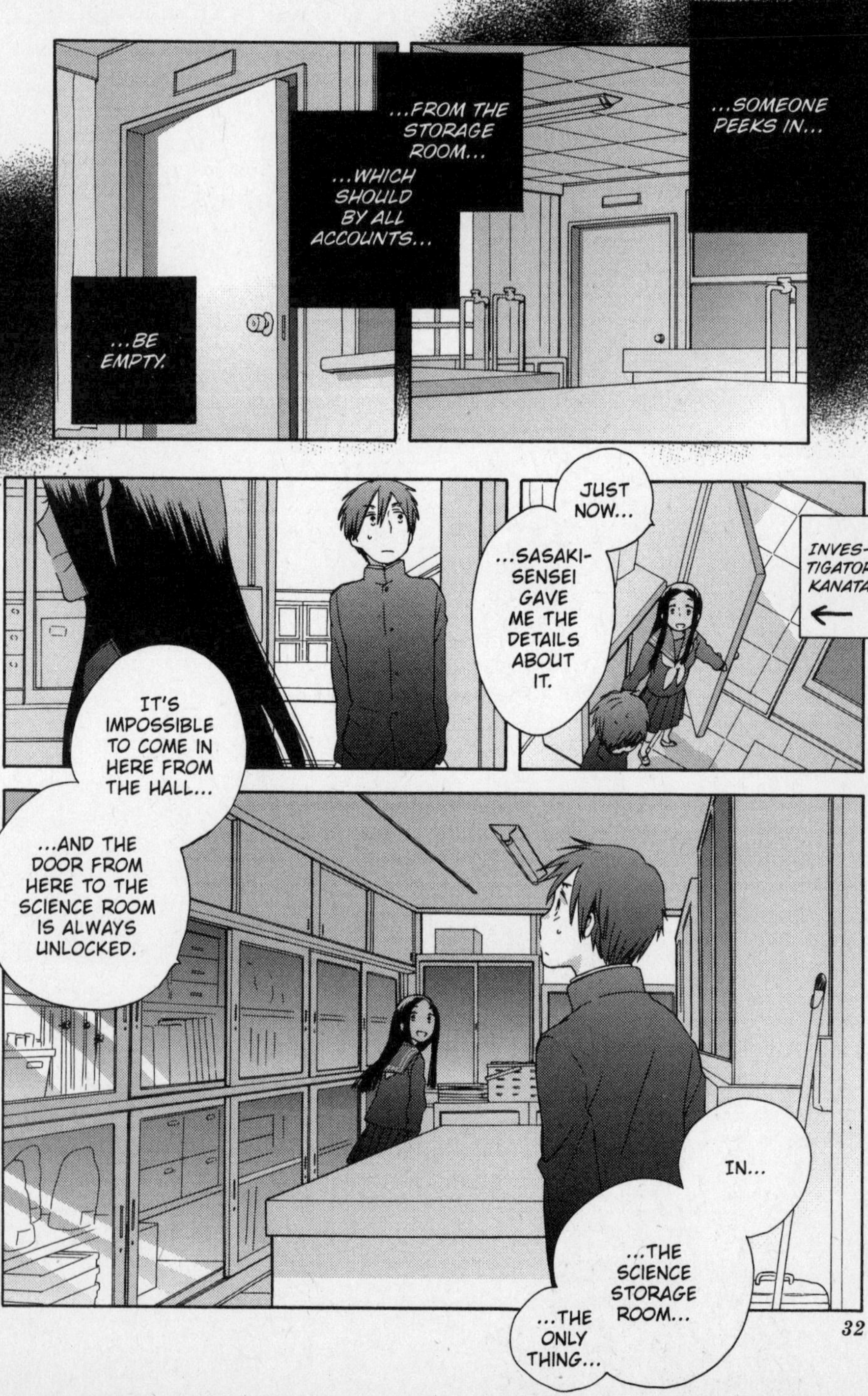
...SOMEONE PEEKS IN...
...FROM THE STORAGE ROOM...
...WHICH SHOULD BY ALL ACCOUNTS...
...BE EMPTY.
JUST NOW...
...SASAKI-SENSEI GAVE ME THE DETAILS ABOUT IT.
INVES-TIGATOR KANATA ←
IT'S IMPOSSIBLE TO COME IN HERE FROM THE HALL...
...AND THE DOOR FROM HERE TO THE SCIENCE ROOM IS ALWAYS UNLOCKED.
IN...
...THE SCIENCE STORAGE ROOM...
...THE ONLY THING...

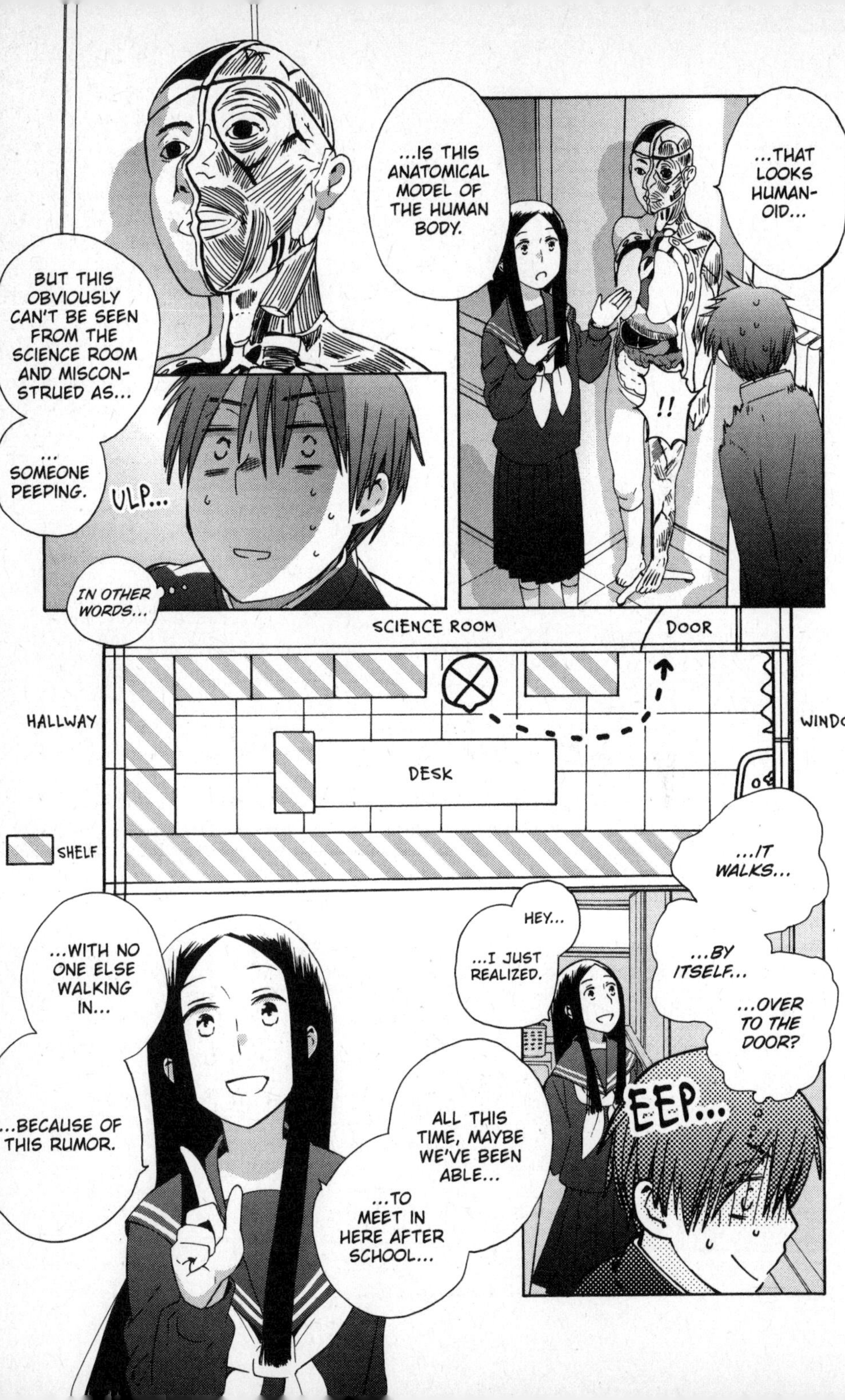
...THAT LOOKS HUMAN-OID...
...IS THIS ANATOMICAL MODEL OF THE HUMAN BODY.
!!
BUT THIS OBVIOUSLY CAN'T BE SEEN FROM THE SCIENCE ROOM AND MISCON-STRUED AS...
...SOMEONE PEEPING.
ULP...
IN OTHER WORDS...
SCIENCE ROOM
DOOR
HALLWAY
WINDOW
DESK
SHELF
HEY...
...I JUST REALIZED.
...IT WALKS...
...BY ITSELF...
...OVER TO THE DOOR?
EEP...
ALL THIS TIME, MAYBE WE'VE BEEN ABLE...
...TO MEET IN HERE AFTER SCHOOL...
...WITH NO ONE ELSE WALKING IN...
...BECAUSE OF THIS RUMOR.

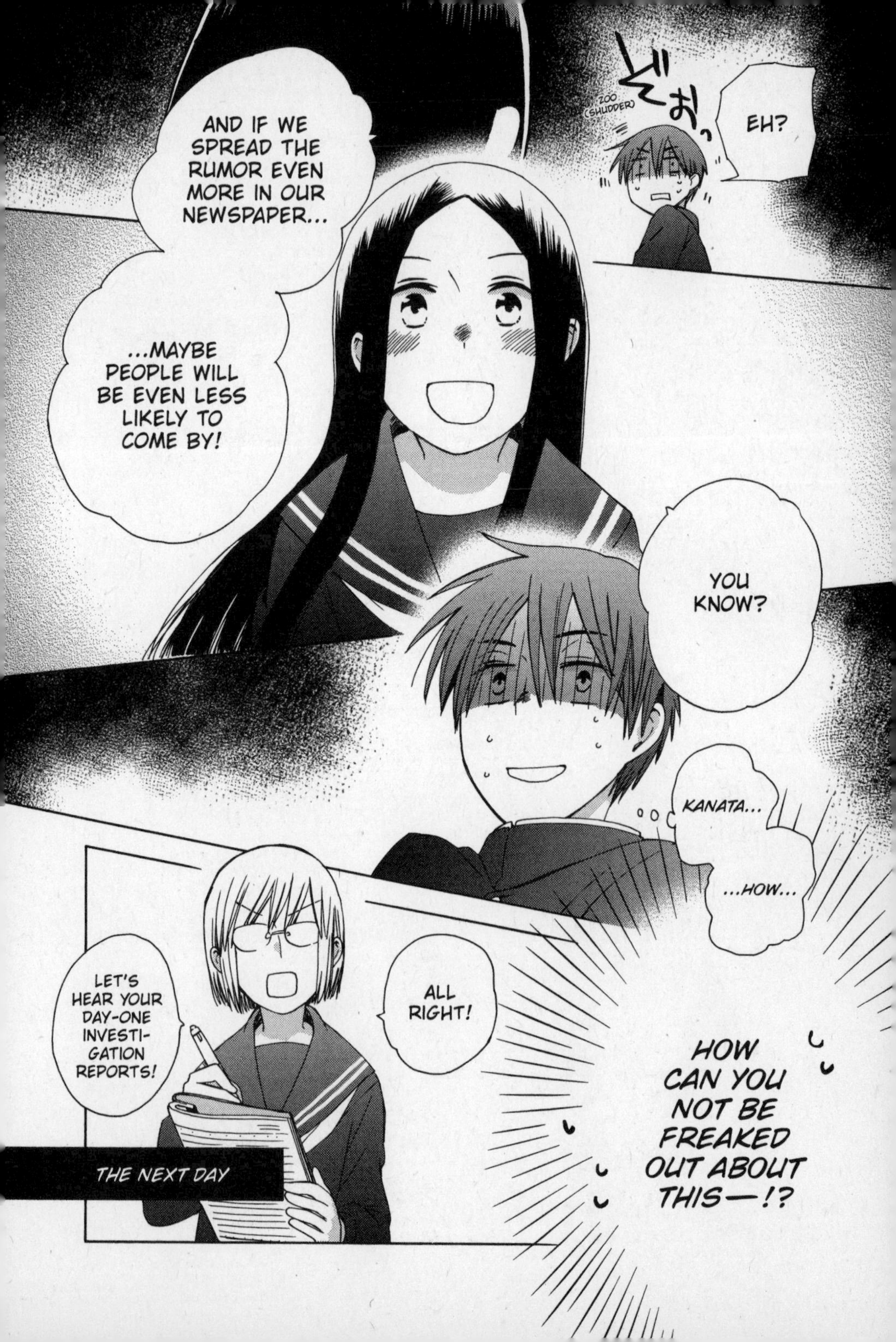
ぞぉっ
ZOO (SHUDDER)
EH?
AND IF WE SPREAD THE RUMOR EVEN MORE IN OUR NEWSPAPER...
...MAYBE PEOPLE WILL BE EVEN LESS LIKELY TO COME BY!
YOU KNOW?
KANATA...
...HOW...
HOW CAN YOU NOT BE FREAKED OUT ABOUT THIS—!?
THE NEXT DAY
ALL RIGHT!
LET'S HEAR YOUR DAY-ONE INVESTIGATION REPORTS!

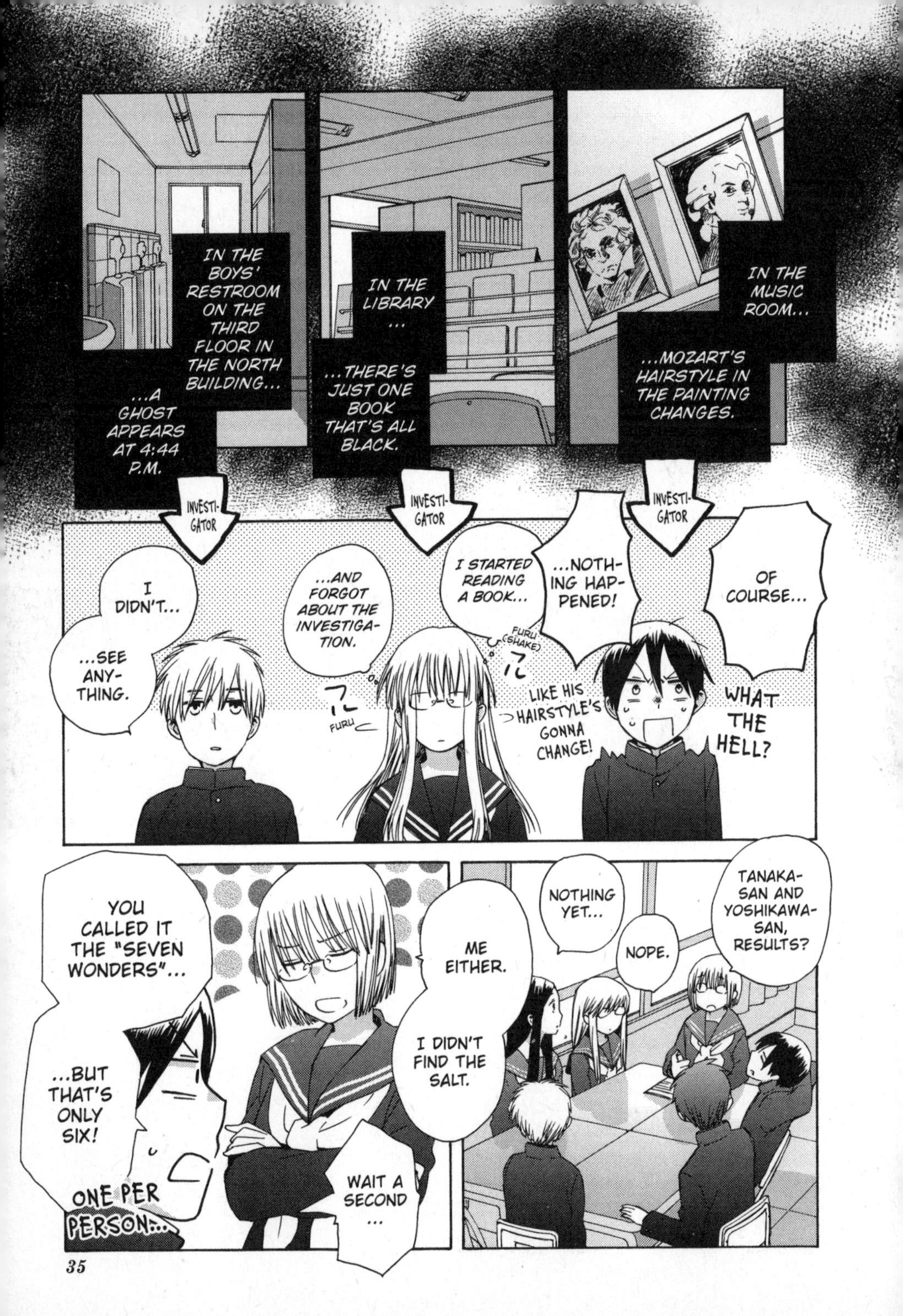
IN THE MUSIC ROOM...
...MOZART'S HAIRSTYLE IN THE PAINTING CHANGES.
IN THE LIBRARY...
...THERE'S JUST ONE BOOK THAT'S ALL BLACK.
IN THE BOYS' RESTROOM ON THE THIRD FLOOR IN THE NORTH BUILDING...
...A GHOST APPEARS AT 4:44 P.M.
INVESTI-GATOR
INVESTI-GATOR
INVESTI-GATOR
OF COURSE...
WHAT THE HELL?
...NOTHING HAPPENED!
LIKE HIS HAIRSTYLE'S GONNA CHANGE!
I STARTED READING A BOOK...
...AND FORGOT ABOUT THE INVESTIGATION.
FURU (SHAKE)
FURU
I DIDN'T...
...SEE ANYTHING.
TANAKA-SAN AND YOSHIKAWA-SAN, RESULTS?
NOTHING YET...
NOPE.
ME EITHER.
I DIDN'T FIND THE SALT.
YOU CALLED IT THE "SEVEN WONDERS"...
...BUT THAT'S ONLY SIX!
WAIT A SECOND...
ONE PER PERSON...

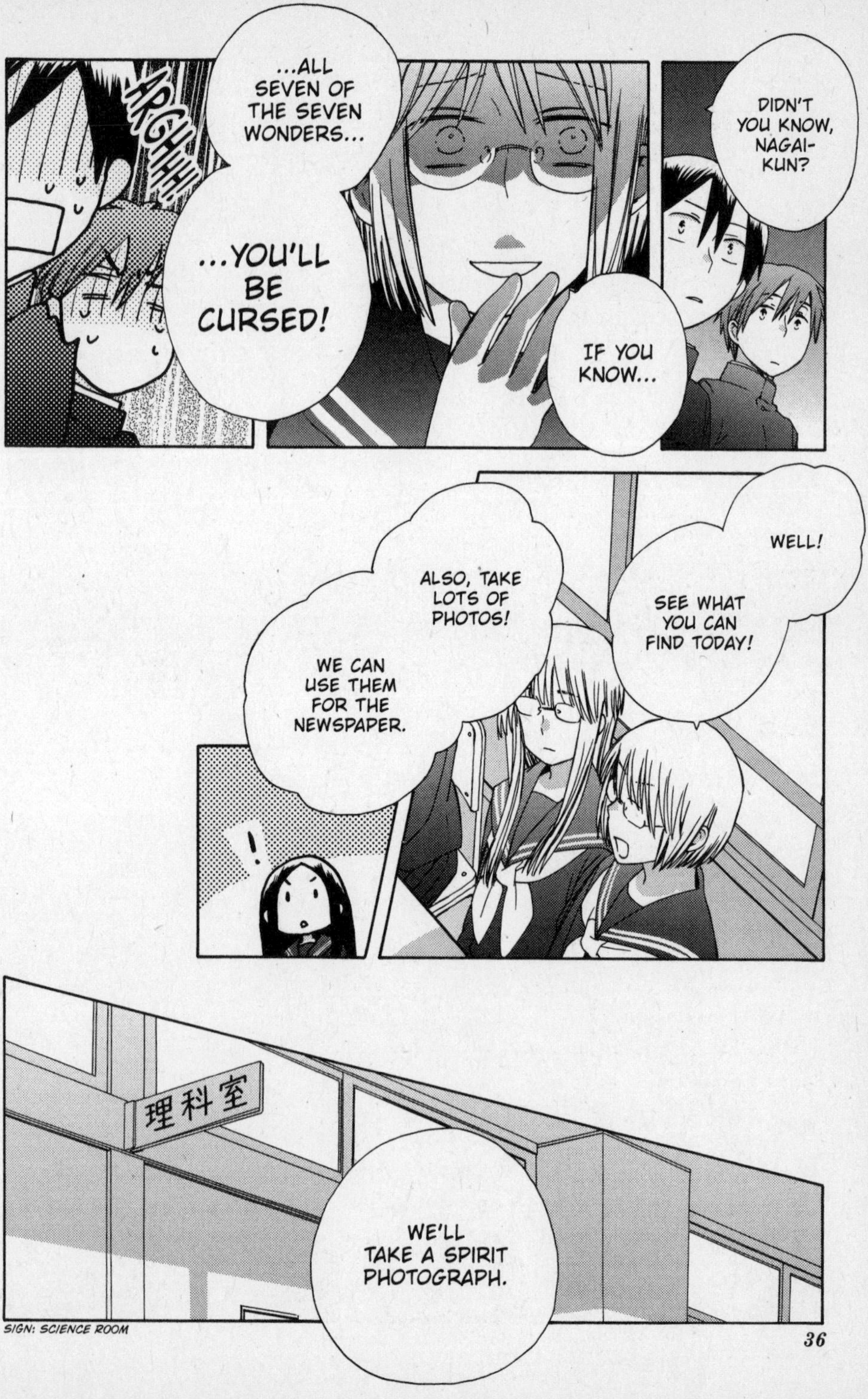
DIDN'T YOU KNOW, NAGAI-KUN?
IF YOU KNOW...
...ALL SEVEN OF THE SEVEN WONDERS...
...YOU'LL BE CURSED!
ARGHHH!
WELL!
SEE WHAT YOU CAN FIND TODAY!
ALSO, TAKE LOTS OF PHOTOS!
WE CAN USE THEM FOR THE NEWSPAPER.
!
理科室
WE'LL TAKE A SPIRIT PHOTOGRAPH.

SIGN: SCIENCE ROOM

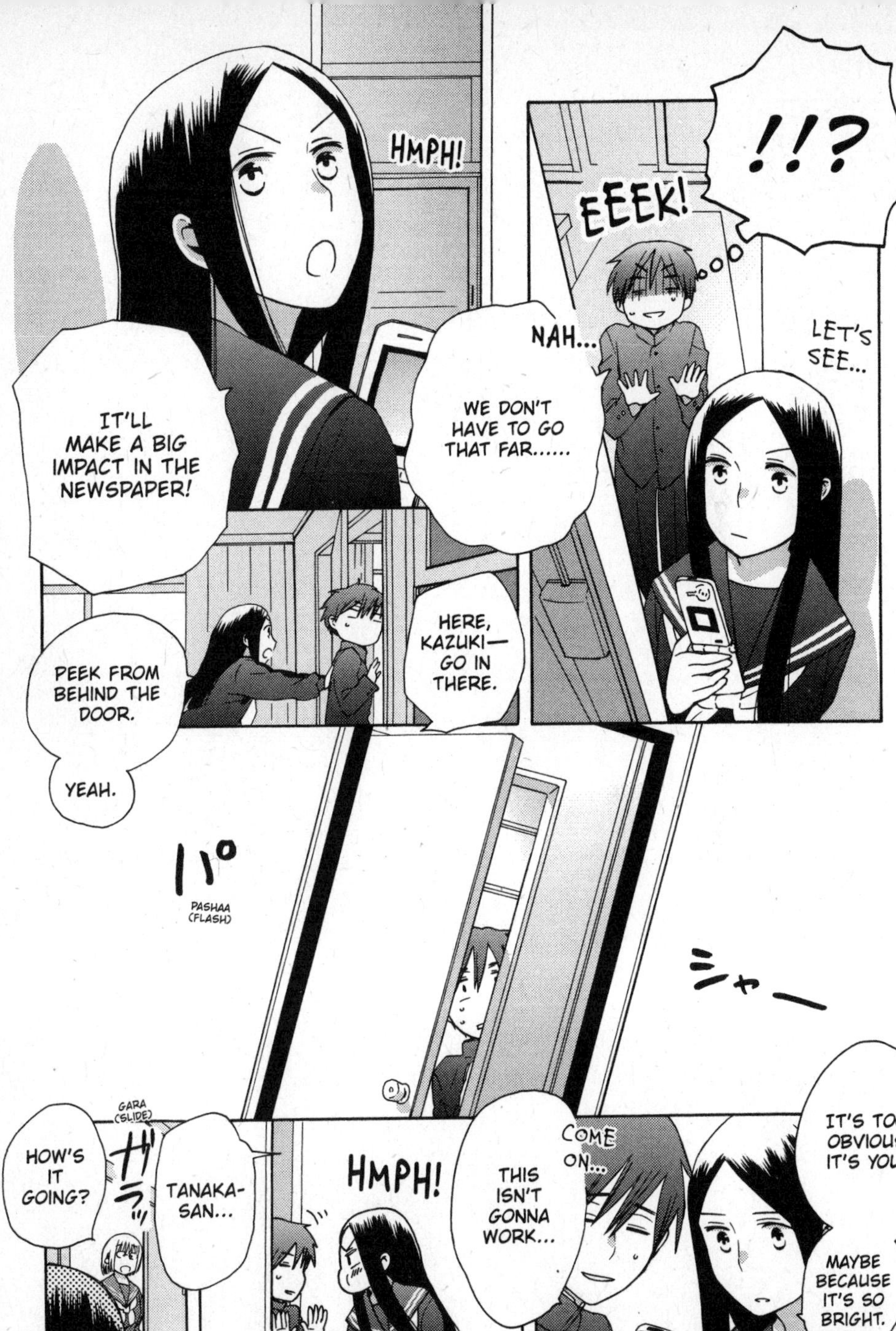
LET'S SEE...
!!?
EEEK!
NAH...
WE DON'T HAVE TO GO THAT FAR......
HMPH!
IT'LL MAKE A BIG IMPACT IN THE NEWSPAPER!
HERE, KAZUKI—GO IN THERE.
PEEK FROM BEHIND THE DOOR.
YEAH.
シャー
パ
PASHAA (FLASH)
IT'S TOO OBVIOUS IT'S YOU.
MAYBE BECAUSE IT'S SO BRIGHT.
COME ON...
THIS ISN'T GONNA WORK...
HMPH!
TANAKA-SAN...
ガラッ
GARA (SLIDE)
HOW'S IT GOING?

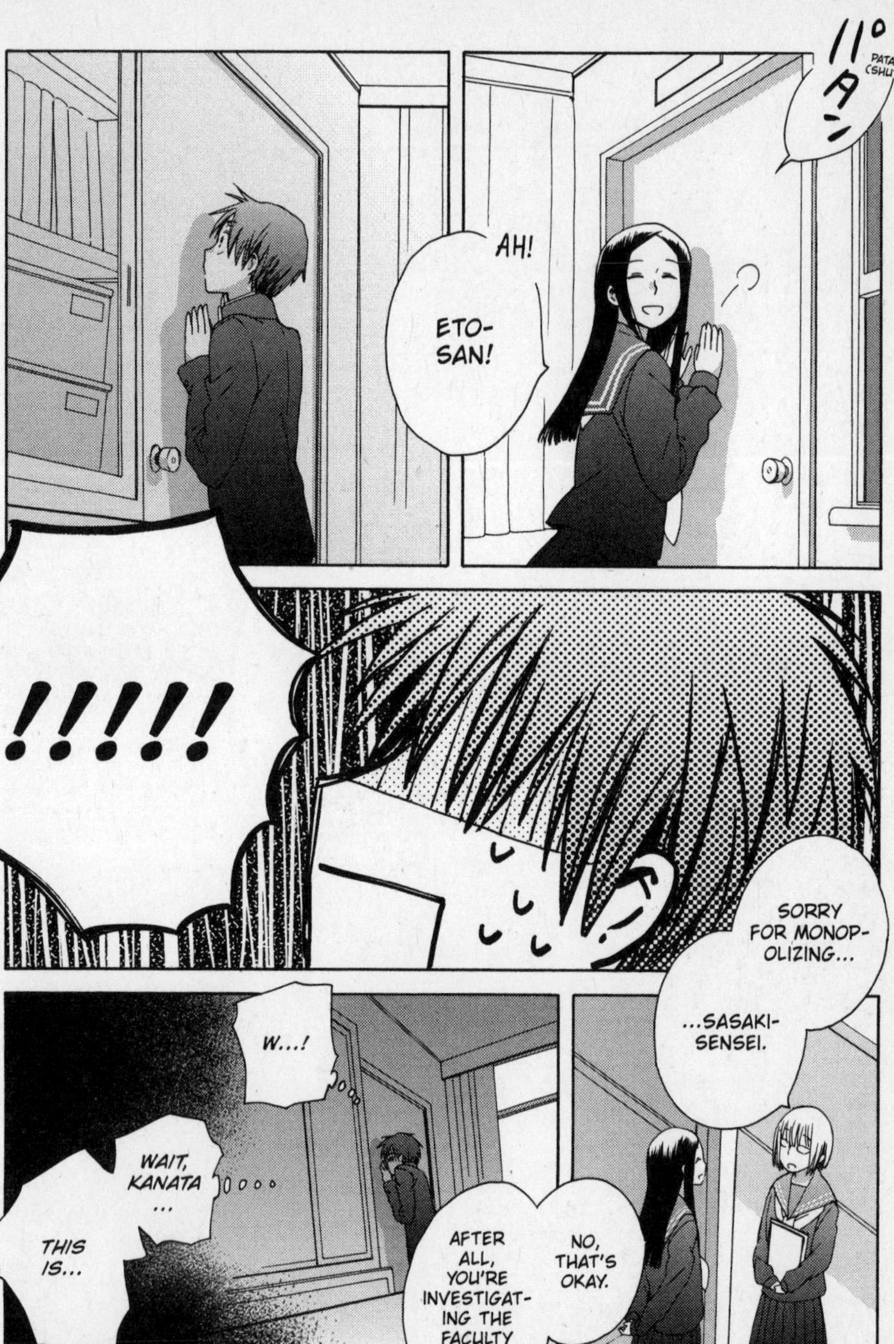
パタン
PATAN (SHUT)
AH!
ETO-SAN!
!!!!!
SORRY FOR MONOP-OLIZING...
...SASAKI-SENSEI.
NO, THAT'S OKAY.
AFTER ALL, YOU'RE INVESTIGAT-ING THE FACULTY ROOM.
W...!
WAIT, KANATA...
THIS IS...

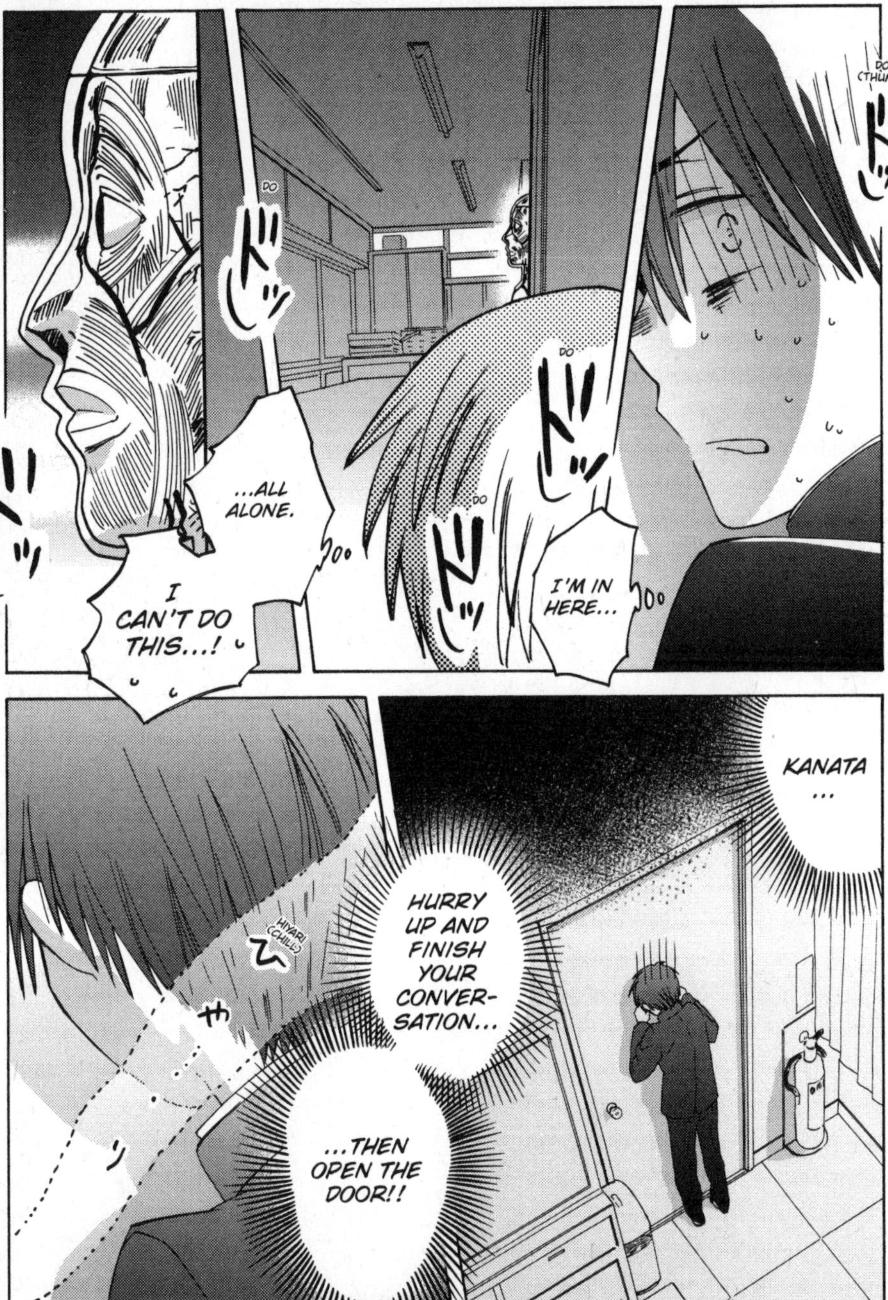
DO (THUMP)
DO
DO
I'M IN HERE...
DO
...ALL ALONE.
DO
I CAN'T DO THIS...!
KANATA ...
HURRY UP AND FINISH YOUR CONVER-SATION...
...THEN OPEN THE DOOR!!
HIYARI (CHILL)

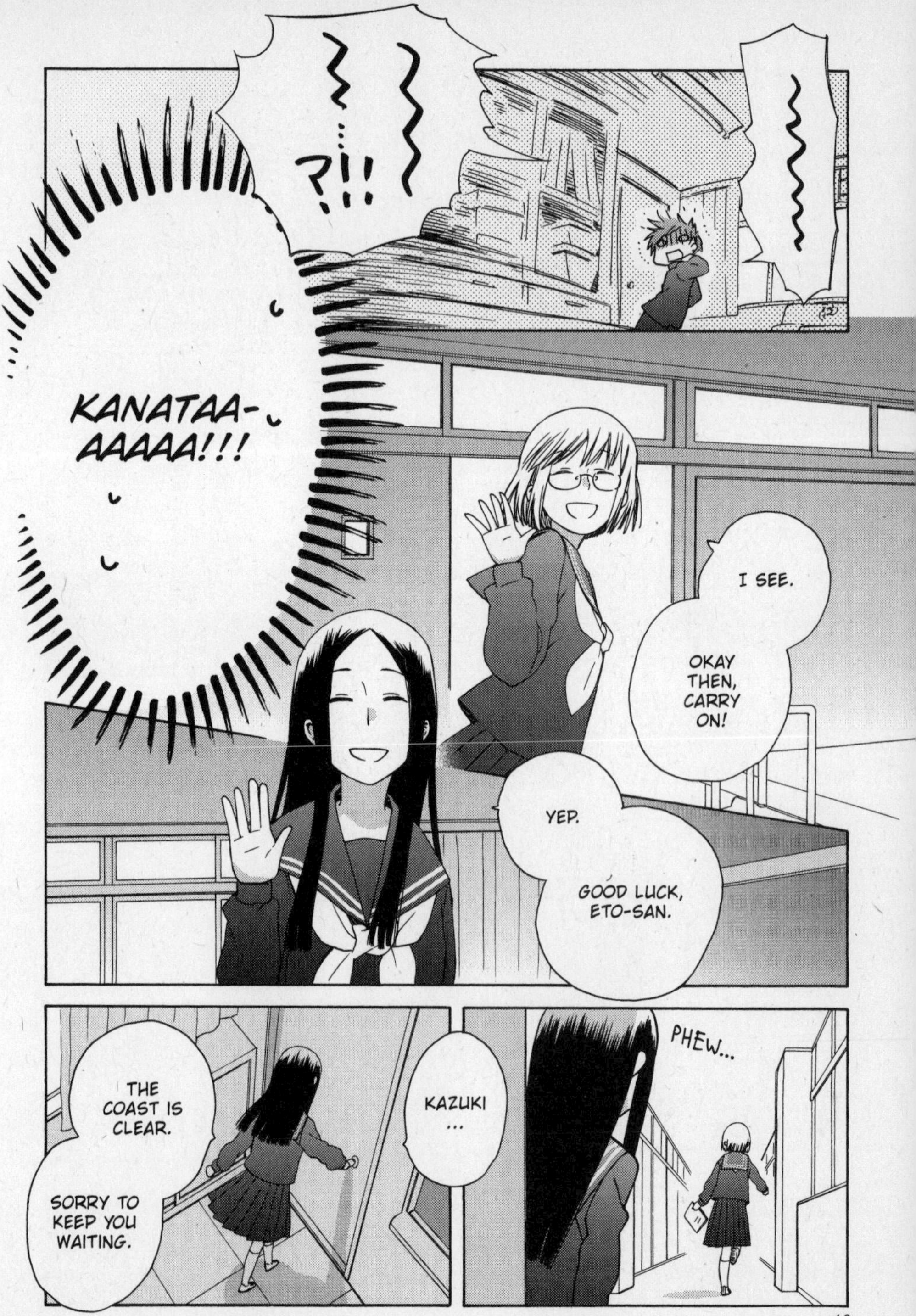
...?!!
KANATAA-AAAAAA!!!
I SEE.
OKAY THEN, CARRY ON!
YEP.
GOOD LUCK, ETO-SAN.
PHEW...
KAZUKI ...
THE COAST IS CLEAR.
SORRY TO KEEP YOU WAITING.

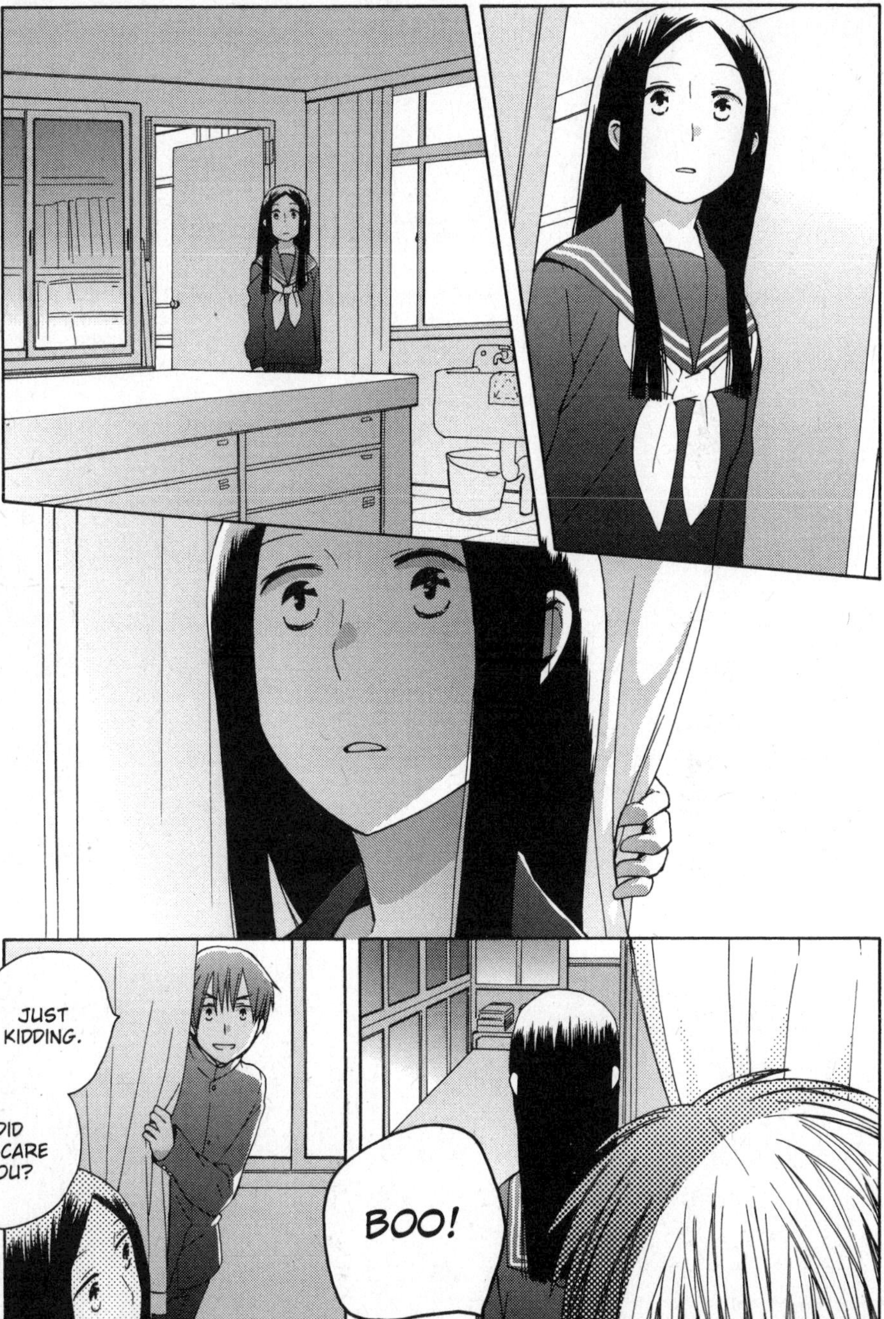
BOO!
JUST KIDDING.
DID I SCARE YOU?

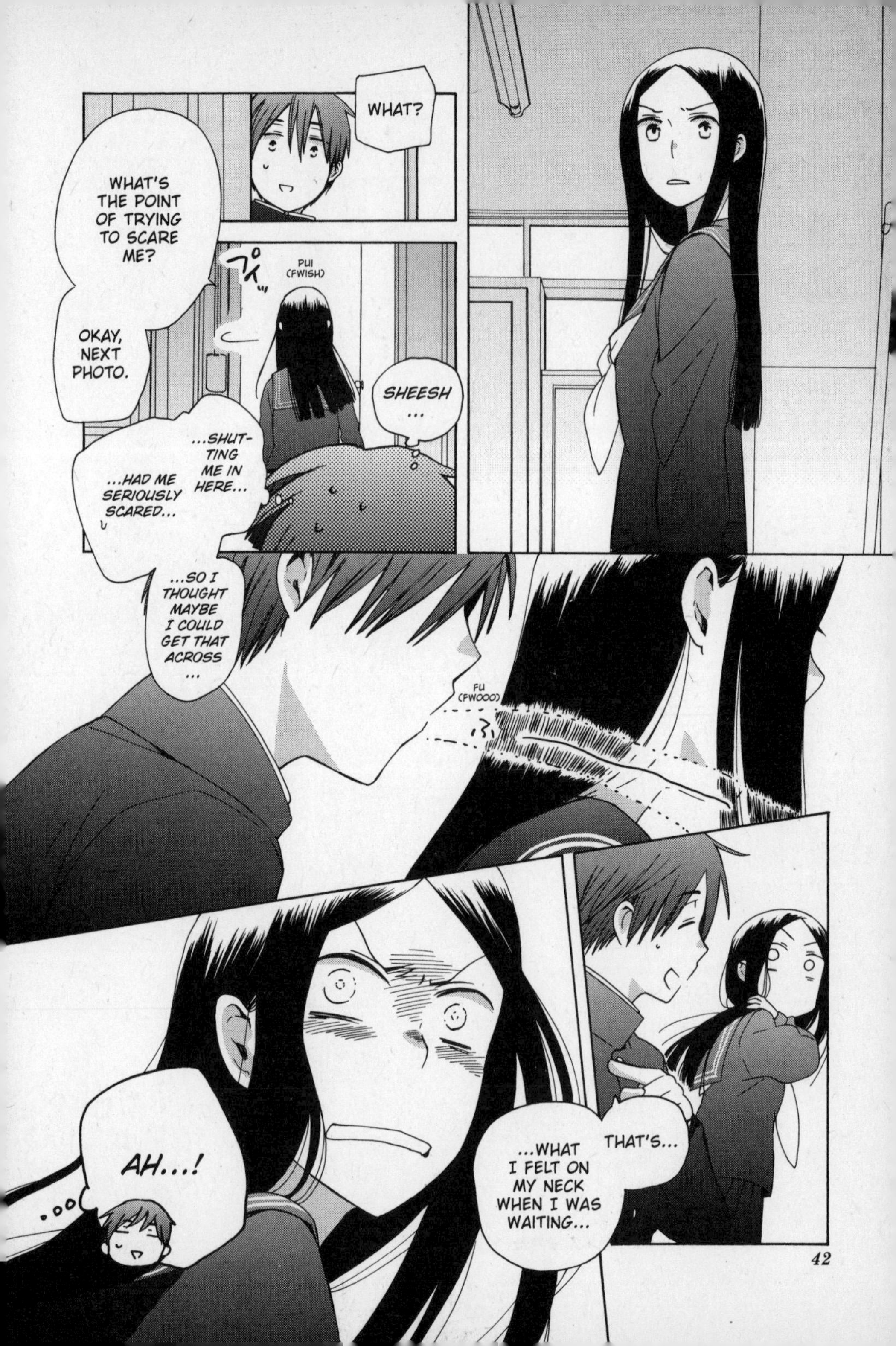
WHAT?
WHAT'S THE POINT OF TRYING TO SCARE ME?
プイ
PUI (FWISH)
OKAY, NEXT PHOTO.
SHEESH ...
...SHUT-TING ME IN HERE...
...HAD ME SERIOUSLY SCARED...
...SO I THOUGHT MAYBE I COULD GET THAT ACROSS...
FU (FWOOO)
ふ
THAT'S...
...WHAT I FELT ON MY NECK WHEN I WAS WAITING...
AH...!

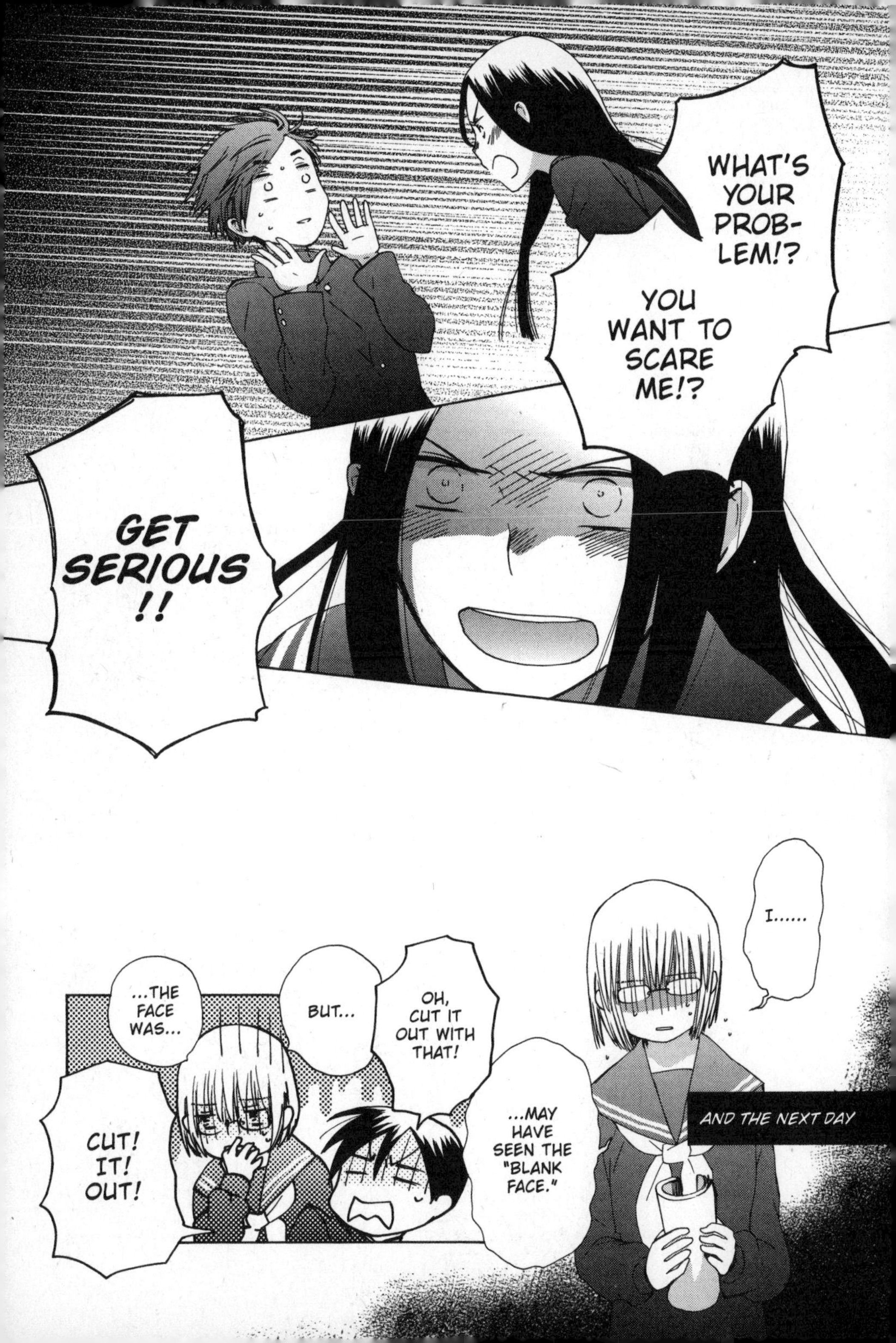
WHAT'S YOUR PROB-LEM!?
YOU WANT TO SCARE ME!?
GET SERIOUS!!
AND THE NEXT DAY
I......
...MAY HAVE SEEN THE "BLANK FACE."
OH, CUT IT OUT WITH THAT!
BUT...
...THE FACE WAS...
CUT! IT! OUT!

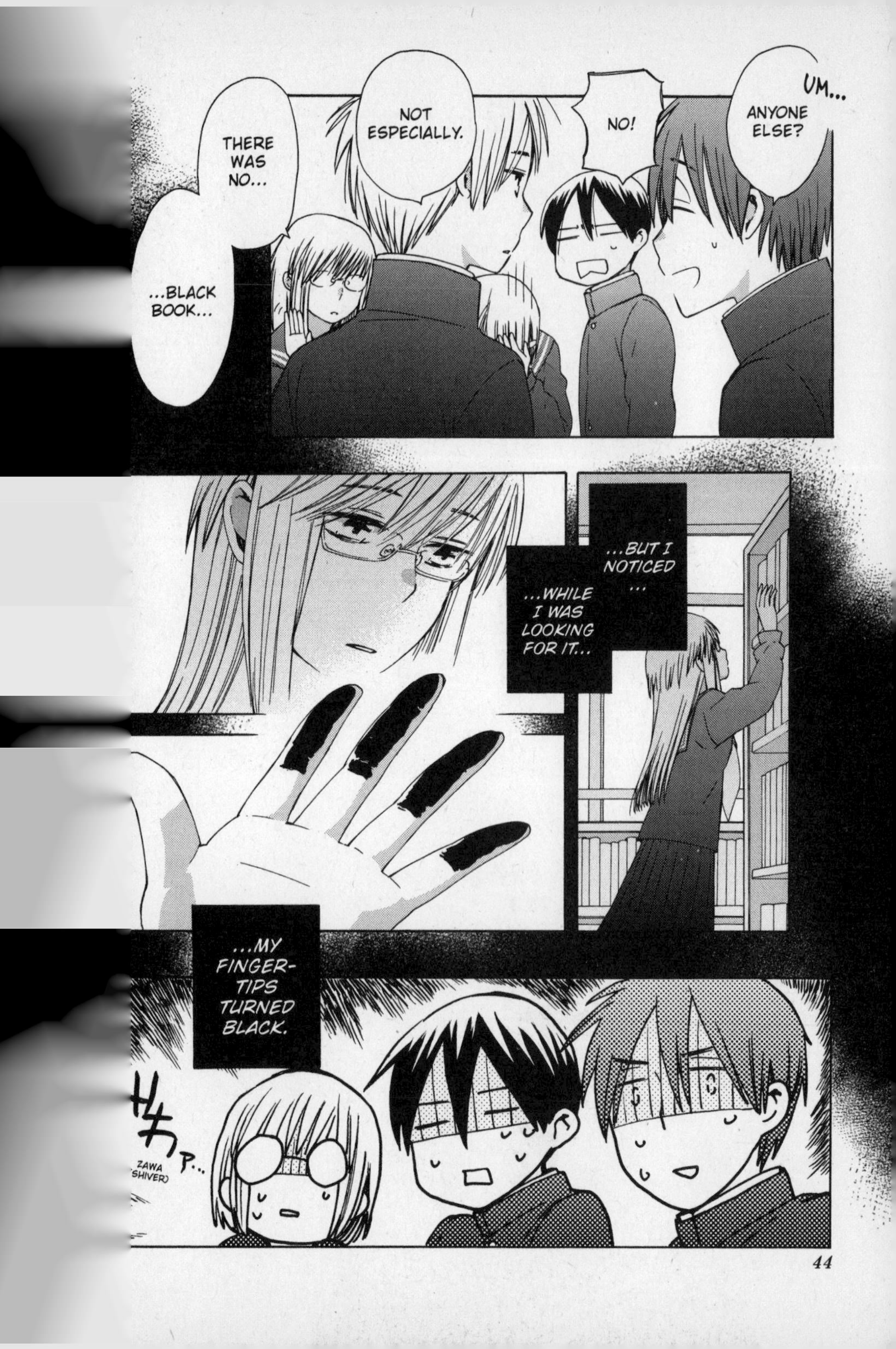
UM... ANYONE ELSE?
NO!
NOT ESPECIALLY.
THERE WAS NO...
...BLACK BOOK...
...BUT I NOTICED ...
...WHILE I WAS LOOKING FOR IT...
...MY FINGER-TIPS TURNED BLACK.
ZAWA (SHIVER)

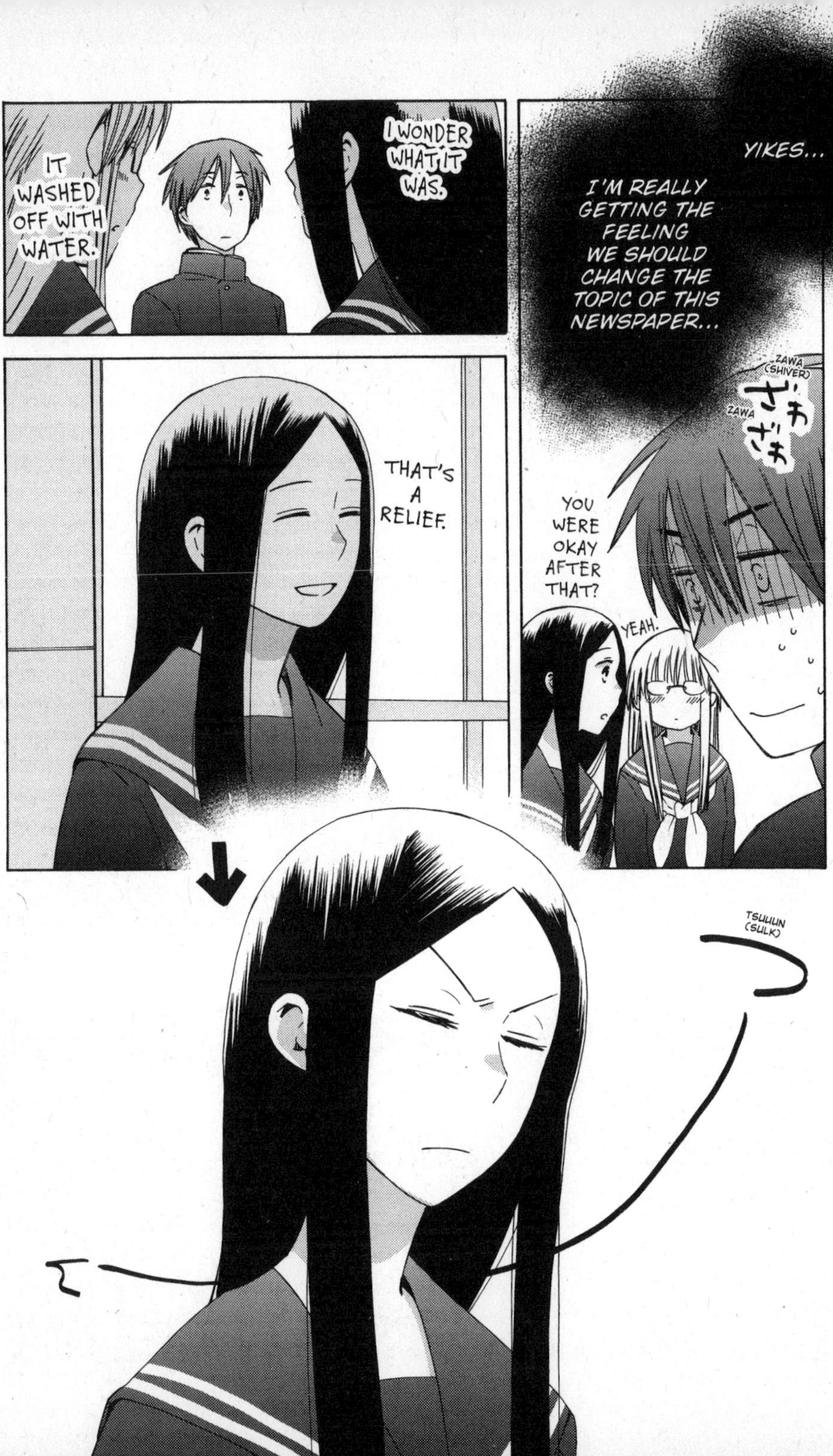
YIKES...
I'M REALLY GETTING THE FEELING WE SHOULD CHANGE THE TOPIC OF THIS NEWSPAPER...
ZAWA (SHIVER) ZAWA
ざわざわ
YOU WERE OKAY AFTER THAT?
YEAH.
I WONDER WHAT IT WAS.
IT WASHED OFF WITH WATER!
THAT'S A RELIEF.
TSUUUN (SULK)

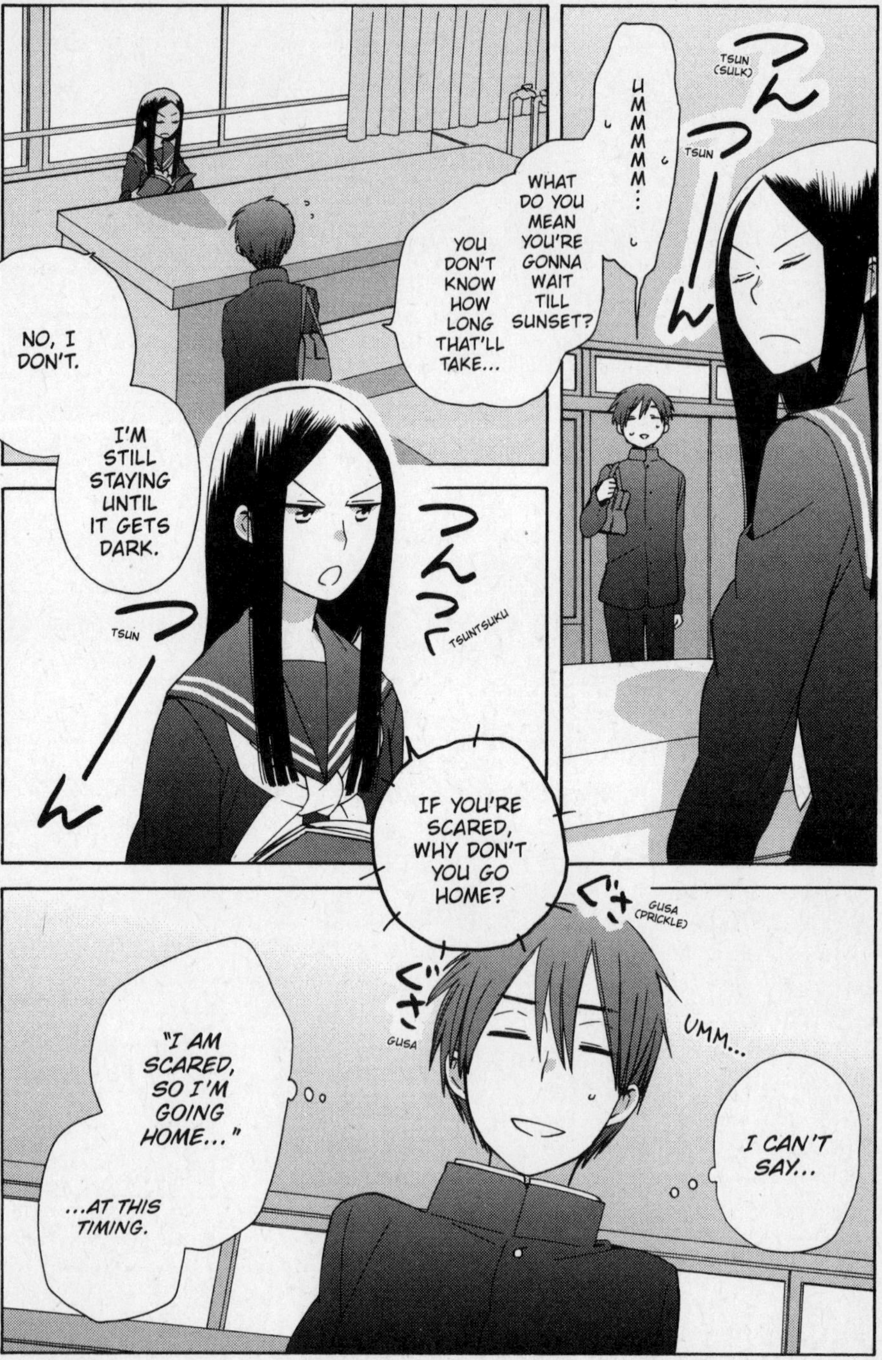

TSUN (SULK)
TSUN
UMMMMMM...
WHAT DO YOU MEAN YOU'RE GONNA WAIT TILL SUNSET?
YOU DON'T KNOW HOW LONG THAT'LL TAKE...
NO, I DON'T.
I'M STILL STAYING UNTIL IT GETS DARK.
TSUNTSUKU
TSUN
IF YOU'RE SCARED, WHY DON'T YOU GO HOME?
GUSA (PRICKLE)
GUSA
UMM...
I CAN'T SAY...
"I AM SCARED, SO I'M GOING HOME..."
...AT THIS TIMING.

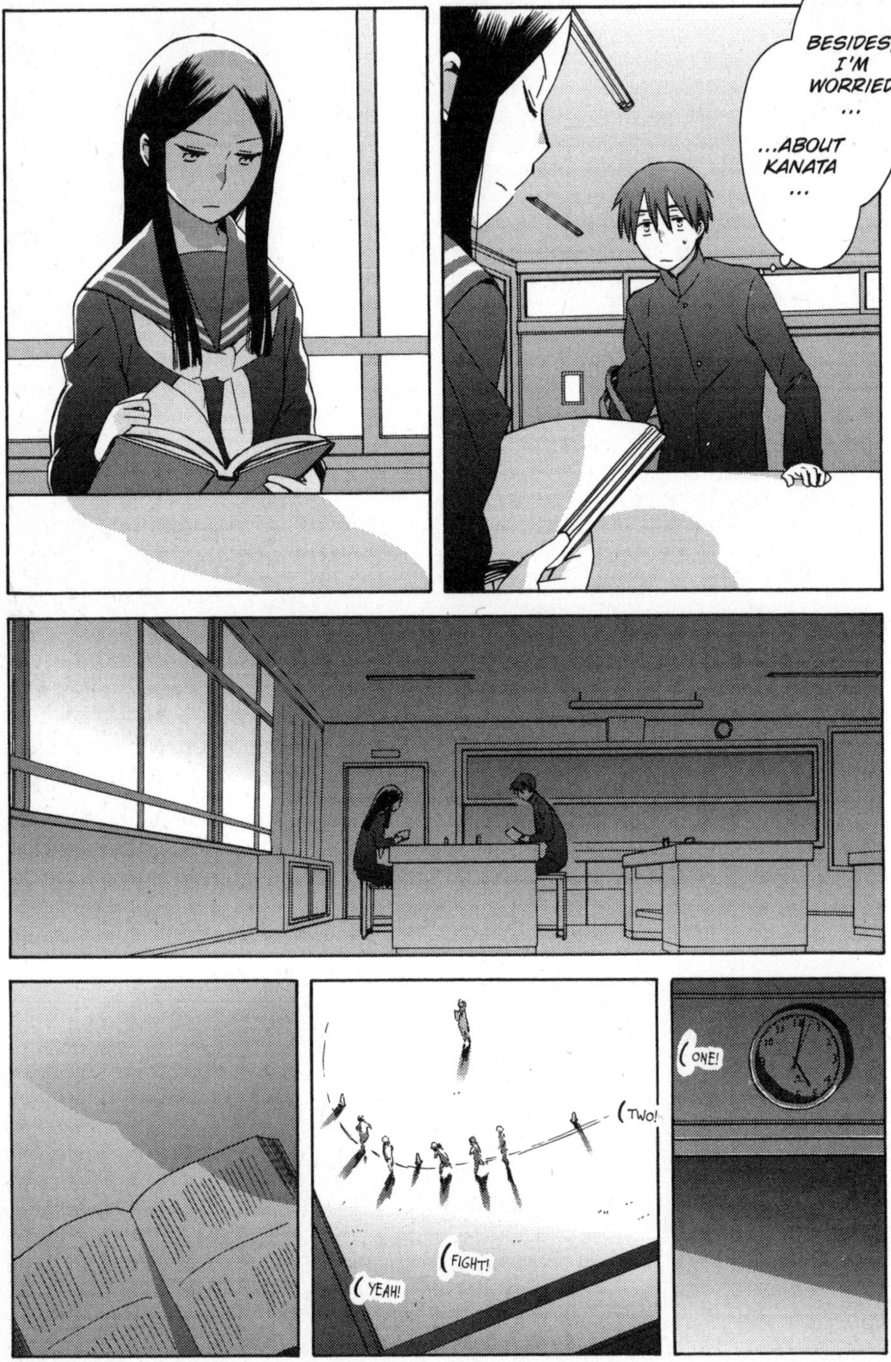
BESIDES, I'M WORRIED ...
...ABOUT KANATA ...
ONE!
TWO!
FIGHT!
YEAH!

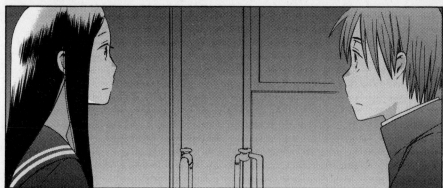

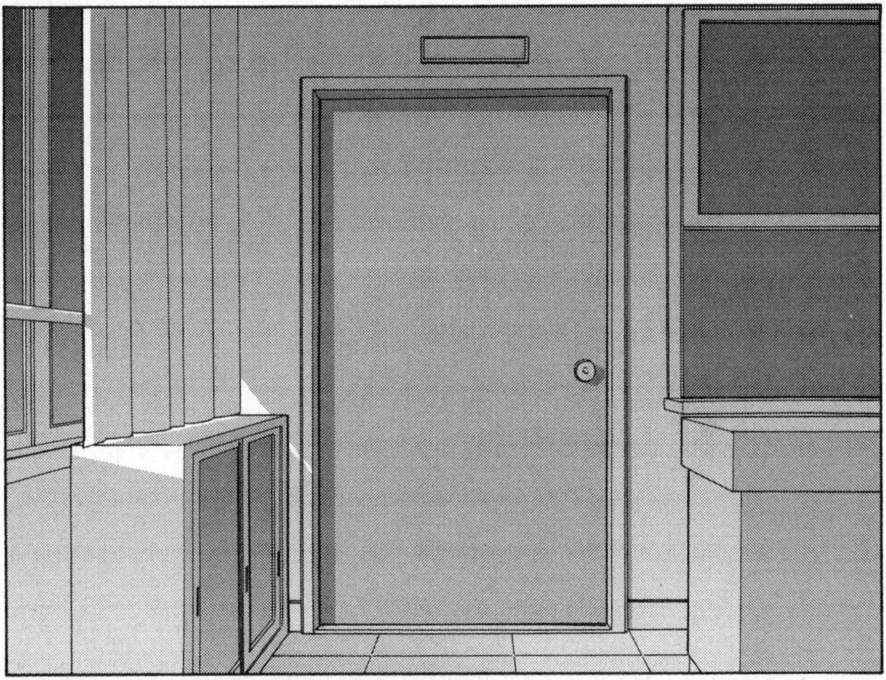

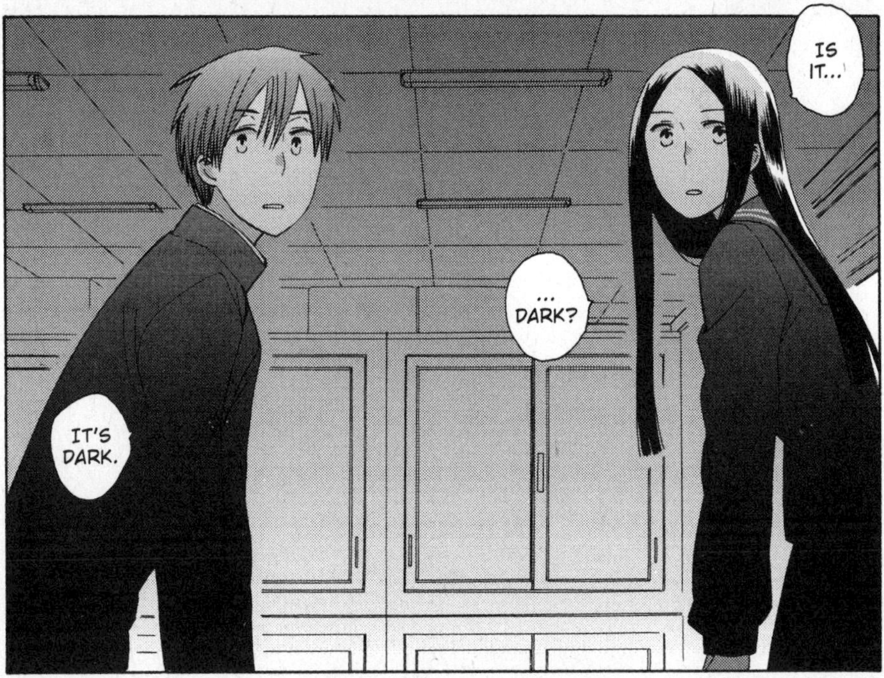
IS IT...
... DARK?
IT'S DARK.

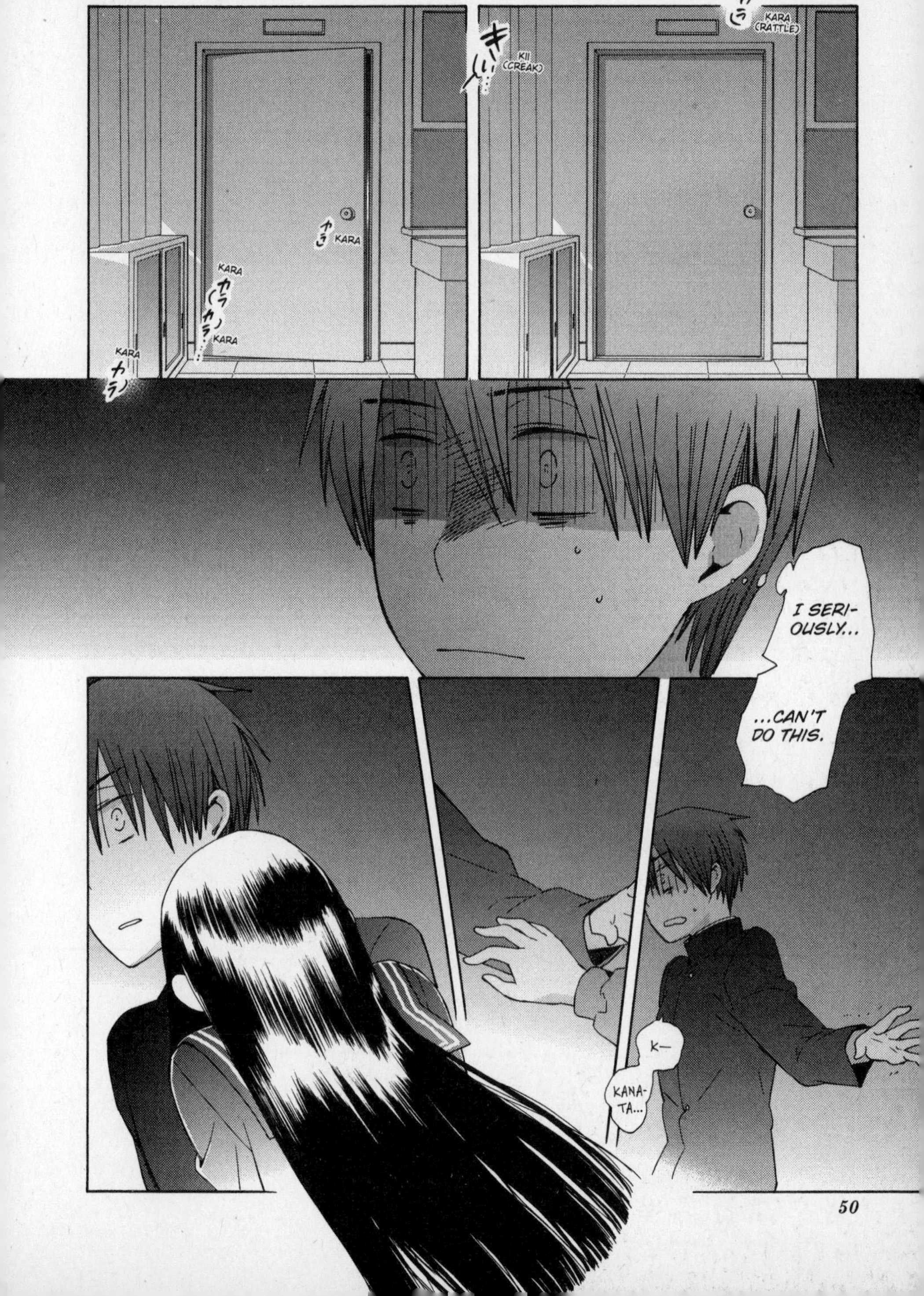
カラ
KARA (RATTLE)
きぃ…
KII (CREAK)
カラ
KARA
カラ (カラ)…
KARA
KARA
カラ
KARA
I SERIOUSLY...
...CAN'T DO THIS.
K—
KANATA...

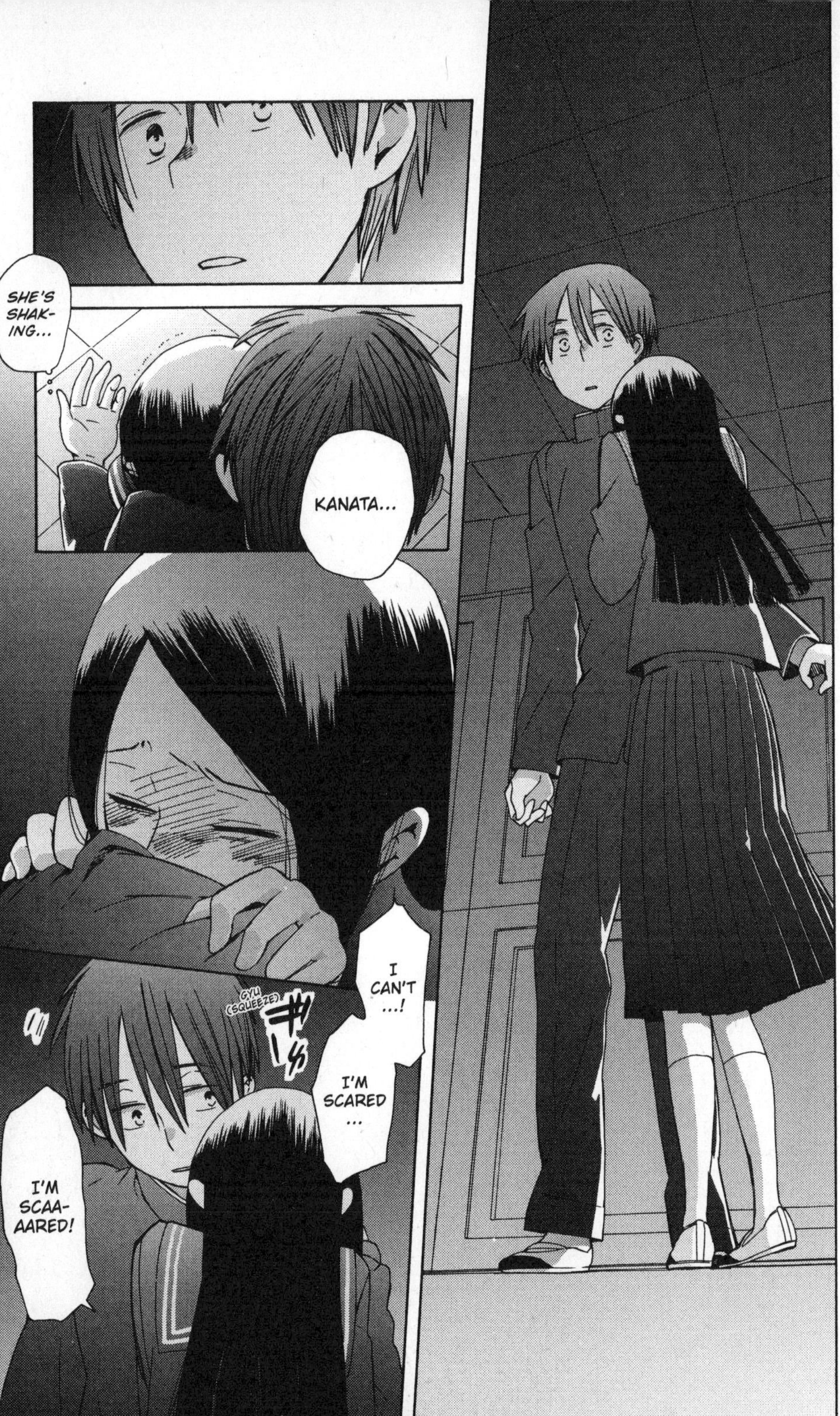
SHE'S SHAK-ING...
KANATA...
I CAN'T ...!
I'M SCARED ...
GYU (SQUEEZE)
I'M SCAA-AARED!

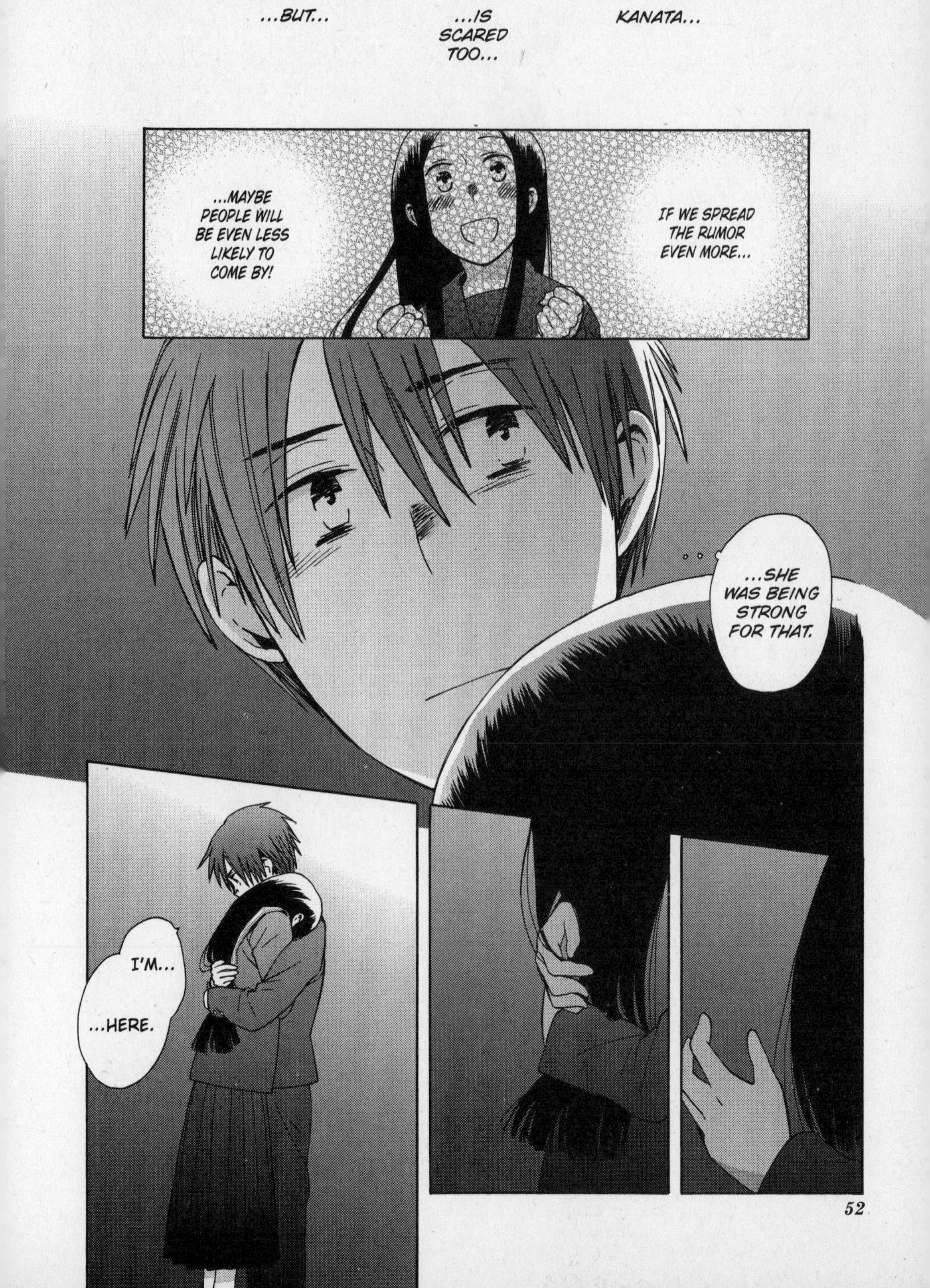
KANATA...
...IS SCARED TOO...
...BUT...
IF WE SPREAD THE RUMOR EVEN MORE...
...MAYBE PEOPLE WILL BE EVEN LESS LIKELY TO COME BY!
...SHE WAS BEING STRONG FOR THAT.
I'M...
...HERE.

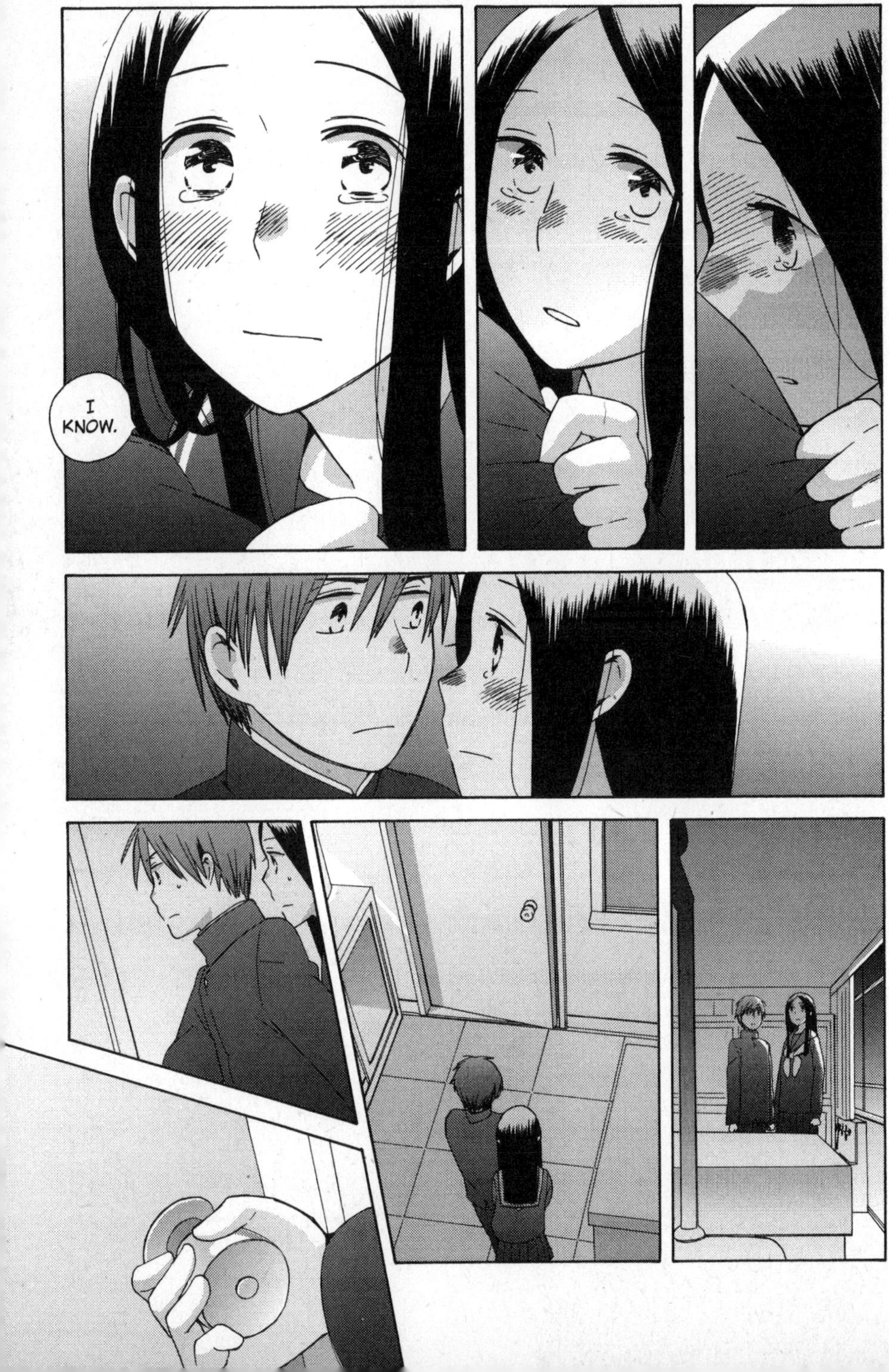
I KNOW.

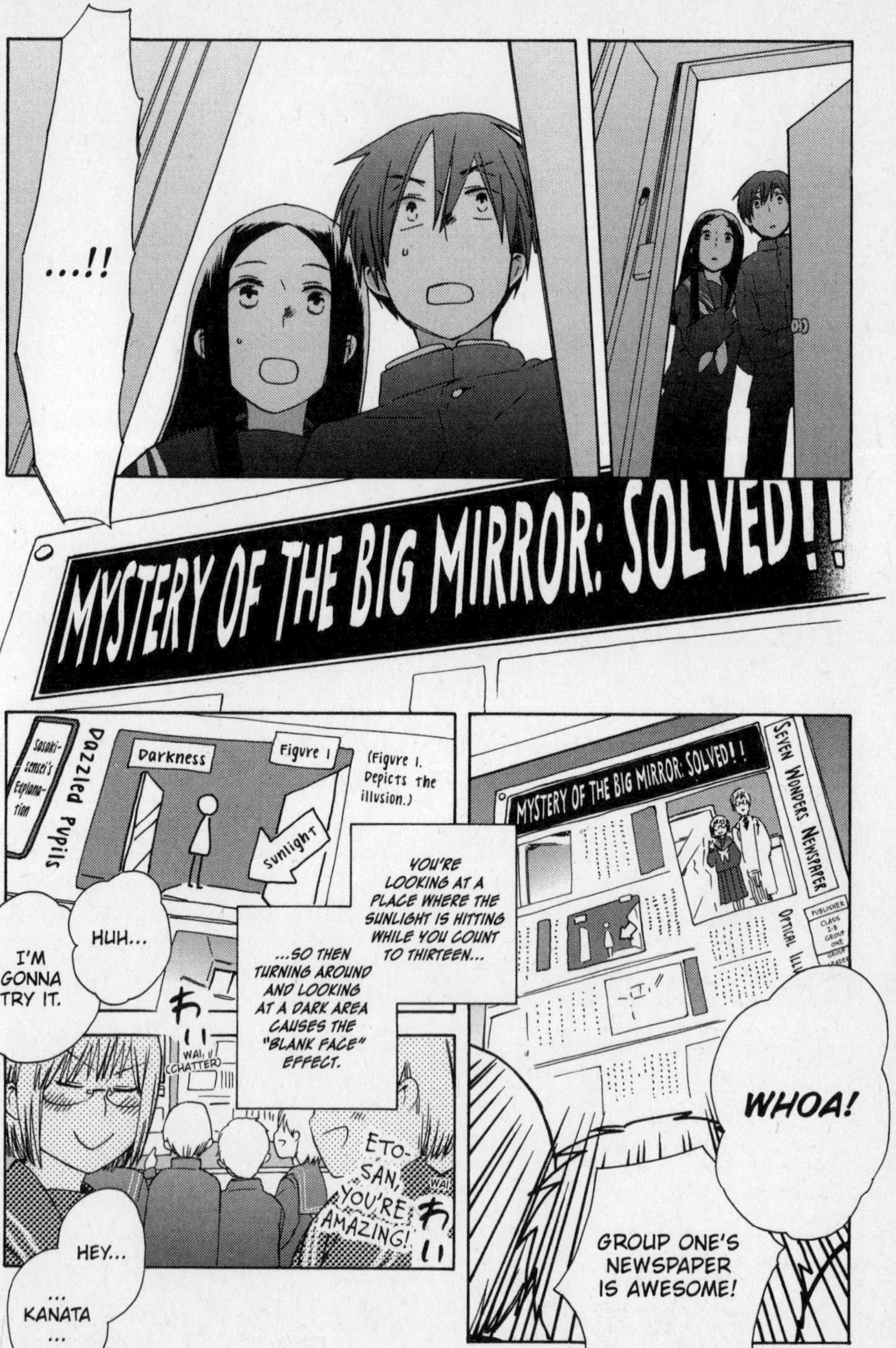
...!!
MYSTERY OF THE BIG MIRROR: SOLVED!!
SEVEN WONDERS NEWSPAPER
MYSTERY OF THE BIG MIRROR: SOLVED!!
PUBLISHER CLASS 2-B GROUP ONE
WHOA!
GROUP ONE'S NEWSPAPER IS AWESOME!
Sasaki-sensei's Explanation
Dazzled Pupils
Figure 1
(Figure 1. Depicts the illusion.)
Darkness
Sunlight
YOU'RE LOOKING AT A PLACE WHERE THE SUNLIGHT IS HITTING WHILE YOU COUNT TO THIRTEEN...
...SO THEN TURNING AROUND AND LOOKING AT A DARK AREA CAUSES THE "BLANK FACE" EFFECT.
HUH...
I'M GONNA TRY IT.
わい WAI
ETO-SAN, YOU'RE AMAZING!
わい WAI (CHATTER)
HEY...
...KANATA...

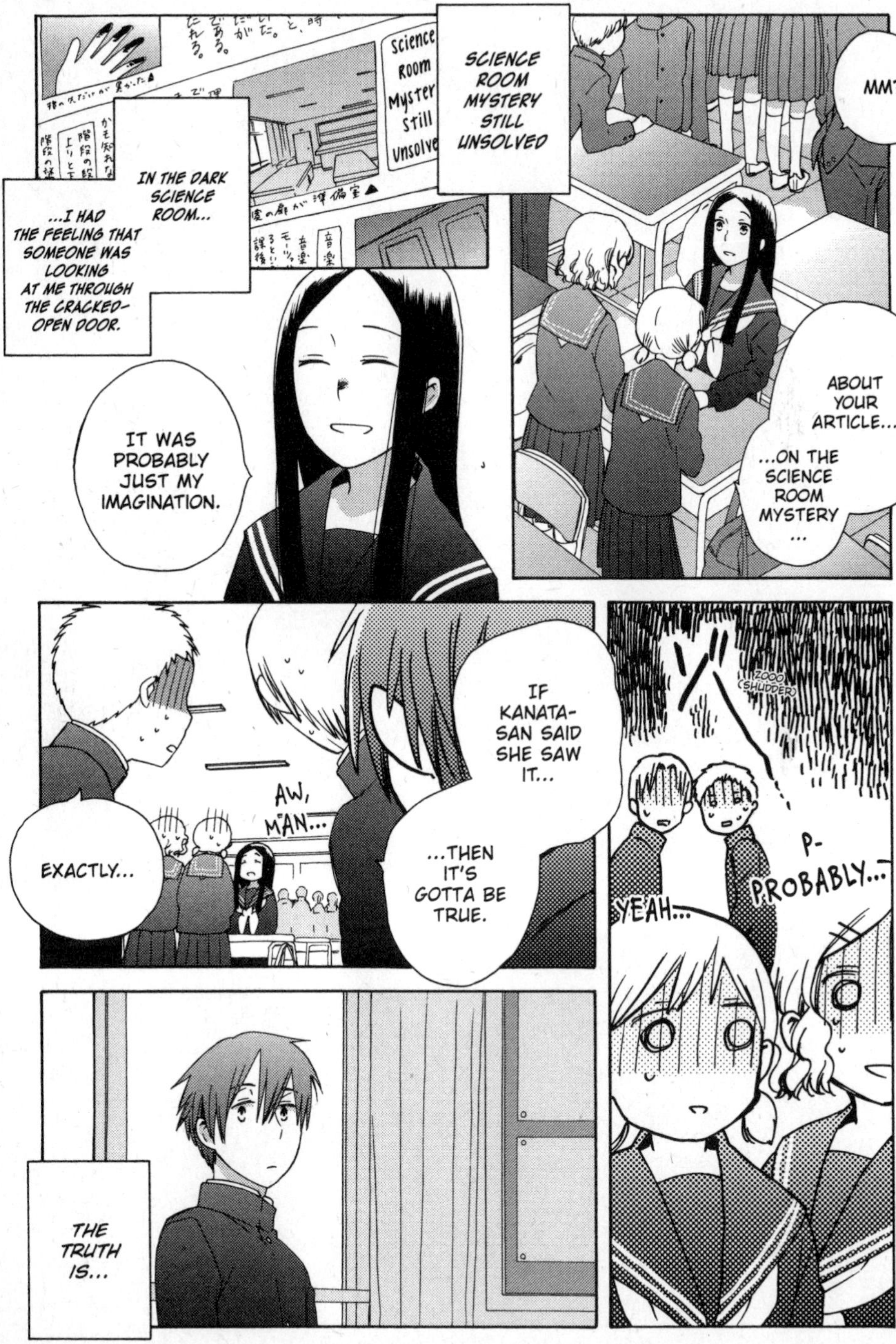
MM?
ABOUT YOUR ARTICLE...
...ON THE SCIENCE ROOM MYSTERY ...
SCIENCE ROOM MYSTERY STILL UNSOLVED
Science Room Mystery Still Unsolve
IN THE DARK SCIENCE ROOM...
...I HAD THE FEELING THAT SOMEONE WAS LOOKING AT ME THROUGH THE CRACKED-OPEN DOOR.
IT WAS PROBABLY JUST MY IMAGINATION.
ZOOO (SHUDDER)
P-PROBABLY...
YEAH...
IF KANATA-SAN SAID SHE SAW IT...
...THEN IT'S GOTTA BE TRUE.
AW, MAN...
EXACTLY...
THE TRUTH IS...

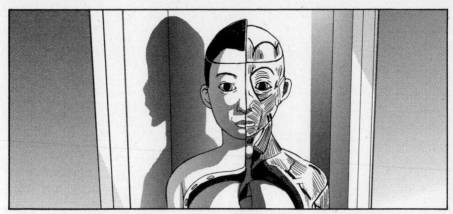

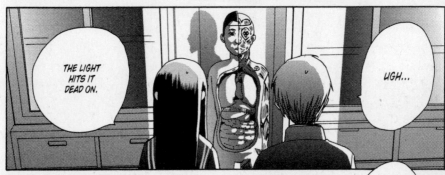

THE LIGHT
HITS IT
DEAD ON.

UGH...

WHEN
IT GETS
DARK LIKE
THIS...

...THE
FLOOD-
LIGHTS
COME ON.

THE ANGLE
IS PERFECT.

AND
ALSO...

...THE BREEZE
COMING FROM
THERE PUSHES
THE DOOR OPEN.

KARA
(RATTLE)
カラ

KARA
カラ

KARA
カラ

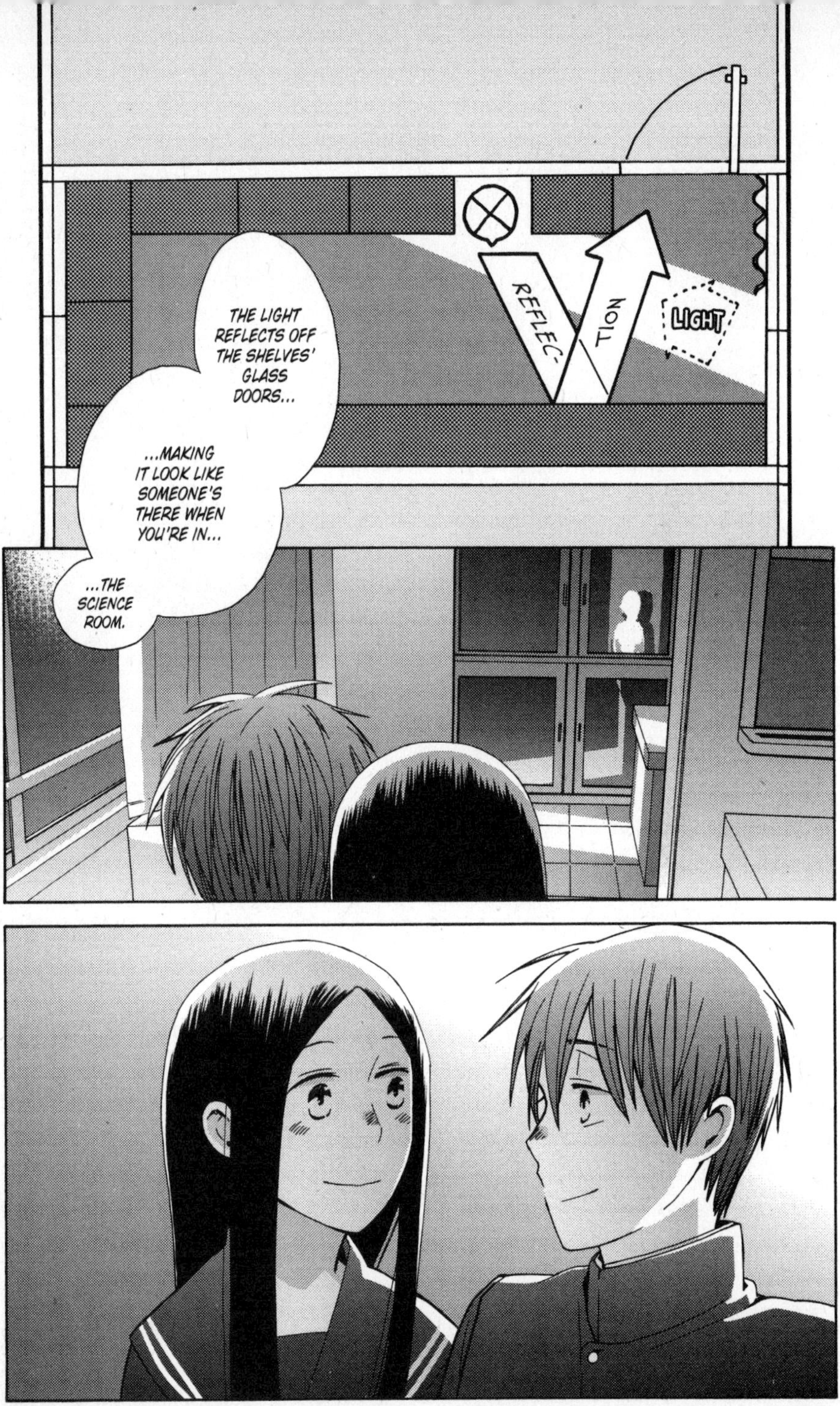
REFLEC-
TION
LIGHT
THE LIGHT REFLECTS OFF THE SHELVES' GLASS DOORS...
...MAKING IT LOOK LIKE SOMEONE'S THERE WHEN YOU'RE IN...
...THE SCIENCE ROOM.

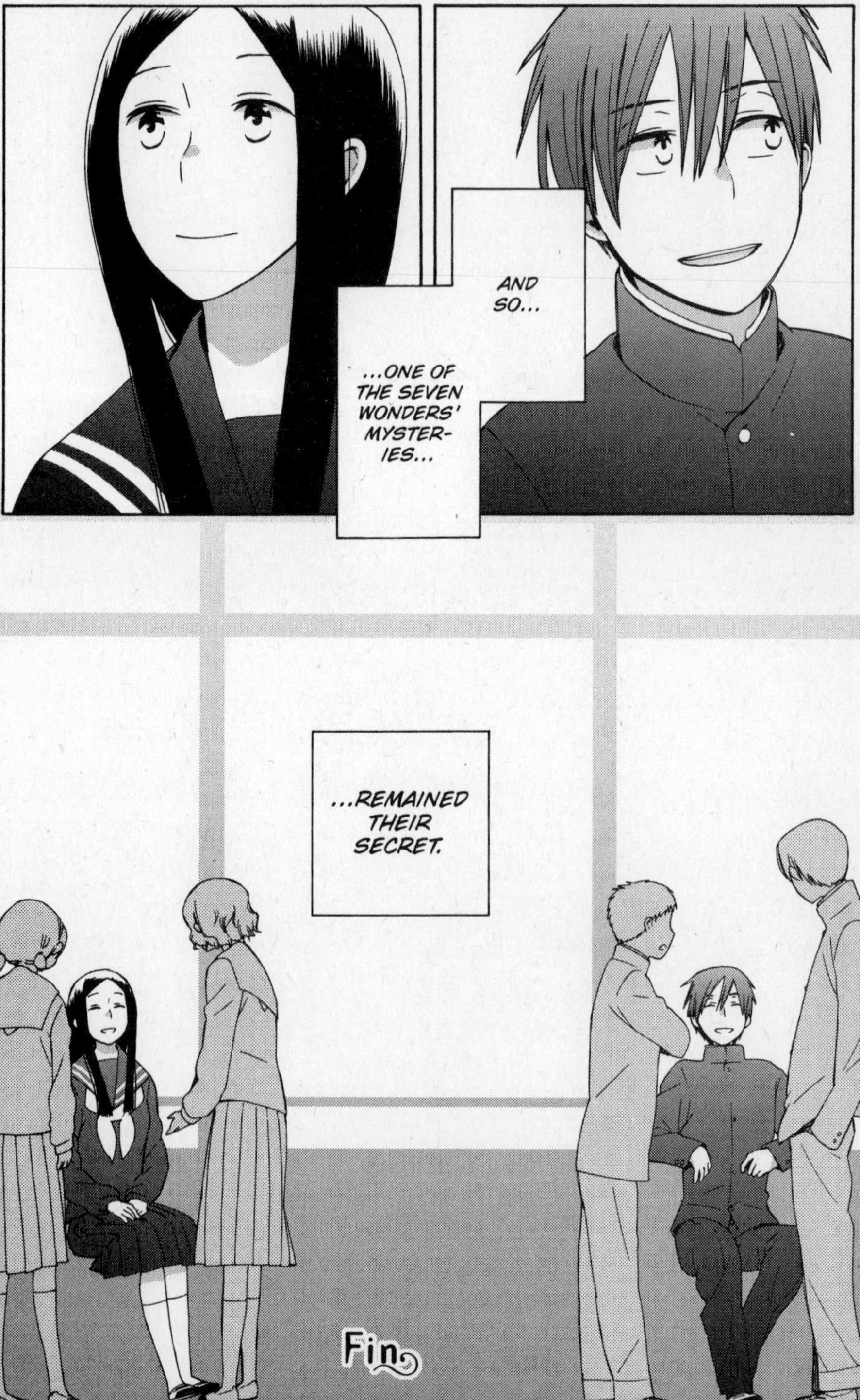
AND SO...
...ONE OF THE SEVEN WONDERS' MYSTER-IES...
...REMAINED THEIR SECRET.
Fin

Love at Fourteen

[Intermission 38]

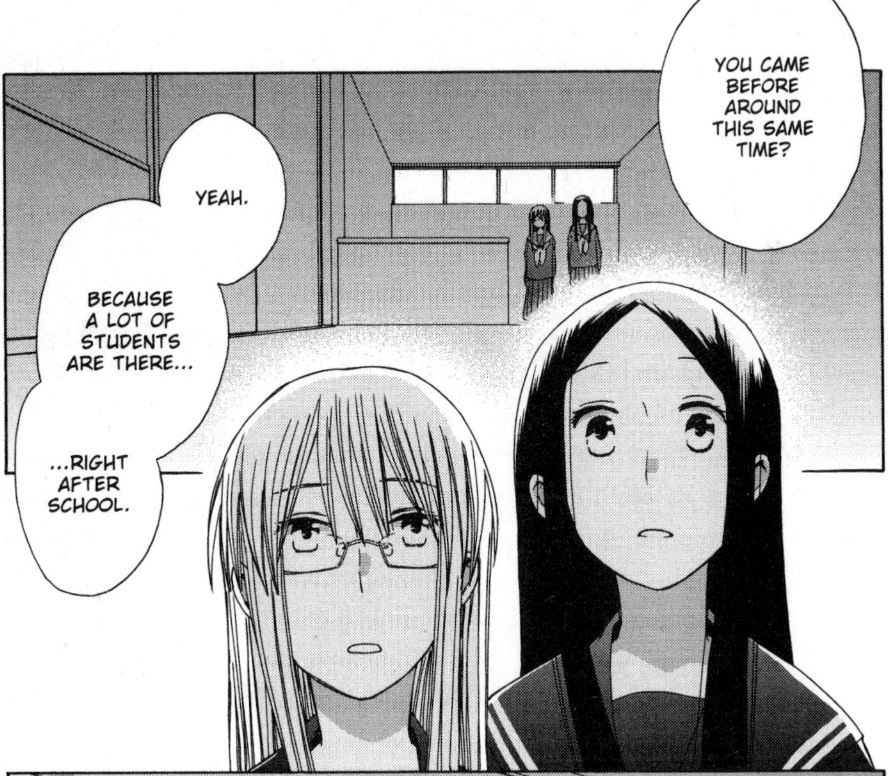
YOU CAME BEFORE AROUND THIS SAME TIME?
YEAH.
BECAUSE A LOT OF STUDENTS ARE THERE...
...RIGHT AFTER SCHOOL.

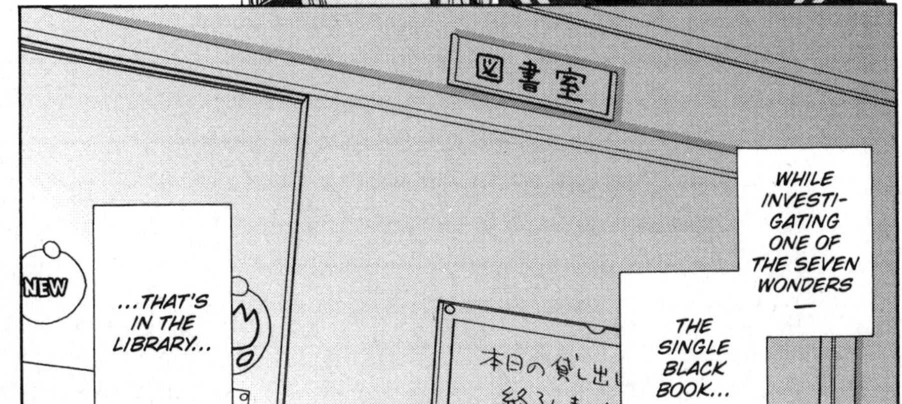
図書室
WHILE INVESTI-GATING ONE OF THE SEVEN WONDERS —
THE SINGLE BLACK BOOK...
...THAT'S IN THE LIBRARY...
NEW

SIGNS: LIBRARY; NO MORE BOOKS MAY BE CHECKED OUT FOR THE DAY

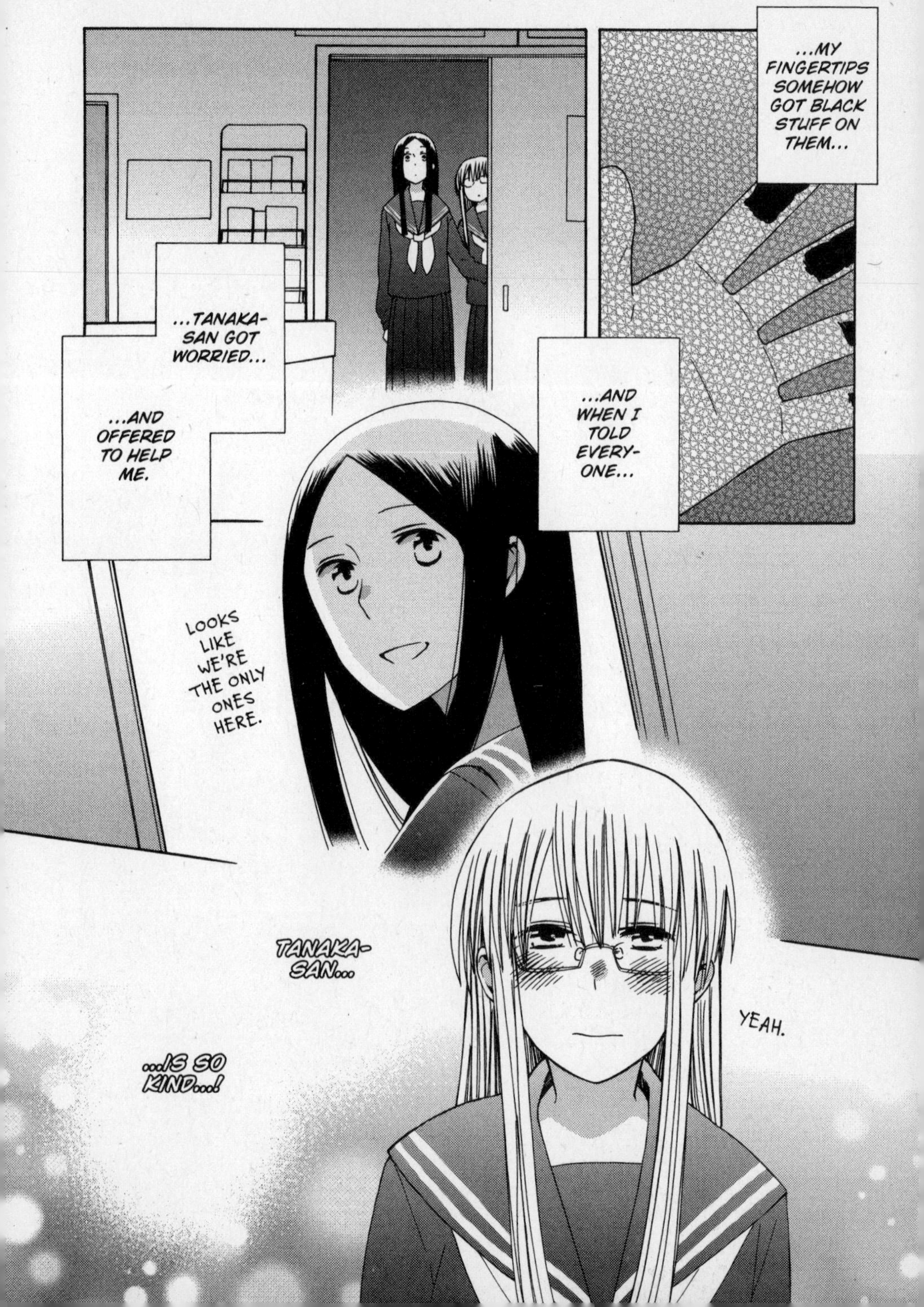
...MY FINGERTIPS SOMEHOW GOT BLACK STUFF ON THEM...
...AND WHEN I TOLD EVERY-ONE...
...TANAKA-SAN GOT WORRIED...
...AND OFFERED TO HELP ME.
LOOKS LIKE WE'RE THE ONLY ONES HERE.
YEAH.
TANAKA-SAN...
...IS SO KIND...!

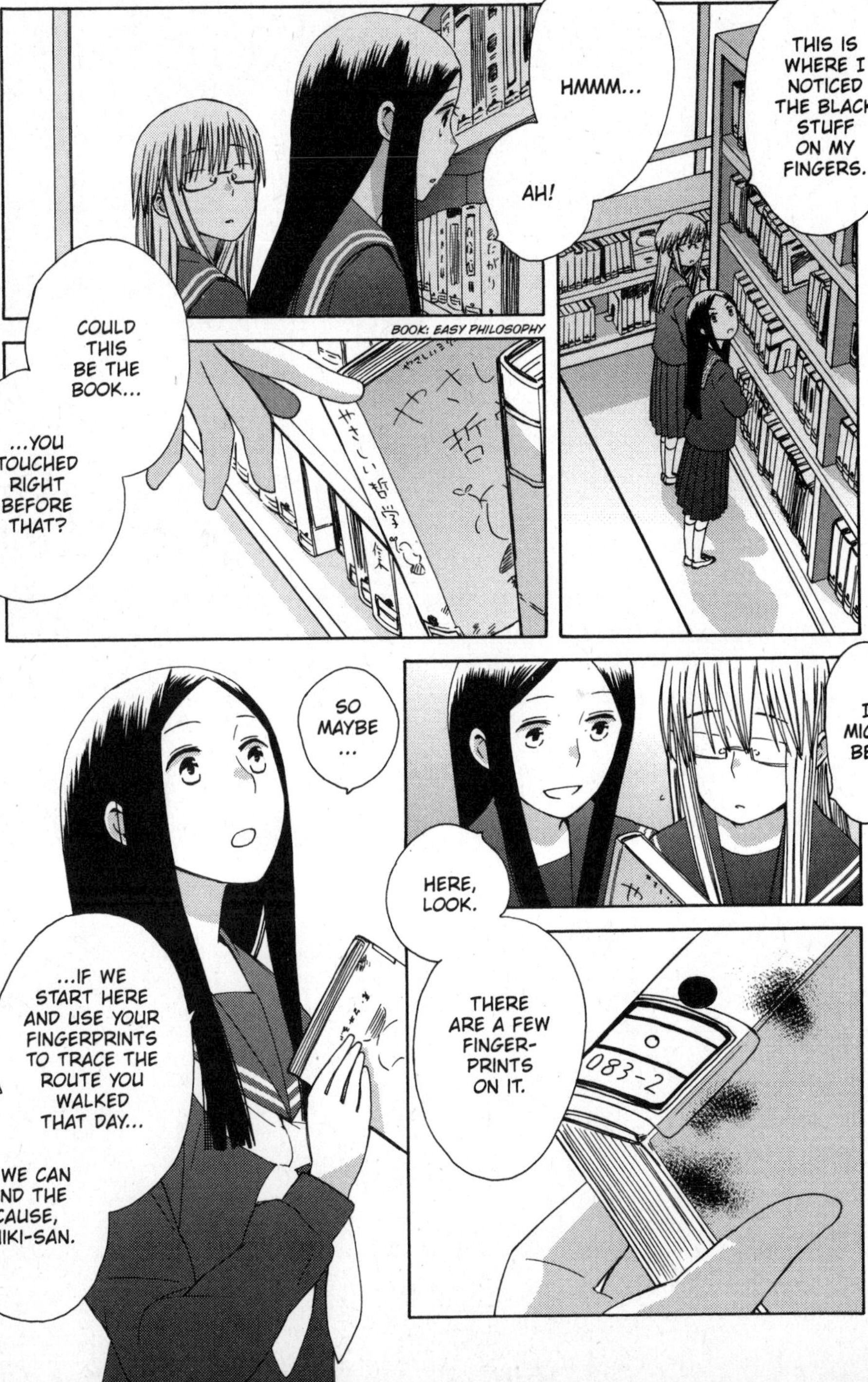
THIS IS WHERE I NOTICED THE BLACK STUFF ON MY FINGERS.
HMMM...
AH!
BOOK: EASY PHILOSOPHY
COULD THIS BE THE BOOK...
...YOU TOUCHED RIGHT BEFORE THAT?
IT MIGHT BE...
HERE, LOOK.
THERE ARE A FEW FINGER-PRINTS ON IT.
083-2
SO MAYBE...
...IF WE START HERE AND USE YOUR FINGERPRINTS TO TRACE THE ROUTE YOU WALKED THAT DAY...
...WE CAN FIND THE CAUSE, SHIKI-SAN.

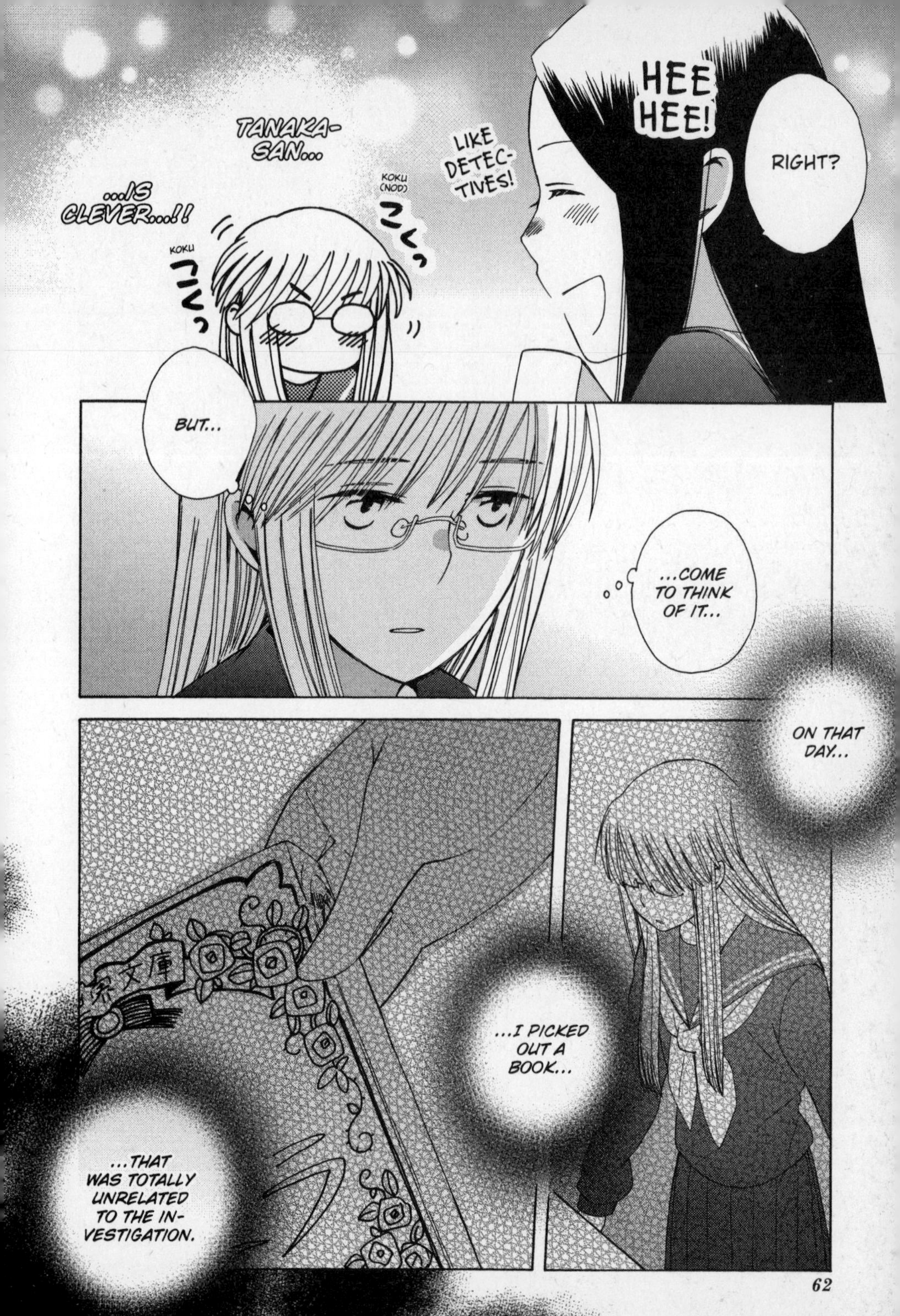
RIGHT?
HEE HEE!
LIKE DETECTIVES!
KOKU (NOD)
こくっ
KOKU
こくっ
TANAKA-SAN...
...IS CLEVER...!!
BUT...
...COME TO THINK OF IT...
ON THAT DAY...
...I PICKED OUT A BOOK...
...THAT WAS TOTALLY UNRELATED TO THE INVESTIGATION.

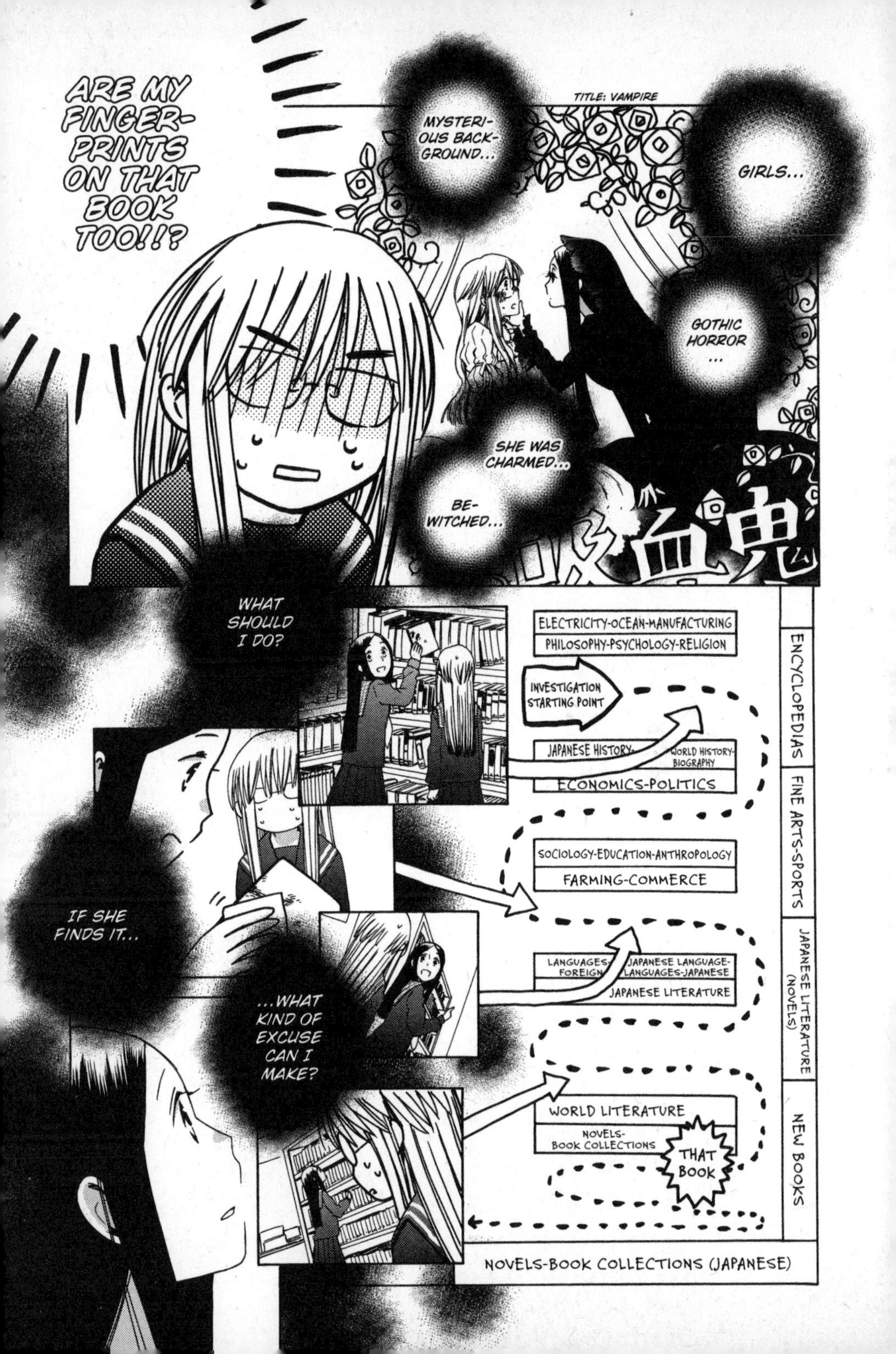
TITLE: VAMPIRE
GIRLS...
MYSTERIOUS BACKGROUND...
GOTHIC HORROR...
吸血鬼
SHE WAS CHARMED...
BEWITCHED...
ARE MY FINGERPRINTS ON THAT BOOK TOO!!?
ENCYCLOPEDIAS
ELECTRICITY-OCEAN-MANUFACTURING
PHILOSOPHY-PSYCHOLOGY-RELIGION
INVESTIGATION STARTING POINT
JAPANESE HISTORY-
WORLD HISTORY-BIOGRAPHY
ECONOMICS-POLITICS
WHAT SHOULD I DO?
FINE ARTS-SPORTS
SOCIOLOGY-EDUCATION-ANTHROPOLOGY
FARMING-COMMERCE
JAPANESE LITERATURE (NOVELS)
LANGUAGES-FOREIGN
JAPANESE LANGUAGE-LANGUAGES-JAPANESE
JAPANESE LITERATURE
IF SHE FINDS IT...
NEW BOOKS
WORLD LITERATURE
NOVELS-BOOK COLLECTIONS
THAT BOOK
NOVELS-BOOK COLLECTIONS (JAPANESE)
...WHAT KIND OF EXCUSE CAN I MAKE?

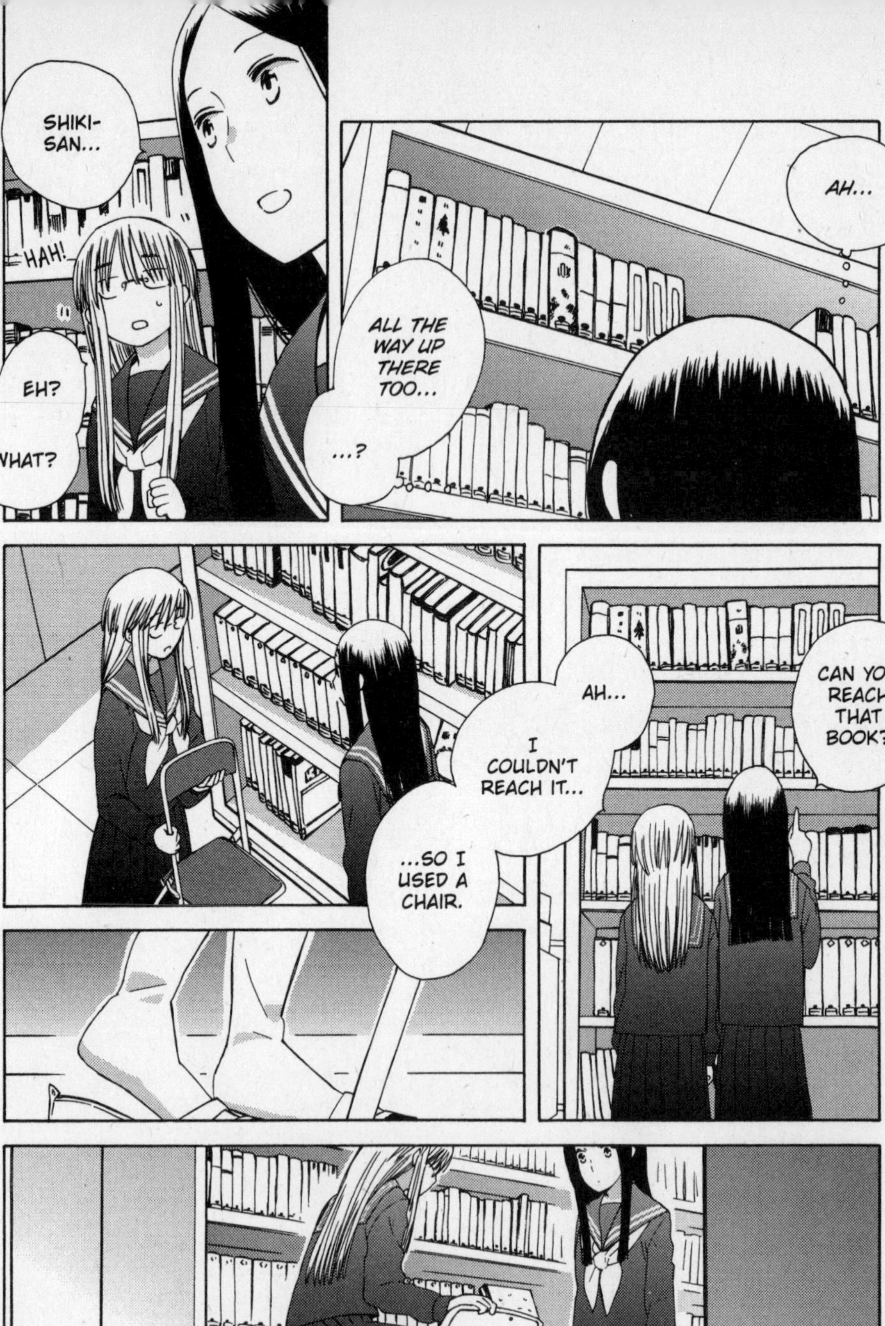
AH...
ALL THE WAY UP THERE TOO...
...?
SHIKI-SAN...
HAH!
EH?
WHAT?
CAN YOU REACH THAT BOOK?
AH...
I COULDN'T REACH IT...
...SO I USED A CHAIR.

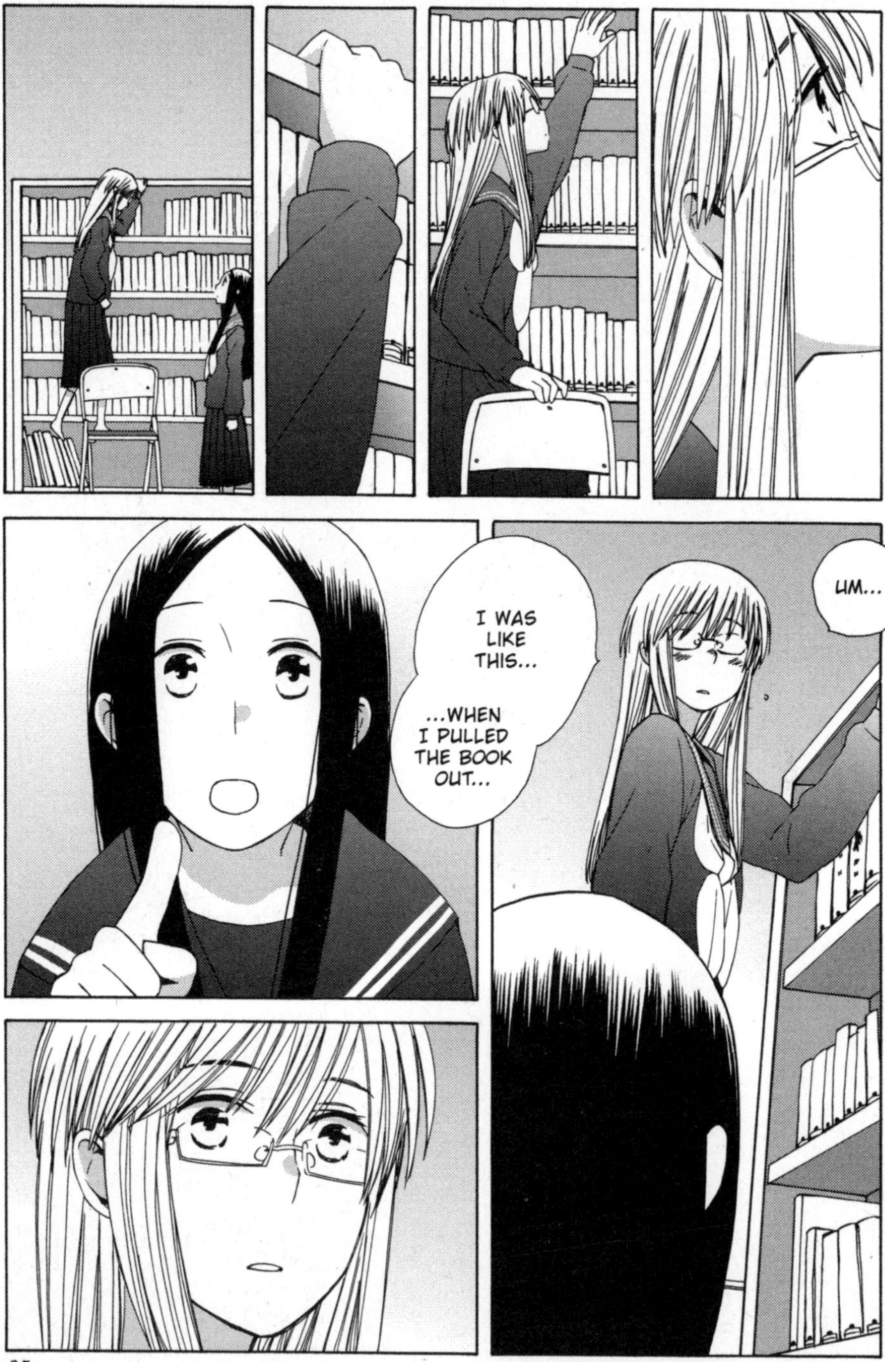
UM...
I WAS LIKE THIS...
...WHEN I PULLED THE BOOK OUT...

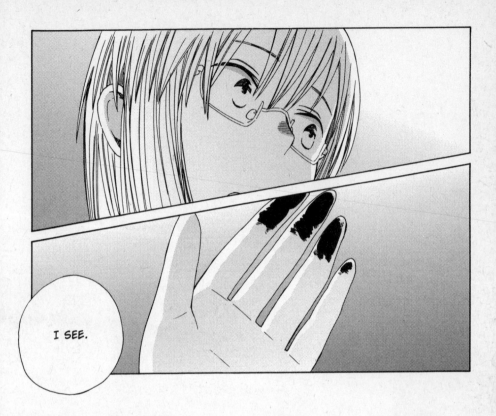

I SEE.

IT SEEMS THIS IS THE ONLY PART THEY DIDN'T CLEAN.

LOOK AT ALL THIS DUST.

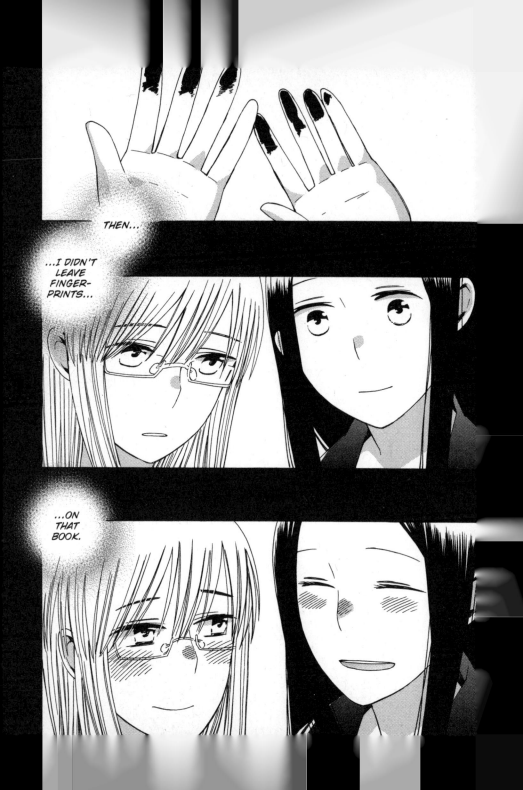

THEN...

...I DIDN'T LEAVE FINGER-PRINTS...

...ON THAT BOOK.

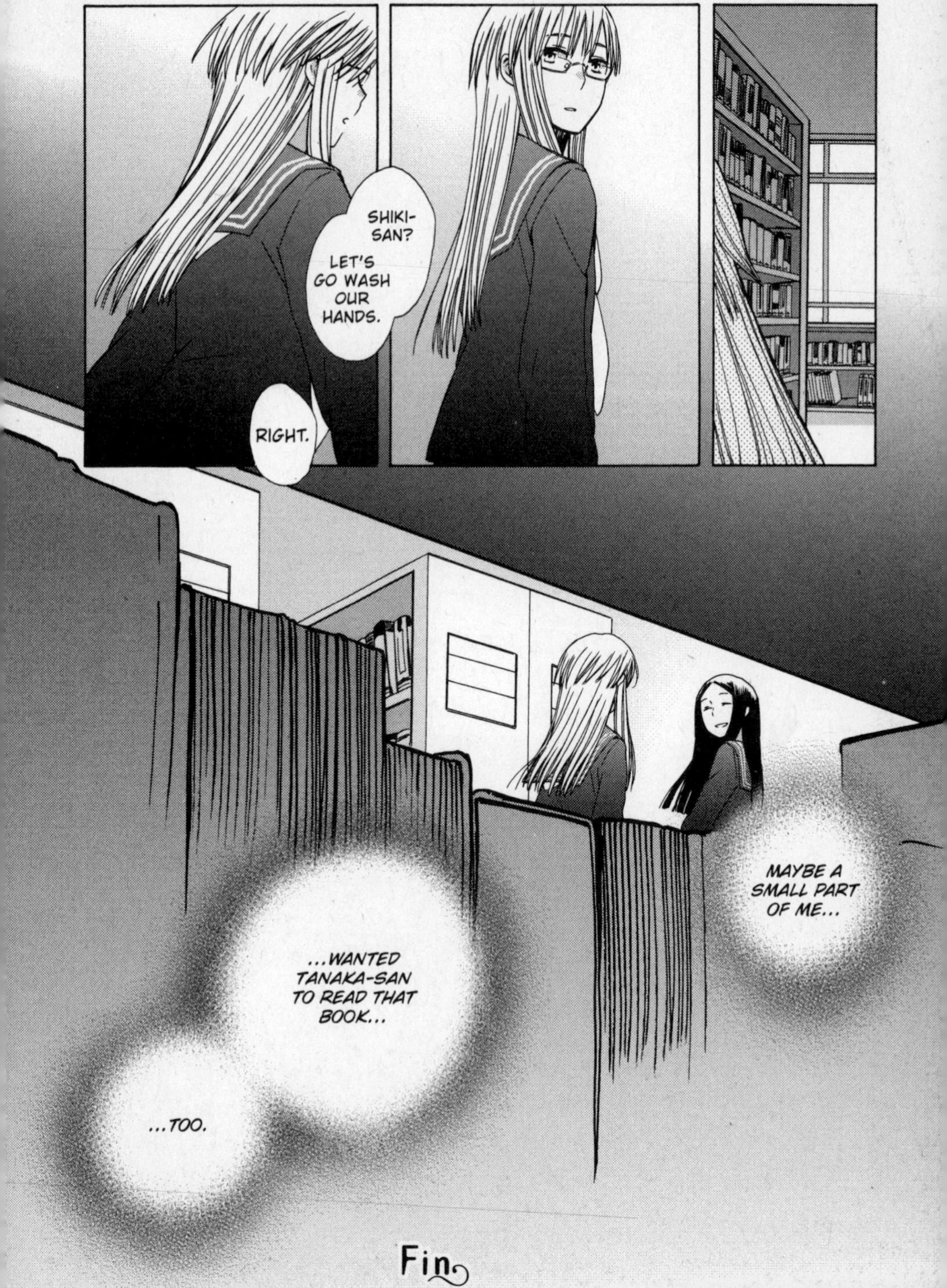
SHIKI-SAN? LET'S GO WASH OUR HANDS.
RIGHT.
MAYBE A SMALL PART OF ME...
...WANTED TANAKA-SAN TO READ THAT BOOK...
...TOO.
Fin

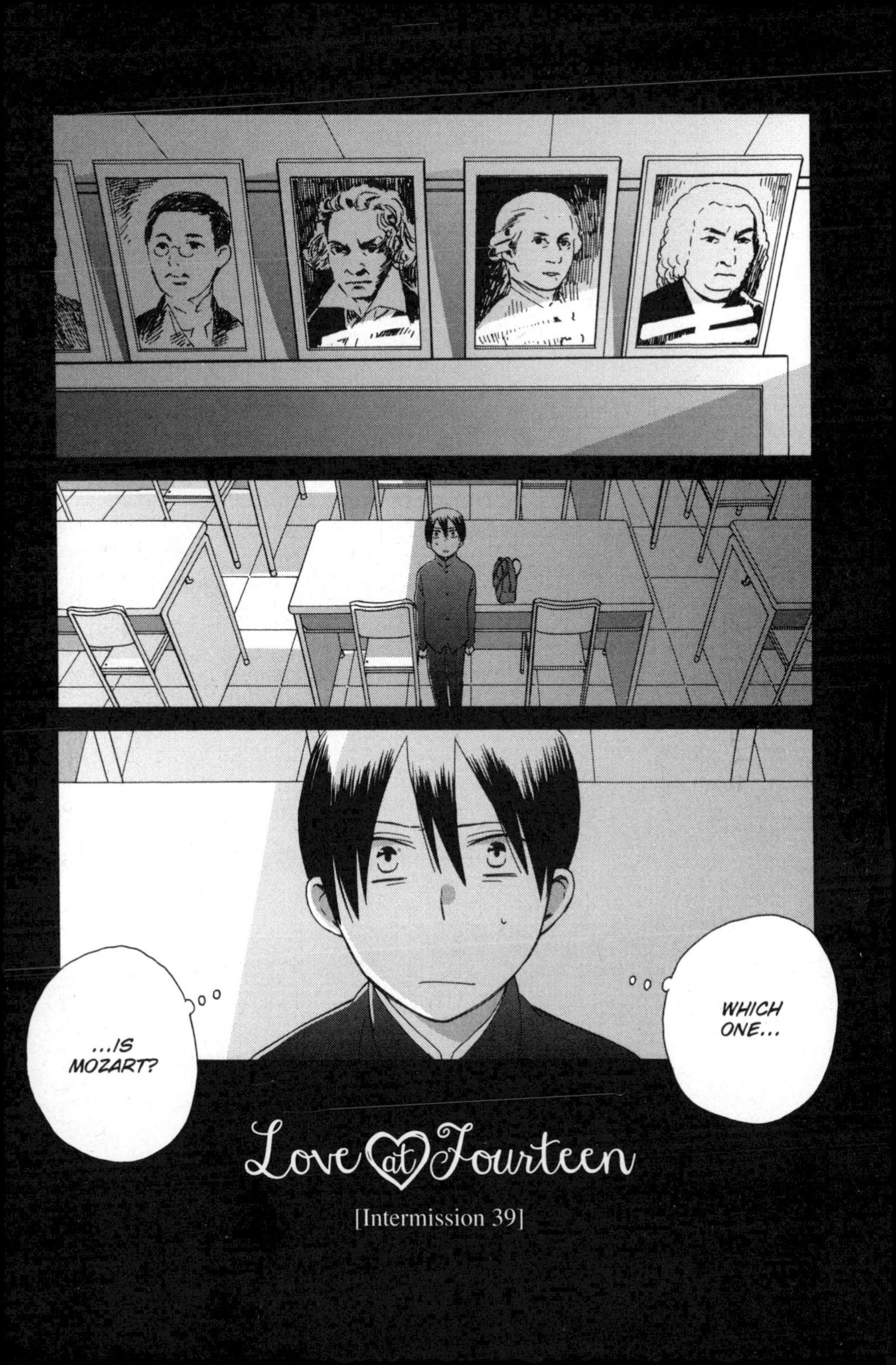
WHICH ONE...
...IS MOZART?

Love at Fourteen

[Intermission 39]

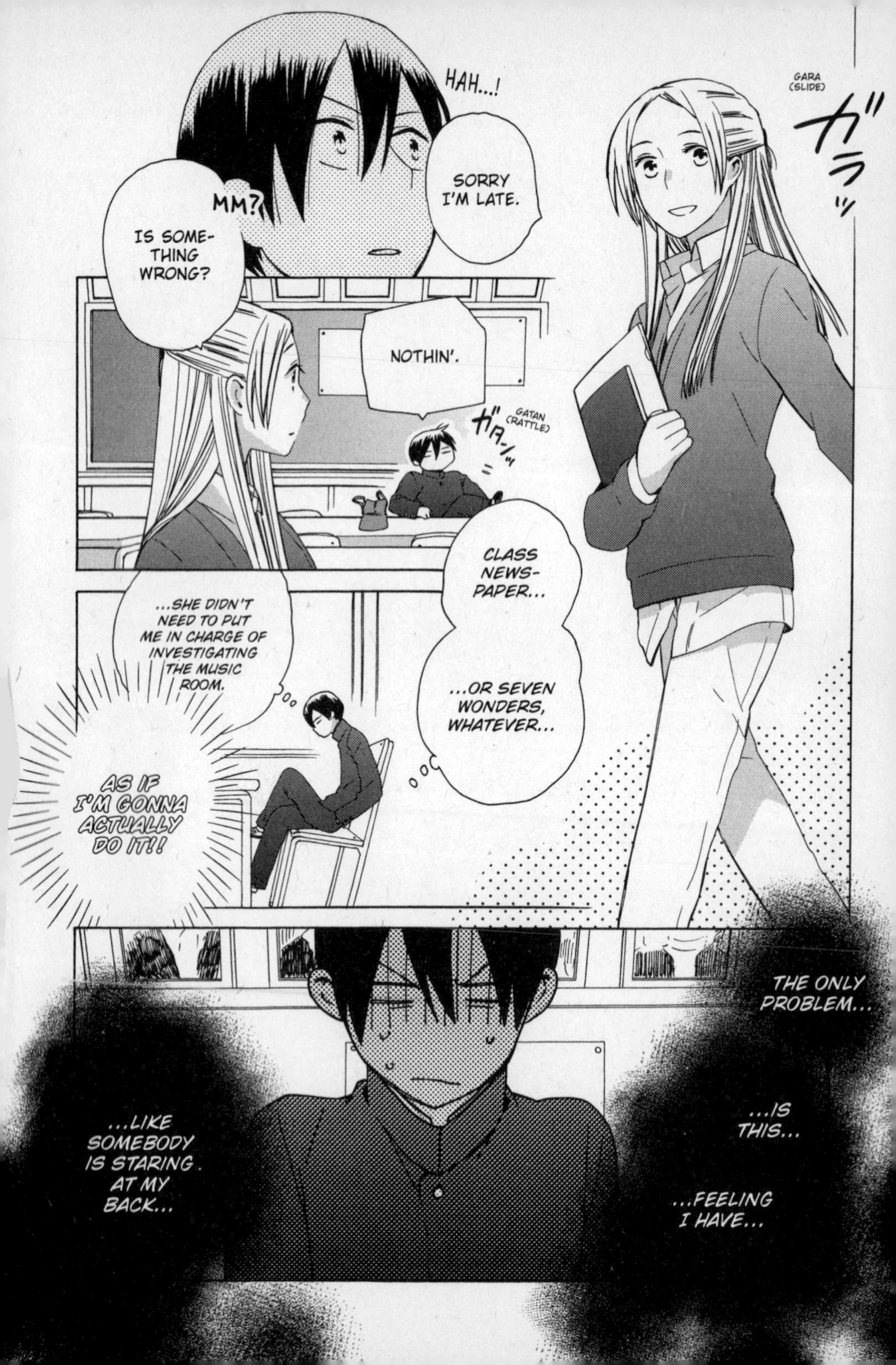
GARA (SLIDE)
ガラッ
HAH...!
SORRY I'M LATE.
MM?
IS SOME-THING WRONG?
NOTHIN'.
GATAN (RATTLE)
ガタン
CLASS NEWS-PAPER...
...OR SEVEN WONDERS, WHATEVER...
...SHE DIDN'T NEED TO PUT ME IN CHARGE OF INVESTIGATING THE MUSIC ROOM.
AS IF I'M GONNA ACTUALLY DO IT!!
THE ONLY PROBLEM...
...IS THIS...
...FEELING I HAVE...
...LIKE SOMEBODY IS STARING AT MY BACK...

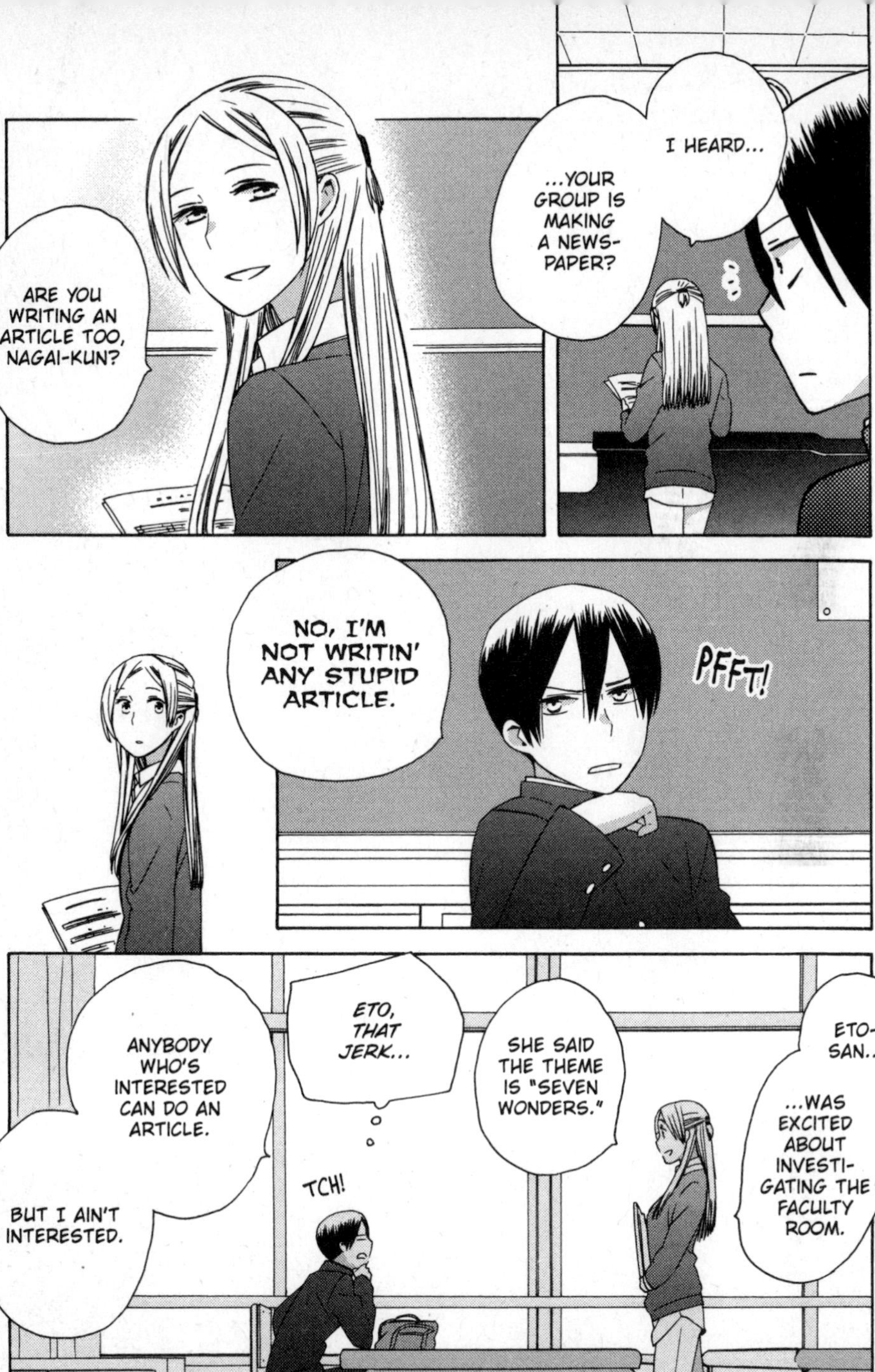
I HEARD...
...YOUR GROUP IS MAKING A NEWS-PAPER?
ARE YOU WRITING AN ARTICLE TOO, NAGAI-KUN?
PFFT!
NO, I'M NOT WRITIN' ANY STUPID ARTICLE.
ETO-SAN...
...WAS EXCITED ABOUT INVESTI-GATING THE FACULTY ROOM.
SHE SAID THE THEME IS "SEVEN WONDERS."
ETO, THAT JERK...
TCH!
ANYBODY WHO'S INTERESTED CAN DO AN ARTICLE.
BUT I AIN'T INTERESTED.

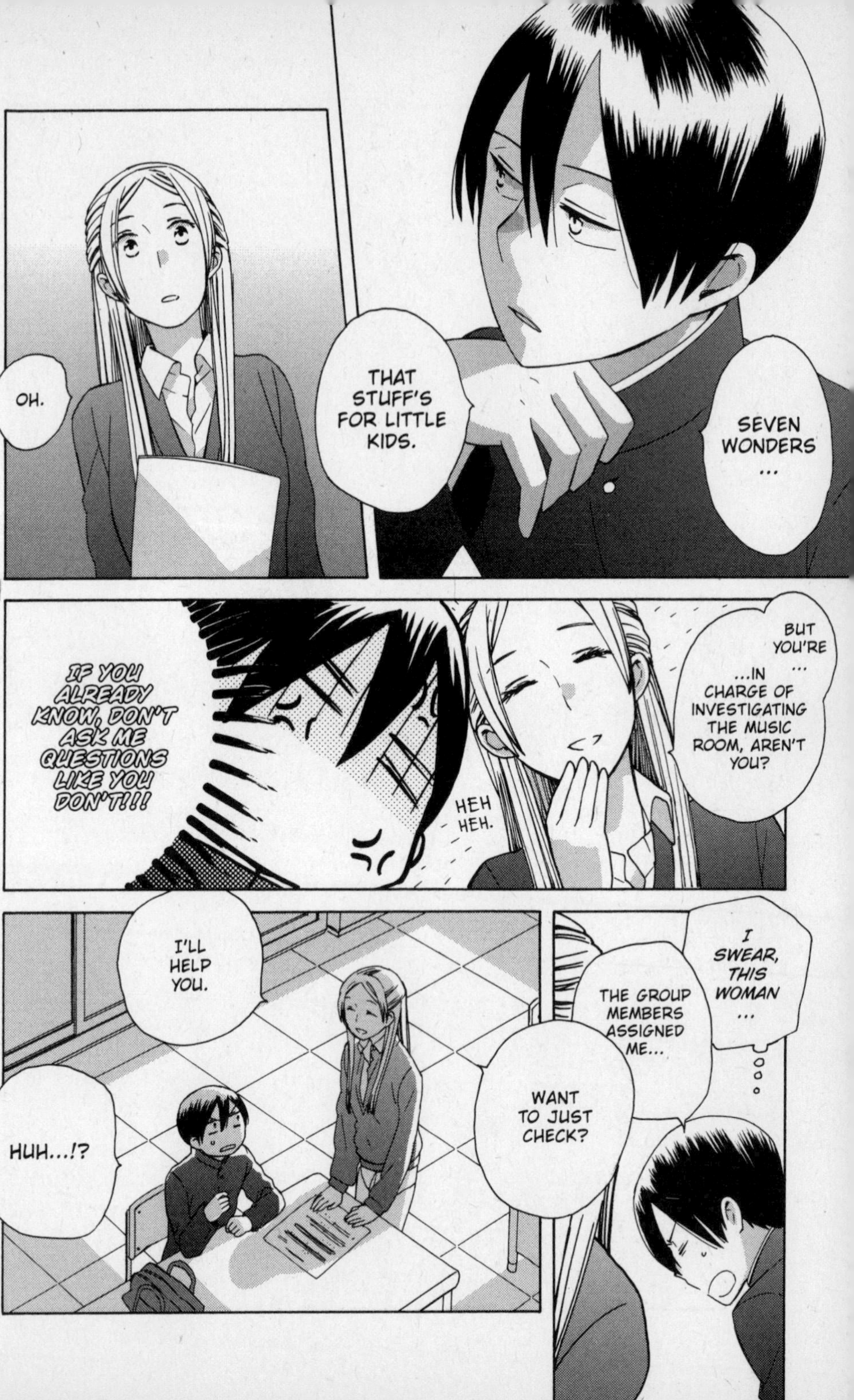

SEVEN WONDERS ...
THAT STUFF'S FOR LITTLE KIDS.
OH.
BUT YOU'RE ...
...IN CHARGE OF INVESTIGATING THE MUSIC ROOM, AREN'T YOU?
HEH HEH.
IF YOU ALREADY KNOW, DON'T ASK ME QUESTIONS LIKE YOU DON'T!!!
I SWEAR, THIS WOMAN ...
THE GROUP MEMBERS ASSIGNED ME...
WANT TO JUST CHECK?
I'LL HELP YOU.
HUH...!?

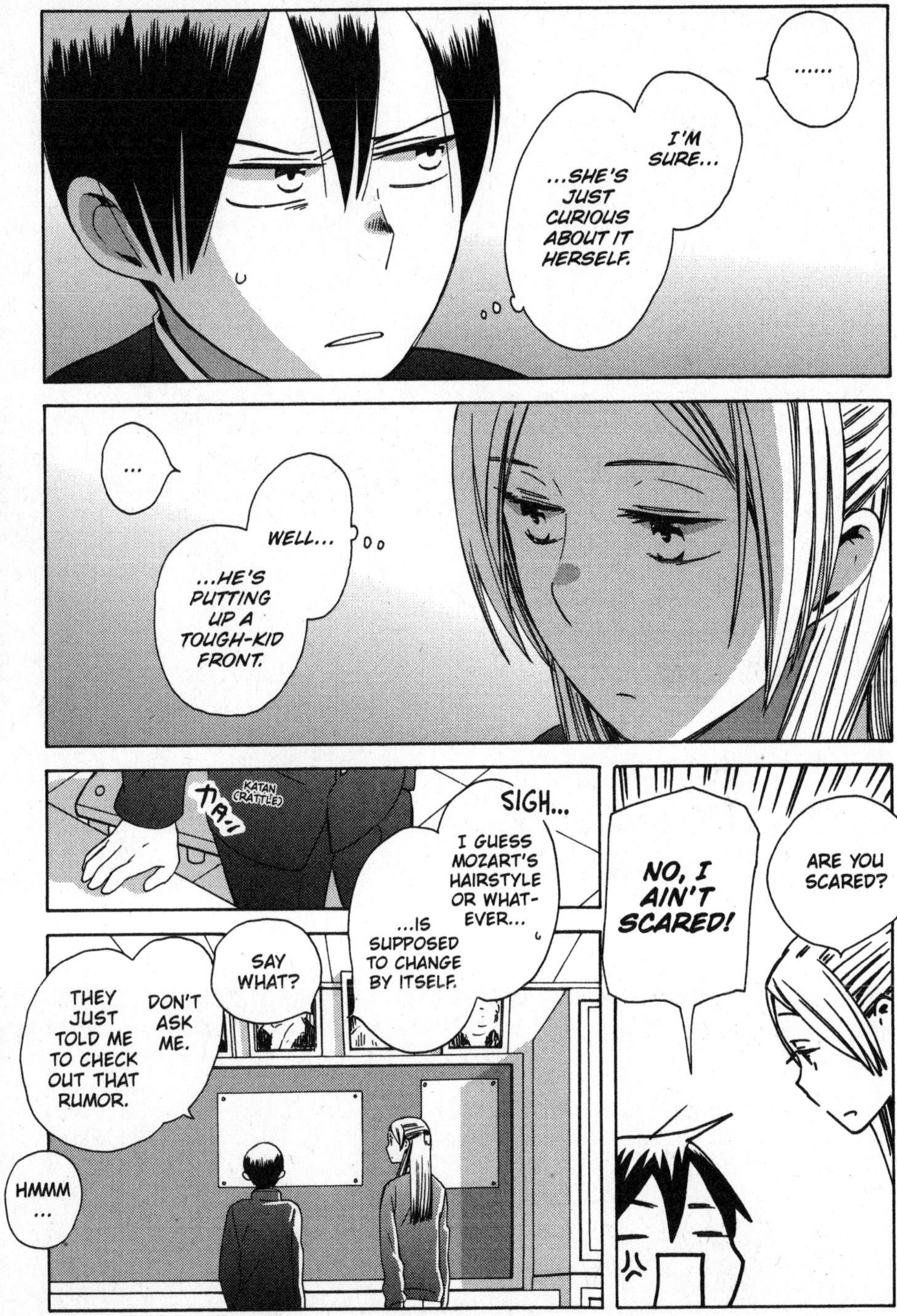
......
I'M SURE...
...SHE'S JUST CURIOUS ABOUT IT HERSELF.
...
WELL...
...HE'S PUTTING UP A TOUGH-KID FRONT.
ARE YOU SCARED?
NO, I AIN'T SCARED!
KATAN (RATTLE)
SIGH...
I GUESS MOZART'S HAIRSTYLE OR WHATEVER...
...IS SUPPOSED TO CHANGE BY ITSELF.
SAY WHAT?
DON'T ASK ME.
THEY JUST TOLD ME TO CHECK OUT THAT RUMOR.
HMMM...

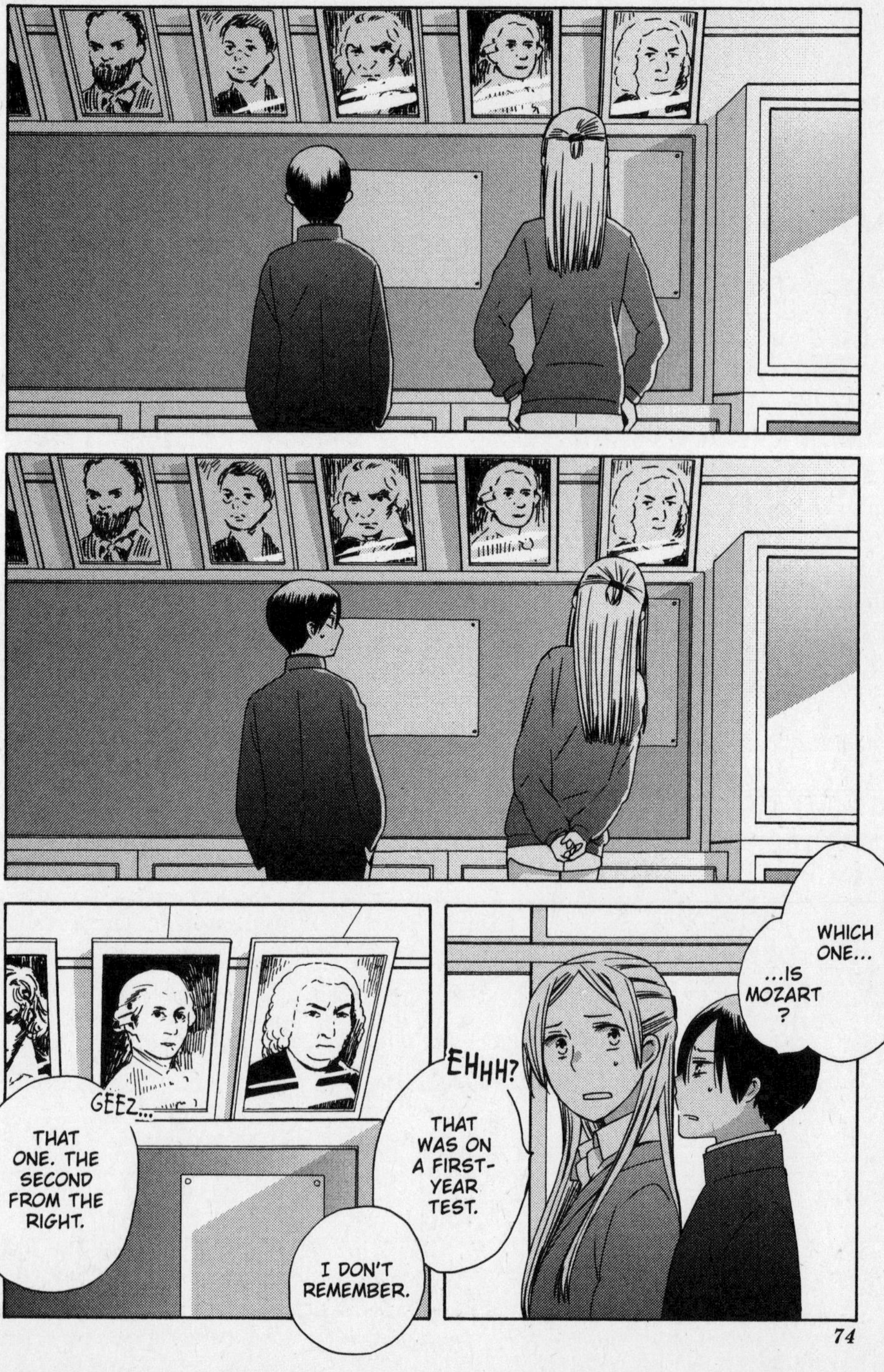
WHICH ONE...
...IS MOZART?
EHHH?
THAT WAS ON A FIRST-YEAR TEST.
I DON'T REMEMBER.
GEEZ...
THAT ONE. THE SECOND FROM THE RIGHT.

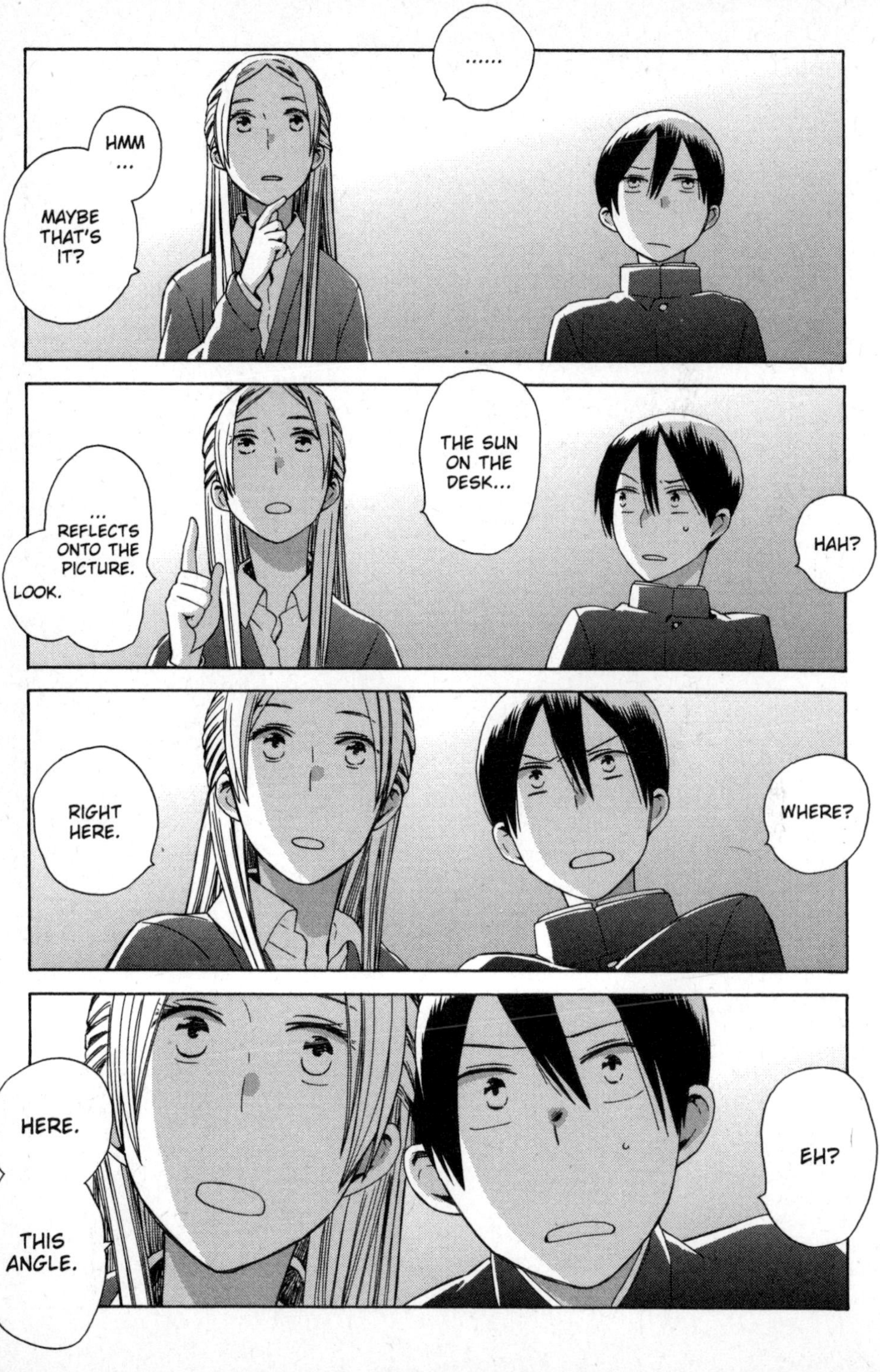
......
HMM ...
MAYBE THAT'S IT?
THE SUN ON THE DESK...
... REFLECTS ONTO THE PICTURE.
LOOK.
HAH?
WHERE?
RIGHT HERE.
EH?
HERE.
THIS ANGLE.

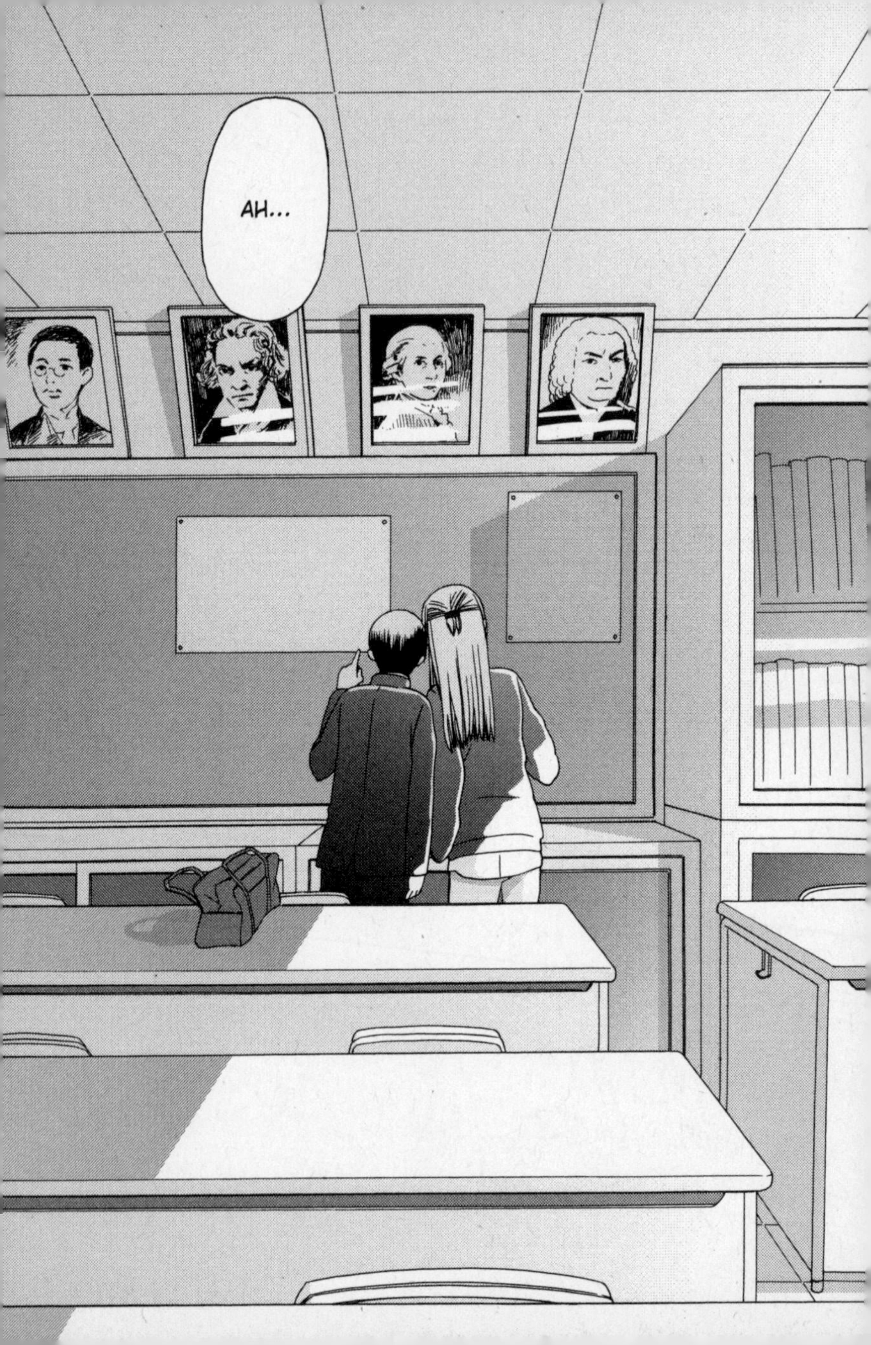
AH...

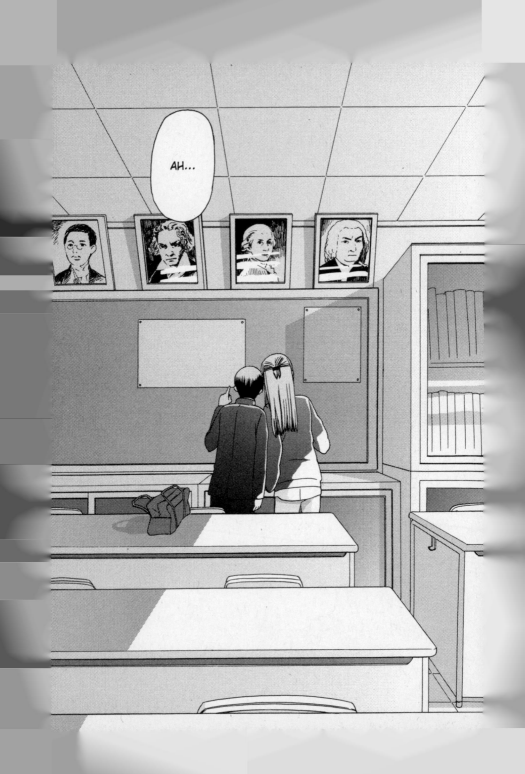

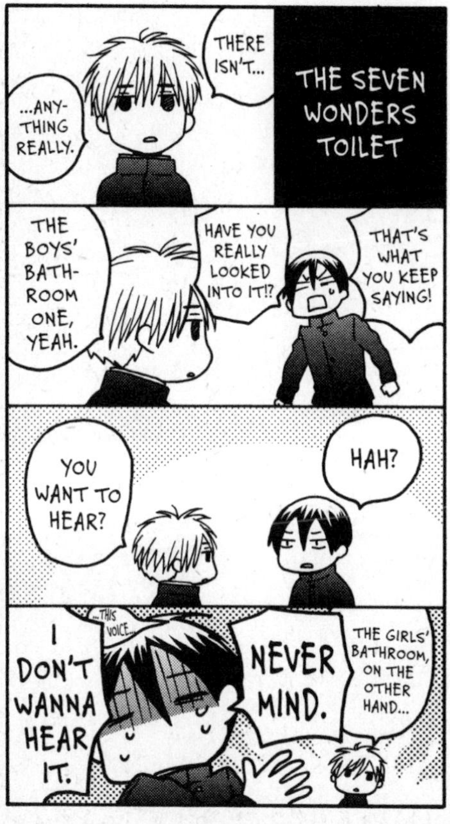
THE SEVEN WONDERS TOILET
THERE ISN'T...
...ANYTHING REALLY.
THAT'S WHAT YOU KEEP SAYING!
HAVE YOU REALLY LOOKED INTO IT!?
THE BOYS' BATHROOM ONE, YEAH.
HAH?
YOU WANT TO HEAR?
THE GIRLS' BATHROOM, ON THE OTHER HAND...
NEVER MIND.
...THIS VOICE...
I DON'T WANNA HEAR IT.

Love at Fourteen

Fuka Mizutani

Love at Fourteen

[Chapter 31]

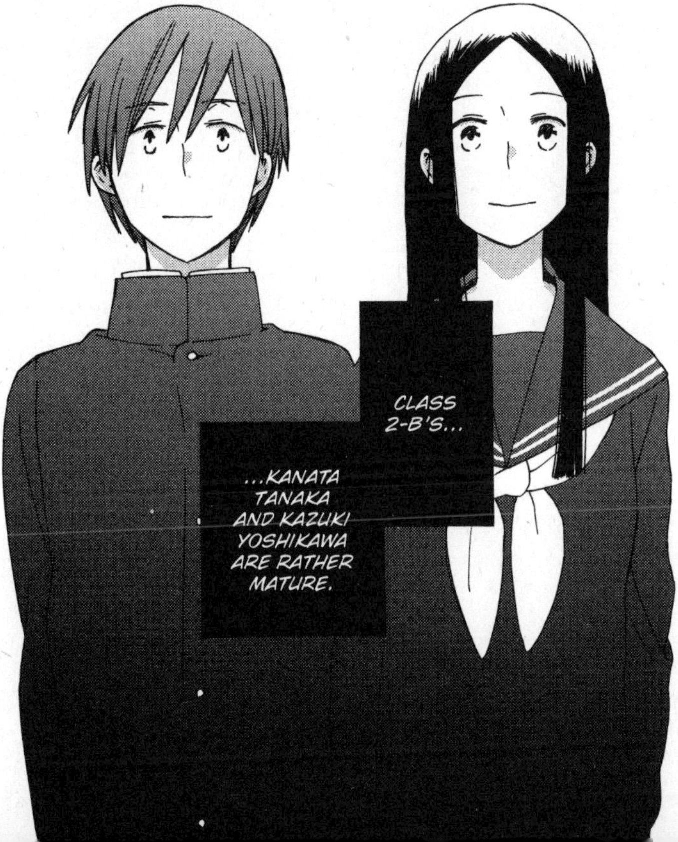
CLASS 2-B'S...
...KANATA TANAKA AND KAZUKI YOSHIKAWA ARE RATHER MATURE.

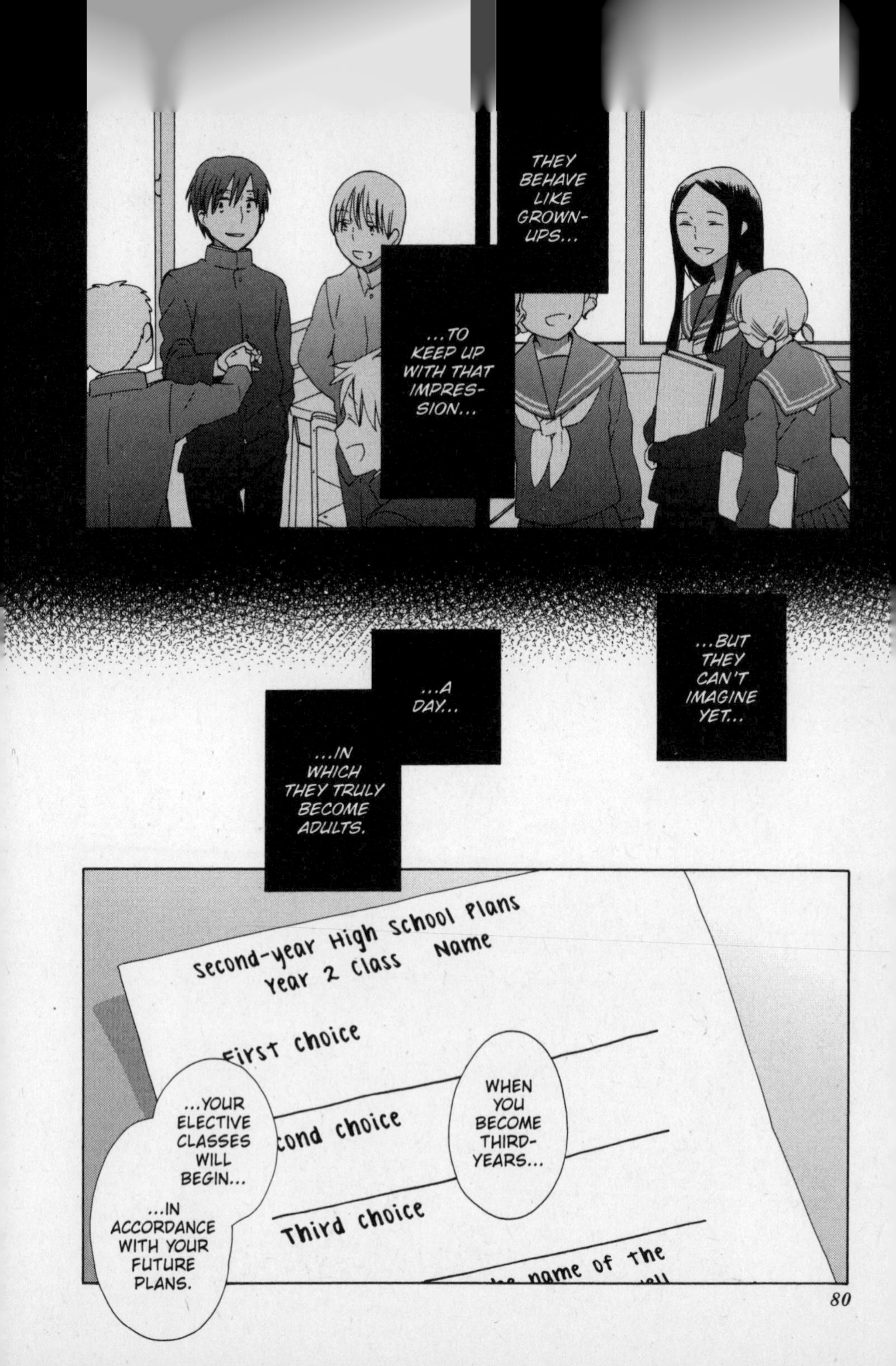
THEY BEHAVE LIKE GROWN-UPS...
...TO KEEP UP WITH THAT IMPRESSION...
...BUT THEY CAN'T IMAGINE YET...
...A DAY...
...IN WHICH THEY TRULY BECOME ADULTS.
Second-year High School Plans
Year 2 Class Name
First choice
cond choice
Third choice
WHEN YOU BECOME THIRD-YEARS...
...YOUR ELECTIVE CLASSES WILL BEGIN...
...IN ACCORDANCE WITH YOUR FUTURE PLANS.

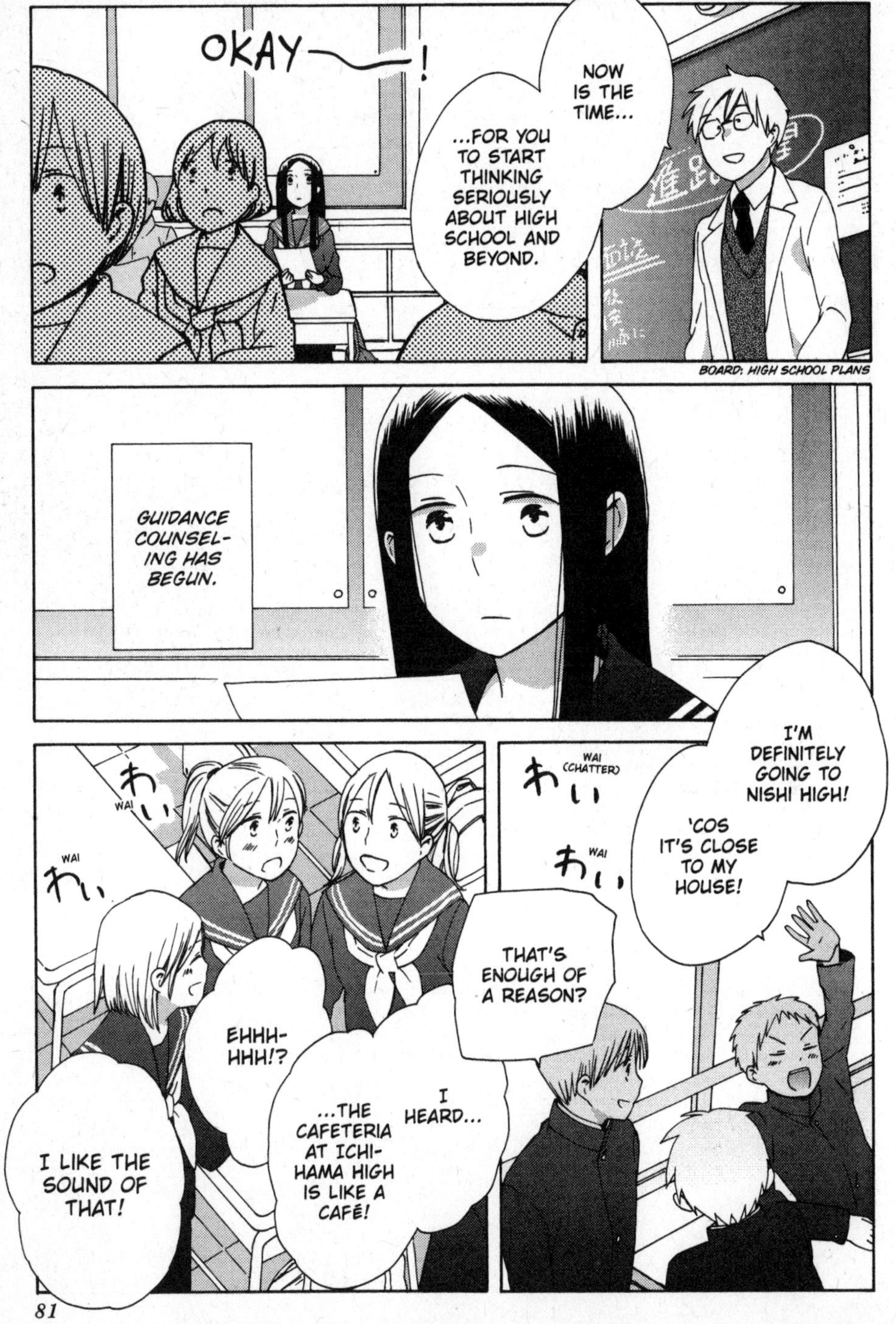
NOW IS THE TIME...
...FOR YOU TO START THINKING SERIOUSLY ABOUT HIGH SCHOOL AND BEYOND.
OKAY~!
BOARD: HIGH SCHOOL PLANS
GUIDANCE COUNSEL-ING HAS BEGUN.
WAI (CHATTER)
WAI
I'M DEFINITELY GOING TO NISHI HIGH!
'COS IT'S CLOSE TO MY HOUSE!
THAT'S ENOUGH OF A REASON?
WAI
WAI
I HEARD...
...THE CAFETERIA AT ICHI-HAMA HIGH IS LIKE A CAFÉ!
EHHH-HHH!?
I LIKE THE SOUND OF THAT!

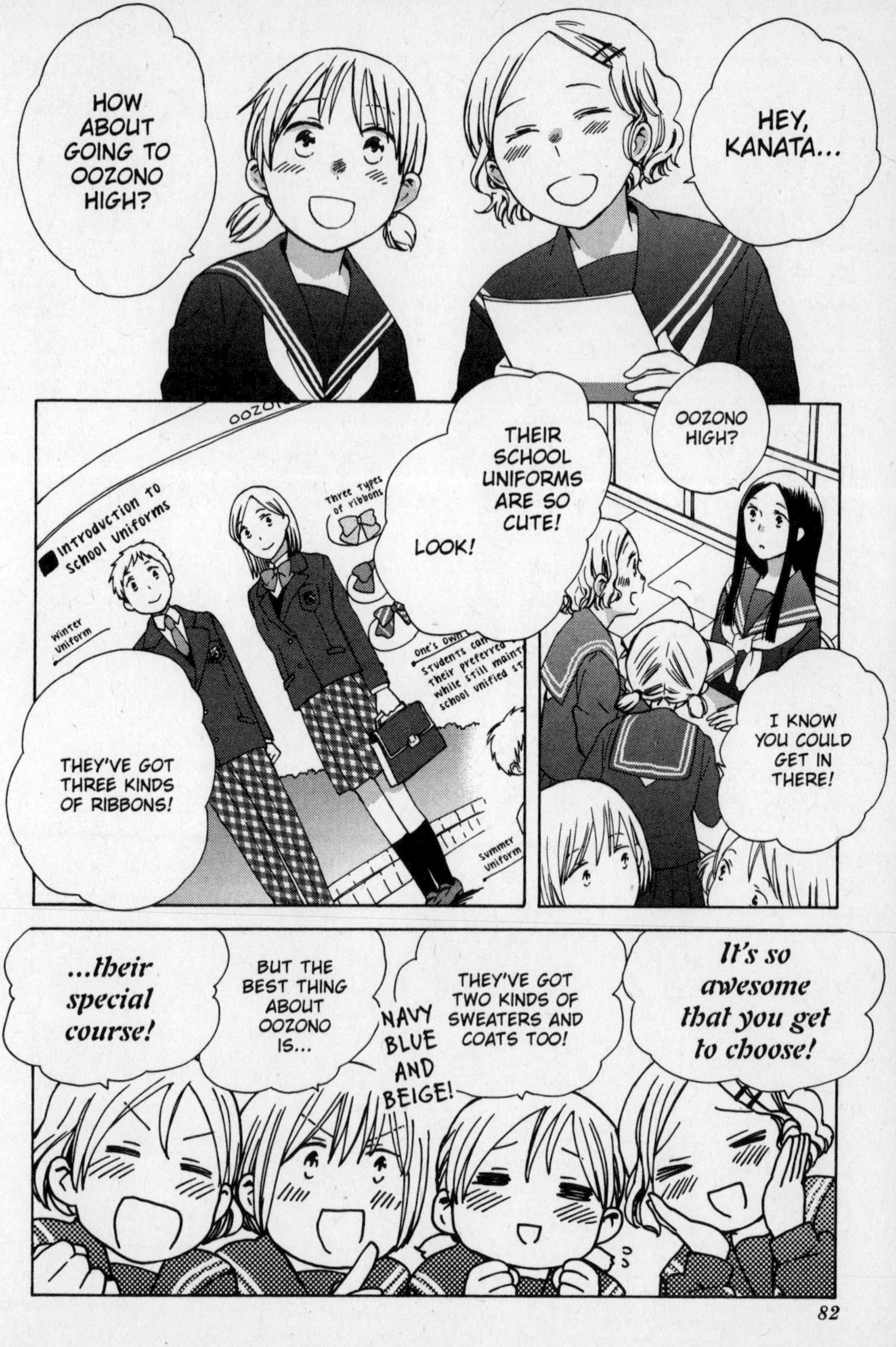

HEY, KANATA...
HOW ABOUT GOING TO OOZONO HIGH?
OOZONO HIGH?
I KNOW YOU COULD GET IN THERE!
THEIR SCHOOL UNIFORMS ARE SO CUTE!
LOOK!
Introduction to School Uniforms
Three Types of Ribbons
Winter Uniform
Summer Uniform
THEY'VE GOT THREE KINDS OF RIBBONS!
It's so awesome that you get to choose!
THEY'VE GOT TWO KINDS OF SWEATERS AND COATS TOO!
NAVY BLUE AND BEIGE!
BUT THE BEST THING ABOUT OOZONO IS...
...their special course!

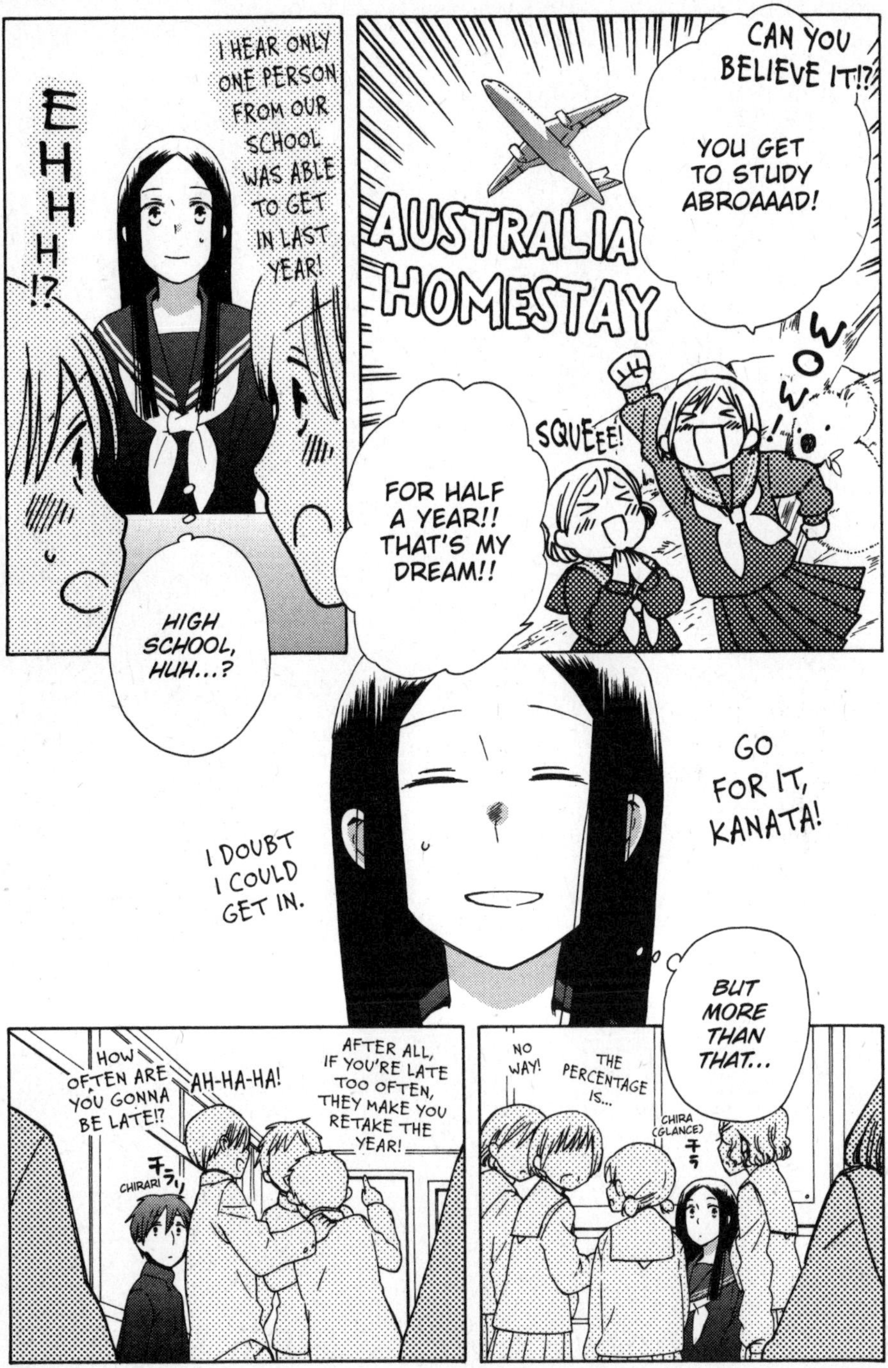
CAN YOU BELIEVE IT!?
YOU GET TO STUDY ABROAAAD!
AUSTRALIA HOMESTAY
WOW!
SQUEEE!
FOR HALF A YEAR!! THAT'S MY DREAM!!
I HEAR ONLY ONE PERSON FROM OUR SCHOOL WAS ABLE TO GET IN LAST YEAR!
EHHH!?
HIGH SCHOOL, HUH...?
GO FOR IT, KANATA!
I DOUBT I COULD GET IN.
BUT MORE THAN THAT...
THE PERCENTAGE IS...
NO WAY!
CHIRA (GLANCE)
チラ
AFTER ALL, IF YOU'RE LATE TOO OFTEN, THEY MAKE YOU RETAKE THE YEAR!
AH-HA-HA!
HOW OFTEN ARE YOU GONNA BE LATE!?
チラリ
CHIRARI

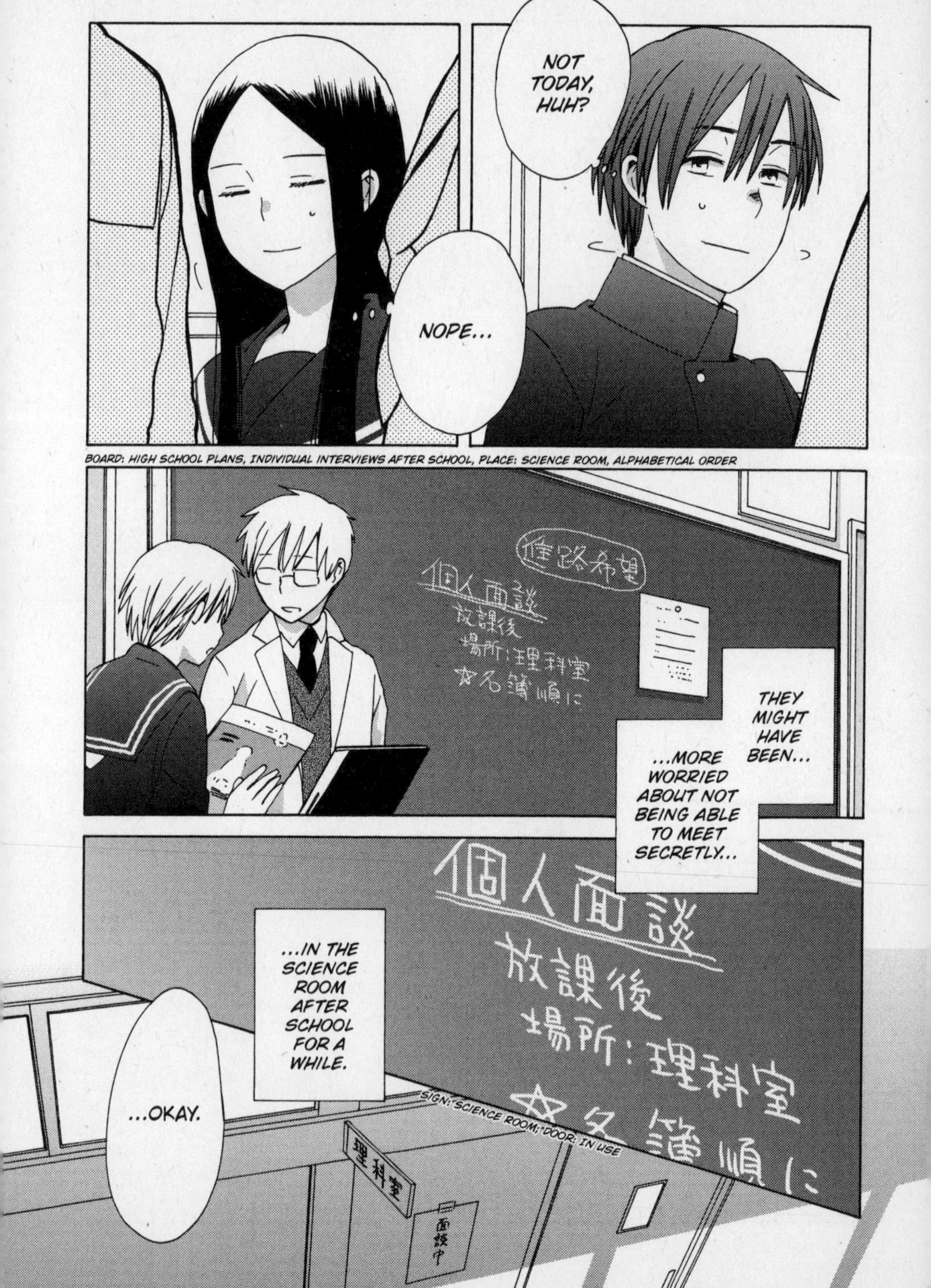
NOT TODAY, HUH?
NOPE...
BOARD: HIGH SCHOOL PLANS, INDIVIDUAL INTERVIEWS AFTER SCHOOL, PLACE: SCIENCE ROOM, ALPHABETICAL ORDER
進路希望
個人面談
放課後
場所：理科室
☆名簿順に
THEY MIGHT HAVE BEEN...
...MORE WORRIED ABOUT NOT BEING ABLE TO MEET SECRETLY...
...IN THE SCIENCE ROOM AFTER SCHOOL FOR A WHILE.
...OKAY.
SIGN: SCIENCE ROOM; DOOR: IN USE
理科室
面談中

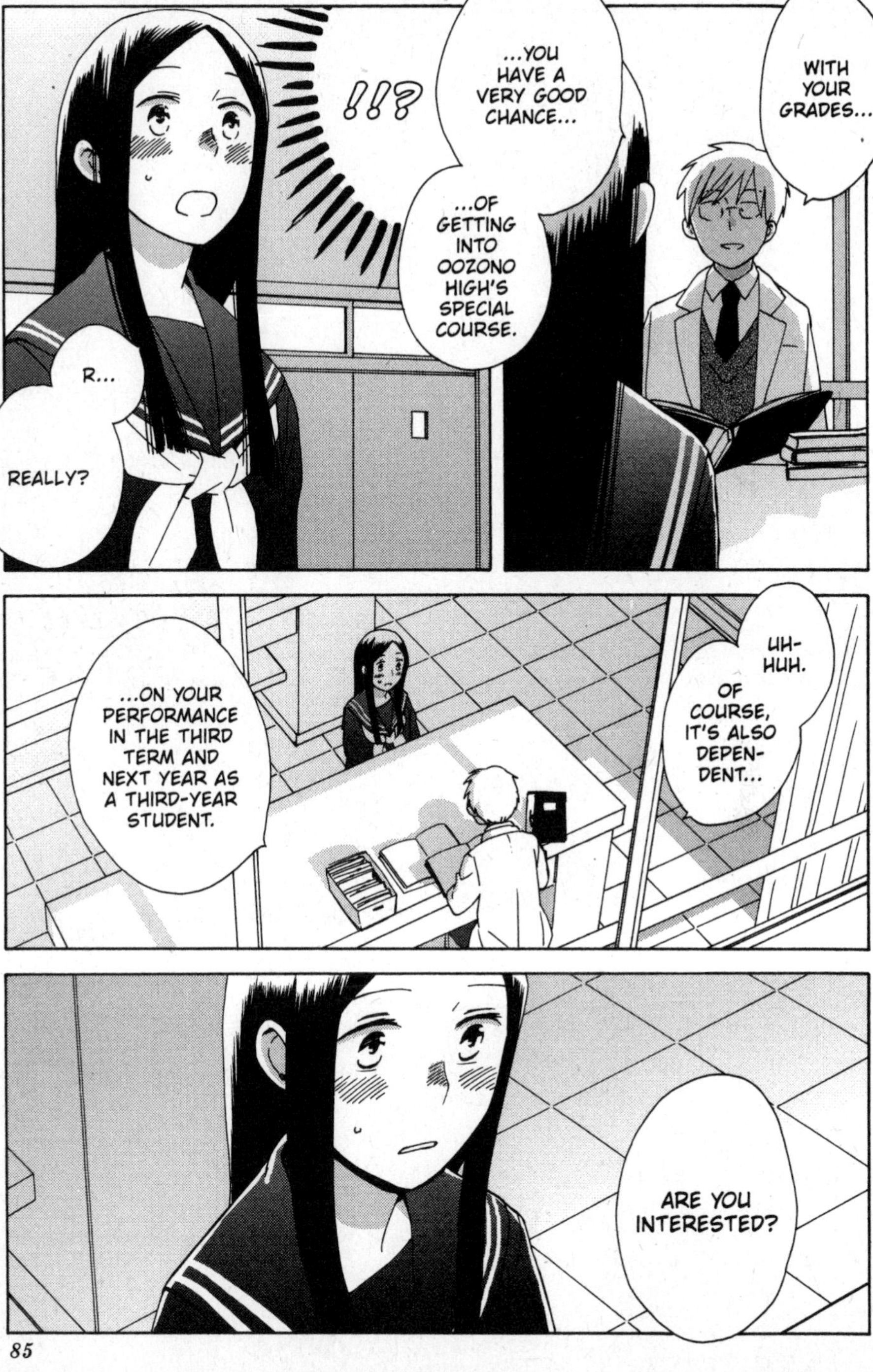
WITH YOUR GRADES...
...YOU HAVE A VERY GOOD CHANCE...
...OF GETTING INTO OOZONO HIGH'S SPECIAL COURSE.
!!?
R...
REALLY?
UH-HUH.
OF COURSE, IT'S ALSO DEPENDENT...
...ON YOUR PERFORMANCE IN THE THIRD TERM AND NEXT YEAR AS A THIRD-YEAR STUDENT.
ARE YOU INTERESTED?

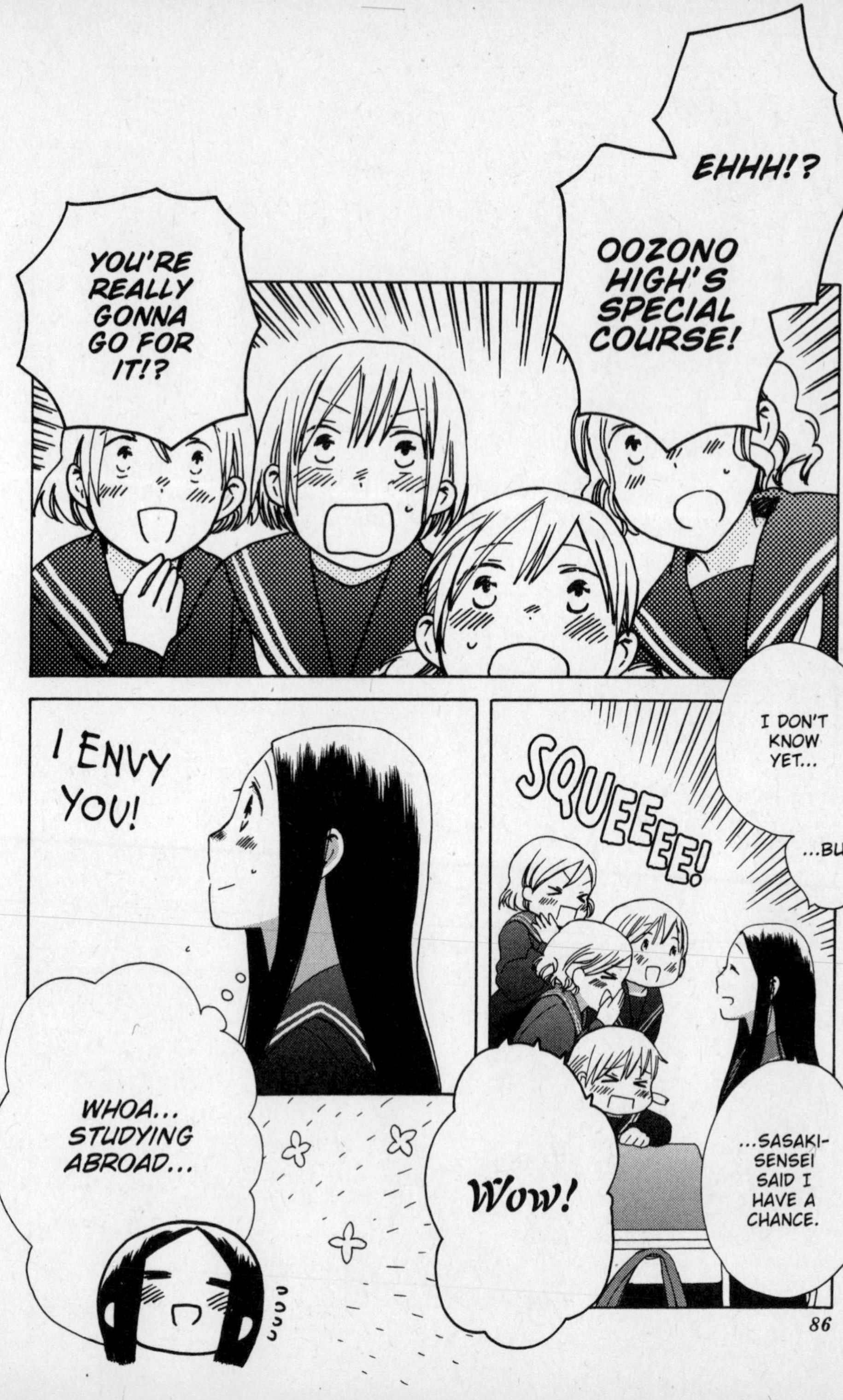
EHHH!?
OOZONO HIGH'S SPECIAL COURSE!
YOU'RE REALLY GONNA GO FOR IT!?
I DON'T KNOW YET...
...BUT...
SQUEEEEEE!
...SASAKI-SENSEI SAID I HAVE A CHANCE.
Wow!
I ENVY YOU!
WHOA... STUDYING ABROAD...

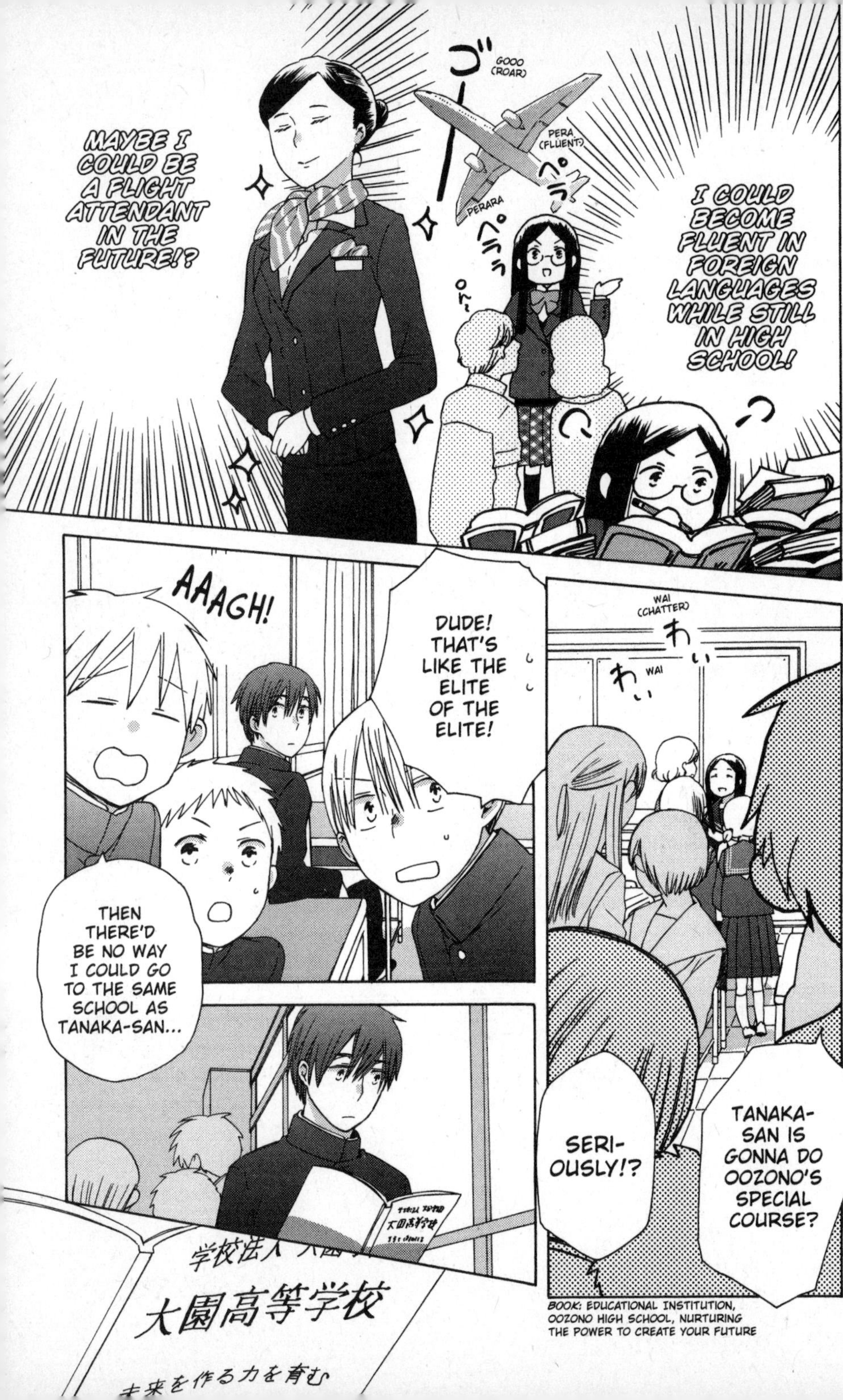
GOOO (ROAR)
PERA (FLUENT)
I COULD BECOME FLUENT IN FOREIGN LANGUAGES WHILE STILL IN HIGH SCHOOL!
PERARA
MAYBE I COULD BE A FLIGHT ATTENDANT IN THE FUTURE!?
WAI (CHATTER)
WAI
TANAKA-SAN IS GONNA DO OOZONO'S SPECIAL COURSE?
SERI-OUSLY!?
DUDE! THAT'S LIKE THE ELITE OF THE ELITE!
AAAGH!
THEN THERE'D BE NO WAY I COULD GO TO THE SAME SCHOOL AS TANAKA-SAN...
学校法人
大園高等学校
未来を作る力を育む
BOOK: EDUCATIONAL INSTITUTION, OOZONO HIGH SCHOOL, NURTURING THE POWER TO CREATE YOUR FUTURE

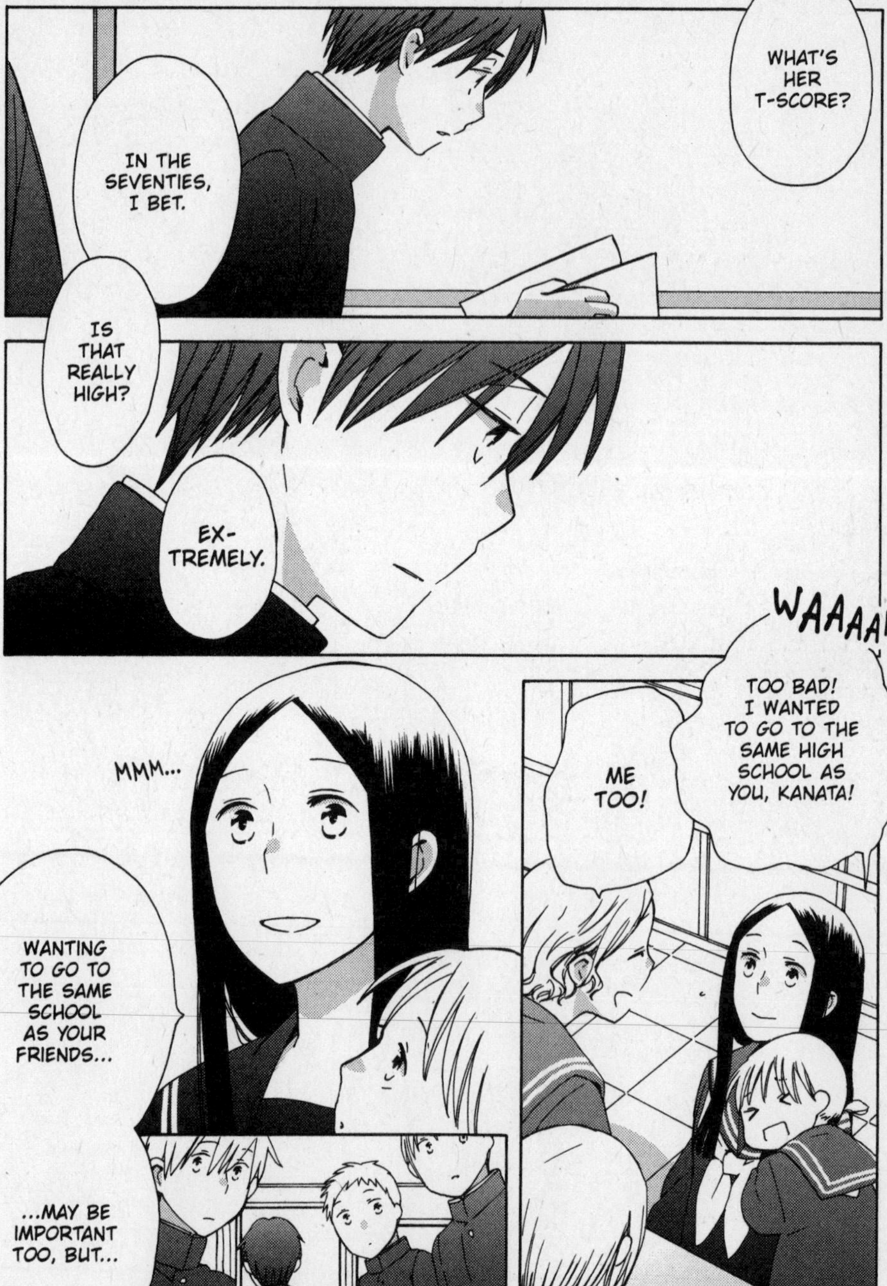
WHAT'S HER T-SCORE?
IN THE SEVENTIES, I BET.
IS THAT REALLY HIGH?
EX-TREMELY.
WAAAAH!
TOO BAD! I WANTED TO GO TO THE SAME HIGH SCHOOL AS YOU, KANATA!
ME TOO!
MMM...
WANTING TO GO TO THE SAME SCHOOL AS YOUR FRIENDS...
...MAY BE IMPORTANT TOO, BUT...

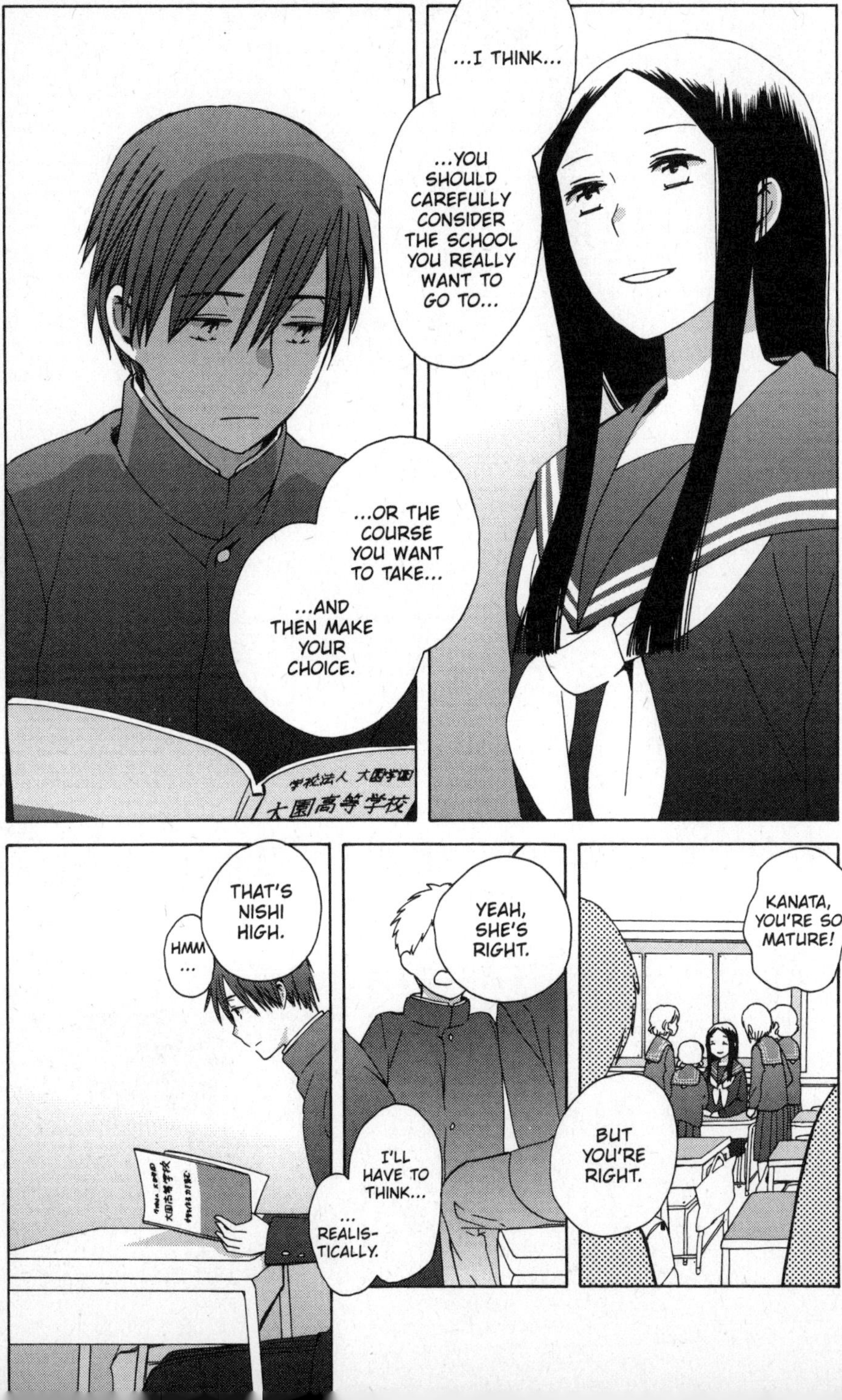
...I THINK...
...YOU SHOULD CAREFULLY CONSIDER THE SCHOOL YOU REALLY WANT TO GO TO...
...OR THE COURSE YOU WANT TO TAKE...
...AND THEN MAKE YOUR CHOICE.
学校法人 大園学園
大園高等学校
KANATA, YOU'RE SO MATURE!
BUT YOU'RE RIGHT.
YEAH, SHE'S RIGHT.
THAT'S NISHI HIGH.
HMM...
I'LL HAVE TO THINK... ...REALISTICALLY.

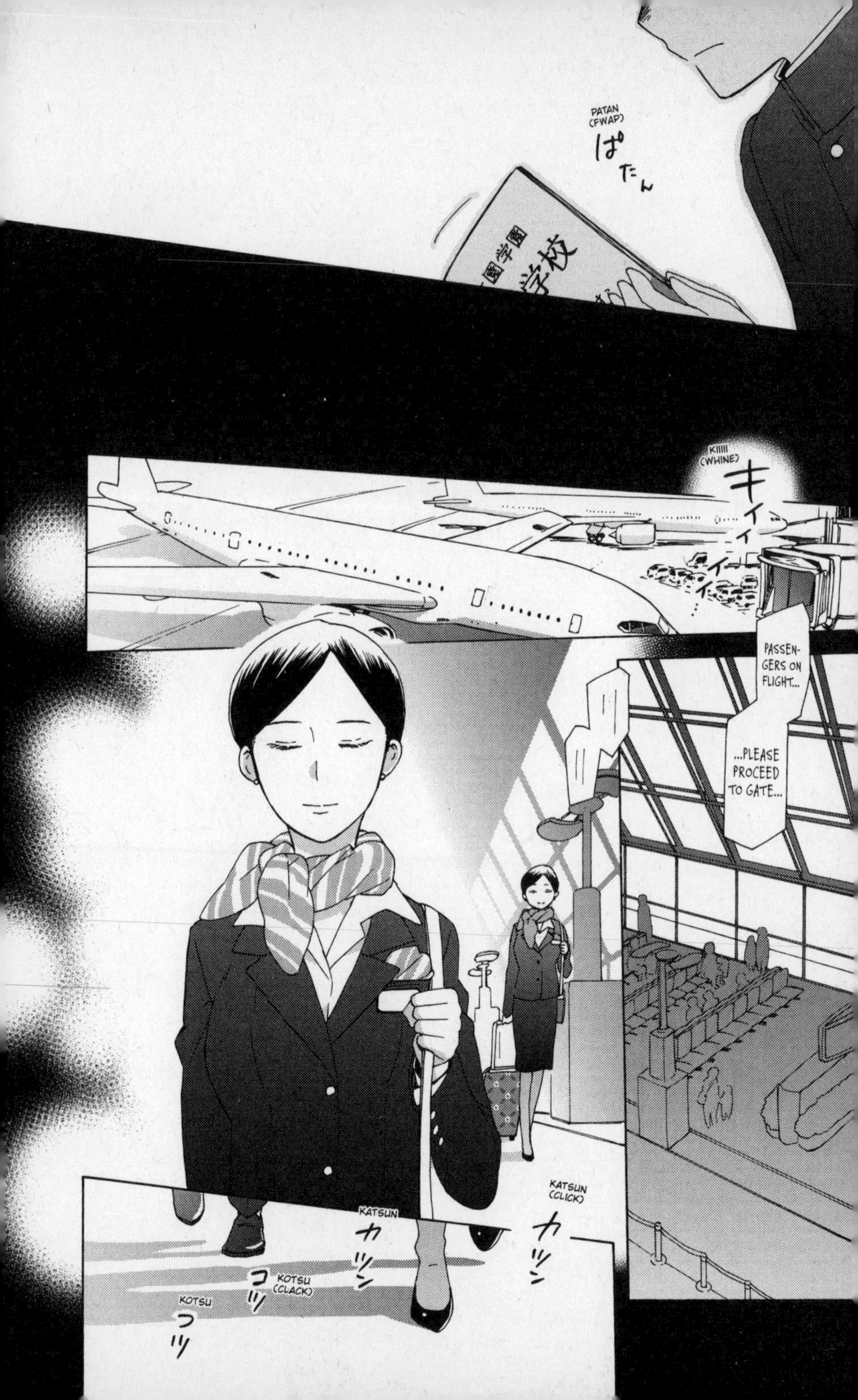
PATAN (FWAP)
ぱたん
KIIII (WHINE)
キイイイ…
PASSEN-GERS ON FLIGHT...
...PLEASE PROCEED TO GATE...
KATSUN (CLICK)
カツン
KATSUN
カツン
KOTSU (CLACK)
コツ
KOTSU
コツ

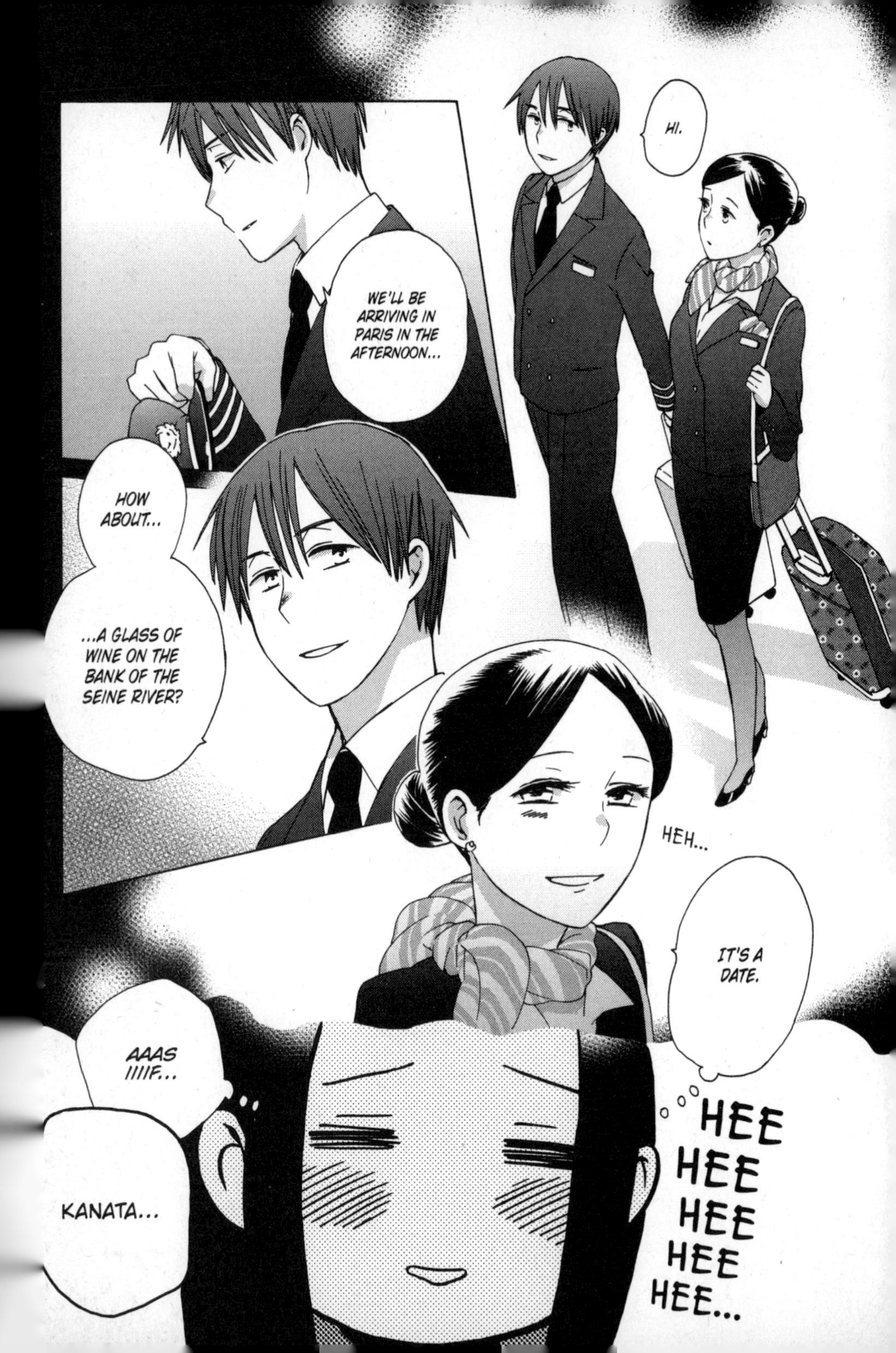
HI.
WE'LL BE ARRIVING IN PARIS IN THE AFTERNOON...
HOW ABOUT...
...A GLASS OF WINE ON THE BANK OF THE SEINE RIVER?
HEH...
IT'S A DATE.
HEE HEE HEE HEE HEE...
AAAS IIIIF...
KANATA...

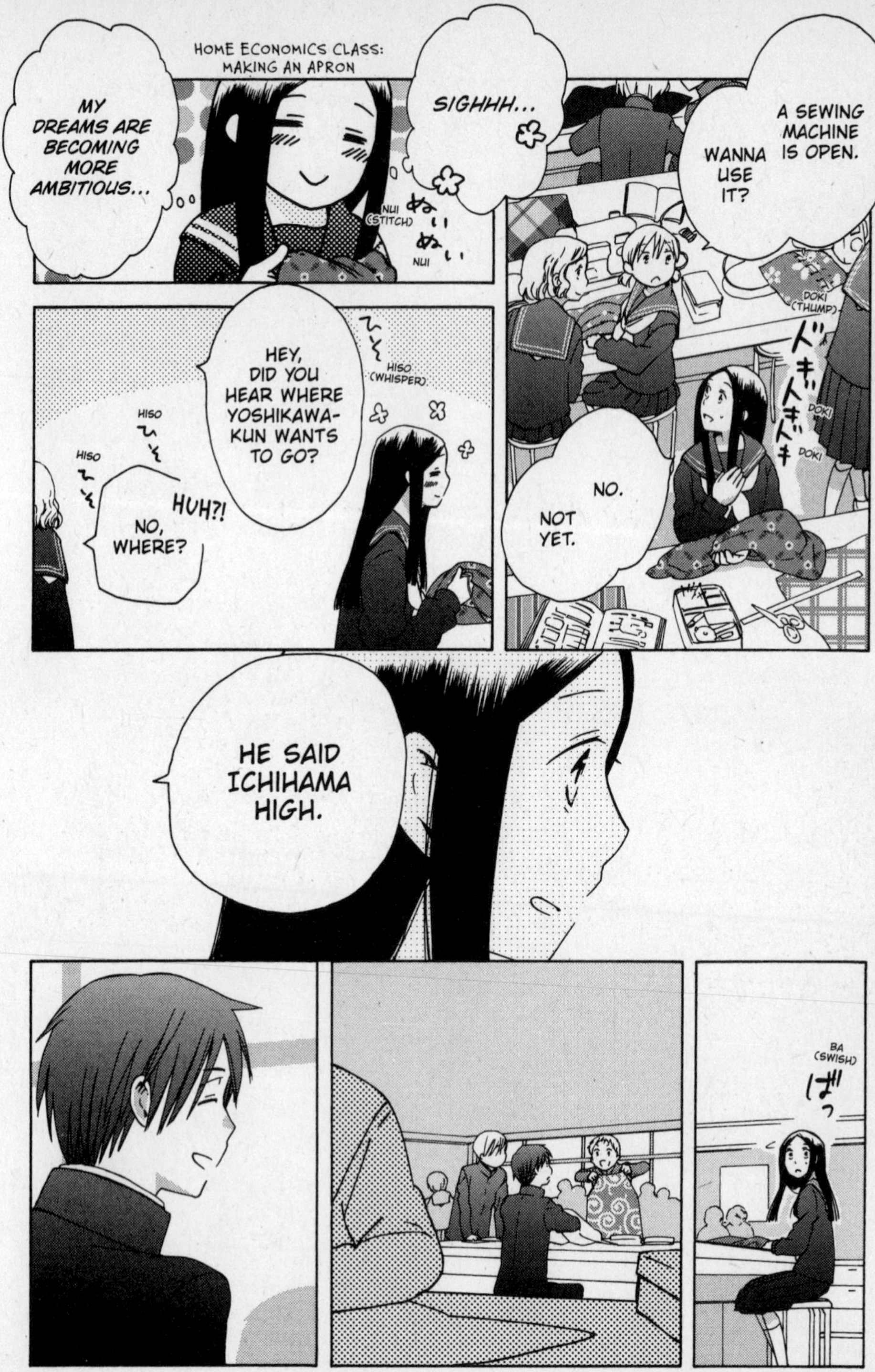
A SEWING MACHINE IS OPEN.
WANNA USE IT?
DOKI (THUMP) ドキ ドキ DOKI DOKI
NO. NOT YET.
HOME ECONOMICS CLASS: MAKING AN APRON
MY DREAMS ARE BECOMING MORE AMBITIOUS...
SIGHHH...
NUI (STITCH) ぬい ぬい NUI
HISO (WHISPER) ひそ
HEY, DID YOU HEAR WHERE YOSHIKAWA-KUN WANTS TO GO?
HISO ひそ
HISO ひそ
HUH?! NO, WHERE?
HE SAID ICHIHAMA HIGH.
BA (SWISH) ばっ

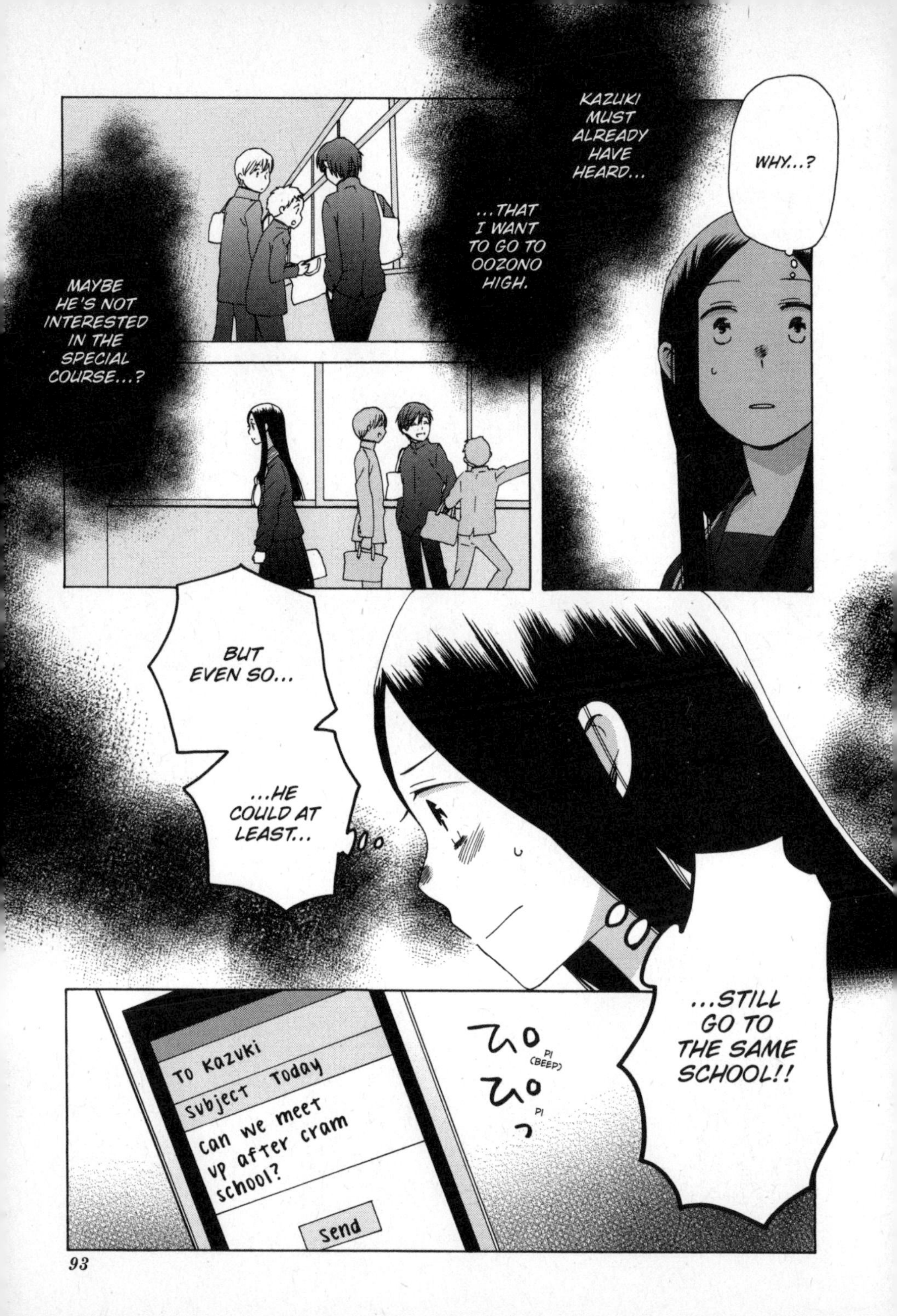
WHY...?
KAZUKI MUST ALREADY HAVE HEARD...
...THAT I WANT TO GO TO OOZONO HIGH.
MAYBE HE'S NOT INTERESTED IN THE SPECIAL COURSE...?
BUT EVEN SO...
...HE COULD AT LEAST...
...STILL GO TO THE SAME SCHOOL!!
PI (BEEP)
PI
To Kazuki
Subject Today
Can we meet up after cram school?
Send

HEY.
FEELS LIKE IT'S BEEN A WHILE...
...SINCE WE WERE LAST ALONE.
I WONDER HOW LONG THE GUIDANCE MEETINGS WILL TAKE.
KAZUKI ...

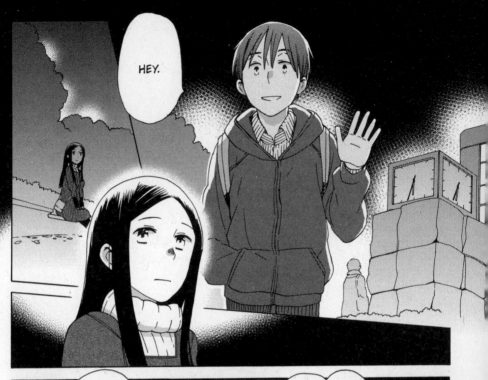

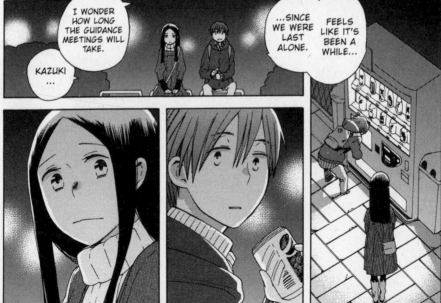

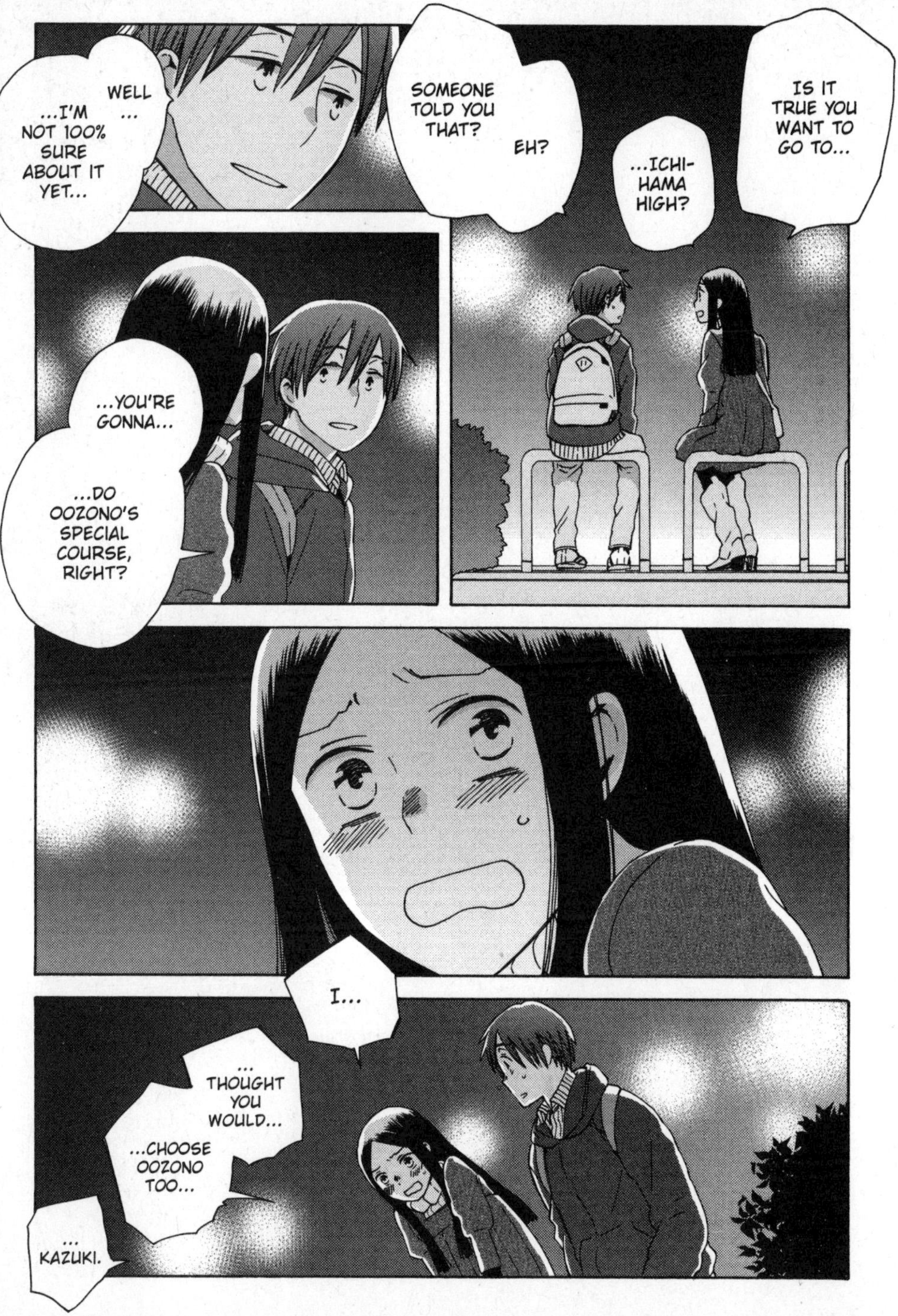
IS IT TRUE YOU WANT TO GO TO...
...ICHI-HAMA HIGH?
EH?
SOMEONE TOLD YOU THAT?
WELL ...
...I'M NOT 100% SURE ABOUT IT YET...
...YOU'RE GONNA...
...DO OOZONO'S SPECIAL COURSE, RIGHT?
I...
...THOUGHT YOU WOULD...
...CHOOSE OOZONO TOO...
...KAZUKI.

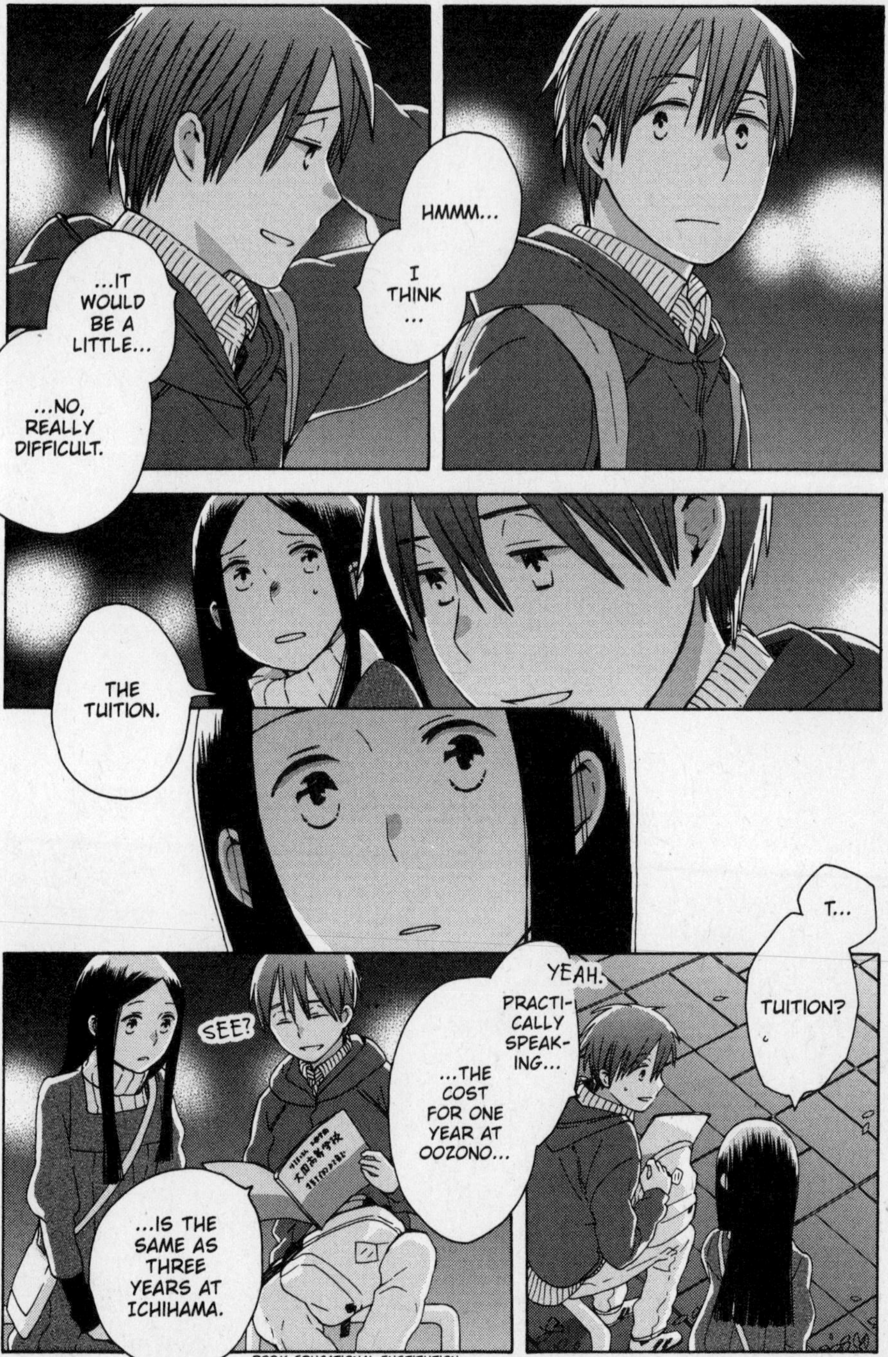
HMMM...
I THINK ...
...IT WOULD BE A LITTLE...
...NO, REALLY DIFFICULT.
THE TUITION.
T...
TUITION?
YEAH.
PRACTI-CALLY SPEAK-ING...
...THE COST FOR ONE YEAR AT OOZONO...
SEE?
...IS THE SAME AS THREE YEARS AT ICHIHAMA.
BOOK: EDUCATIONAL INSTITUTION, OOZONO HIGH SCHOOL, NURTURING THE POWER TO CREATE YOUR FUTURE

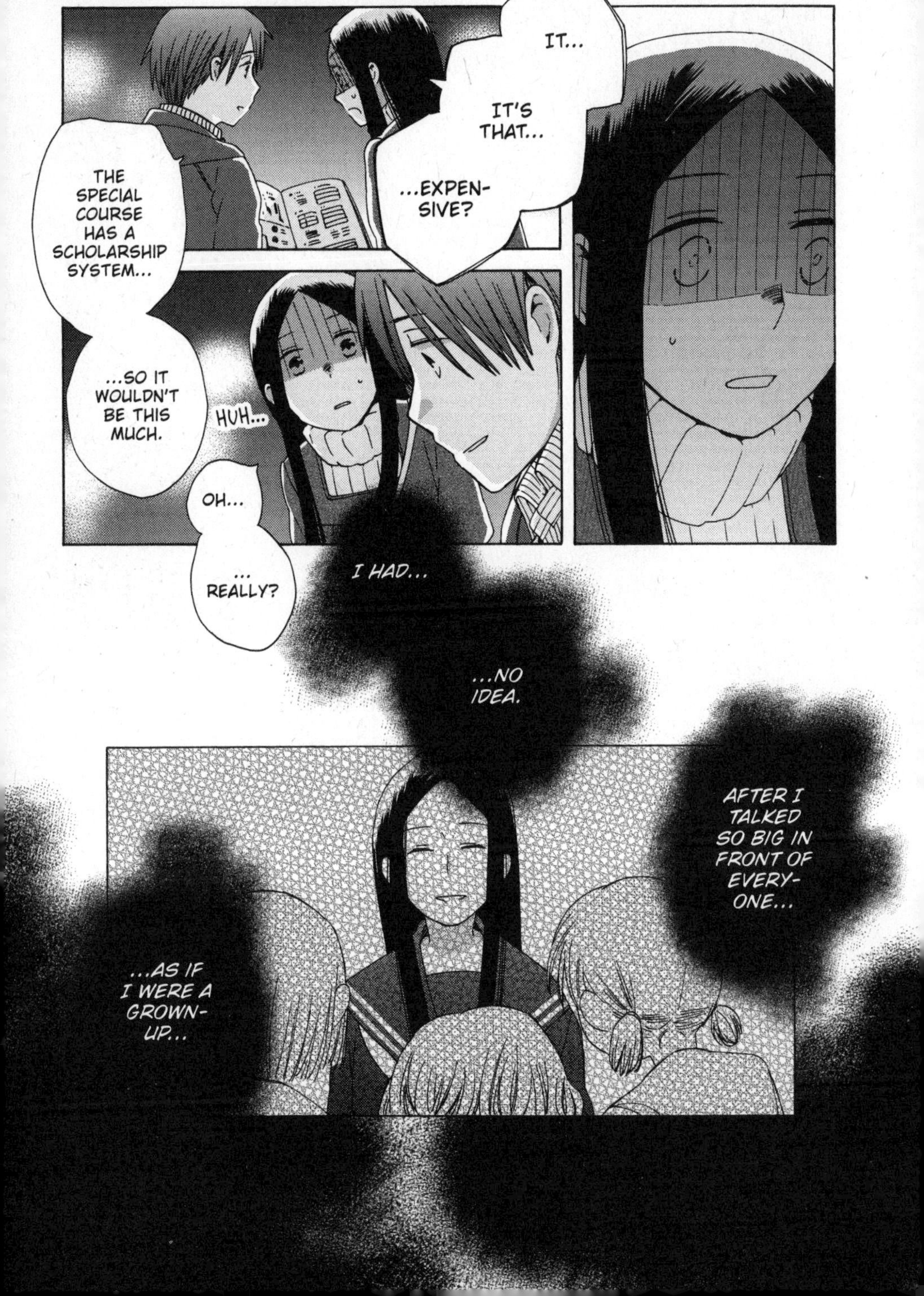
IT...
IT'S THAT...
...EXPENSIVE?
THE SPECIAL COURSE HAS A SCHOLARSHIP SYSTEM...
...SO IT WOULDN'T BE THIS MUCH.
HUH...
OH...
...REALLY?
I HAD...
...NO IDEA.
AFTER I TALKED SO BIG IN FRONT OF EVERYONE...
...AS IF I WERE A GROWN-UP...

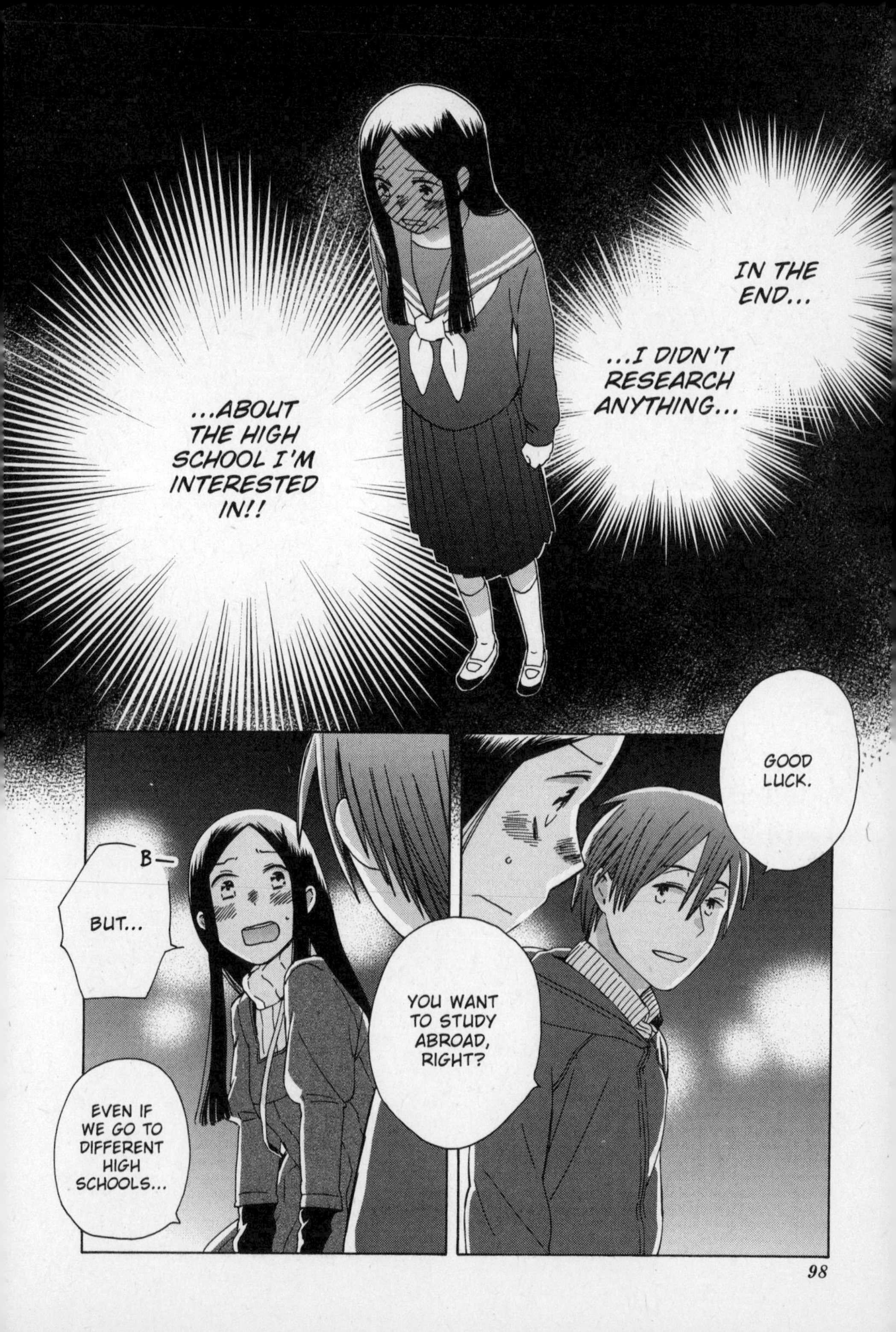
IN THE END...
...I DIDN'T RESEARCH ANYTHING...
...ABOUT THE HIGH SCHOOL I'M INTERESTED IN!!
GOOD LUCK.
YOU WANT TO STUDY ABROAD, RIGHT?
B—
BUT...
EVEN IF WE GO TO DIFFERENT HIGH SCHOOLS...

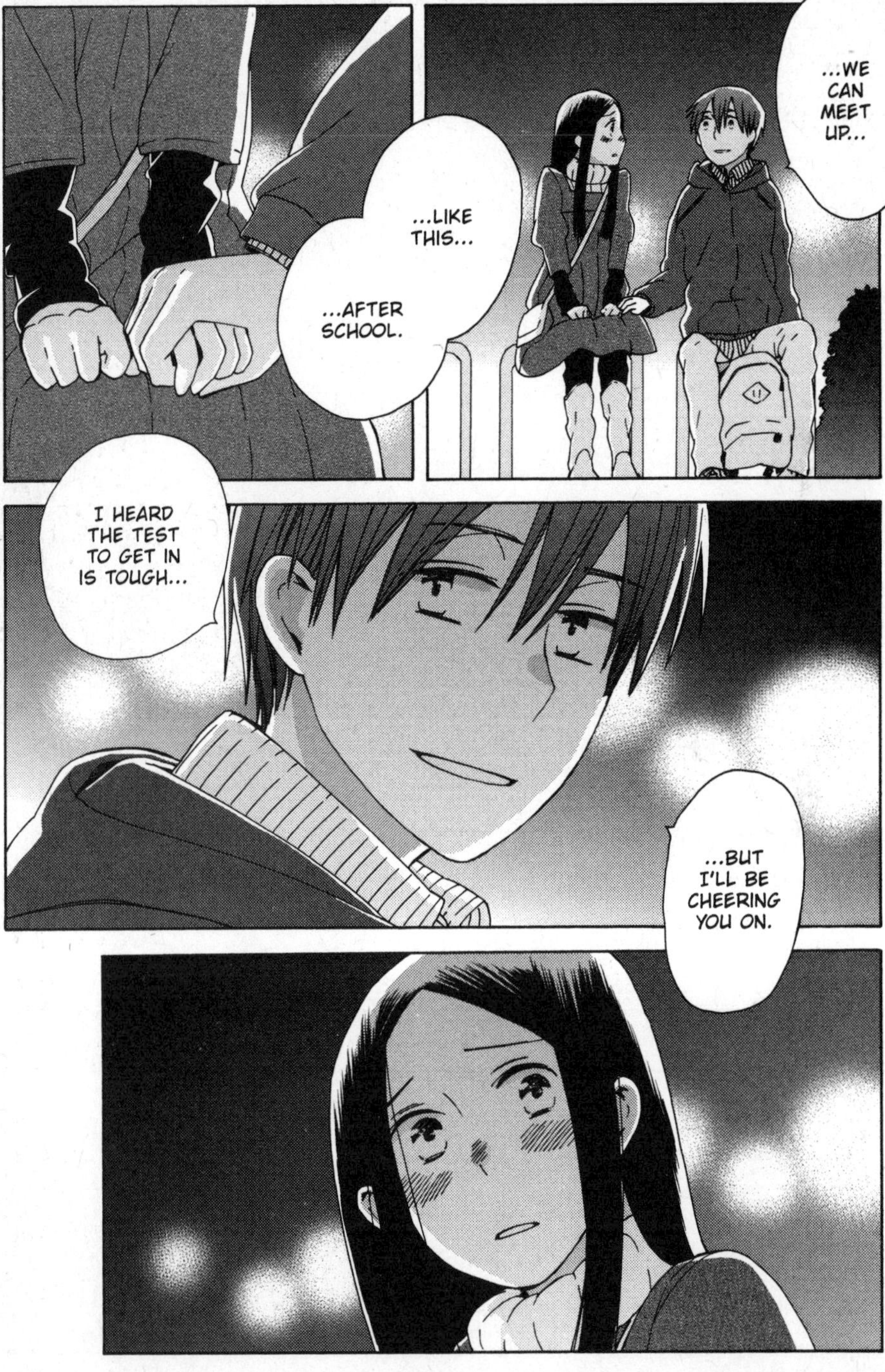
...WE CAN MEET UP...
...LIKE THIS...
...AFTER SCHOOL.
I HEARD THE TEST TO GET IN IS TOUGH...
...BUT I'LL BE CHEERING YOU ON.

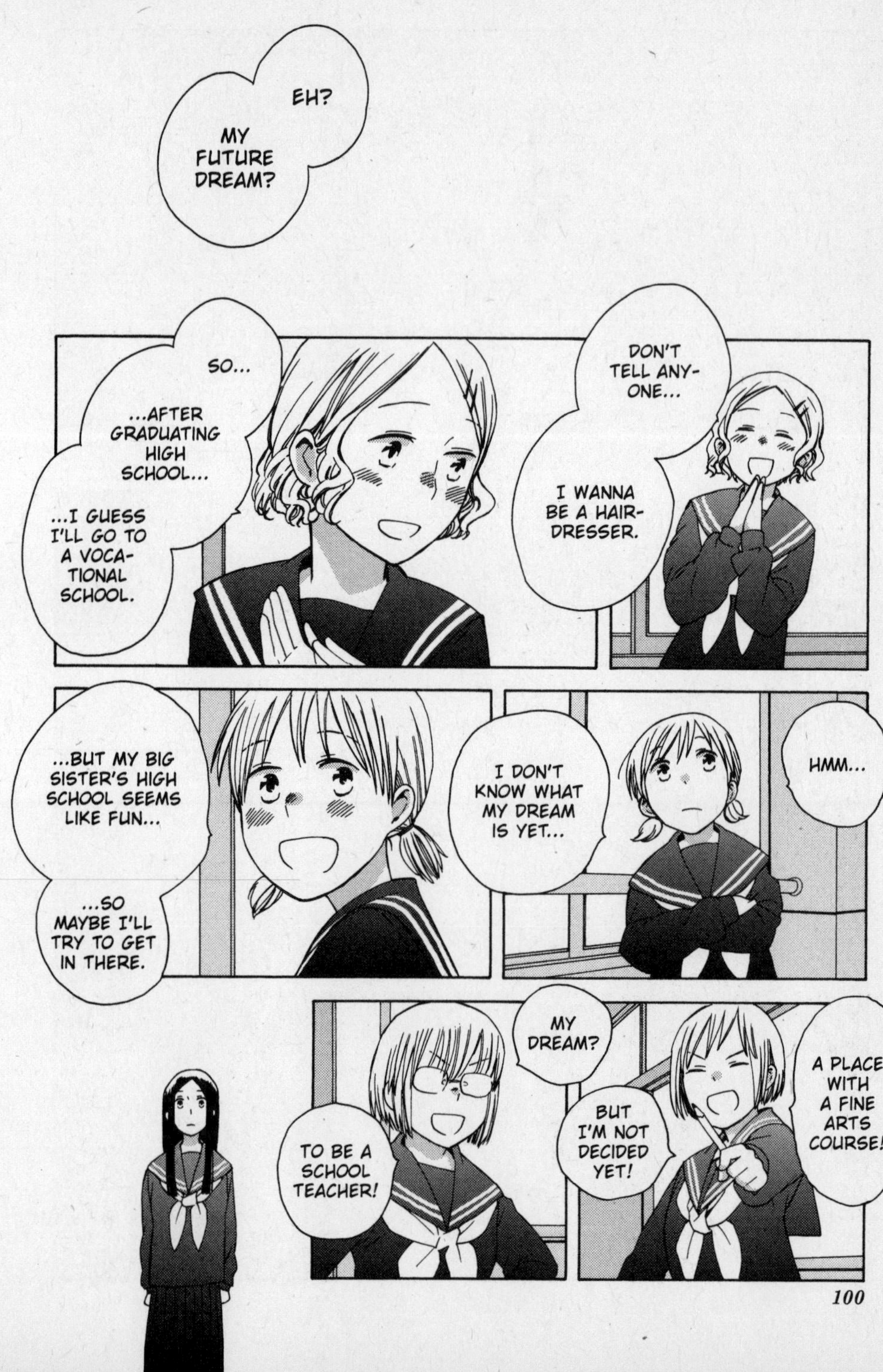
EH? MY FUTURE DREAM?
DON'T TELL ANYONE...
I WANNA BE A HAIRDRESSER.
SO...
...AFTER GRADUATING HIGH SCHOOL...
...I GUESS I'LL GO TO A VOCATIONAL SCHOOL.
HMM...
I DON'T KNOW WHAT MY DREAM IS YET...
...BUT MY BIG SISTER'S HIGH SCHOOL SEEMS LIKE FUN...
...SO MAYBE I'LL TRY TO GET IN THERE.
A PLACE WITH A FINE ARTS COURSE!
BUT I'M NOT DECIDED YET!
MY DREAM?
TO BE A SCHOOL TEACHER!

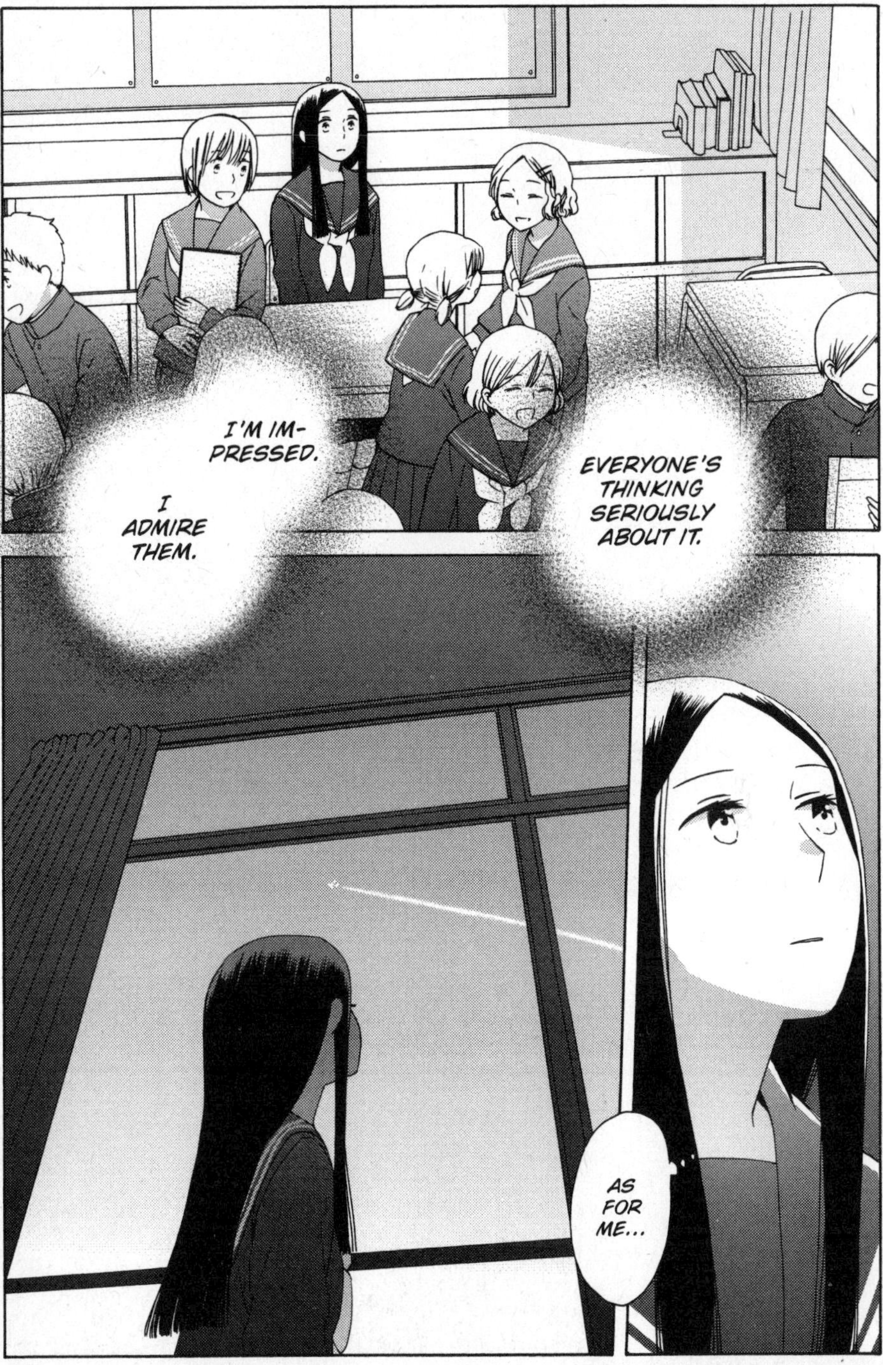
EVERYONE'S THINKING SERIOUSLY ABOUT IT.
I'M IMPRESSED.
I ADMIRE THEM.
AS FOR ME...

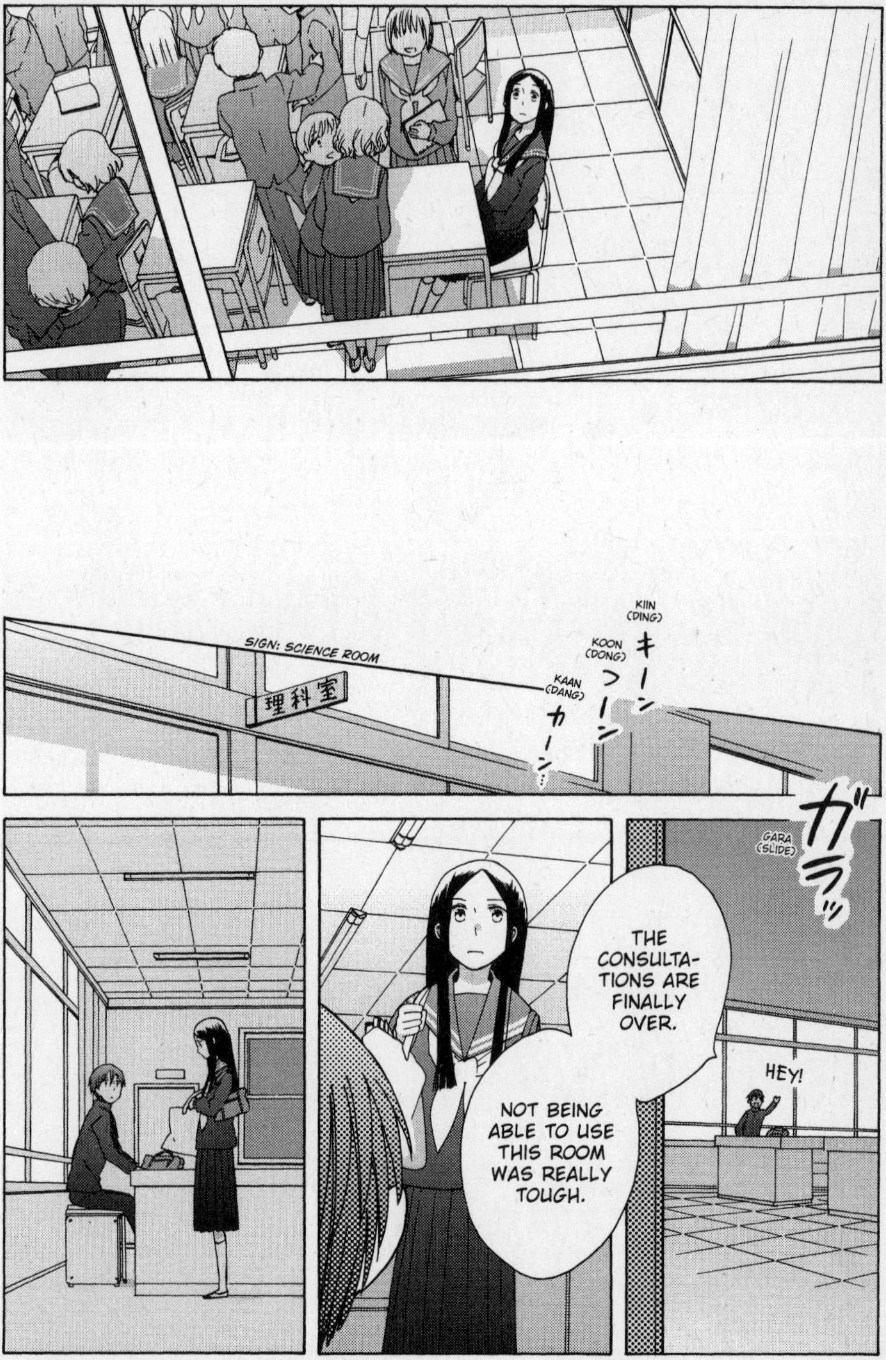
KIIN (DING)
キーン
KOON (DONG)
コーン
KAAN (DANG)
カーン…
SIGN: SCIENCE ROOM
理科室
GARA (SLIDE)
ガラッ
HEY!
THE CONSULTATIONS ARE FINALLY OVER.
NOT BEING ABLE TO USE THIS ROOM WAS REALLY TOUGH.

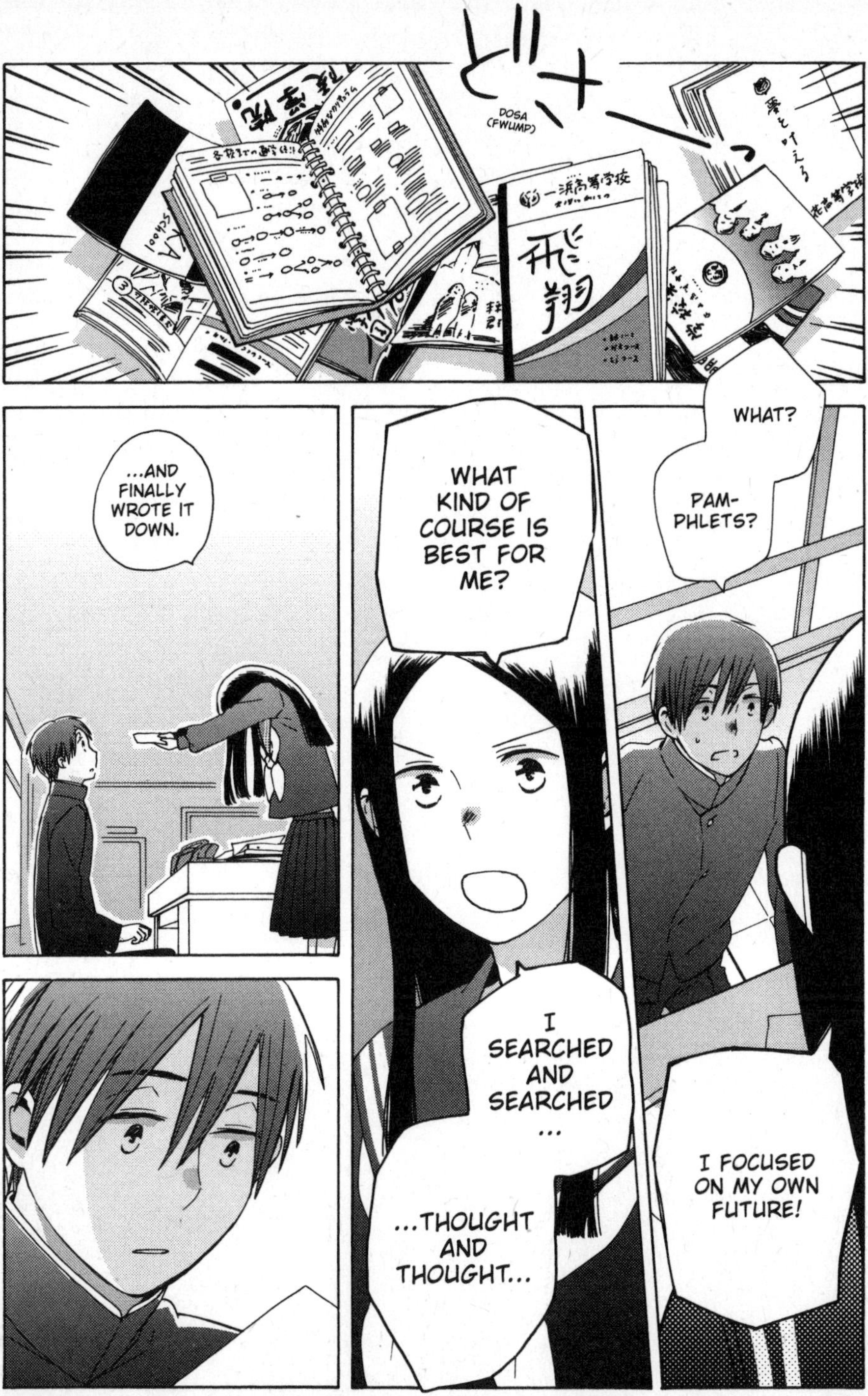
DOSA (FWUMP)
WHAT? PAM-PHLETS?
WHAT KIND OF COURSE IS BEST FOR ME?
I FOCUSED ON MY OWN FUTURE!
I SEARCHED AND SEARCHED...
...THOUGHT AND THOUGHT...
...AND FINALLY WROTE IT DOWN.

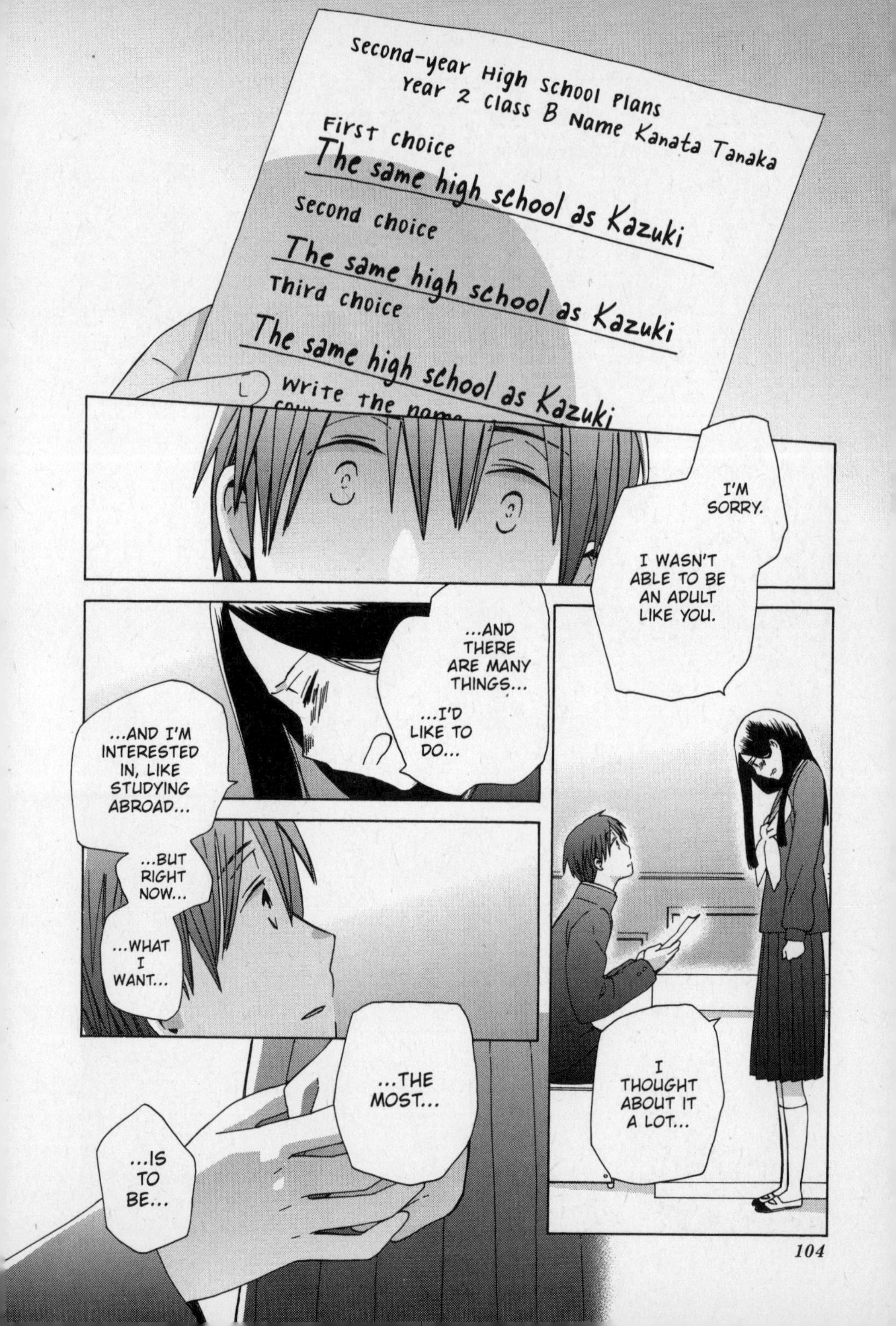

Second-year High School Plans
Year 2 Class B Name Kanata Tanaka
First choice
The same high school as Kazuki
Second choice
The same high school as Kazuki
Third choice
The same high school as Kazuki
Write the name
I'M SORRY.
I WASN'T ABLE TO BE AN ADULT LIKE YOU.
I THOUGHT ABOUT IT A LOT...
...AND THERE ARE MANY THINGS...
...I'D LIKE TO DO...
...AND I'M INTERESTED IN, LIKE STUDYING ABROAD...
...BUT RIGHT NOW...
...WHAT I WANT...
...THE MOST...
...IS TO BE...

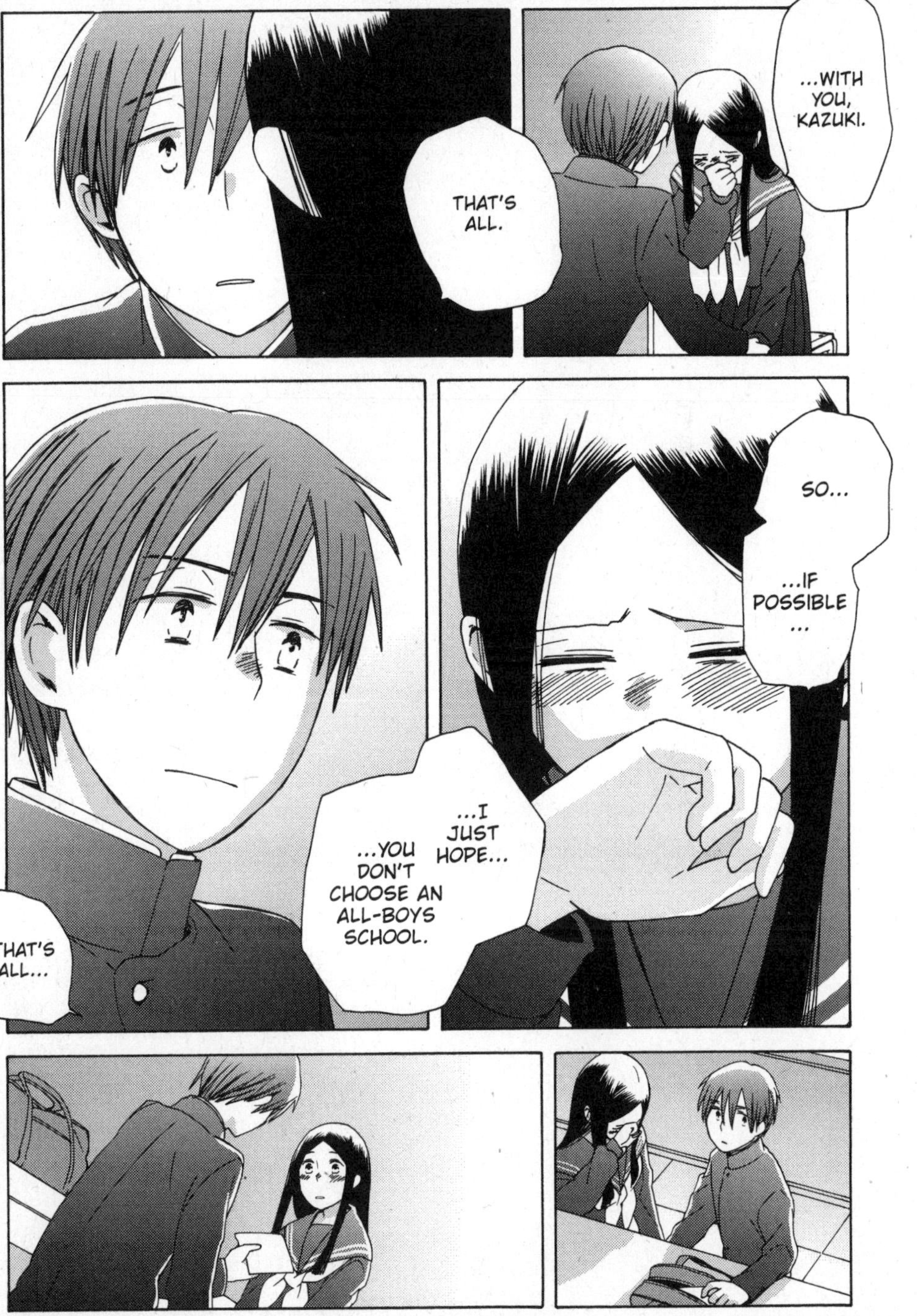
...WITH YOU, KAZUKI.
THAT'S ALL.
SO...
...IF POSSIBLE ...
...I JUST HOPE...
...YOU DON'T CHOOSE AN ALL-BOYS SCHOOL.
THAT'S ALL...

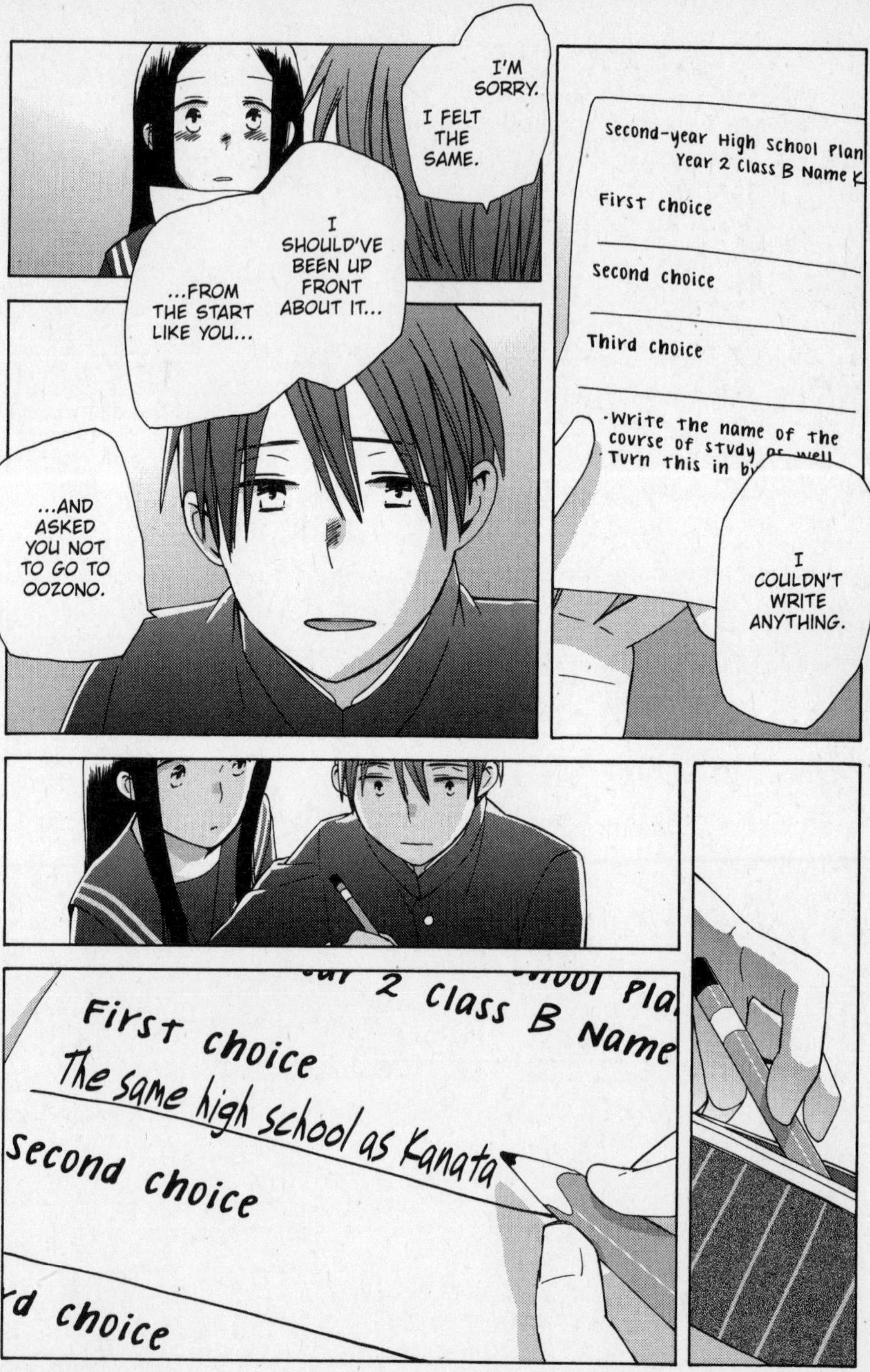

Second-year High School Plan
Year 2 Class B Name K
First choice
Second choice
Third choice
·Write the name of the course of study as well
·Turn this in by
I COULDN'T WRITE ANYTHING.
I'M SORRY.
I FELT THE SAME.
I SHOULD'VE BEEN UP FRONT ABOUT IT...
...FROM THE START LIKE YOU...
...AND ASKED YOU NOT TO GO TO OOZONO.
2 Class B Name
First choice
The same high school as Kanata
Second choice
choice

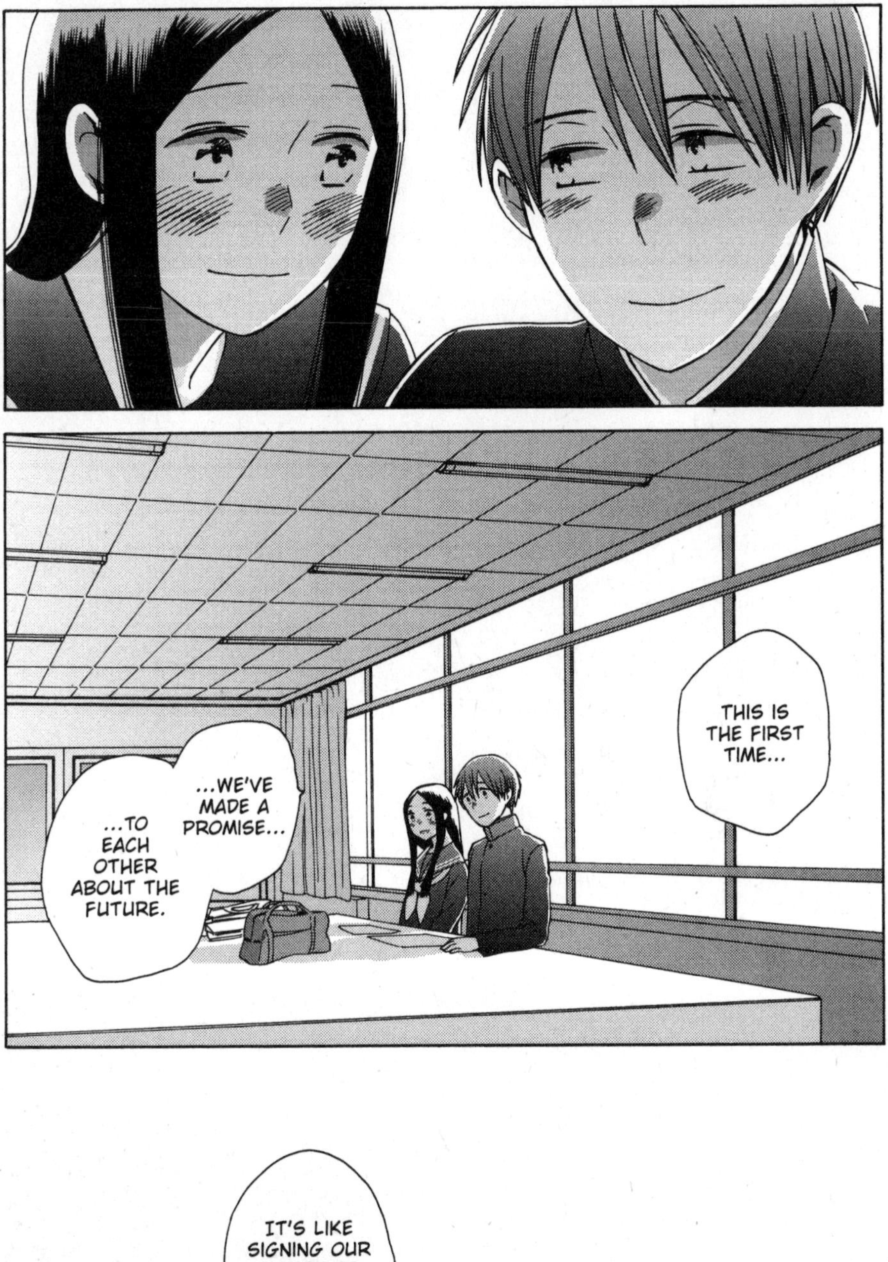
THIS IS THE FIRST TIME...
...WE'VE MADE A PROMISE...
...TO EACH OTHER ABOUT THE FUTURE.
IT'S LIKE SIGNING OUR NAMES AT A WEDDING CEREMONY.

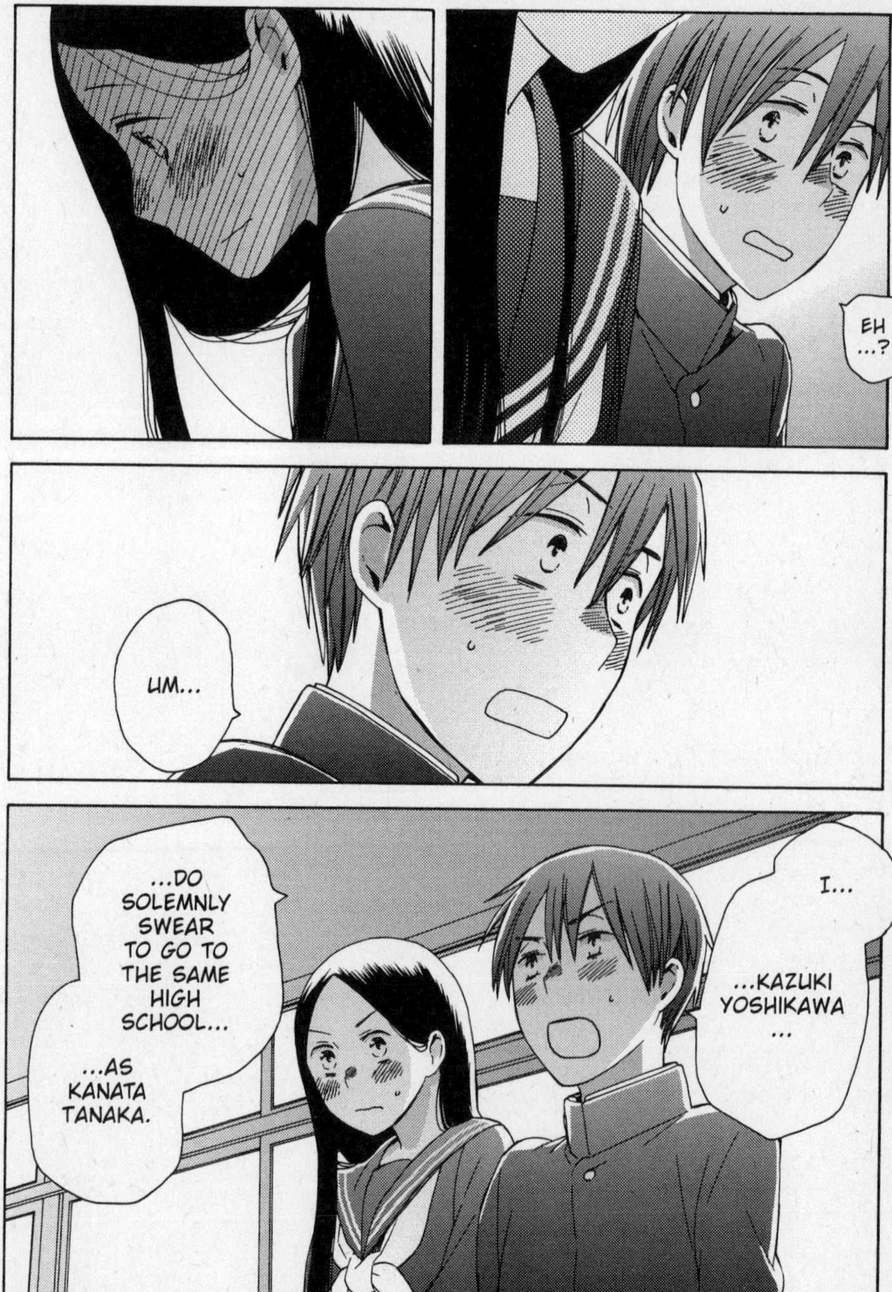
EH ...?
UM...
I...
...KAZUKI YOSHIKAWA ...
...DO SOLEMNLY SWEAR TO GO TO THE SAME HIGH SCHOOL...
...AS KANATA TANAKA.

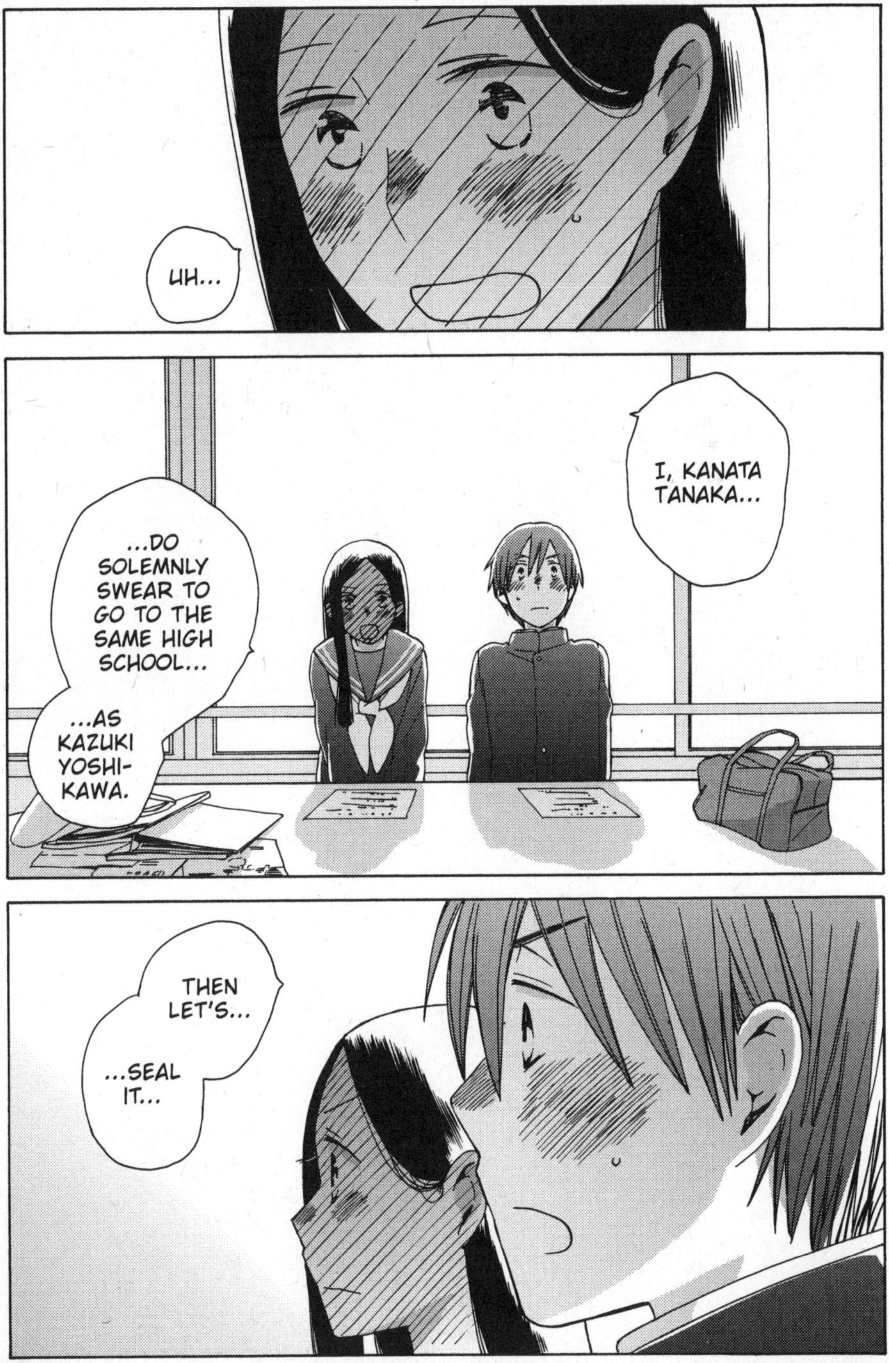
UH...
I, KANATA TANAKA...
...DO SOLEMNLY SWEAR TO GO TO THE SAME HIGH SCHOOL...
...AS KAZUKI YOSHI-KAWA.
THEN LET'S...
...SEAL IT...

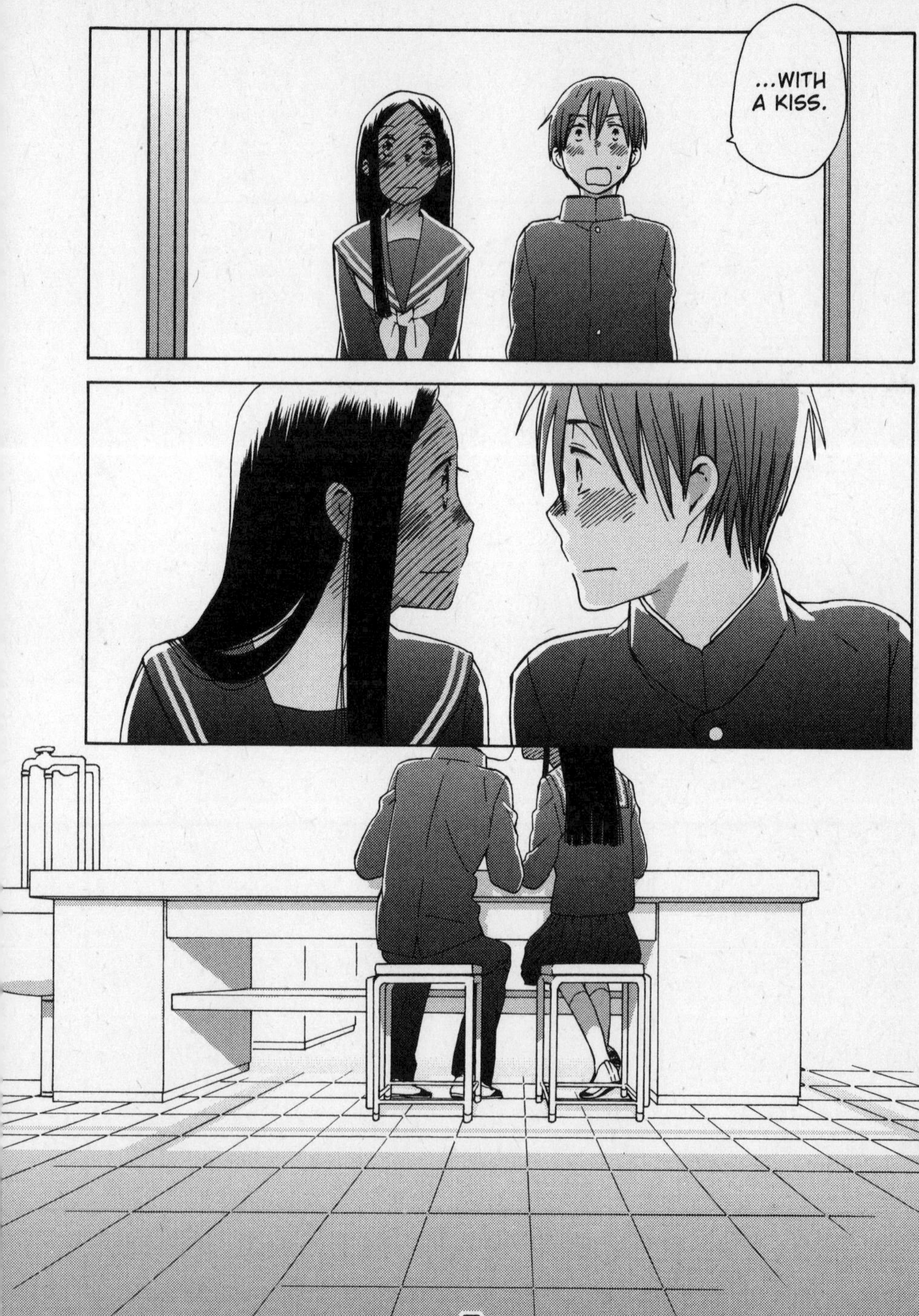
...WITH A KISS.
Fin

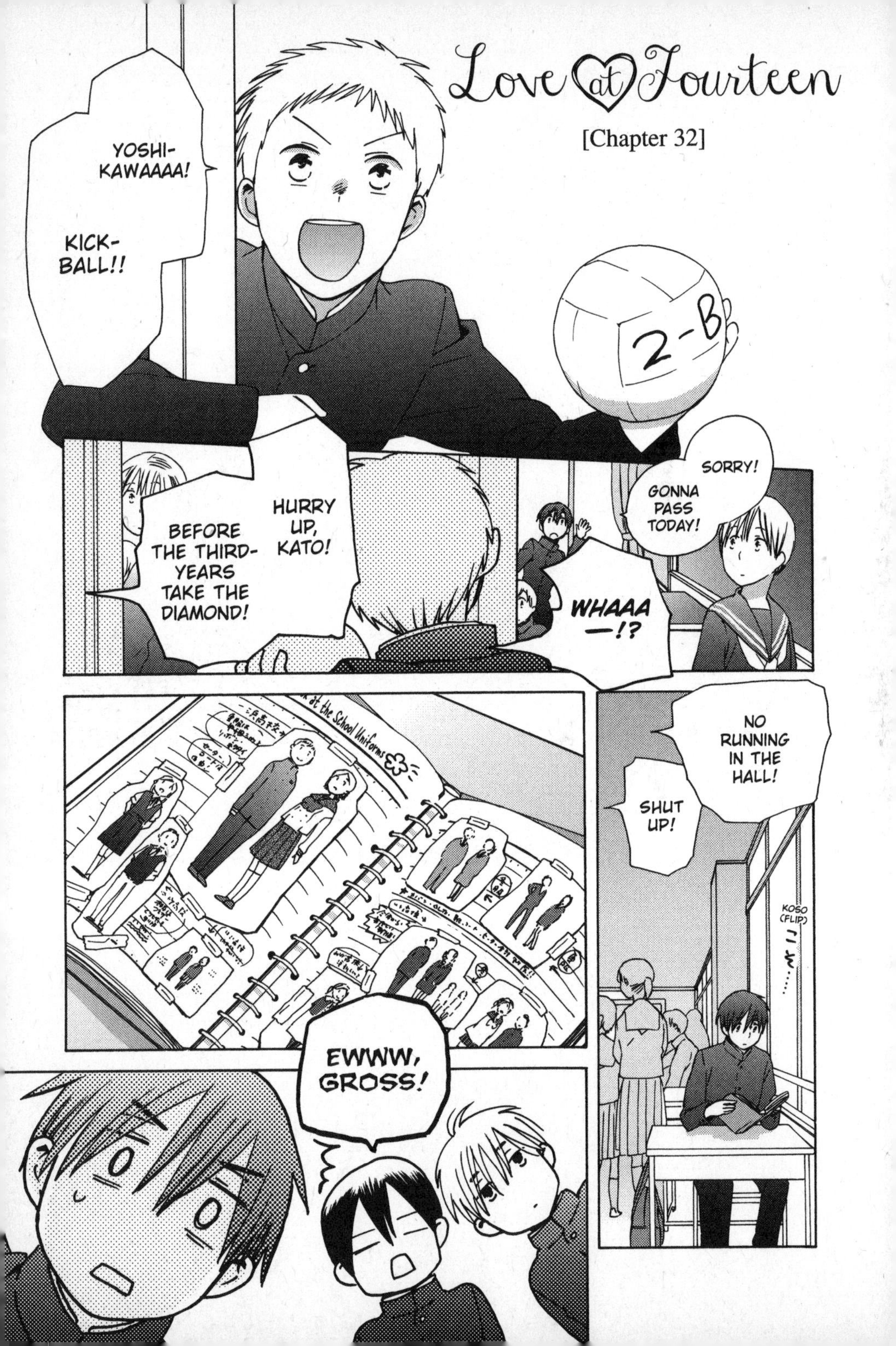
Love at Fourteen
[Chapter 32]
YOSHI-KAWAAAA!
KICK-BALL!!
2-B
SORRY!
GONNA PASS TODAY!
WHAAA—!?
HURRY UP, KATO!
BEFORE THE THIRD-YEARS TAKE THE DIAMOND!
NO RUNNING IN THE HALL!
SHUT UP!
KOSO (FLIP)
こそ……
at the School Uniforms
EWWW, GROSS!

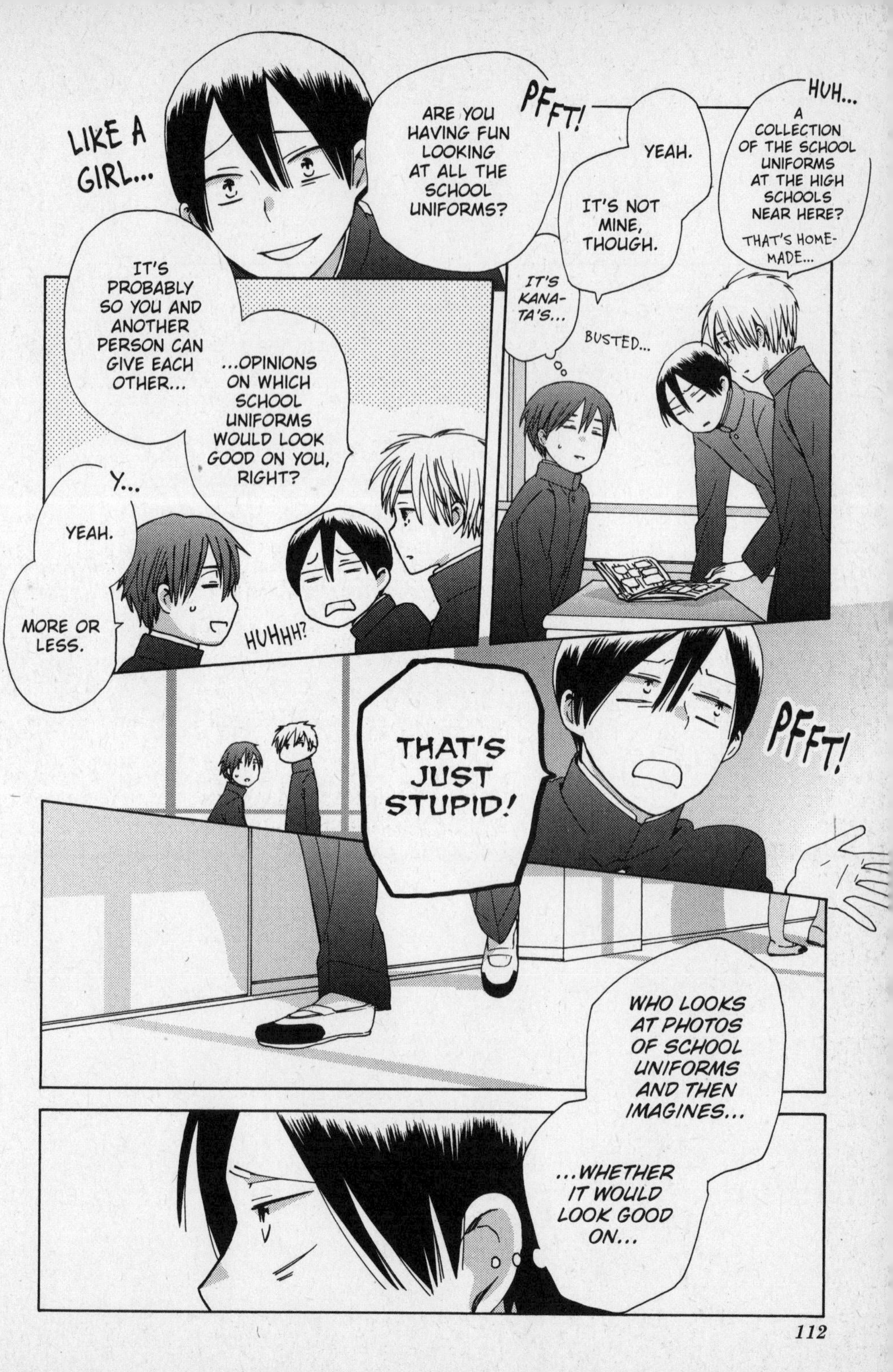

HUH...
A COLLECTION OF THE SCHOOL UNIFORMS AT THE HIGH SCHOOLS NEAR HERE?
THAT'S HOME-MADE...
YEAH.
IT'S NOT MINE, THOUGH.
PFFT!
IT'S KANATA'S...
BUSTED...
ARE YOU HAVING FUN LOOKING AT ALL THE SCHOOL UNIFORMS?
LIKE A GIRL...
IT'S PROBABLY SO YOU AND ANOTHER PERSON CAN GIVE EACH OTHER...
...OPINIONS ON WHICH SCHOOL UNIFORMS WOULD LOOK GOOD ON YOU, RIGHT?
HUHHH?
Y...
YEAH.
MORE OR LESS.
PFFT!
THAT'S JUST STUPID!
WHO LOOKS AT PHOTOS OF SCHOOL UNIFORMS AND THEN IMAGINES...
...WHETHER IT WOULD LOOK GOOD ON...

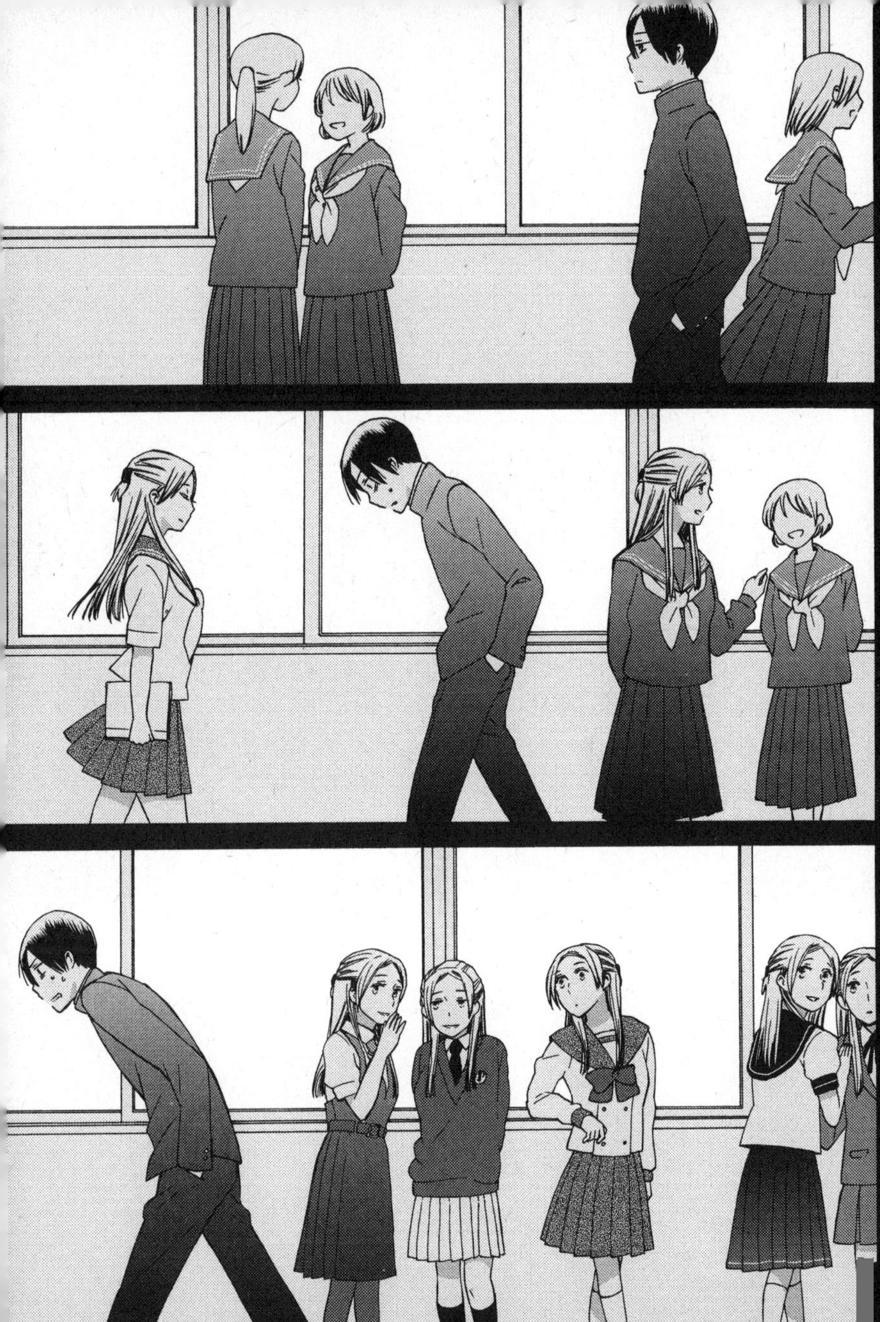

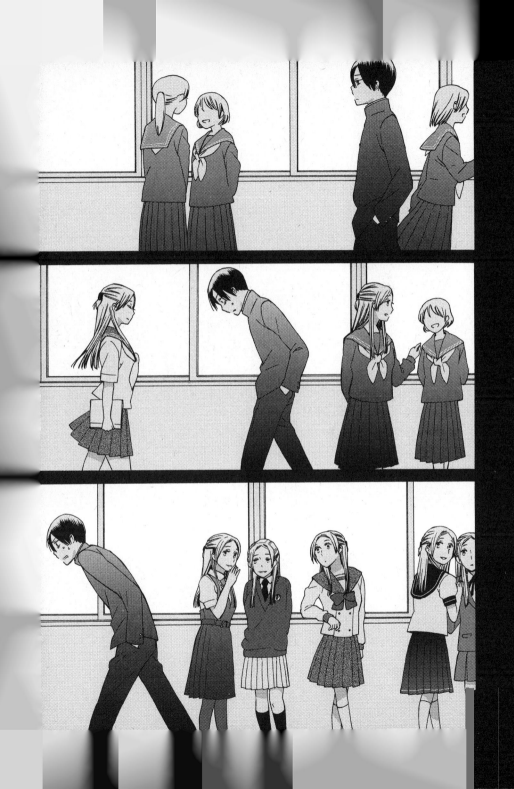

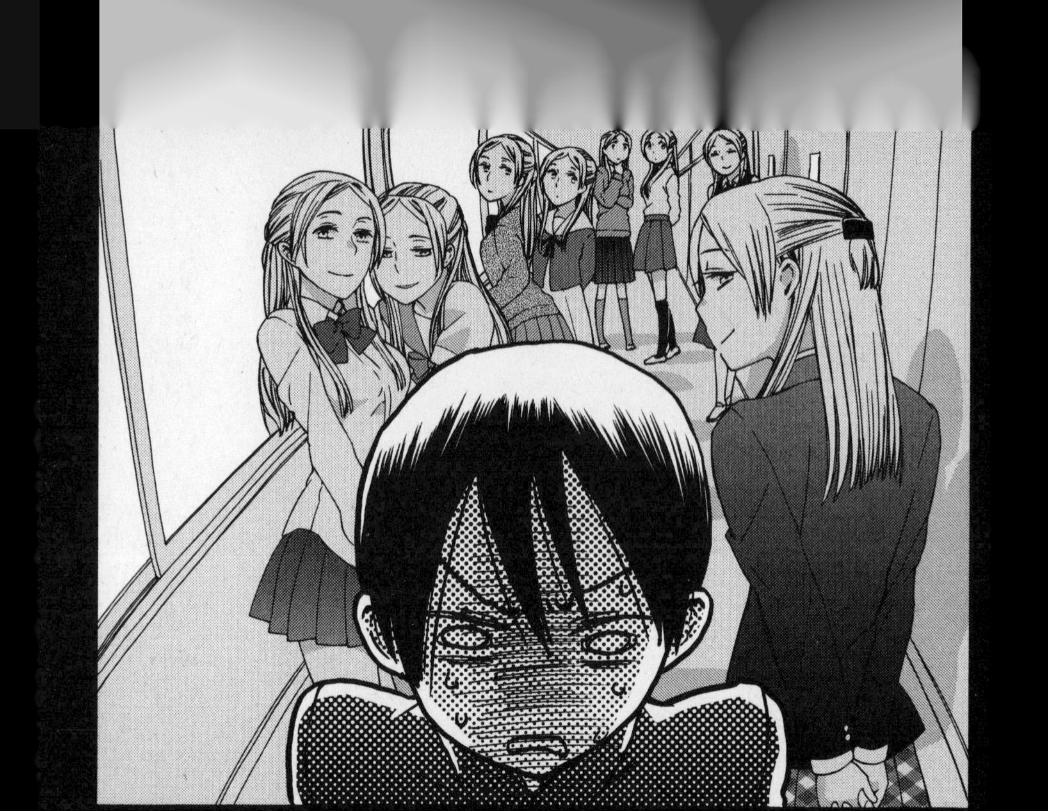

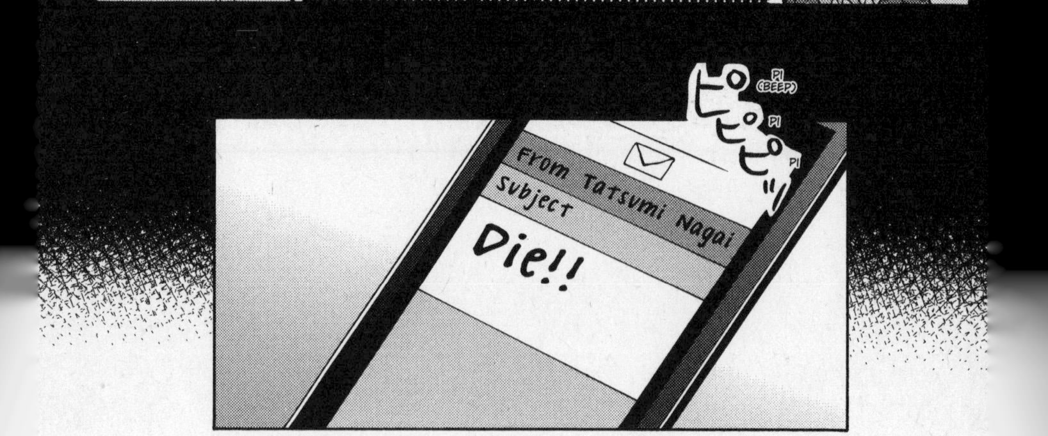
ピピピッ
PI (BEEP) PI PI
From Tatsumi Nagai
Subject
Die!!

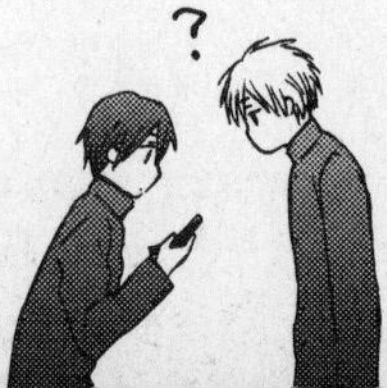
?

Fin

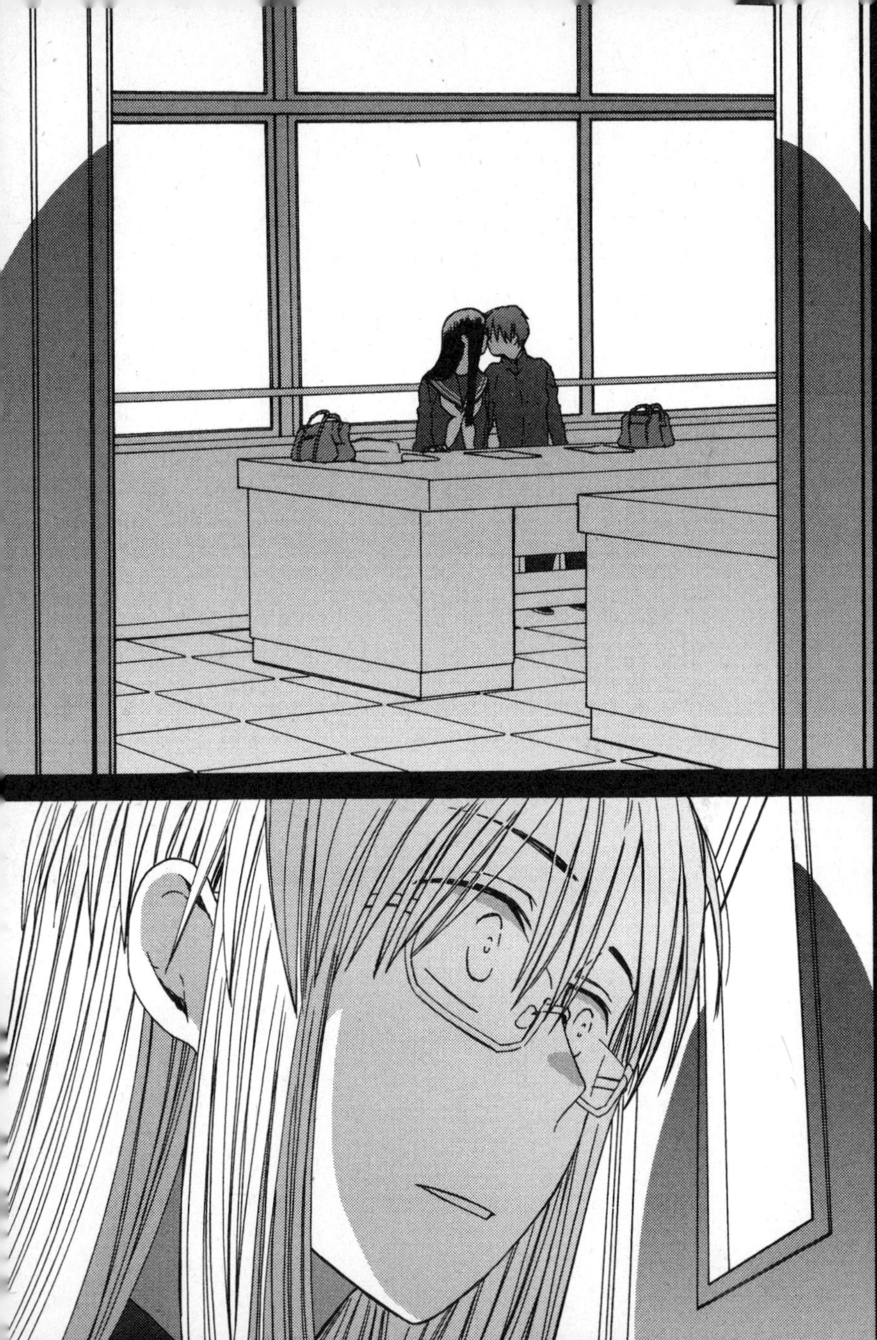

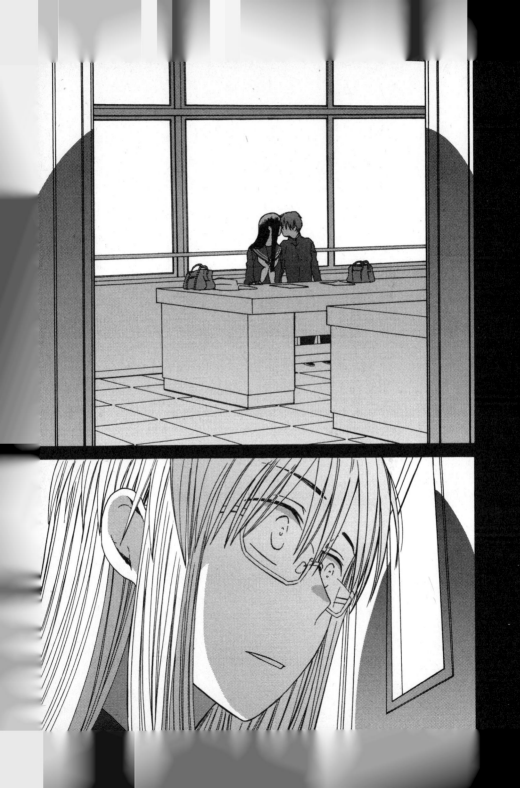

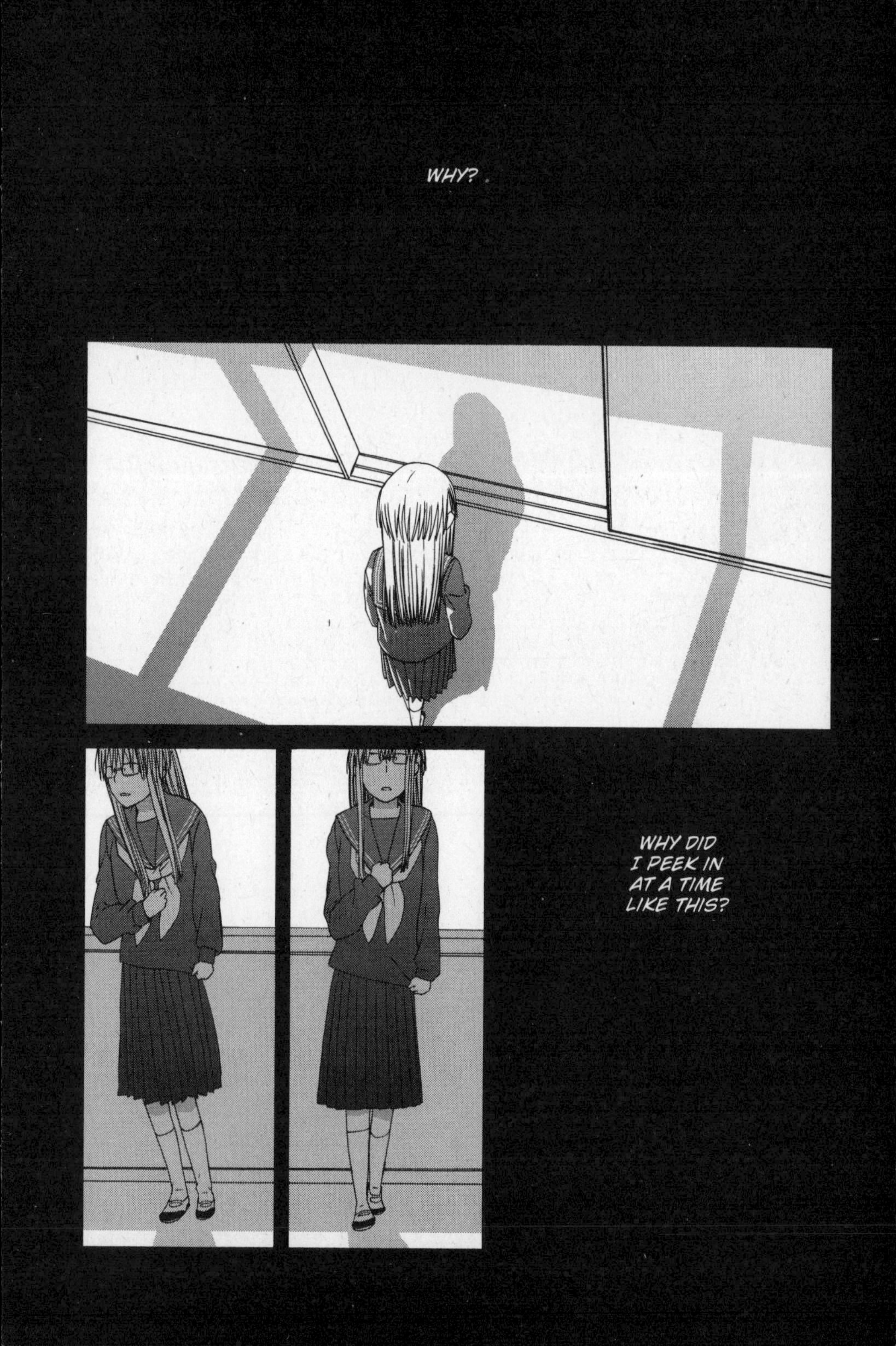
WHY?
WHY DID I PEEK IN AT A TIME LIKE THIS?

I JUST...

...WANTED TO
GET A QUICK
GLIMPSE OF
TANAKA-SAN.

THAT'S
ALL, AND
YET...

Love at Fourteen

[Intermission 40]

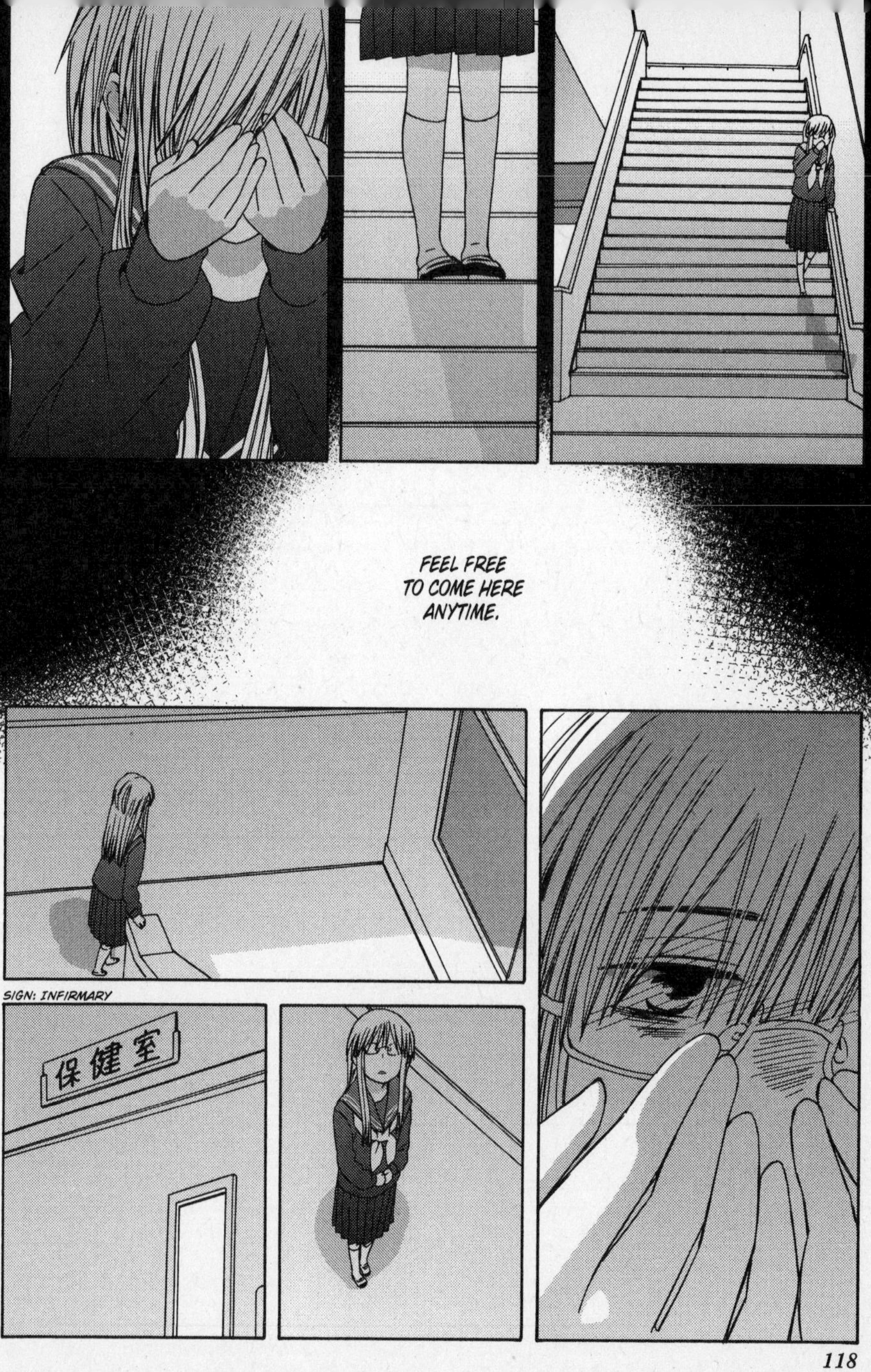
FEEL FREE
TO COME HERE
ANYTIME.
SIGN: INFIRMARY
保健室

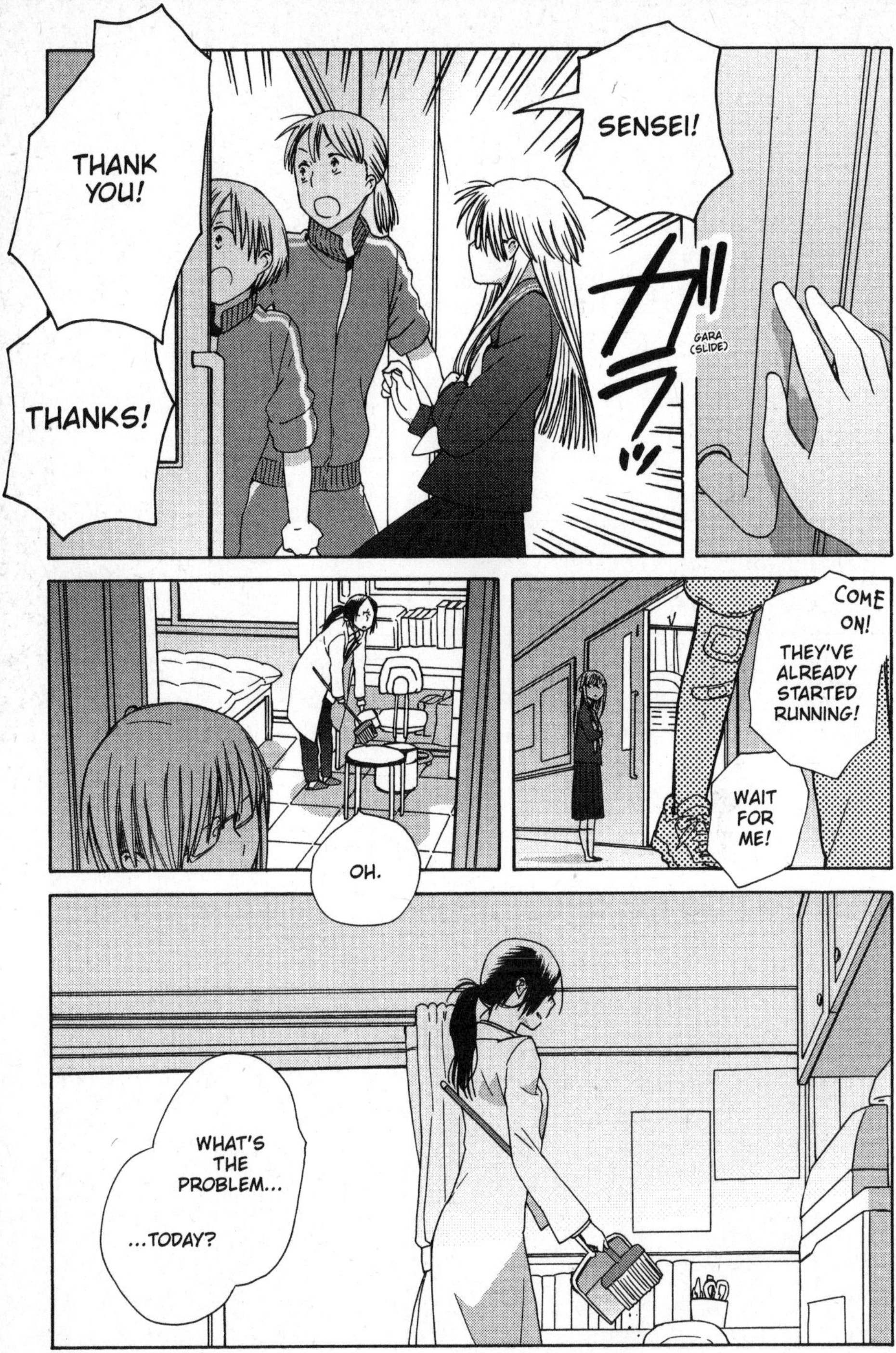
SENSEI!
GARA (SLIDE)
THANK YOU!
THANKS!
COME ON! THEY'VE ALREADY STARTED RUNNING!
WAIT FOR ME!
OH.
WHAT'S THE PROBLEM...
...TODAY?

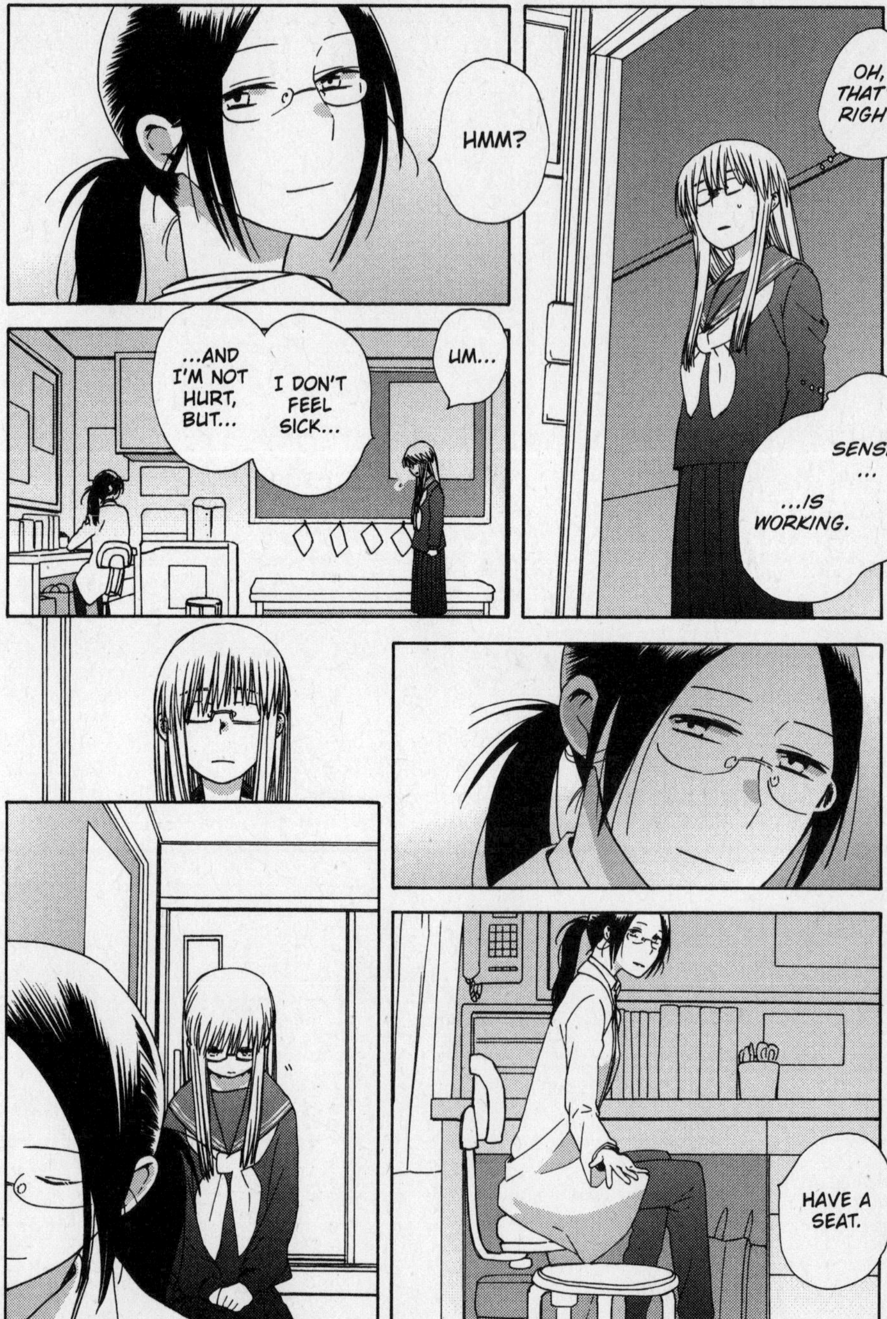
OH, THAT'S RIGHT.
SENSEI...
...IS WORKING.
HMM?
UM...
I DON'T FEEL SICK...
...AND I'M NOT HURT, BUT...
HAVE A SEAT.

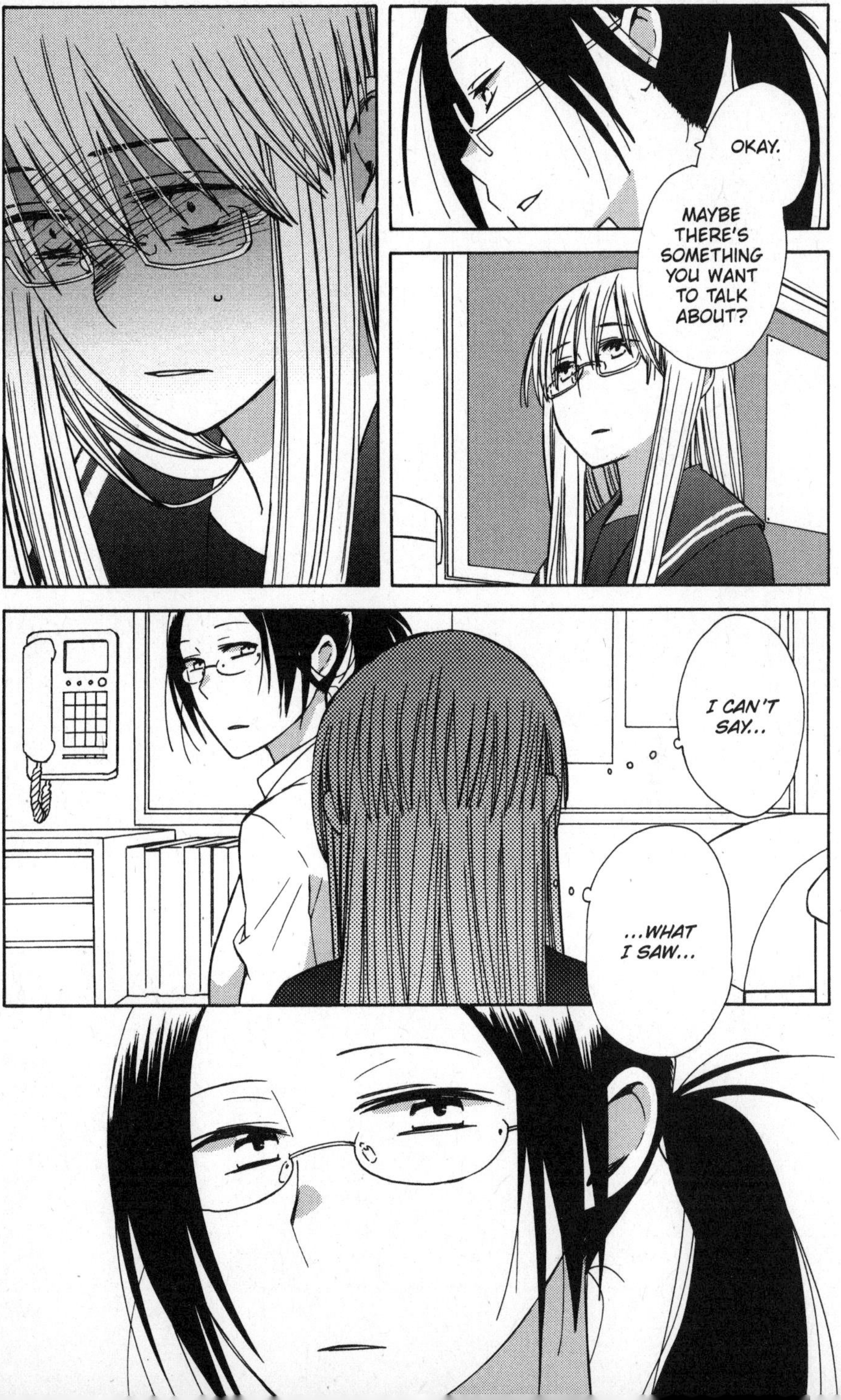
OKAY.
MAYBE THERE'S SOMETHING YOU WANT TO TALK ABOUT?
I CAN'T SAY...
...WHAT I SAW...

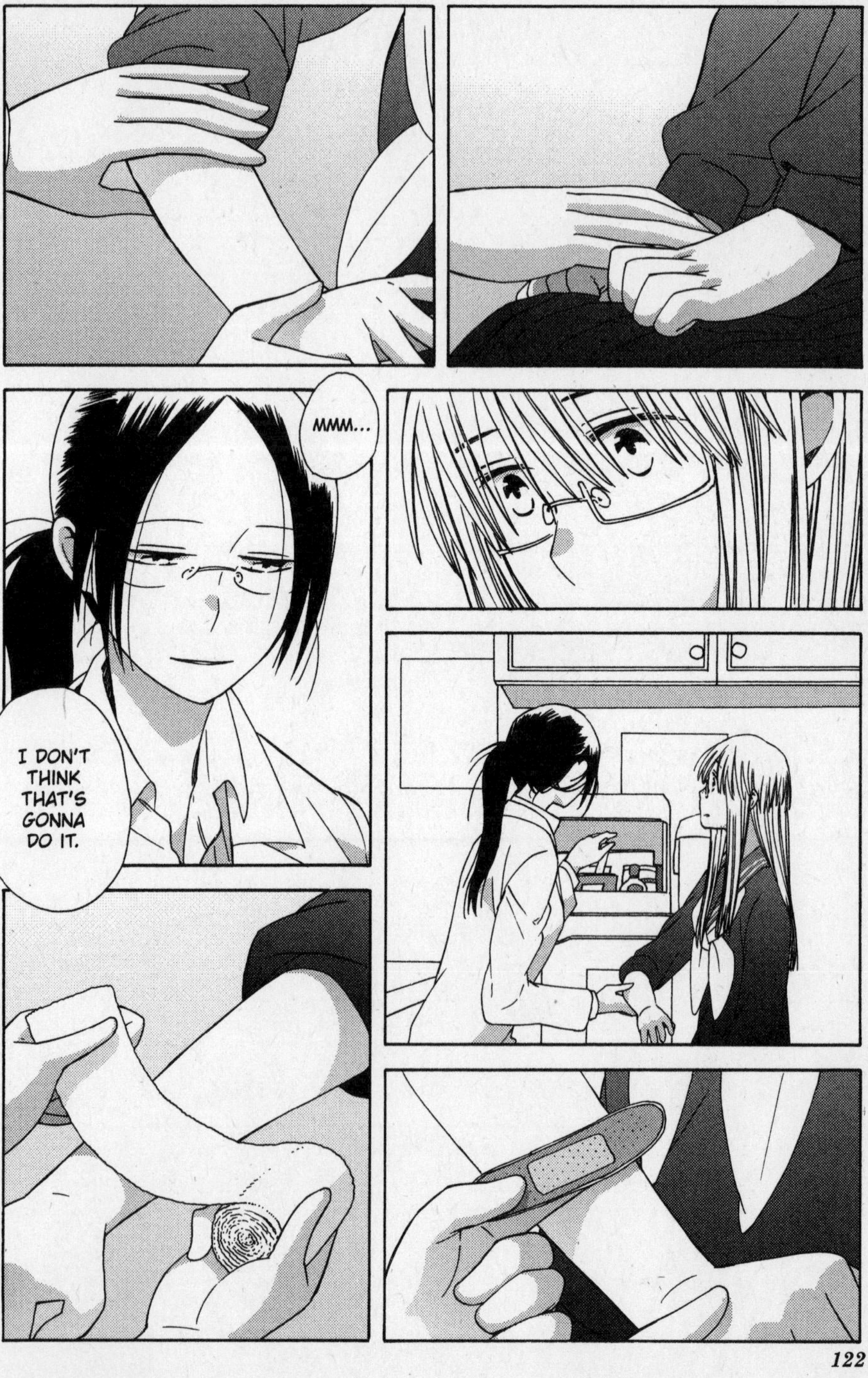
MMM...
I DON'T THINK THAT'S GONNA DO IT.

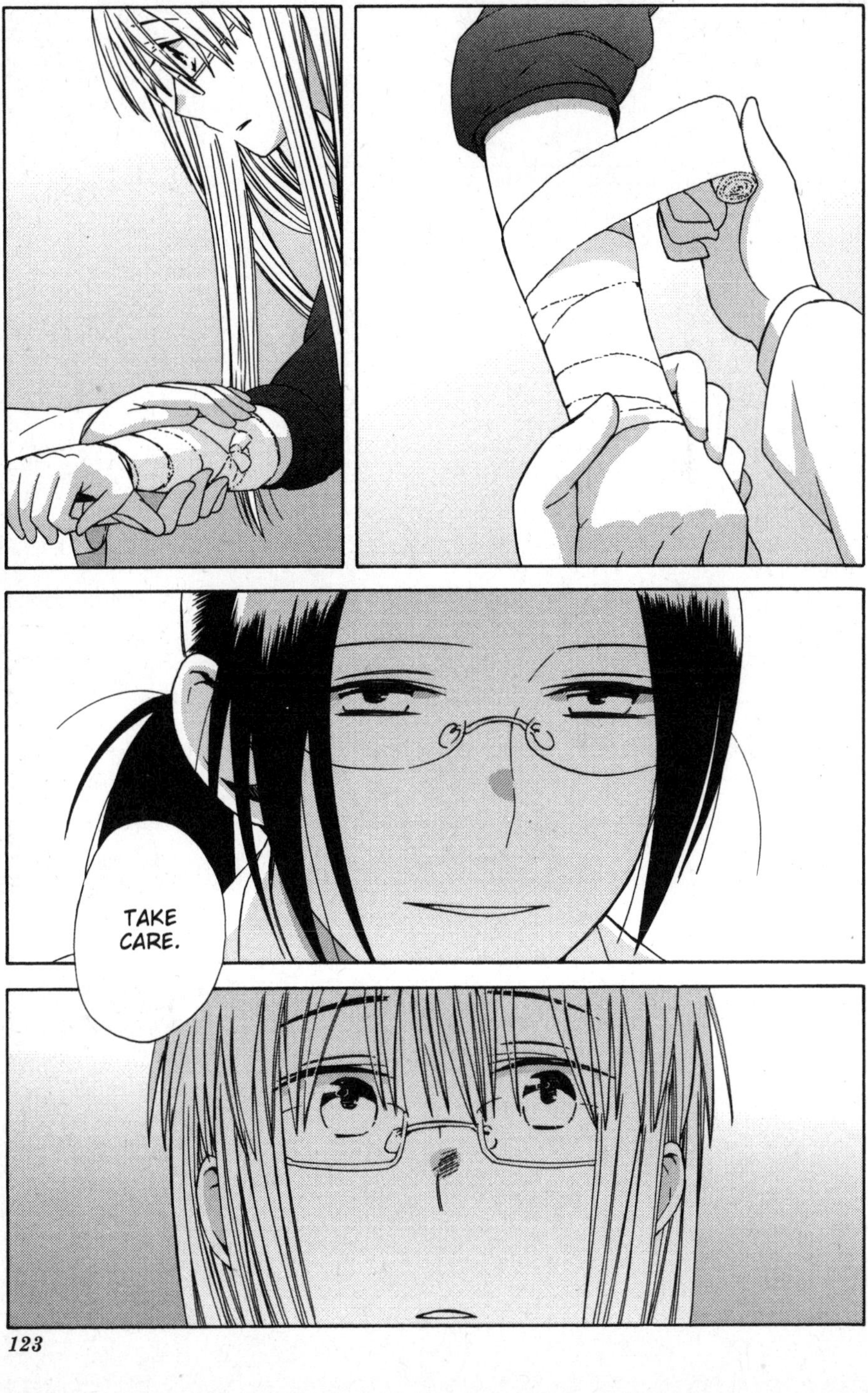
TAKE CARE.

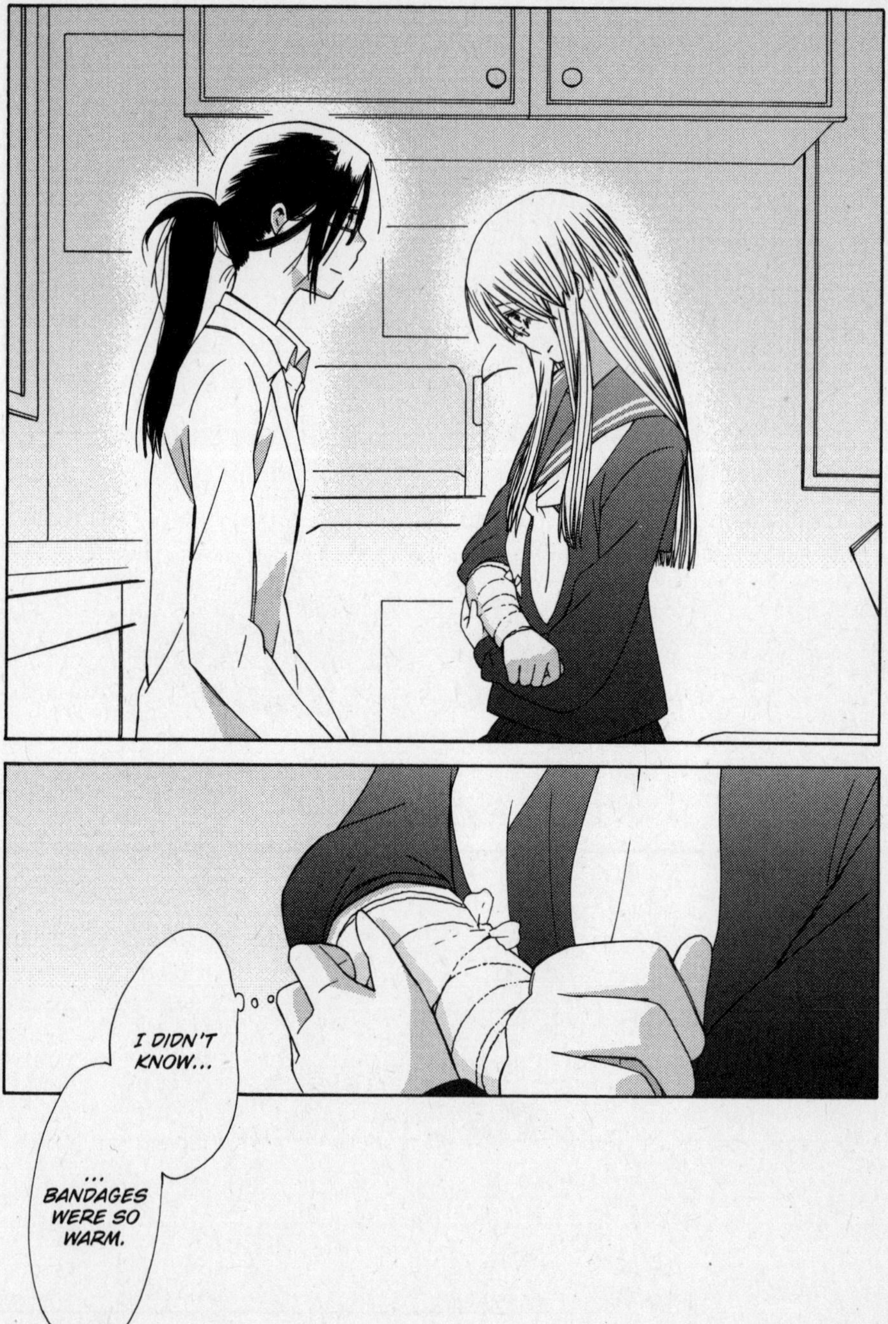
I DIDN'T KNOW...
...BANDAGES WERE SO WARM.

Fin

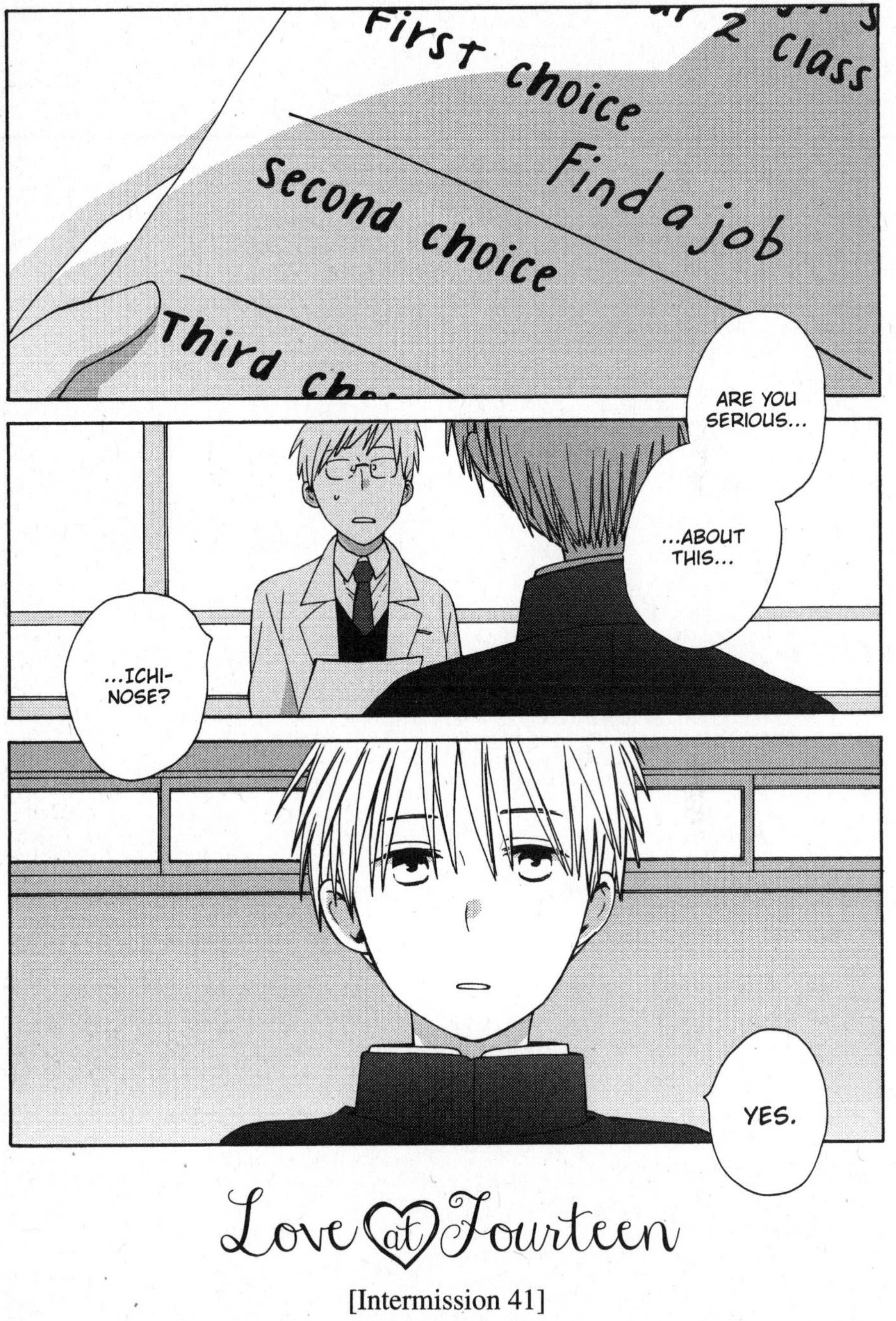
2 Class
First choice
Find a job
Second choice
Third
ARE YOU SERIOUS...
...ABOUT THIS...
...ICHI-NOSE?
YES.

Love at Fourteen

[Intermission 41]

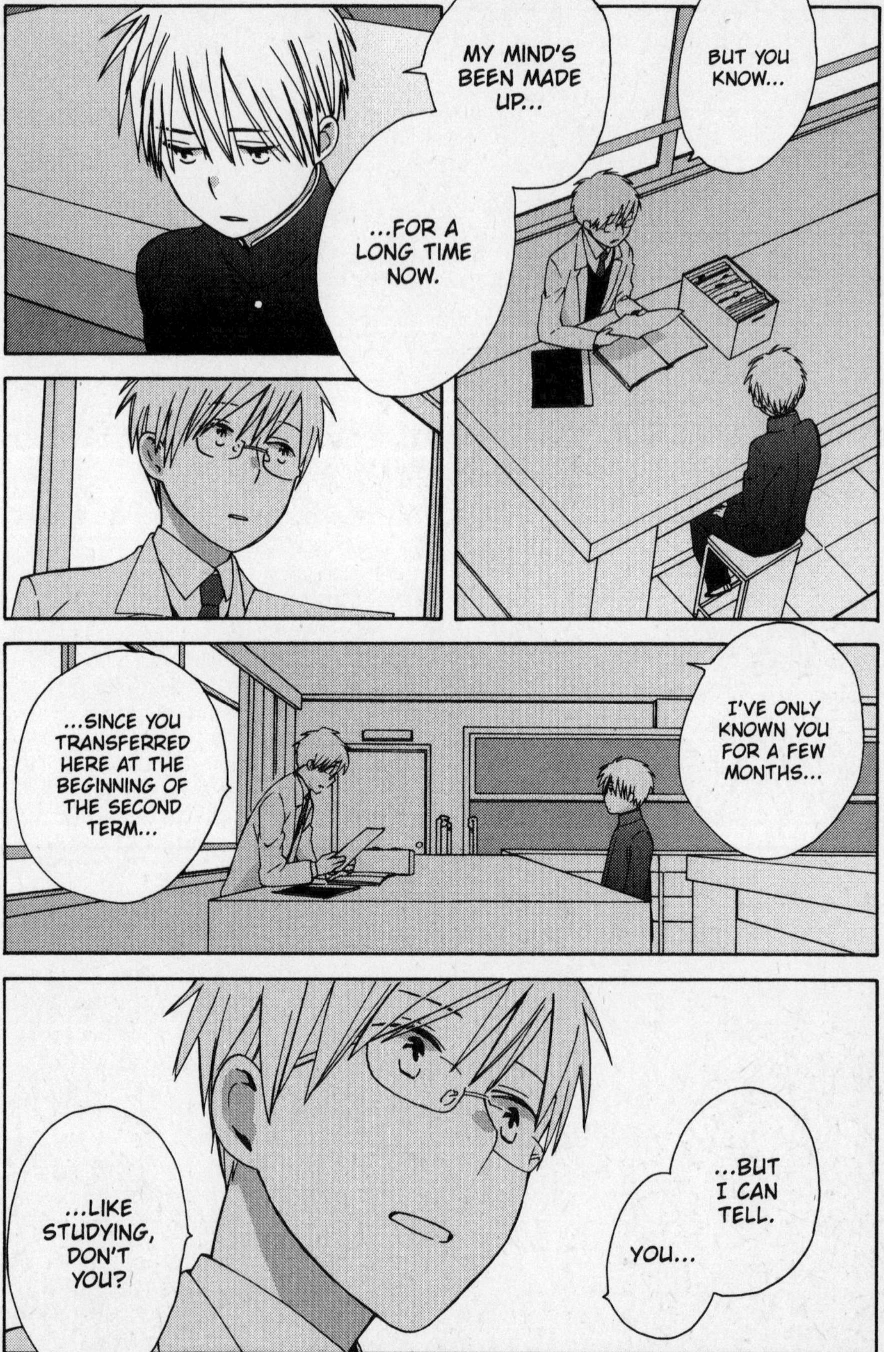
BUT YOU KNOW...
MY MIND'S BEEN MADE UP...
...FOR A LONG TIME NOW.
I'VE ONLY KNOWN YOU FOR A FEW MONTHS...
...SINCE YOU TRANSFERRED HERE AT THE BEGINNING OF THE SECOND TERM...
...BUT I CAN TELL.
YOU...
...LIKE STUDYING, DON'T YOU?

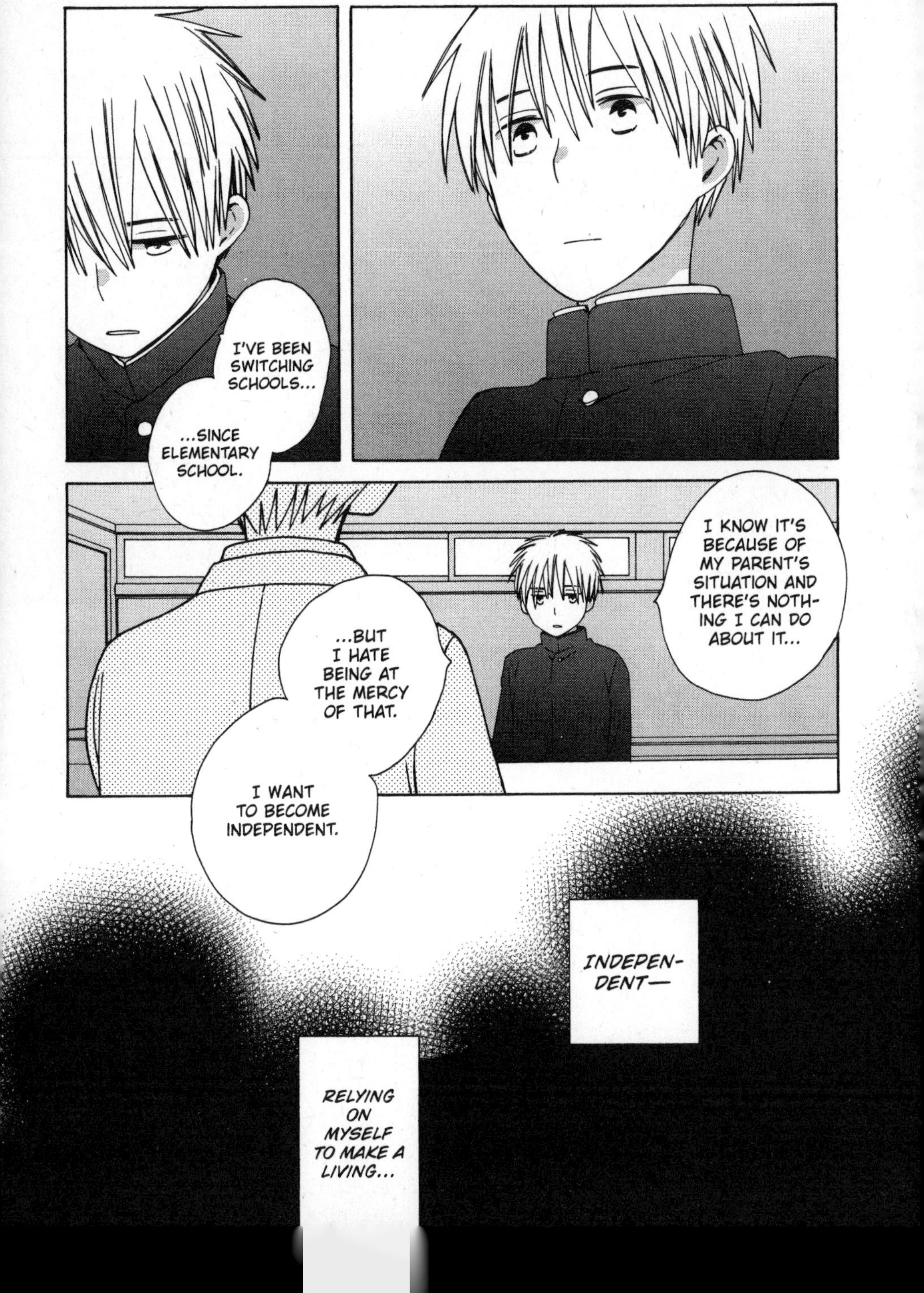
I'VE BEEN SWITCHING SCHOOLS...
...SINCE ELEMENTARY SCHOOL.
I KNOW IT'S BECAUSE OF MY PARENT'S SITUATION AND THERE'S NOTHING I CAN DO ABOUT IT...
...BUT I HATE BEING AT THE MERCY OF THAT.
I WANT TO BECOME INDEPENDENT.
INDEPENDENT—
RELYING ON MYSELF TO MAKE A LIVING...

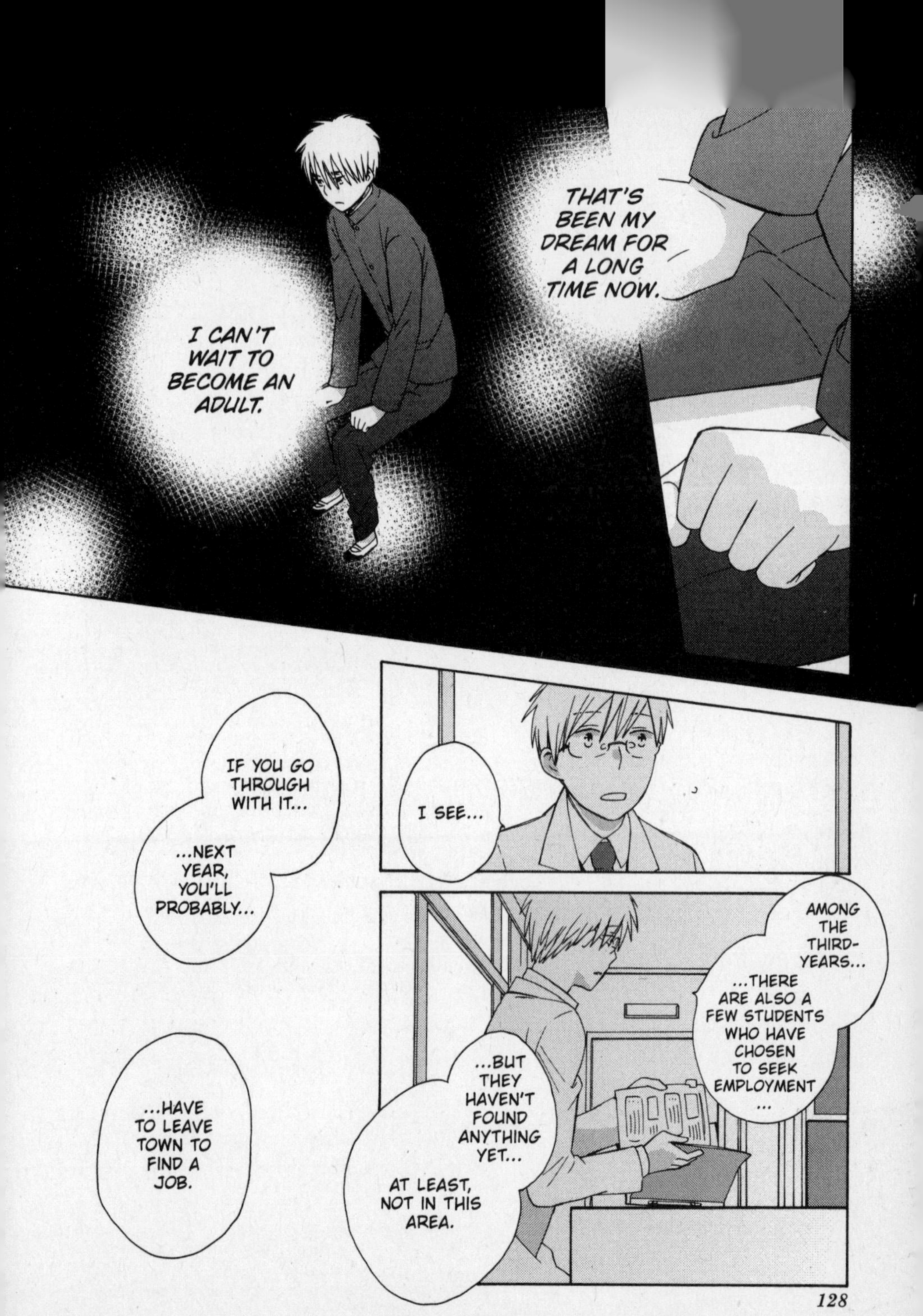
THAT'S BEEN MY DREAM FOR A LONG TIME NOW.
I CAN'T WAIT TO BECOME AN ADULT.
I SEE...
IF YOU GO THROUGH WITH IT...
...NEXT YEAR, YOU'LL PROBABLY...
AMONG THE THIRD-YEARS...
...THERE ARE ALSO A FEW STUDENTS WHO HAVE CHOSEN TO SEEK EMPLOYMENT...
...BUT THEY HAVEN'T FOUND ANYTHING YET...
AT LEAST, NOT IN THIS AREA.
...HAVE TO LEAVE TOWN TO FIND A JOB.

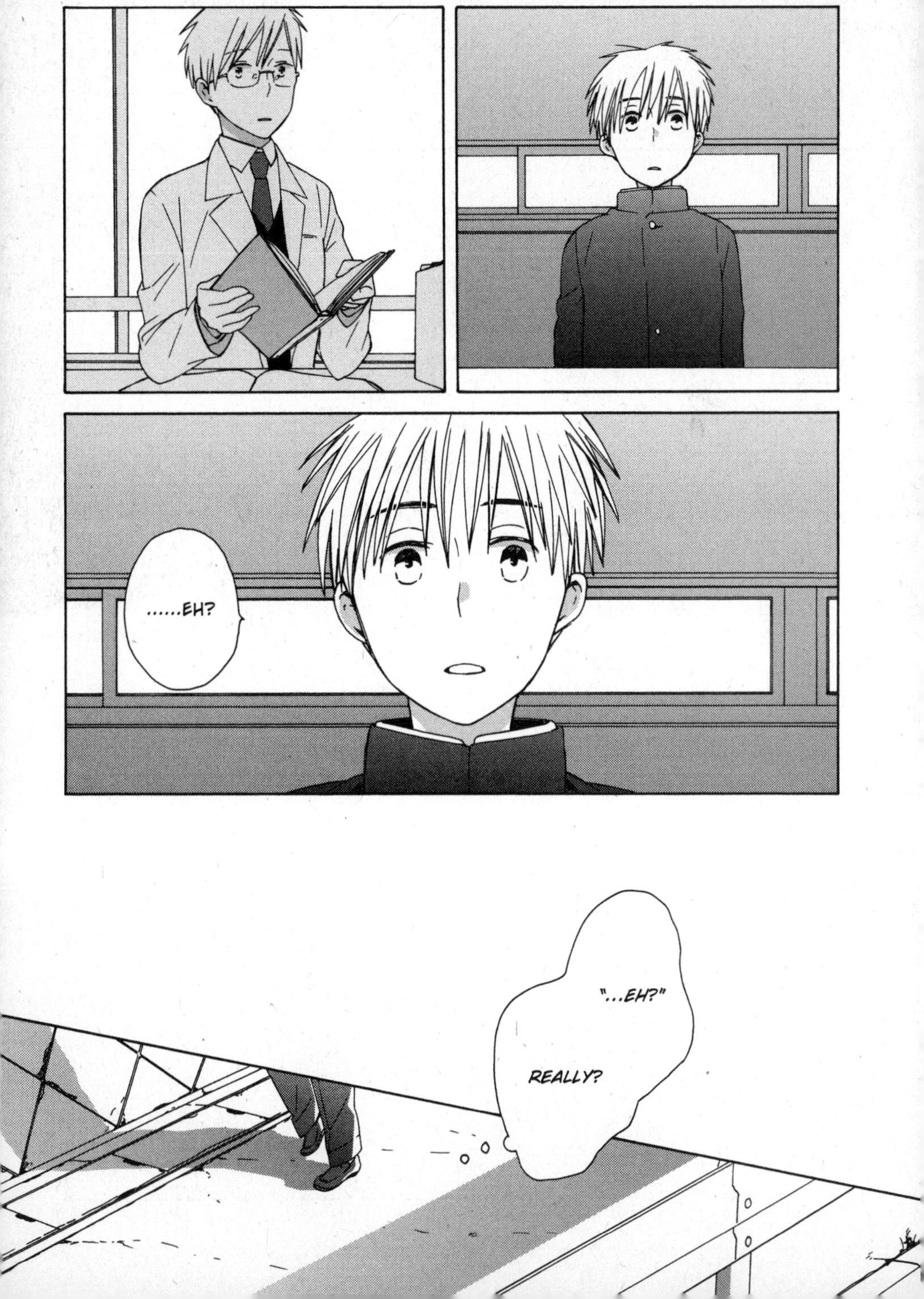
......EH?
"...EH?"
REALLY?

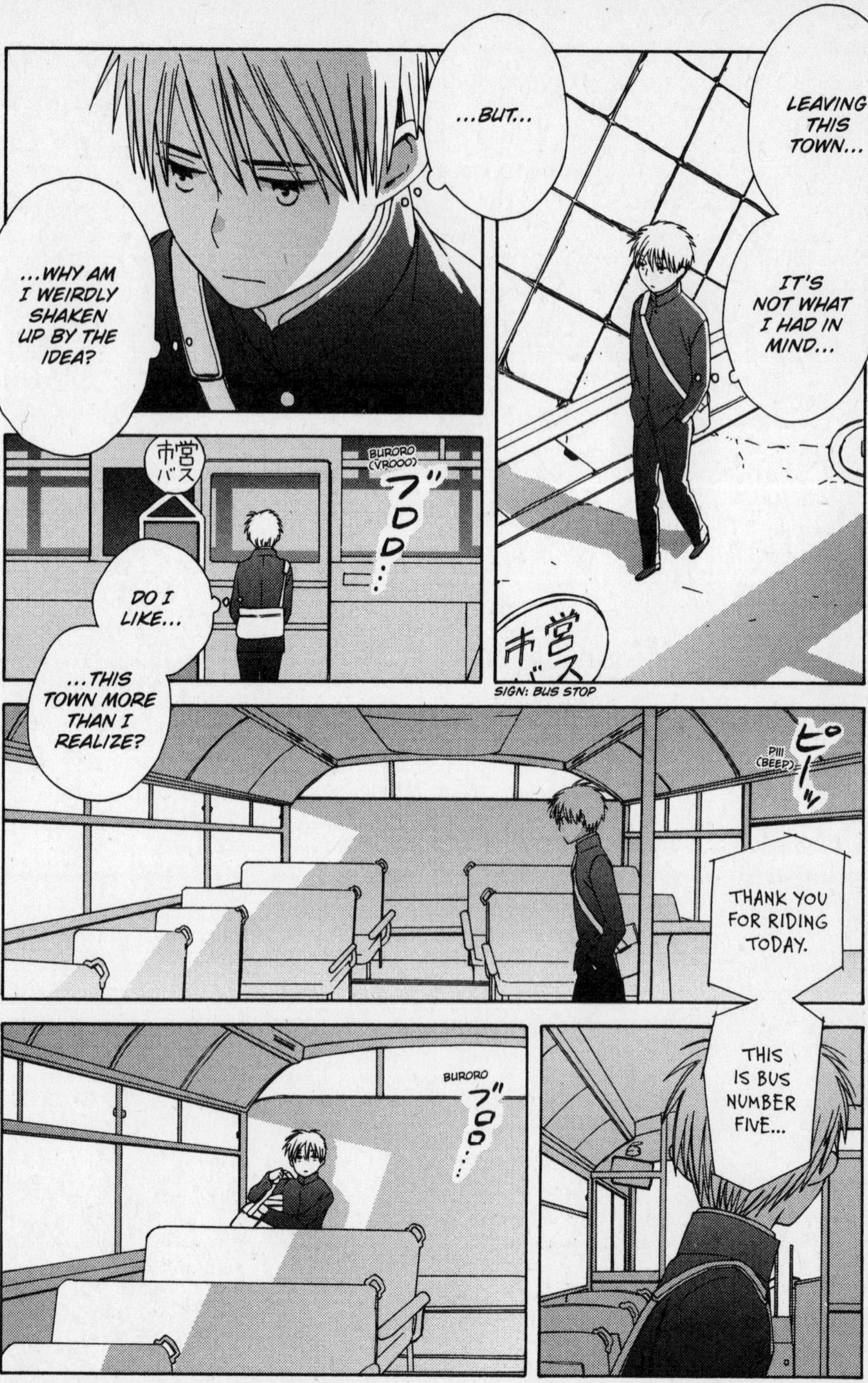
LEAVING THIS TOWN...
IT'S NOT WHAT I HAD IN MIND...
...BUT...
...WHY AM I WEIRDLY SHAKEN UP BY THE IDEA?
SIGN: BUS STOP
BURORO (VROOO)
ブロロ...
DO I LIKE...
...THIS TOWN MORE THAN I REALIZE?
PIII (BEEP)
ピーッ
THANK YOU FOR RIDING TODAY.
THIS IS BUS NUMBER FIVE...
BURORO
ブロロ...

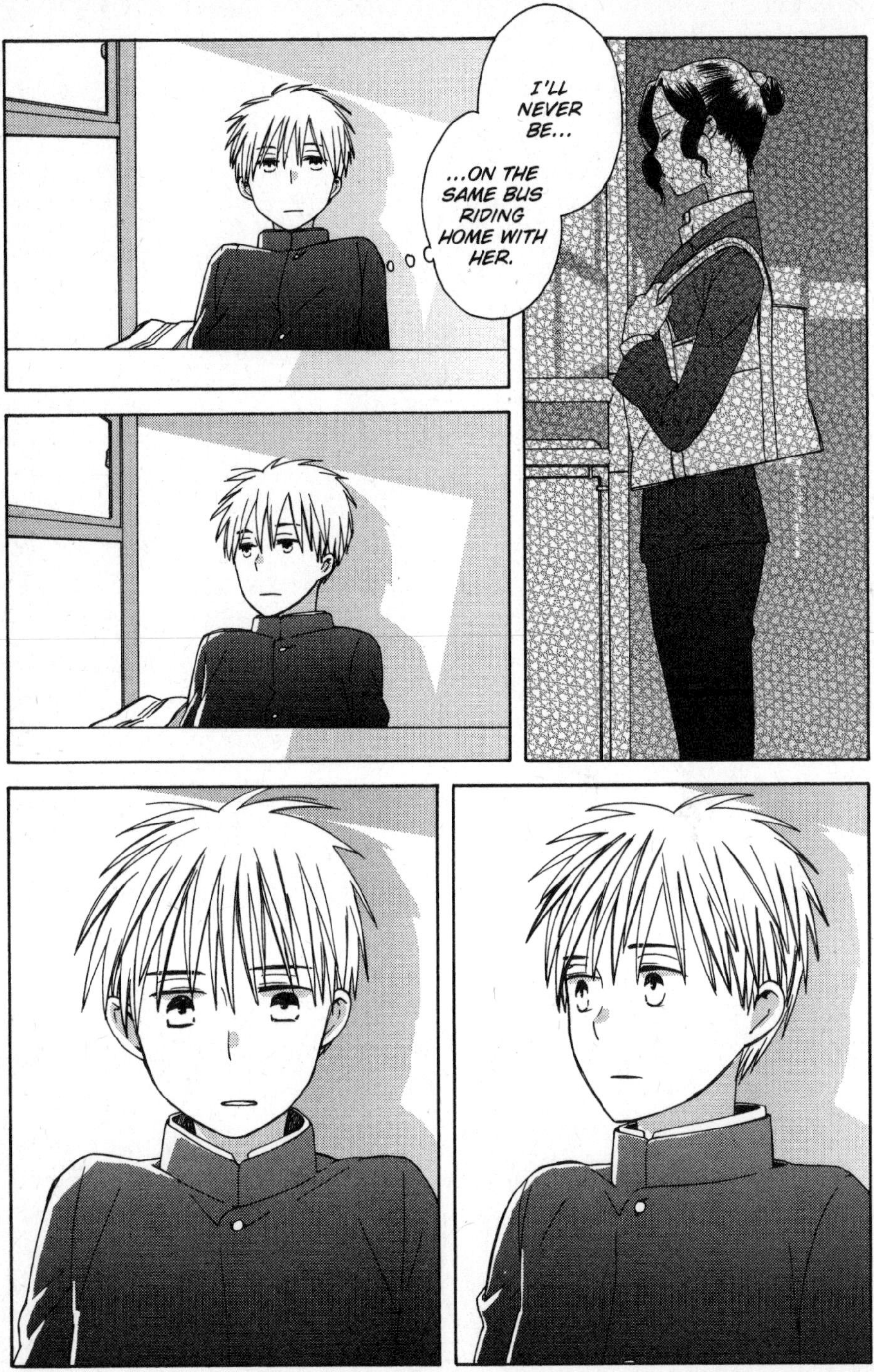
I'LL NEVER BE... ...ON THE SAME BUS RIDING HOME WITH HER.

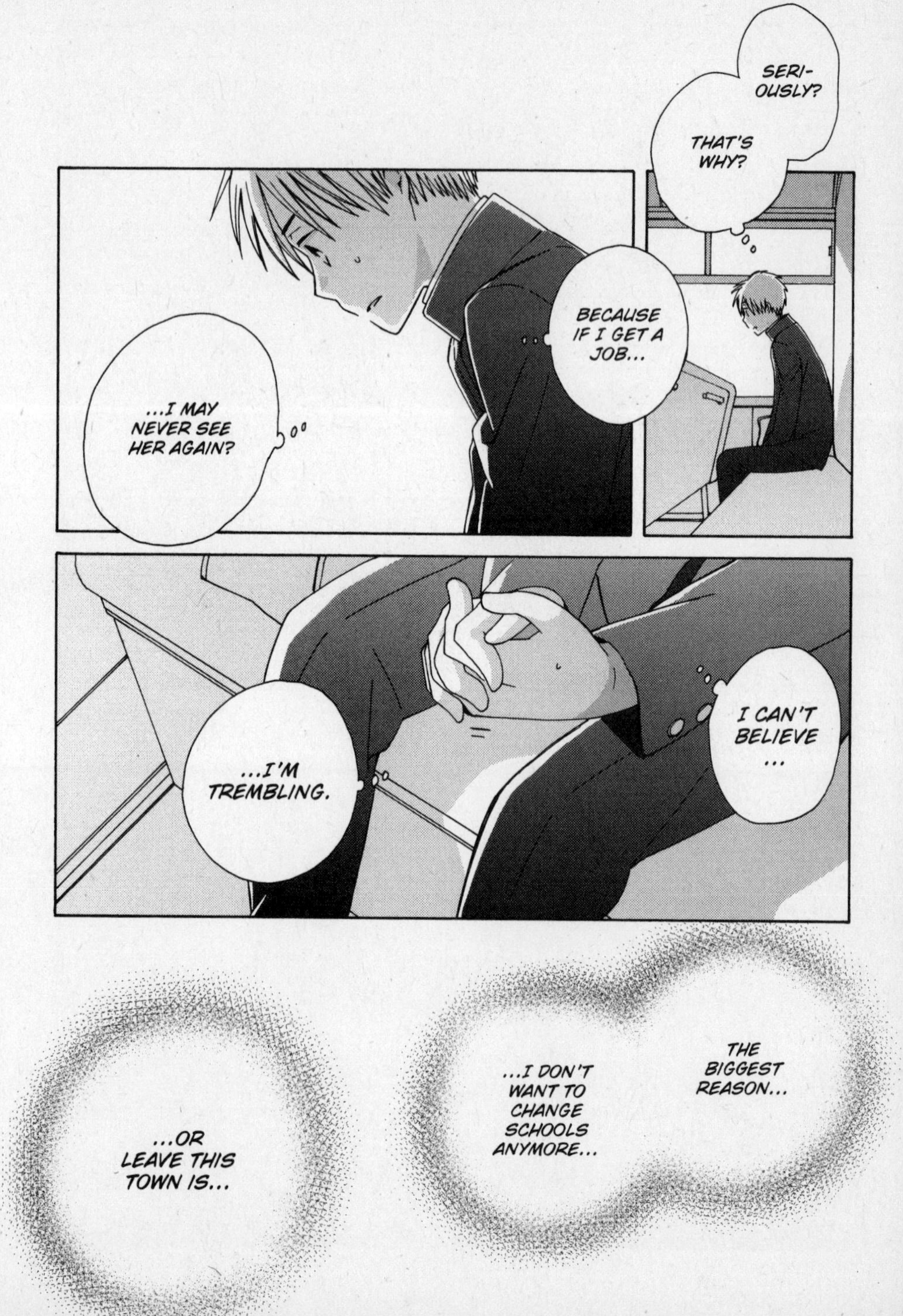
SERI-OUSLY? THAT'S WHY?
BECAUSE IF I GET A JOB...
...I MAY NEVER SEE HER AGAIN?
I CAN'T BELIEVE...
...I'M TREMBLING.
THE BIGGEST REASON...
...I DON'T WANT TO CHANGE SCHOOLS ANYMORE...
...OR LEAVE THIS TOWN IS...

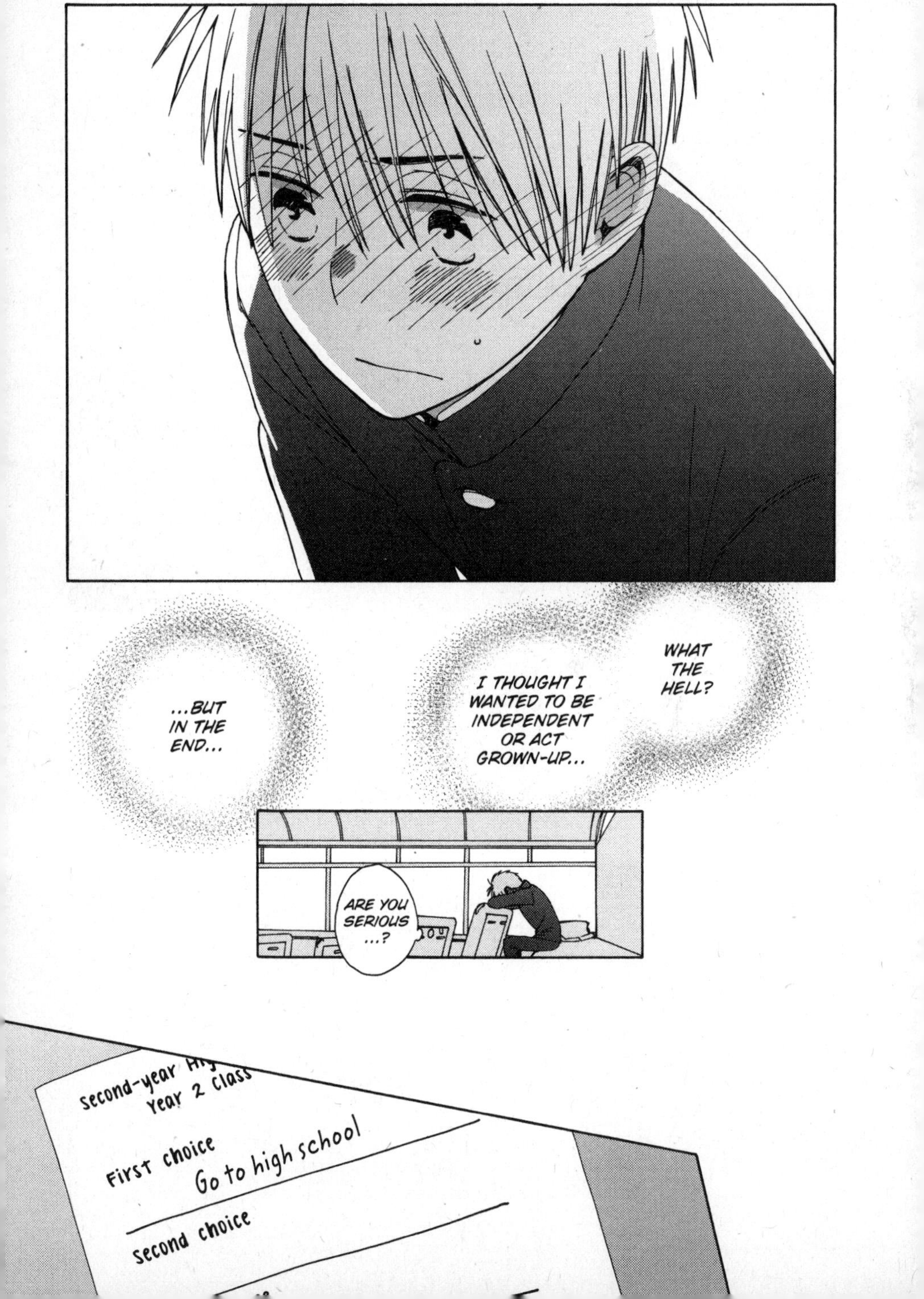
WHAT THE HELL?
I THOUGHT I WANTED TO BE INDEPENDENT OR ACT GROWN-UP...
...BUT IN THE END...
ARE YOU SERIOUS ...?
Second-year
Year 2 Class
First choice
Go to high school
Second choice

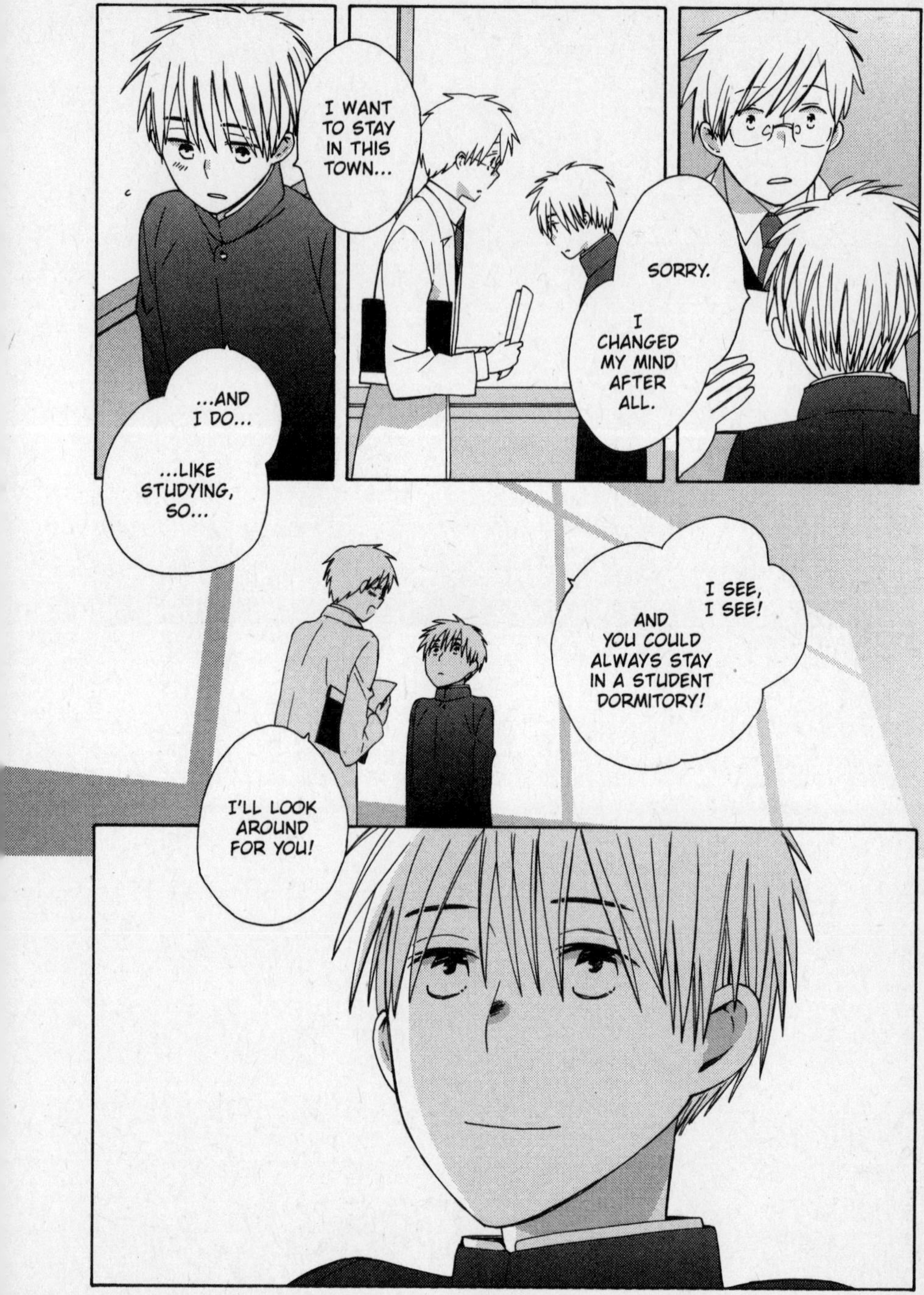
SORRY.
I CHANGED MY MIND AFTER ALL.
I WANT TO STAY IN THIS TOWN...
...AND I DO...
...LIKE STUDYING, SO...
I SEE, I SEE!
AND YOU COULD ALWAYS STAY IN A STUDENT DORMITORY!
I'LL LOOK AROUND FOR YOU!

Fin

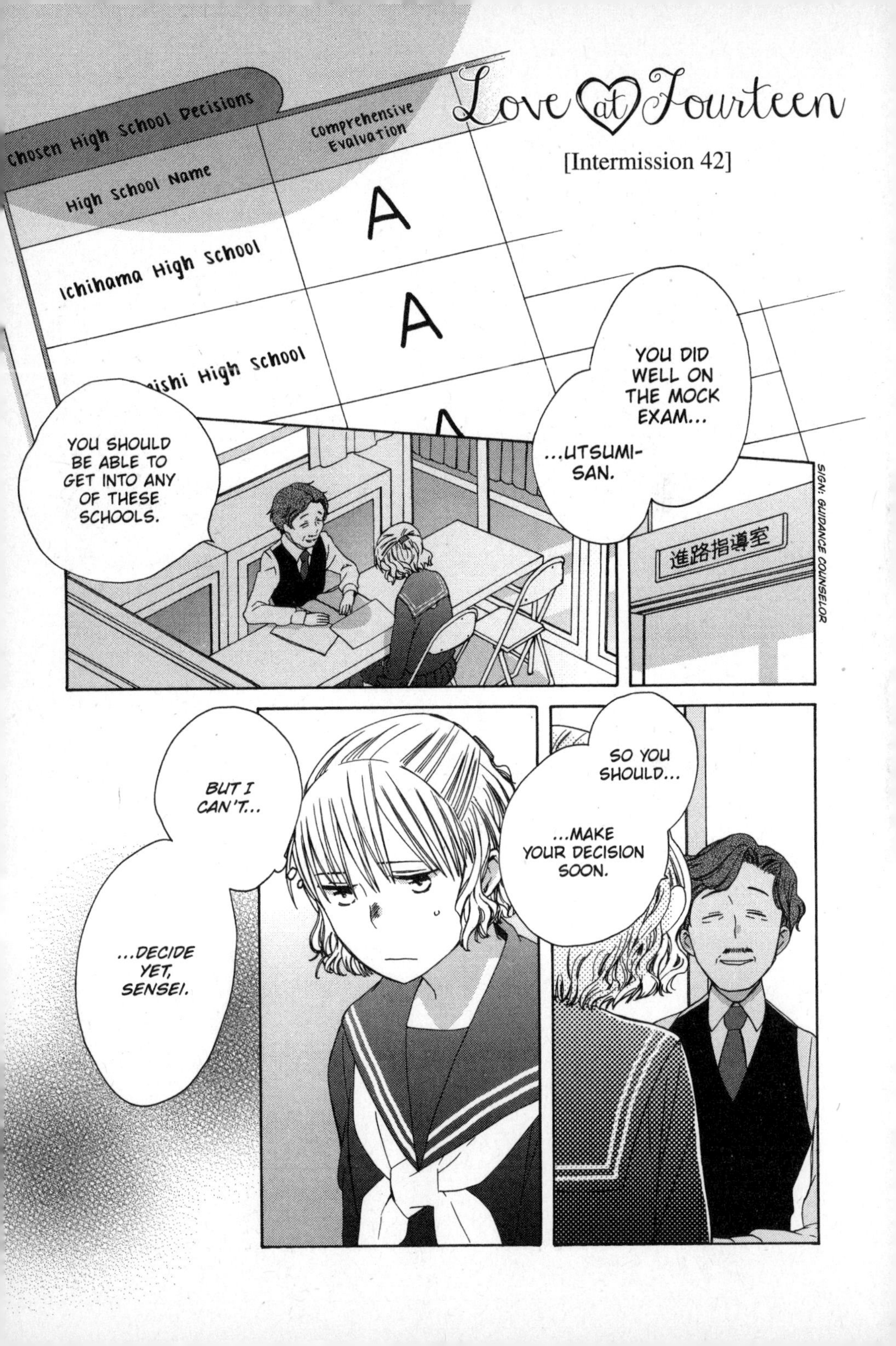
Love at Fourteen
[Intermission 42]
Chosen High School Decisions
High School Name
Comprehensive Evaluation
Ichihama High School
A
nishi High School
A
YOU DID WELL ON THE MOCK EXAM...
...UTSUMI-SAN.
進路指導室
SIGN: GUIDANCE COUNSELOR
YOU SHOULD BE ABLE TO GET INTO ANY OF THESE SCHOOLS.
SO YOU SHOULD...
...MAKE YOUR DECISION SOON.
BUT I CAN'T...
...DECIDE YET, SENSEI.

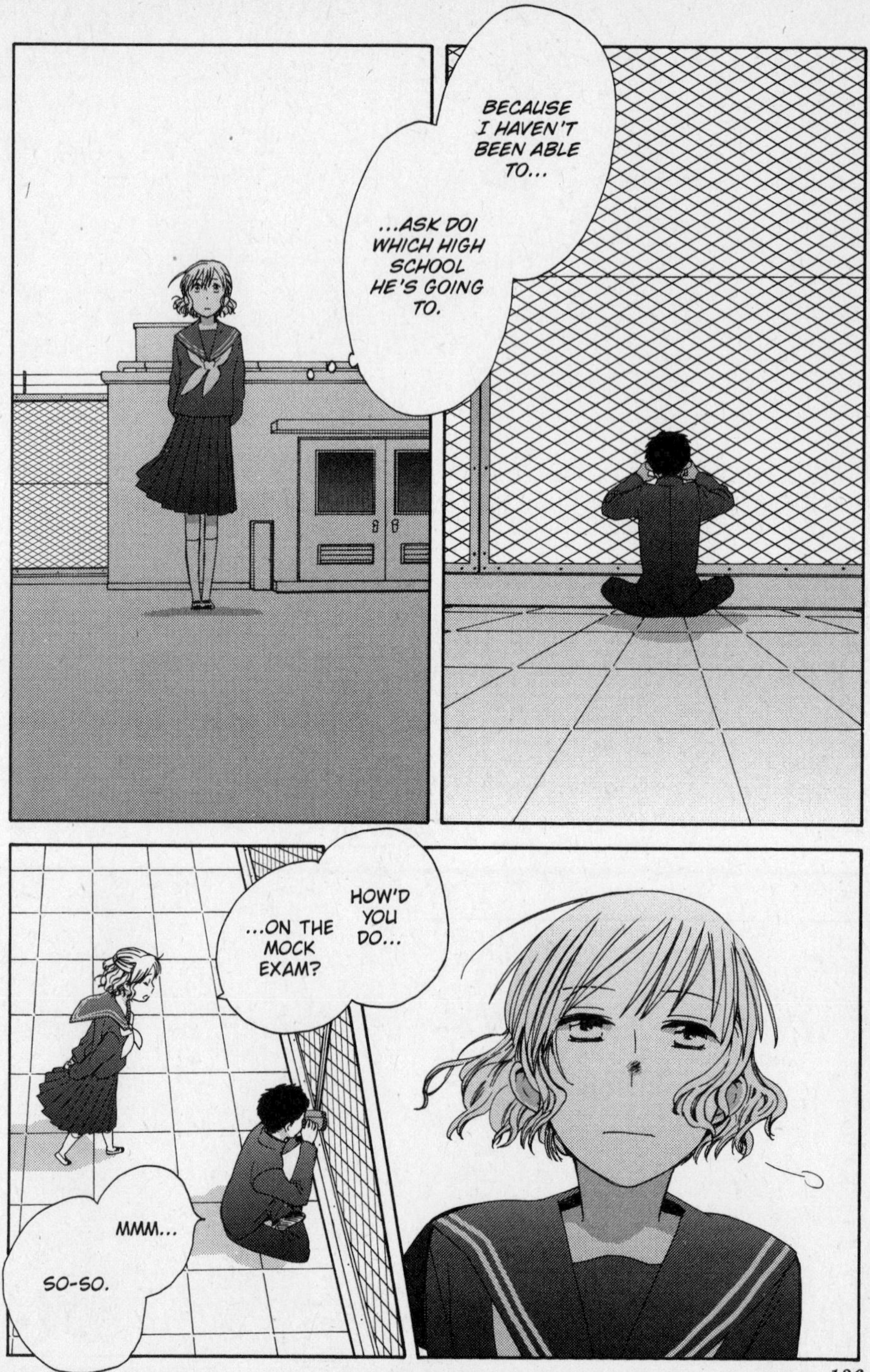
BECAUSE I HAVEN'T BEEN ABLE TO...
...ASK DOI WHICH HIGH SCHOOL HE'S GOING TO.
HOW'D YOU DO...
...ON THE MOCK EXAM?
MMM...
SO-SO.

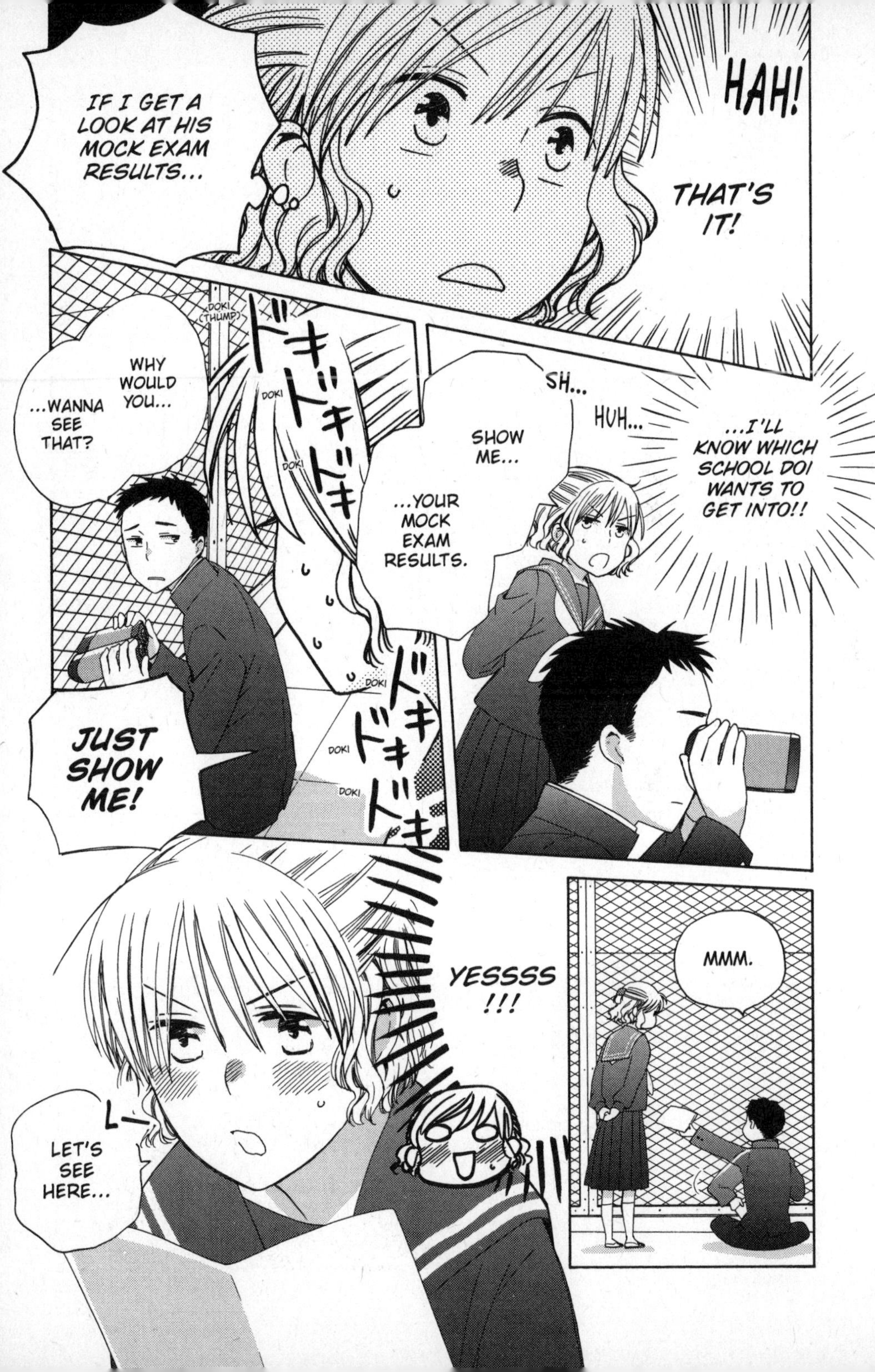
HAH!
THAT'S IT!
IF I GET A LOOK AT HIS MOCK EXAM RESULTS...
...I'LL KNOW WHICH SCHOOL DOI WANTS TO GET INTO!!
HUH...
SH...
SHOW ME...
...YOUR MOCK EXAM RESULTS.
DOKI (THUMP)
ドキッドキドキ
DOKI
DOKI
WHY WOULD YOU...
...WANNA SEE THAT?
ドキドキ
DOKI
DOKI
DOKI
JUST SHOW ME!
MMM.
YESSSS!!!
L—
LET'S SEE HERE...

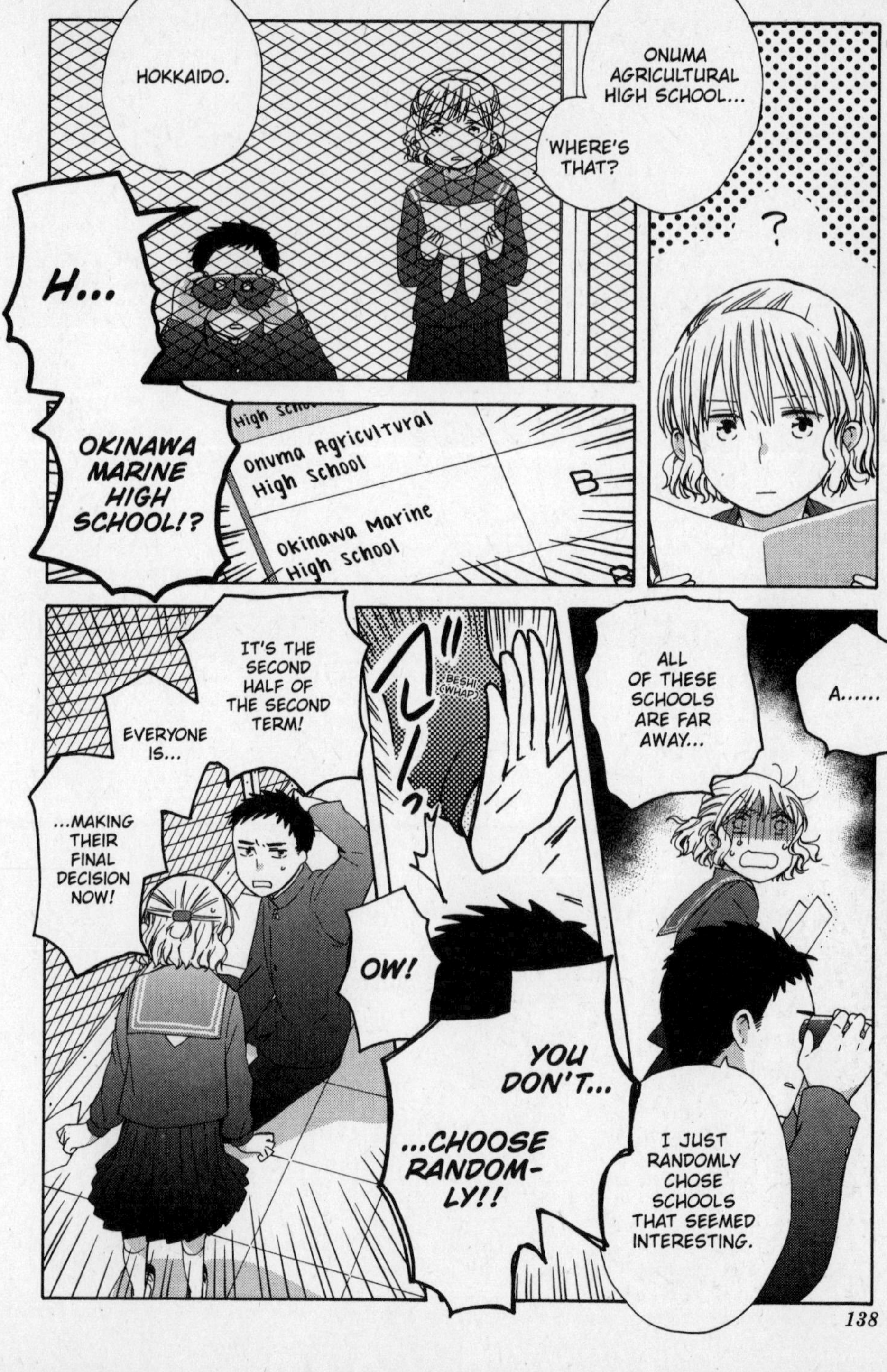
ONUMA AGRICULTURAL HIGH SCHOOL...
WHERE'S THAT?
?
HOKKAIDO.
H...
High School
Onuma Agricultural High School
B
Okinawa Marine High School
OKINAWA MARINE HIGH SCHOOL!?
A......
ALL OF THESE SCHOOLS ARE FAR AWAY...
I JUST RANDOMLY CHOSE SCHOOLS THAT SEEMED INTERESTING.
BESHI (WHAP)
OW!
YOU DON'T...
...CHOOSE RANDOM-LY!!
IT'S THE SECOND HALF OF THE SECOND TERM!
EVERYONE IS...
...MAKING THEIR FINAL DECISION NOW!

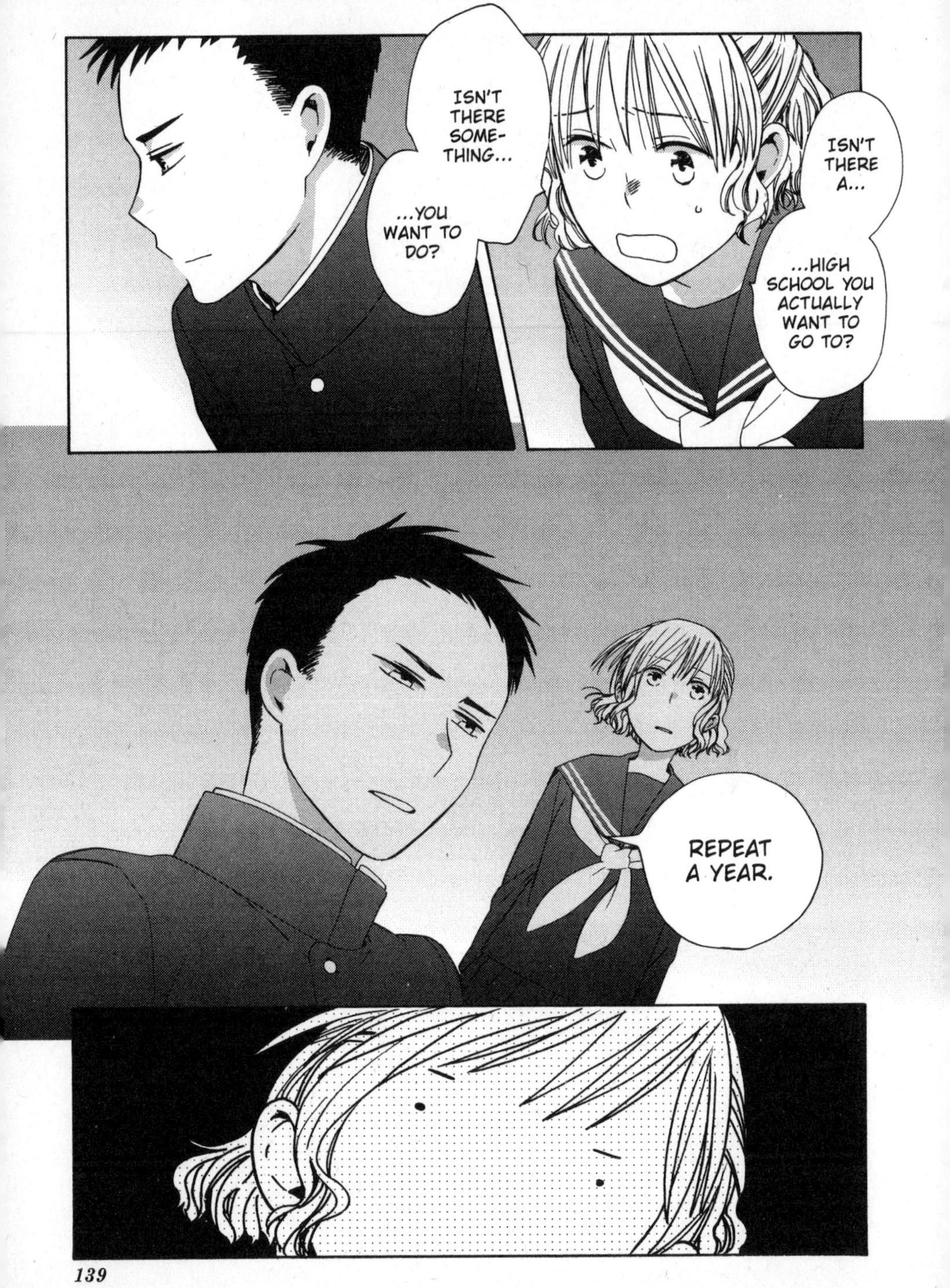
ISN'T THERE A...
...HIGH SCHOOL YOU ACTUALLY WANT TO GO TO?
ISN'T THERE SOMETHING...
...YOU WANT TO DO?
REPEAT A YEAR.

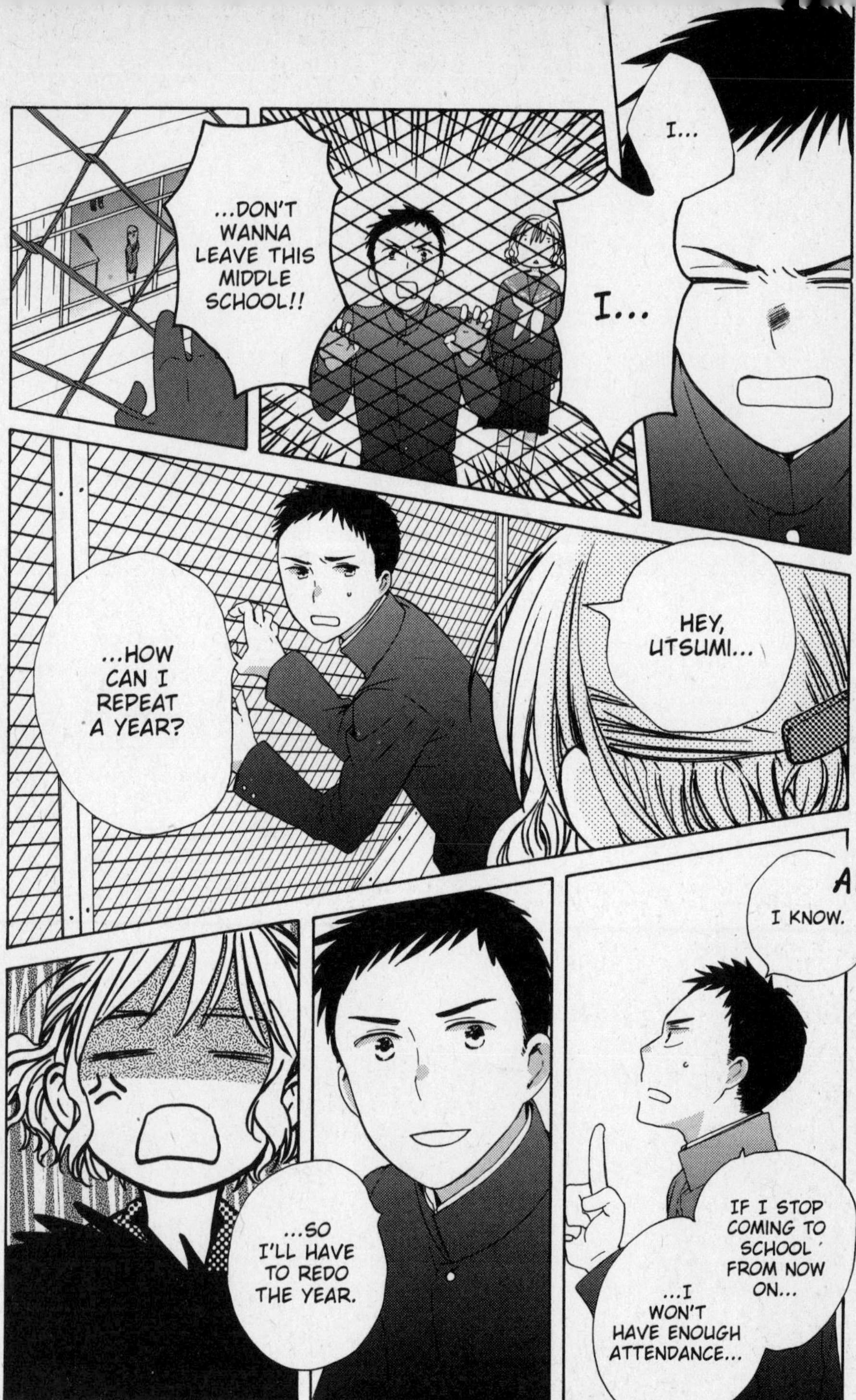
I...
I...
...DON'T WANNA LEAVE THIS MIDDLE SCHOOL!!
HEY, UTSUMI...
...HOW CAN I REPEAT A YEAR?
AH!
I KNOW.
IF I STOP COMING TO SCHOOL FROM NOW ON...
...I WON'T HAVE ENOUGH ATTENDANCE...
...SO I'LL HAVE TO REDO THE YEAR.

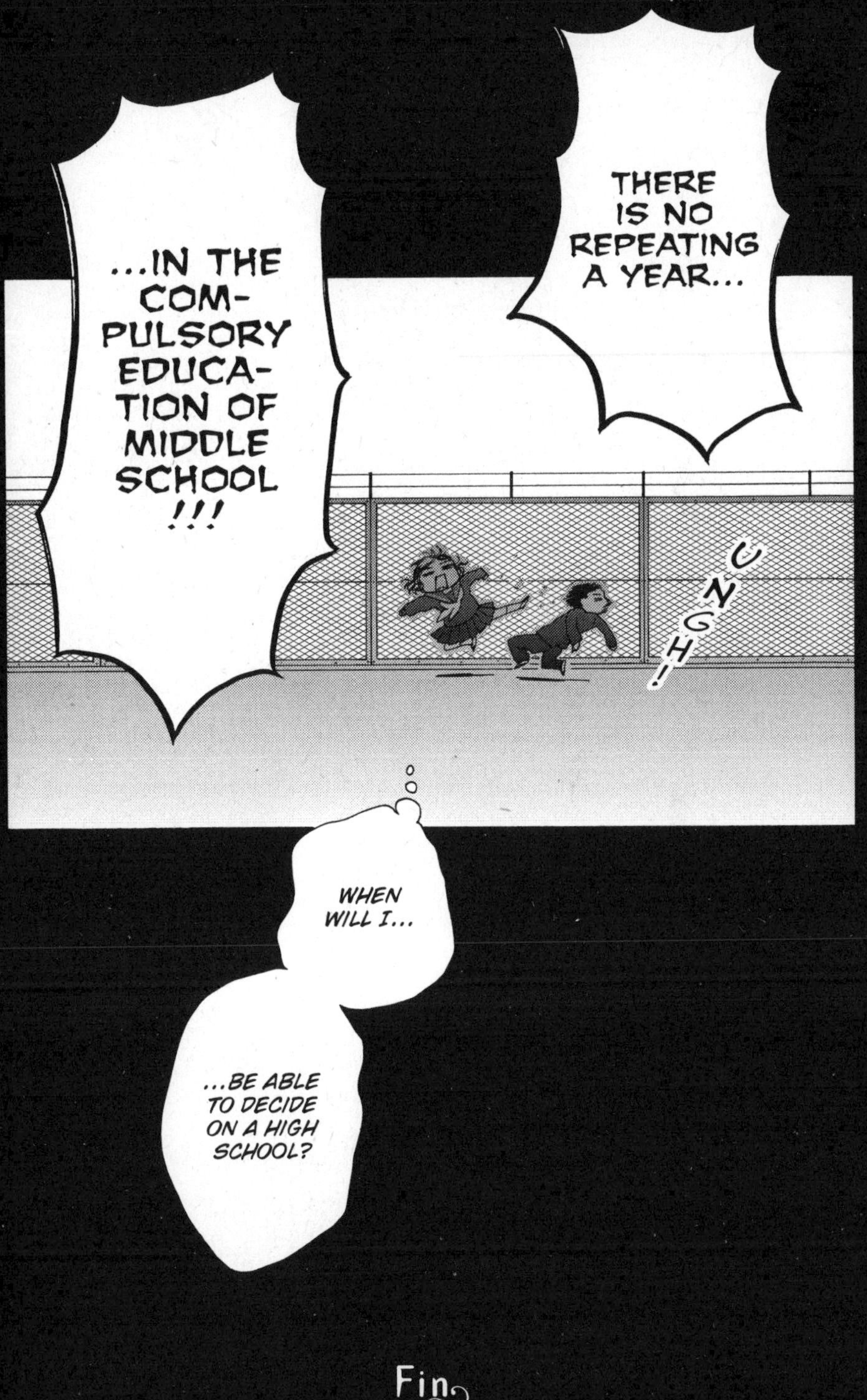
THERE IS NO REPEATING A YEAR...
...IN THE COM-PULSORY EDUCATION OF MIDDLE SCHOOL!!!
UNGH!
WHEN WILL I...
...BE ABLE TO DECIDE ON A HIGH SCHOOL?
Fin

Love at Fourteen

Fuka Mizutani

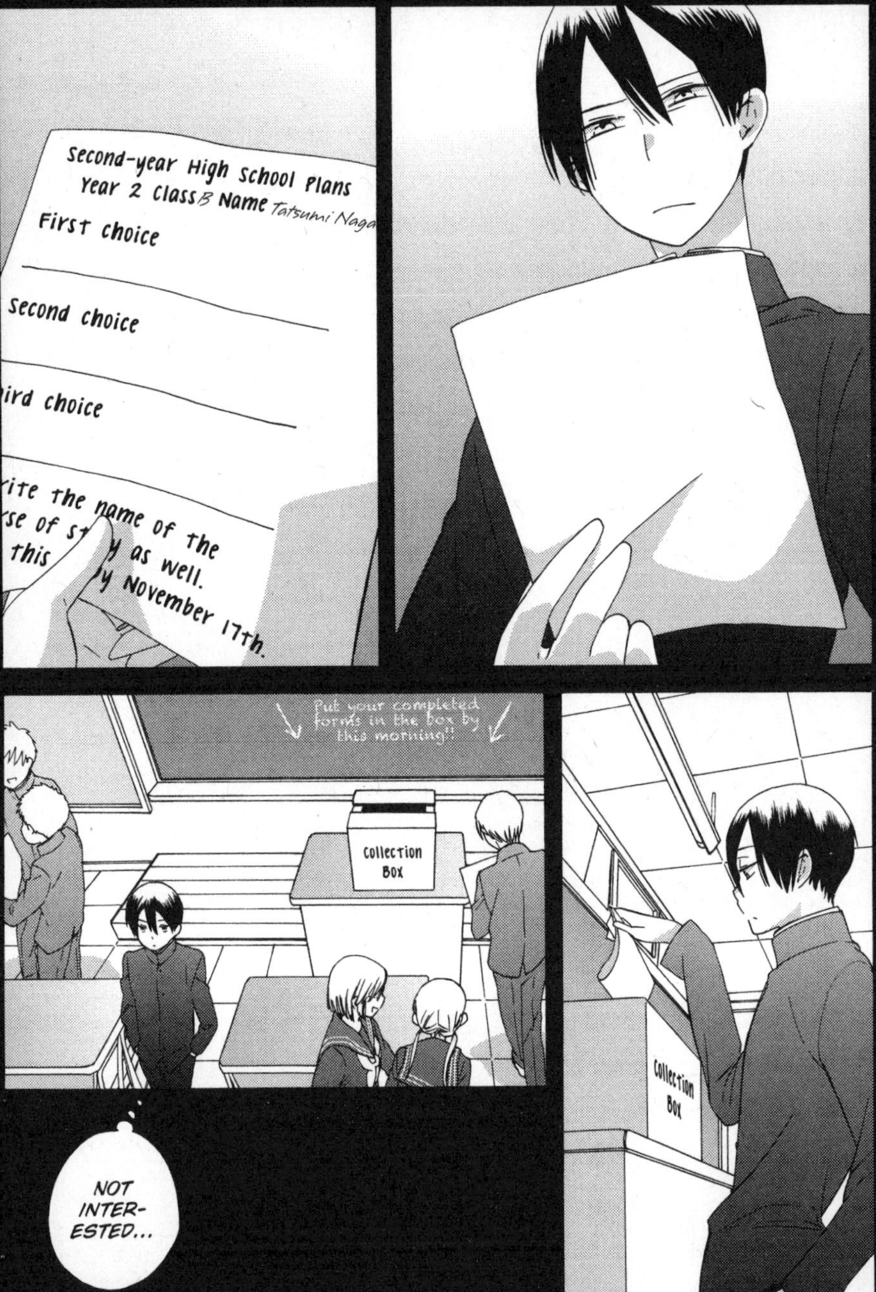
Second-year High School Plans
Year 2 Class B Name Tatsumi Naga
First choice
Second choice
ird choice
rite the name of the
rse of st y as well.
this y November 17th.
Collection Box
Put your completed forms in the box by this morning!!
Collection Box
NOT INTER-ESTED...

Love at Fourteen

[Chapter 33]

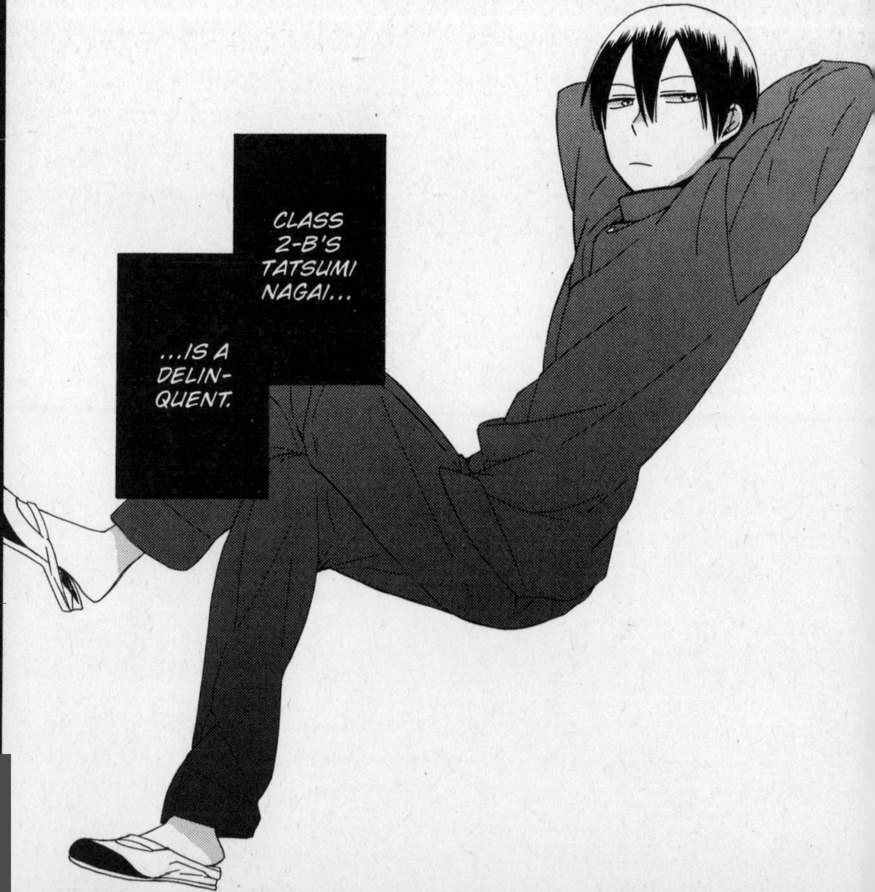
CLASS 2-B'S TATSUMI NAGAI...
...IS A DELIN-QUENT.

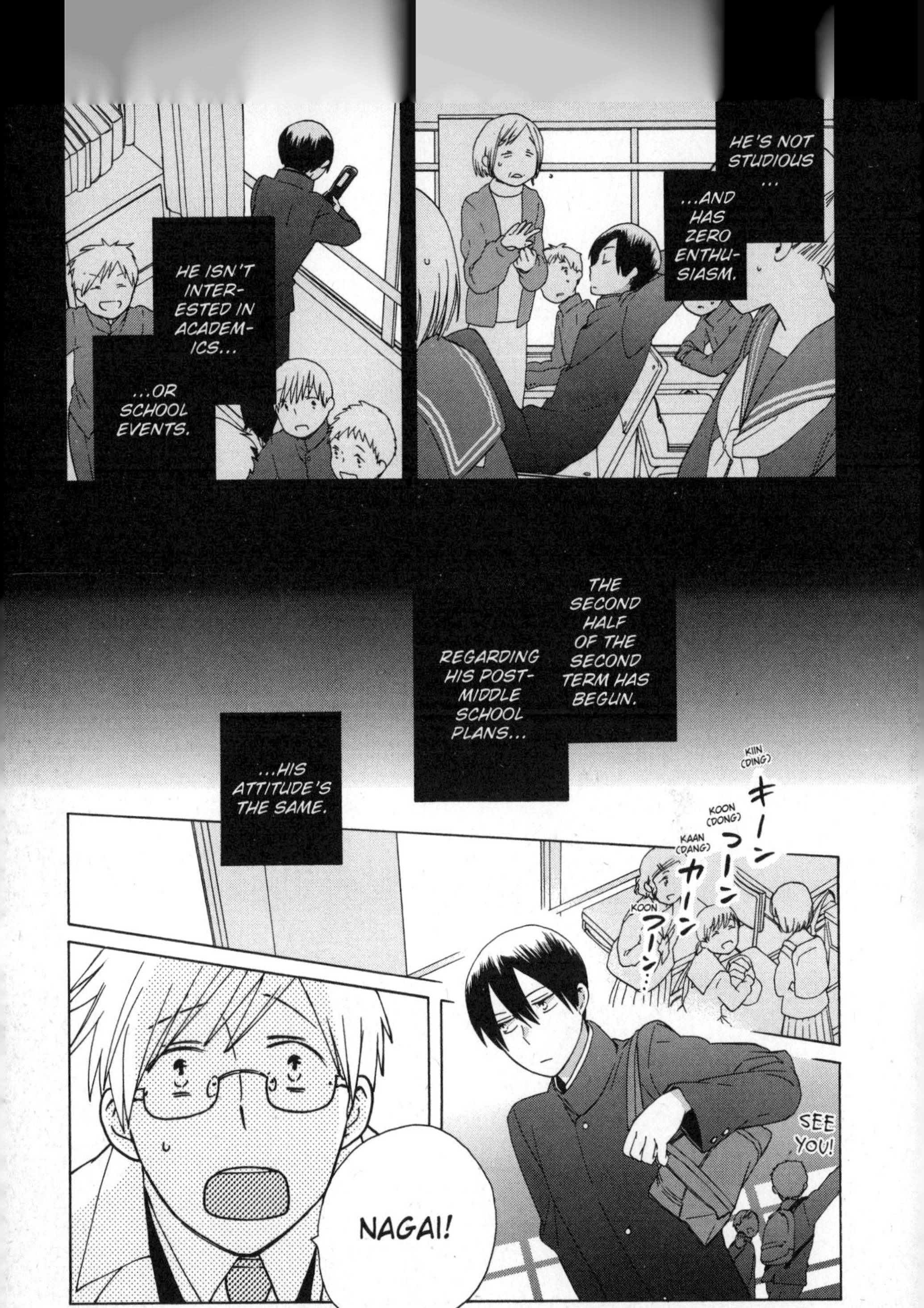

HE'S NOT STUDIOUS...
...AND HAS ZERO ENTHUSIASM.
HE ISN'T INTERESTED IN ACADEMICS...
...OR SCHOOL EVENTS.
THE SECOND HALF OF THE SECOND TERM HAS BEGUN.
REGARDING HIS POST-MIDDLE SCHOOL PLANS...
...HIS ATTITUDE'S THE SAME.
KIIN (DING)
キーン
KOON (DONG)
コーン
KAAN (DANG)
カーン
KOON
コーン...
SEE YOU!
NAGAI!

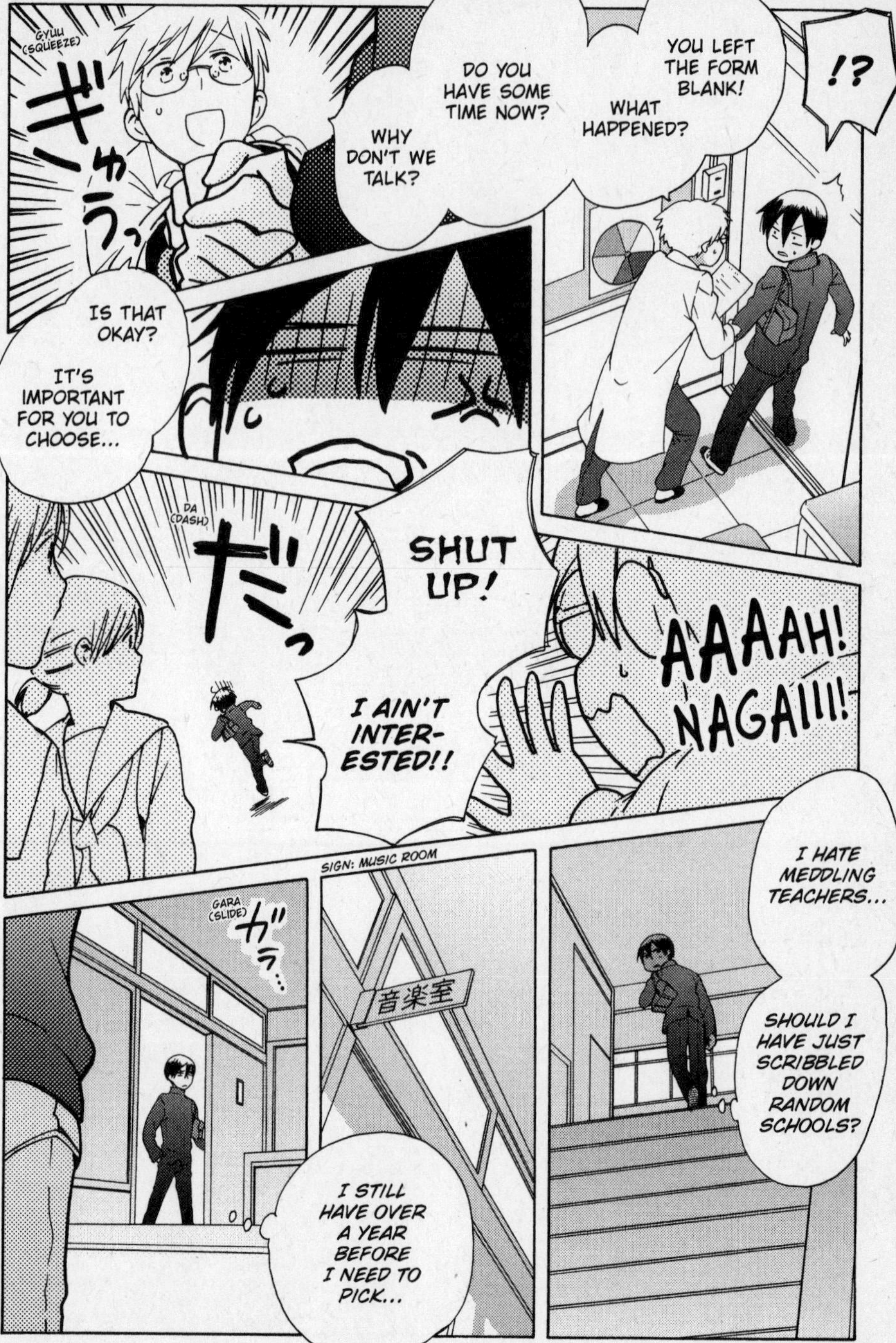
!?
YOU LEFT THE FORM BLANK!
WHAT HAPPENED?
DO YOU HAVE SOME TIME NOW?
WHY DON'T WE TALK?
GYUU (SQUEEZE)
ぎゅうっ
IS THAT OKAY?
IT'S IMPORTANT FOR YOU TO CHOOSE...
SHUT UP!
I AIN'T INTERESTED!!
AAAAH! NAGAI!!!
DA (DASH)
だっ
I HATE MEDDLING TEACHERS...
SHOULD I HAVE JUST SCRIBBLED DOWN RANDOM SCHOOLS?
SIGN: MUSIC ROOM
音楽室
I STILL HAVE OVER A YEAR BEFORE I NEED TO PICK...
GARA (SLIDE)
ガラ...

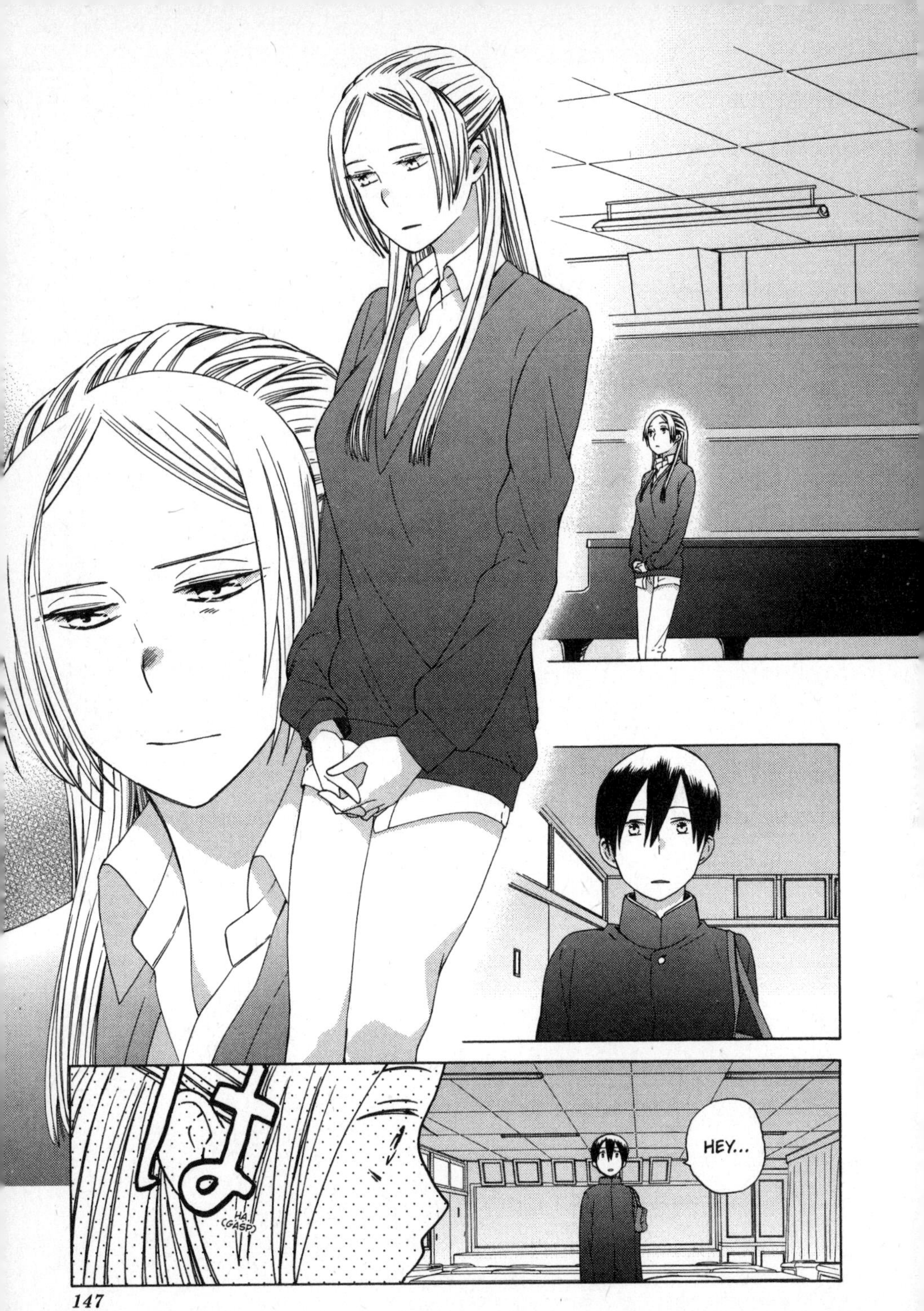
HA (GASP)
HEY...

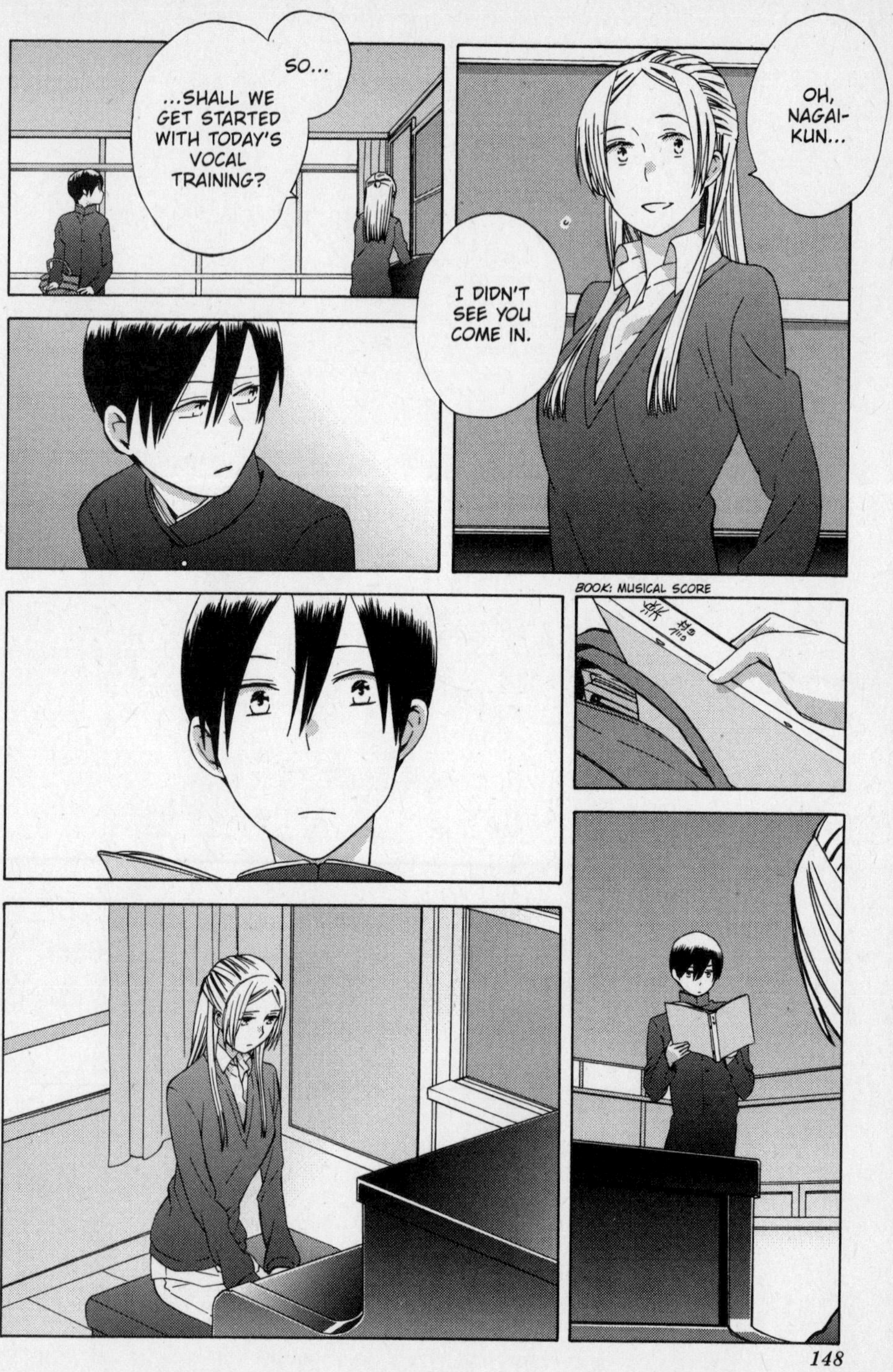
OH, NAGAI-KUN...
I DIDN'T SEE YOU COME IN.
SO...
...SHALL WE GET STARTED WITH TODAY'S VOCAL TRAINING?
BOOK: MUSICAL SCORE

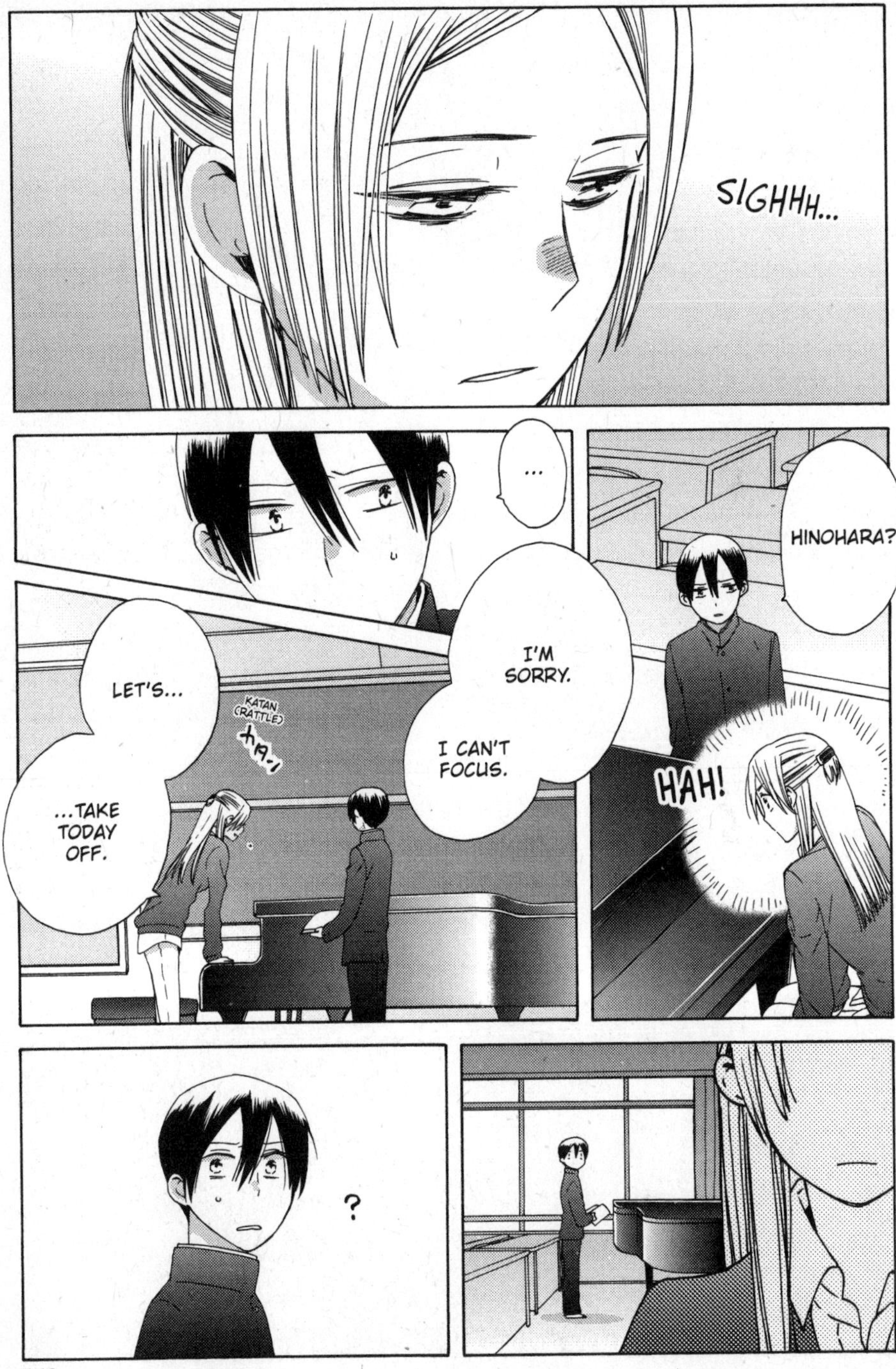
SIGHHH...
HINOHARA?
HAH!
...
I'M SORRY.
I CAN'T FOCUS.
LET'S...
KATAN (RATTLE)
...TAKE TODAY OFF.
?

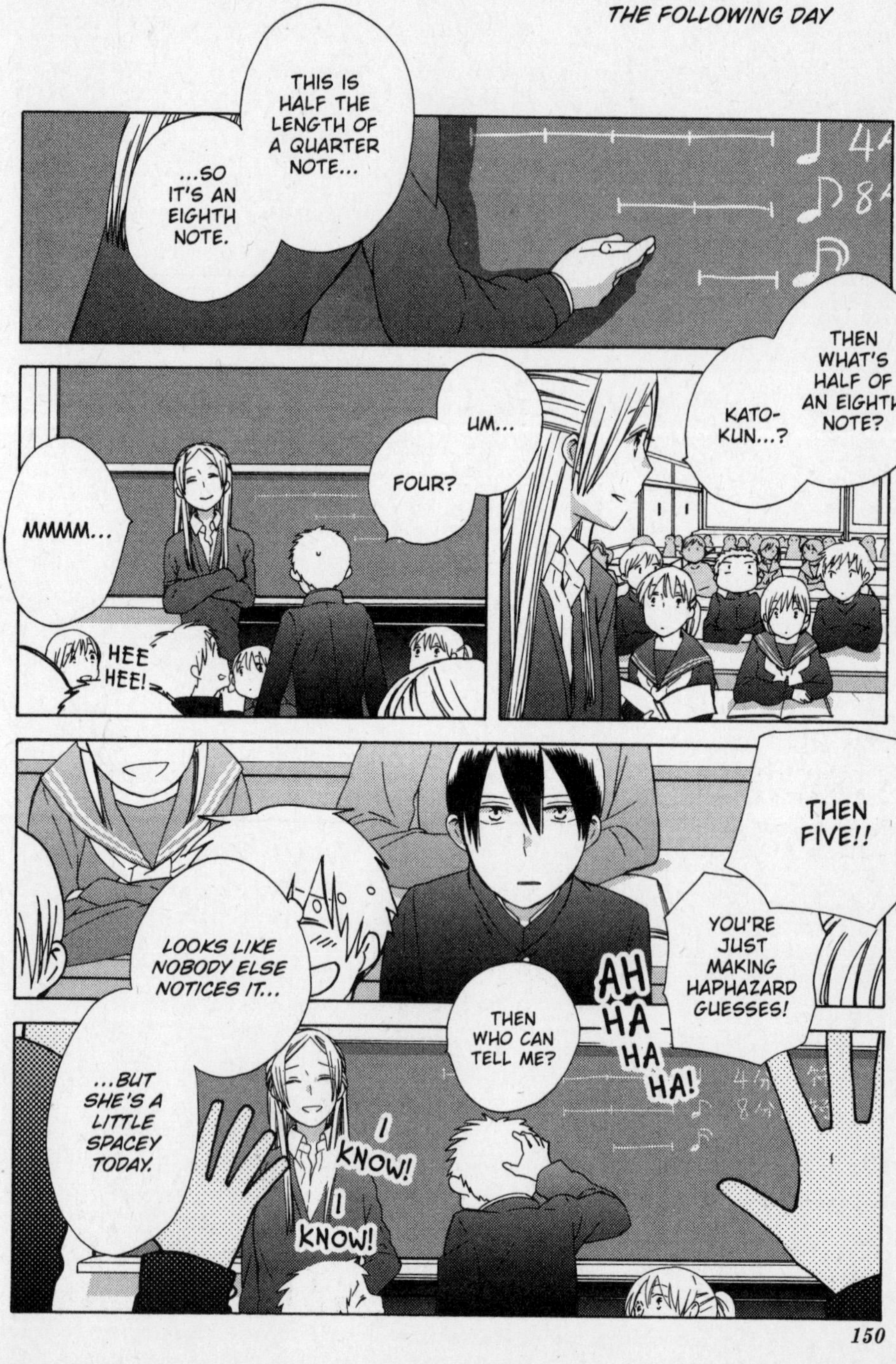
THE FOLLOWING DAY
THIS IS HALF THE LENGTH OF A QUARTER NOTE...
...SO IT'S AN EIGHTH NOTE.
THEN WHAT'S HALF OF AN EIGHTH NOTE?
KATO-KUN...?
UM...
FOUR?
MMMM...
HEE HEE!
THEN FIVE!!
YOU'RE JUST MAKING HAPHAZARD GUESSES!
AH HA HA HA!
LOOKS LIKE NOBODY ELSE NOTICES IT...
THEN WHO CAN TELL ME?
I KNOW!
I KNOW!
...BUT SHE'S A LITTLE SPACEY TODAY.

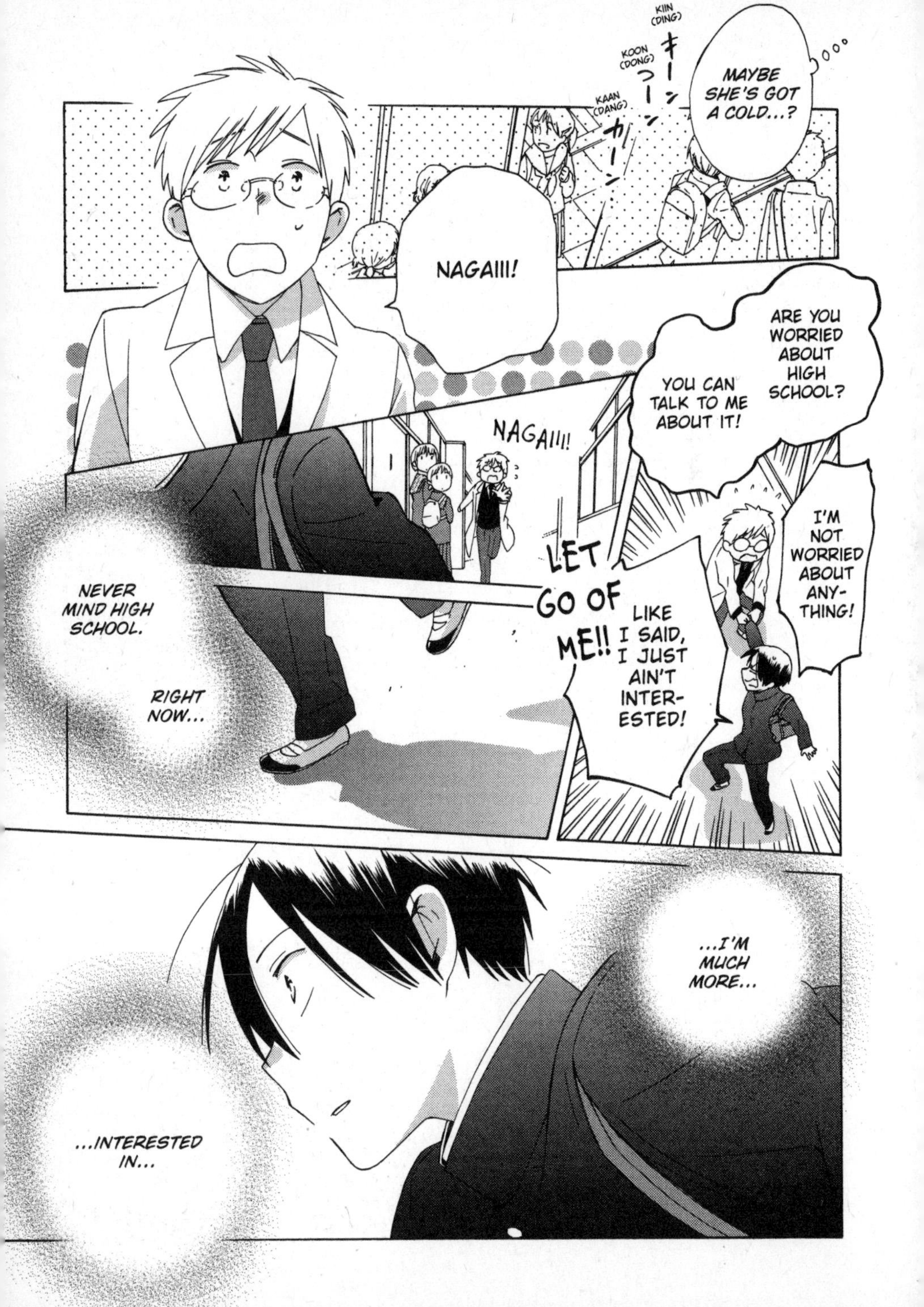
KIIN (DING)
KOON (DONG)
KAAN (DANG)
MAYBE SHE'S GOT A COLD...?
NAGAIII!
NAGAIII!!
ARE YOU WORRIED ABOUT HIGH SCHOOL?
YOU CAN TALK TO ME ABOUT IT!
I'M NOT WORRIED ABOUT ANYTHING!
LIKE I SAID, I JUST AIN'T INTERESTED!
LET GO OF ME!!
NEVER MIND HIGH SCHOOL.
RIGHT NOW...
...I'M MUCH MORE...
...INTERESTED IN...

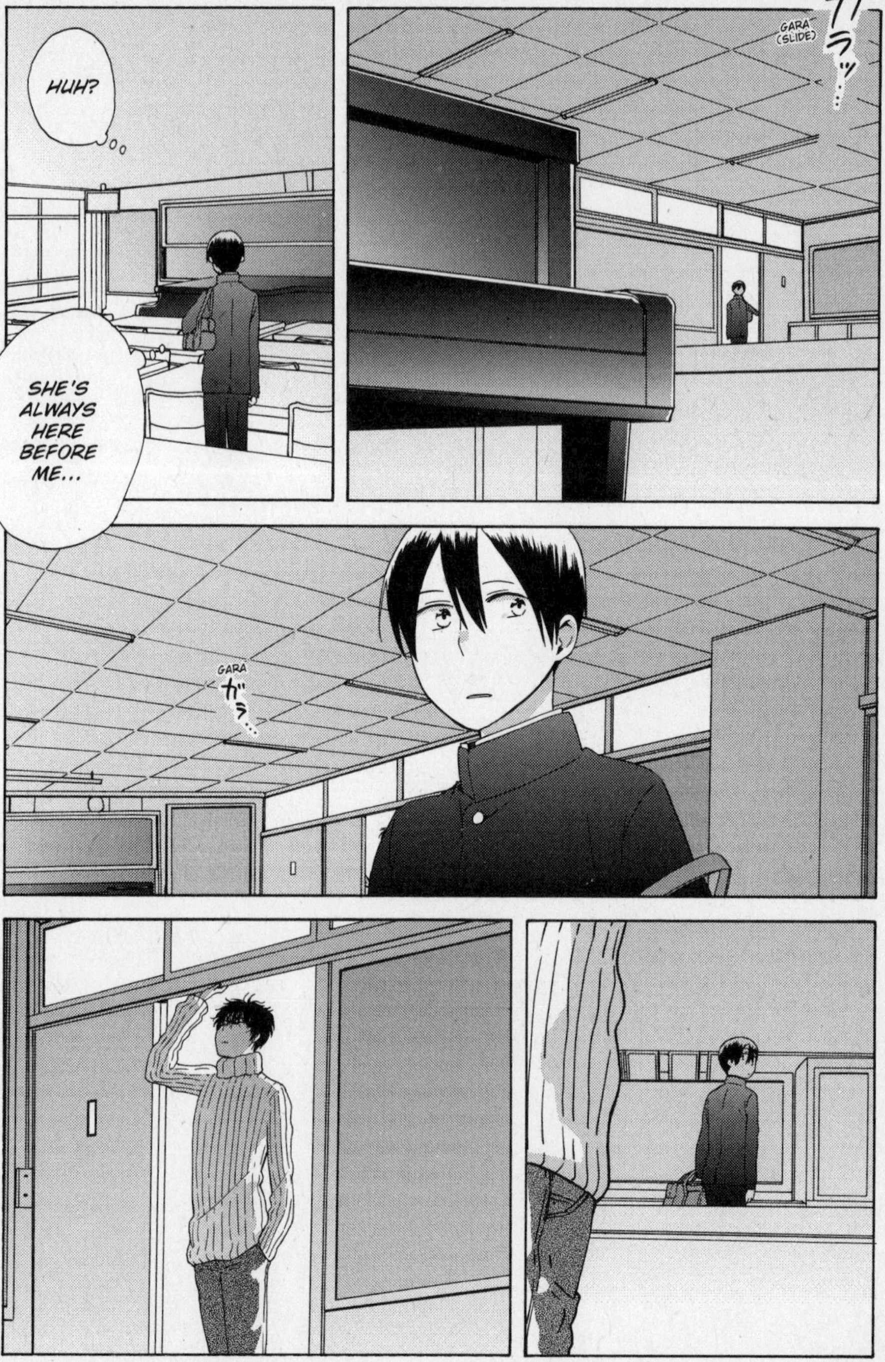
ガラッ…
GARA (SLIDE)
HUH?
SHE'S ALWAYS HERE BEFORE ME...
ガラ…
GARA

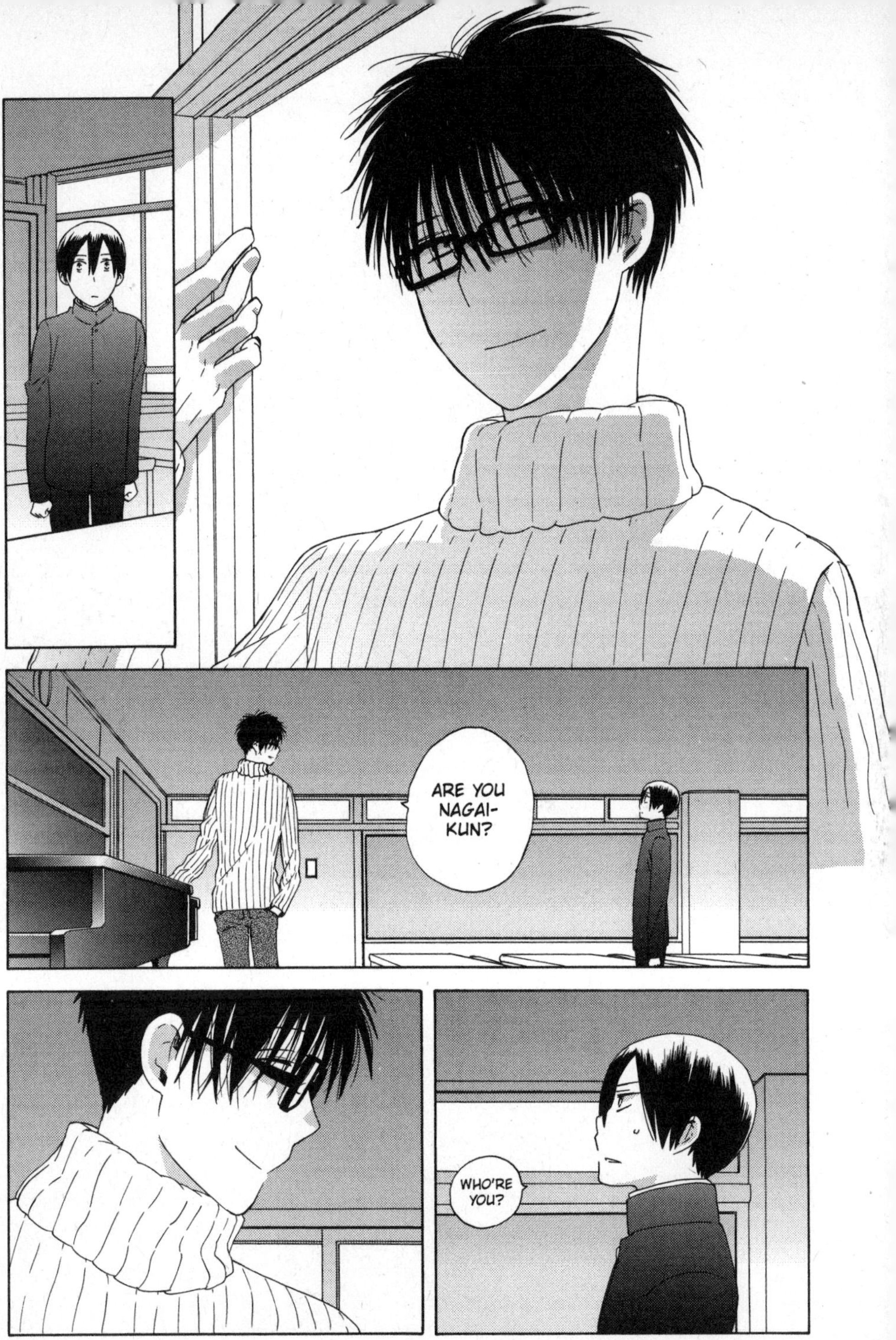
ARE YOU NAGAI-KUN?
WHO'RE YOU?

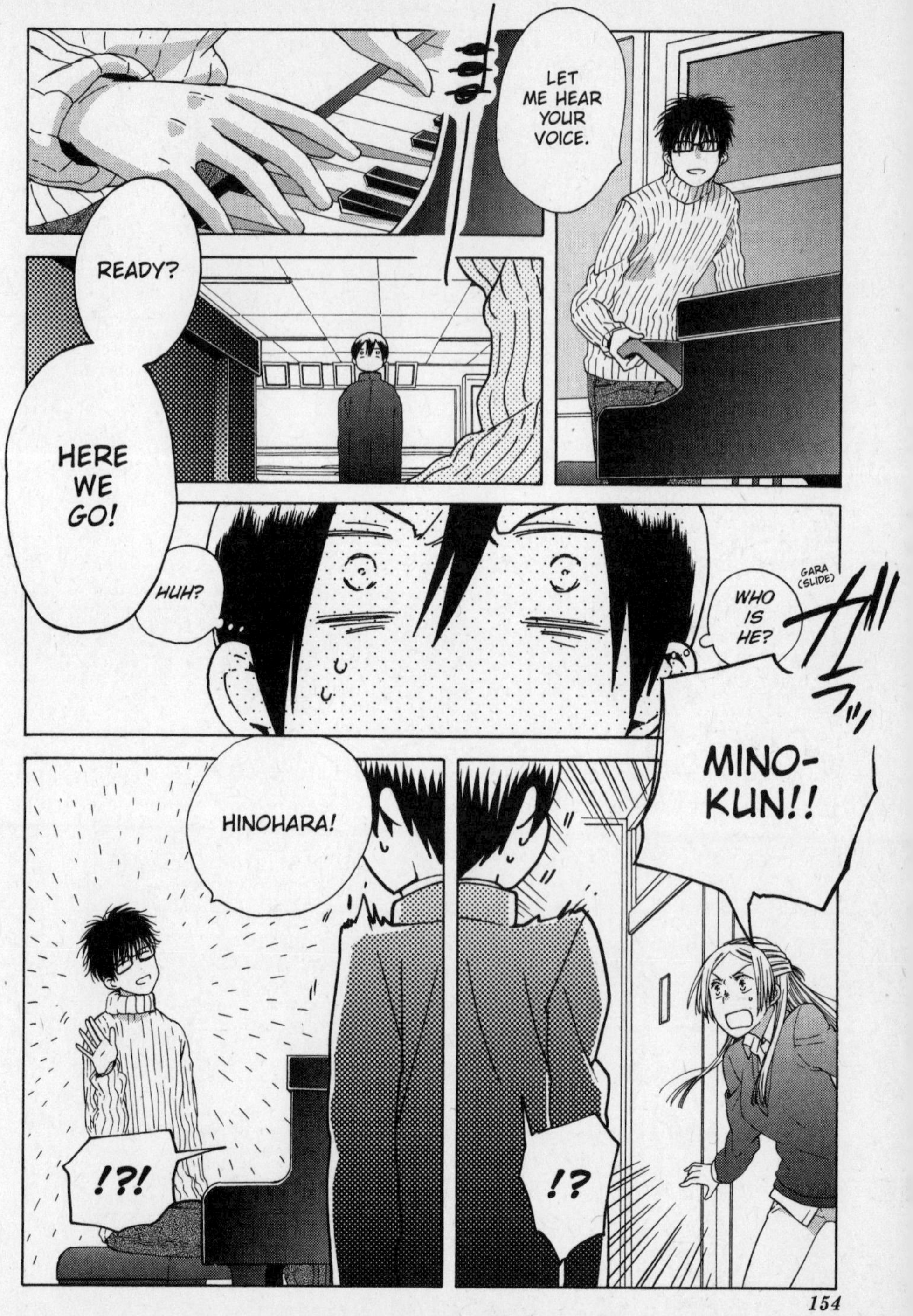

LET ME HEAR YOUR VOICE.
READY?
HERE WE GO!
GARA (SLIDE)
WHO IS HE?
HUH?
MINO-KUN!!
!?
HINOHARA!
!?!

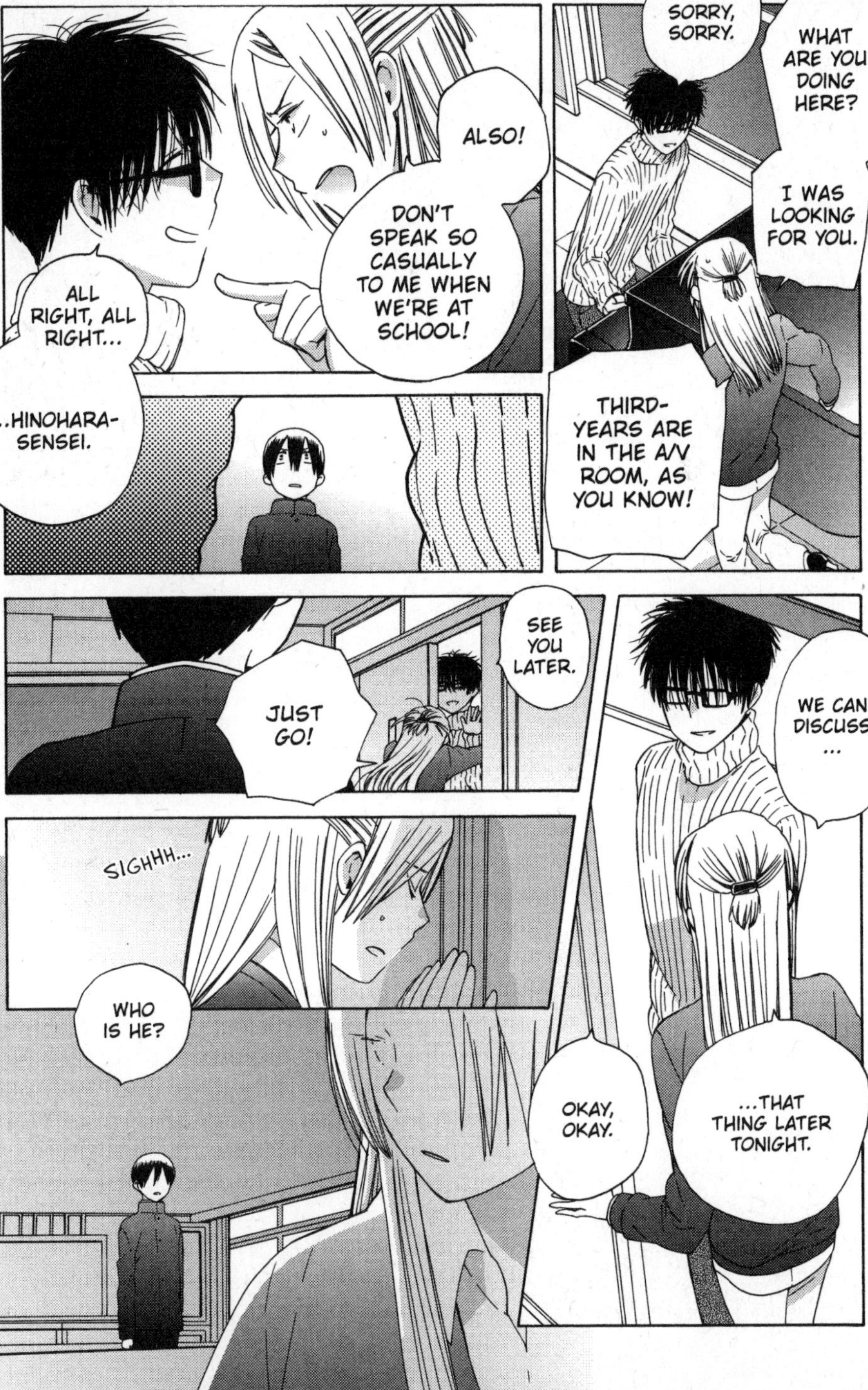
WHAT ARE YOU DOING HERE?
I WAS LOOKING FOR YOU.
THIRD-YEARS ARE IN THE A/V ROOM, AS YOU KNOW!
SORRY, SORRY.
ALSO!
DON'T SPEAK SO CASUALLY TO ME WHEN WE'RE AT SCHOOL!
ALL RIGHT, ALL RIGHT...
...HINOHARA-SENSEI.
WE CAN DISCUSS ...
...THAT THING LATER TONIGHT.
OKAY, OKAY.
SEE YOU LATER.
JUST GO!
SIGHHH...
WHO IS HE?

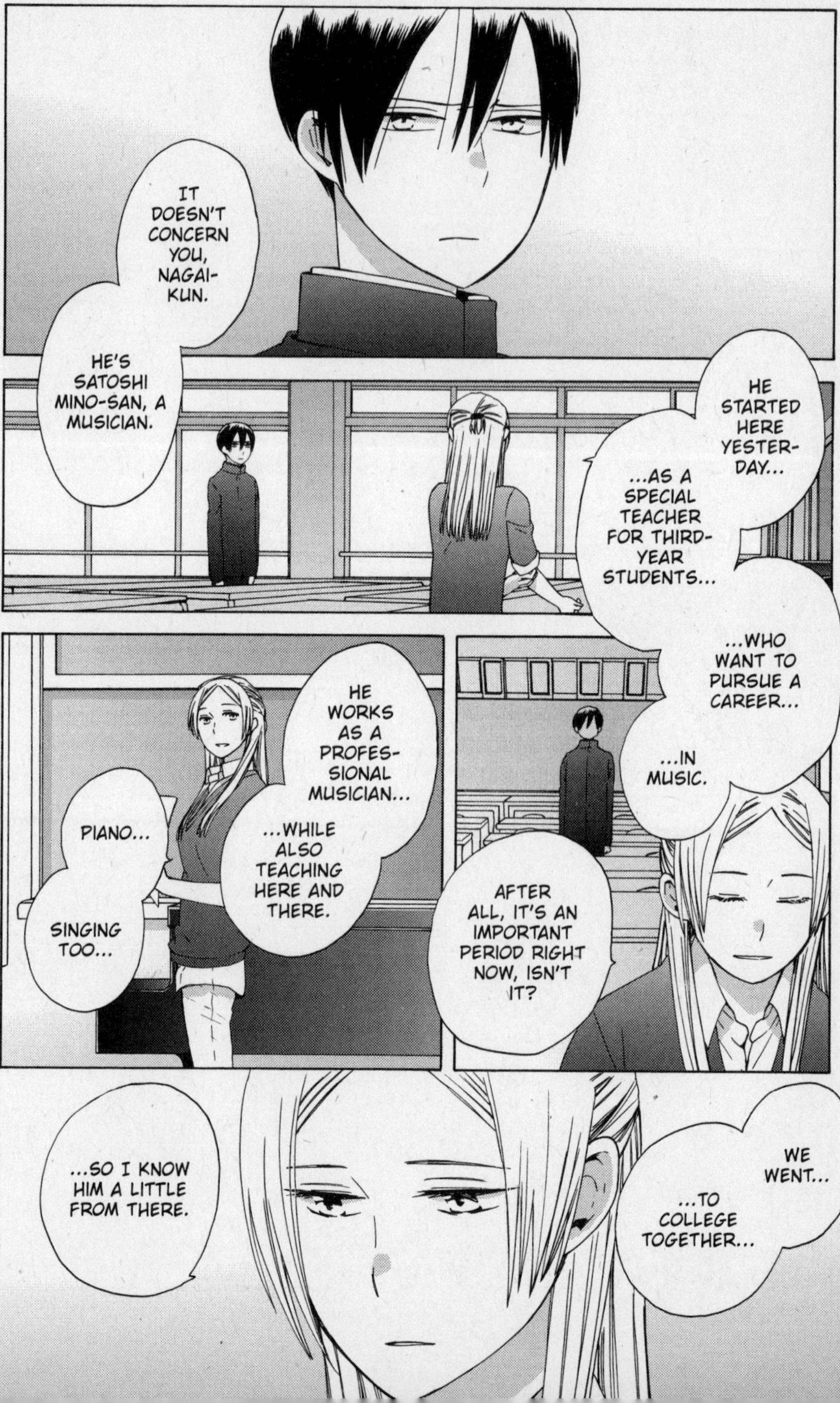
IT DOESN'T CONCERN YOU, NAGAI-KUN.
HE'S SATOSHI MINO-SAN, A MUSICIAN.
HE STARTED HERE YESTER-DAY...
...AS A SPECIAL TEACHER FOR THIRD-YEAR STUDENTS...
...WHO WANT TO PURSUE A CAREER...
...IN MUSIC.
AFTER ALL, IT'S AN IMPORTANT PERIOD RIGHT NOW, ISN'T IT?
HE WORKS AS A PROFES-SIONAL MUSICIAN...
...WHILE ALSO TEACHING HERE AND THERE.
PIANO...
SINGING TOO...
WE WENT...
...TO COLLEGE TOGETHER...
...SO I KNOW HIM A LITTLE FROM THERE.

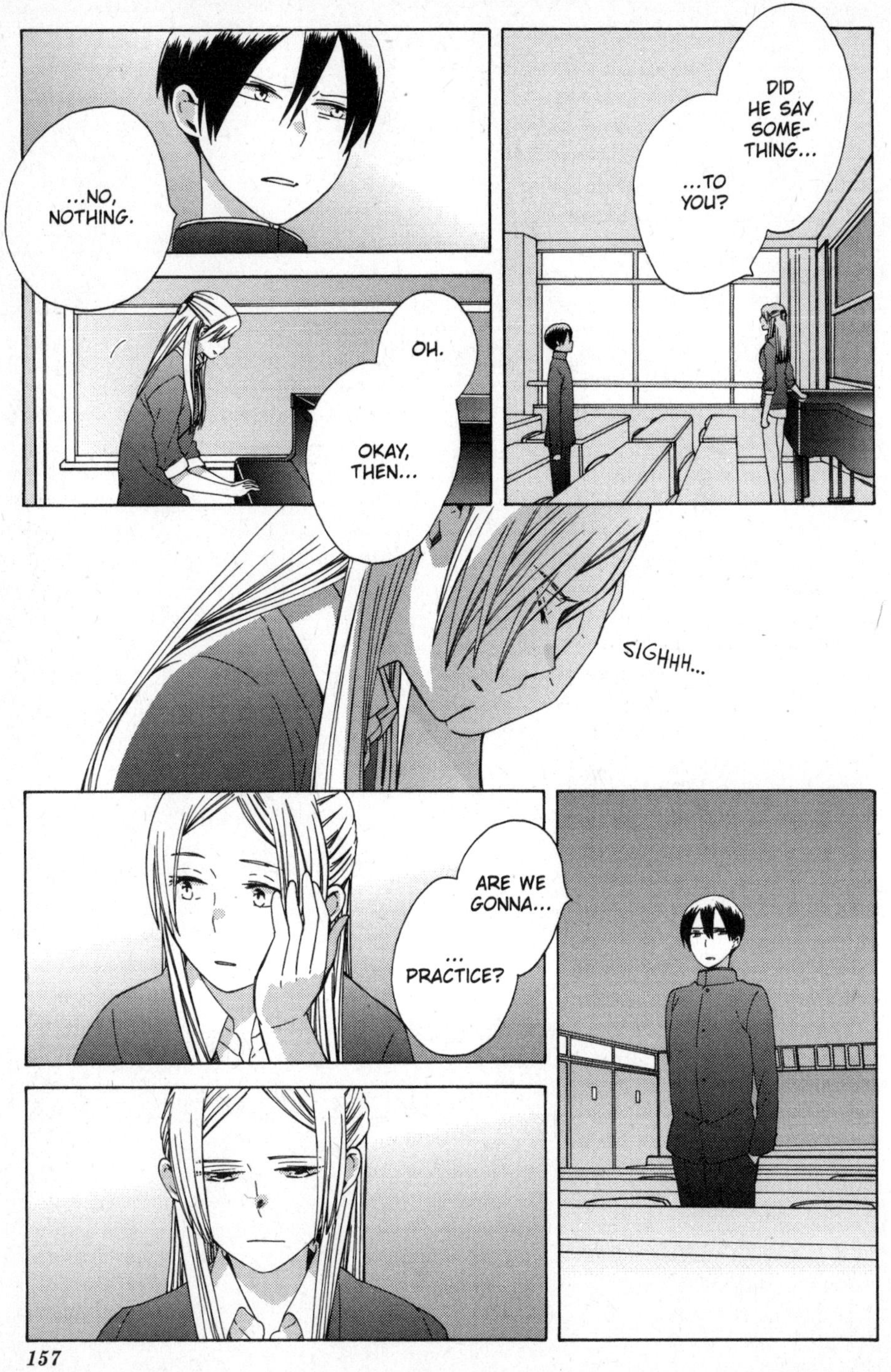
DID HE SAY SOME-THING...
...TO YOU?
...NO, NOTHING.
OH.
OKAY, THEN...
SIGHHH...
ARE WE GONNA...
... PRACTICE?

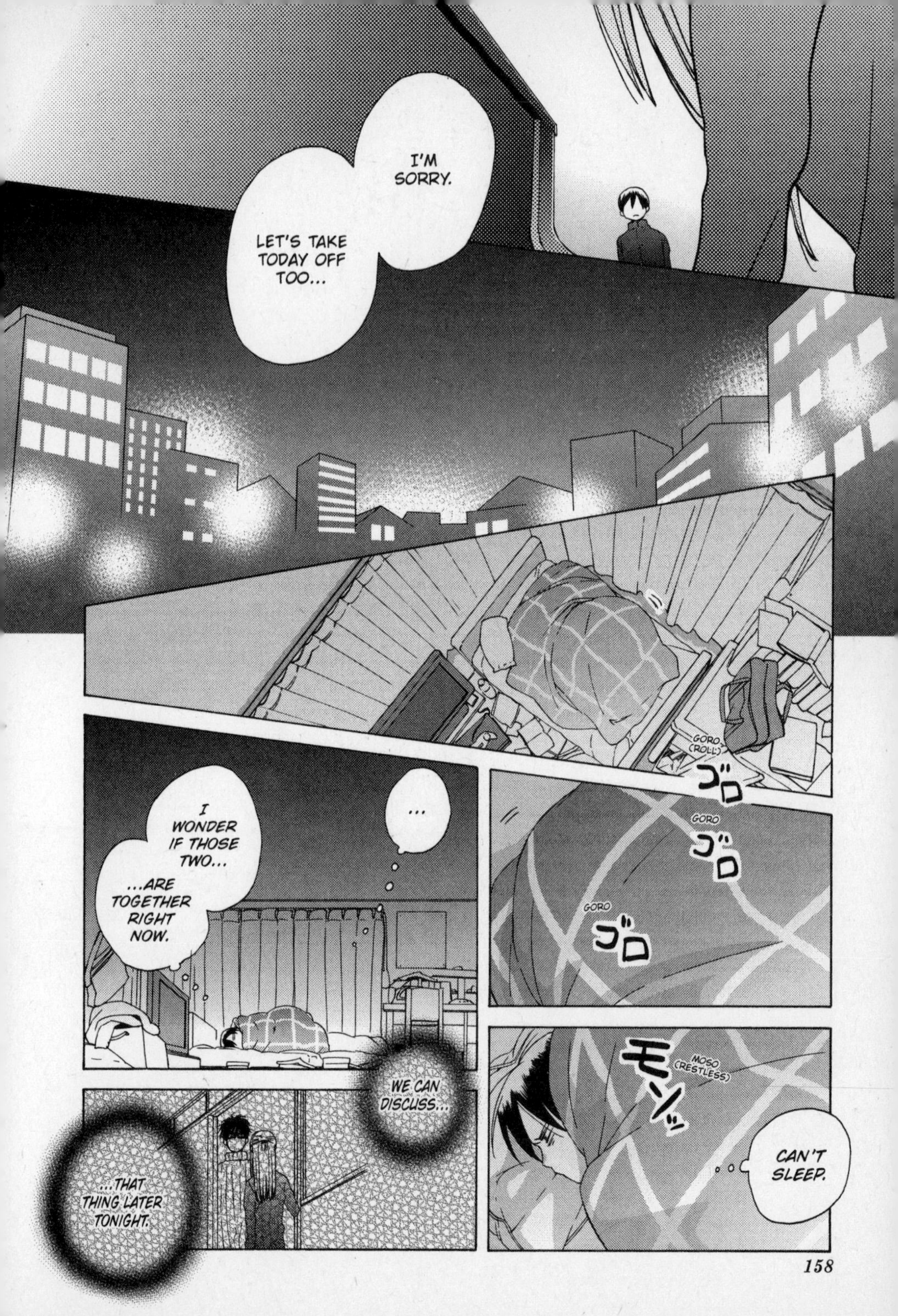

I'M SORRY.
LET'S TAKE TODAY OFF TOO...
GORO (ROLL:)
ゴロ
GORO
ゴロ
GORO
ゴロ
MOSO (RESTLESS)
モソッ
CAN'T SLEEP.
...
I WONDER IF THOSE TWO...
...ARE TOGETHER RIGHT NOW.
WE CAN DISCUSS...
...THAT THING LATER TONIGHT.

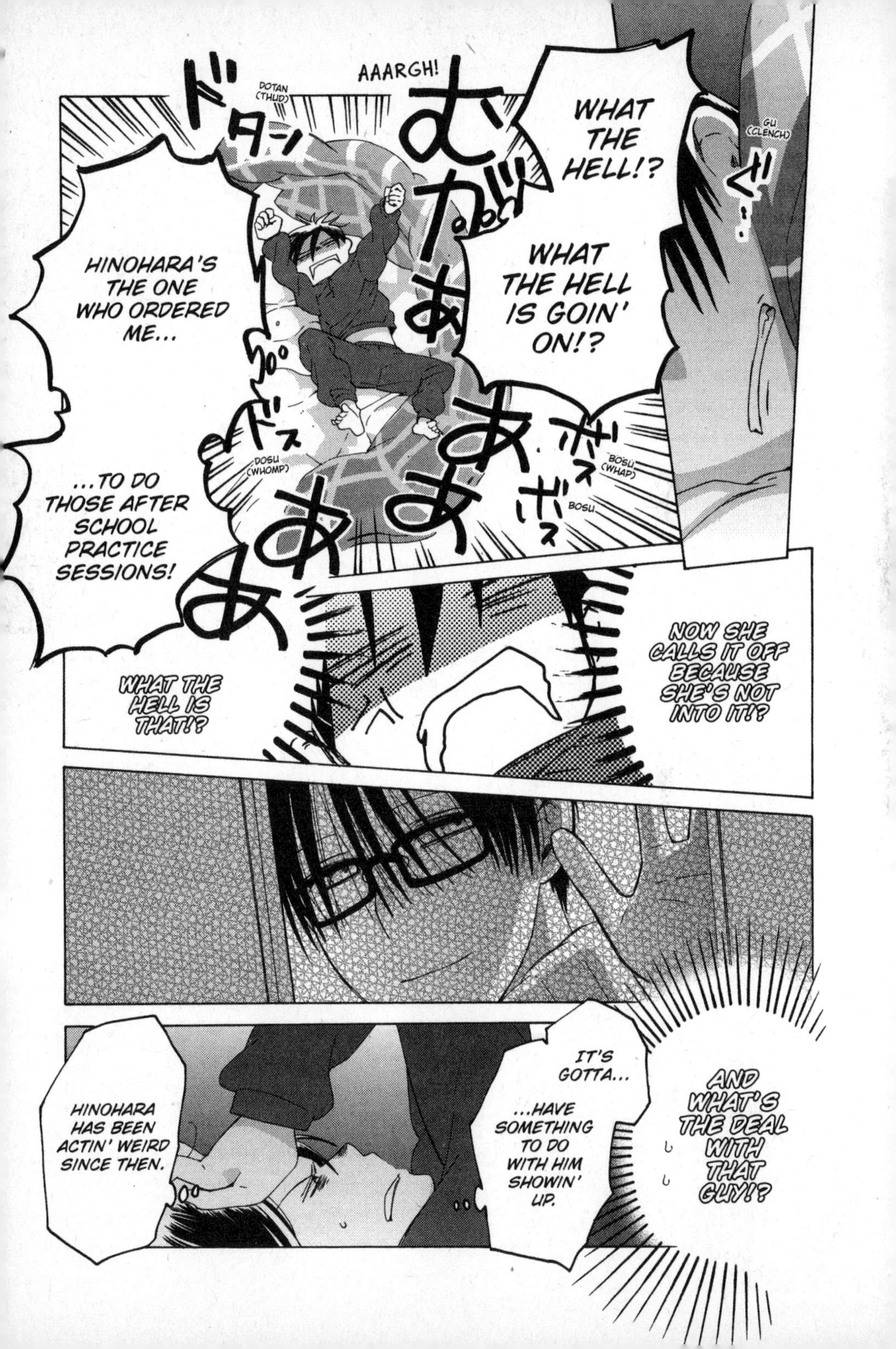
GU (CLENCH)
WHAT THE HELL!?
WHAT THE HELL IS GOIN' ON!?
AAARGH!
DOTAN (THUD)
BOSU (WHAP)
BOSU
DOSU (WHOMP)
HINOHARA'S THE ONE WHO ORDERED ME...
...TO DO THOSE AFTER SCHOOL PRACTICE SESSIONS!
NOW SHE CALLS IT OFF BECAUSE SHE'S NOT INTO IT!?
WHAT THE HELL IS THAT!?
AND WHAT'S THE DEAL WITH THAT GUY!?
IT'S GOTTA...
...HAVE SOMETHING TO DO WITH HIM SHOWIN' UP.
HINOHARA HAS BEEN ACTIN' WEIRD SINCE THEN.

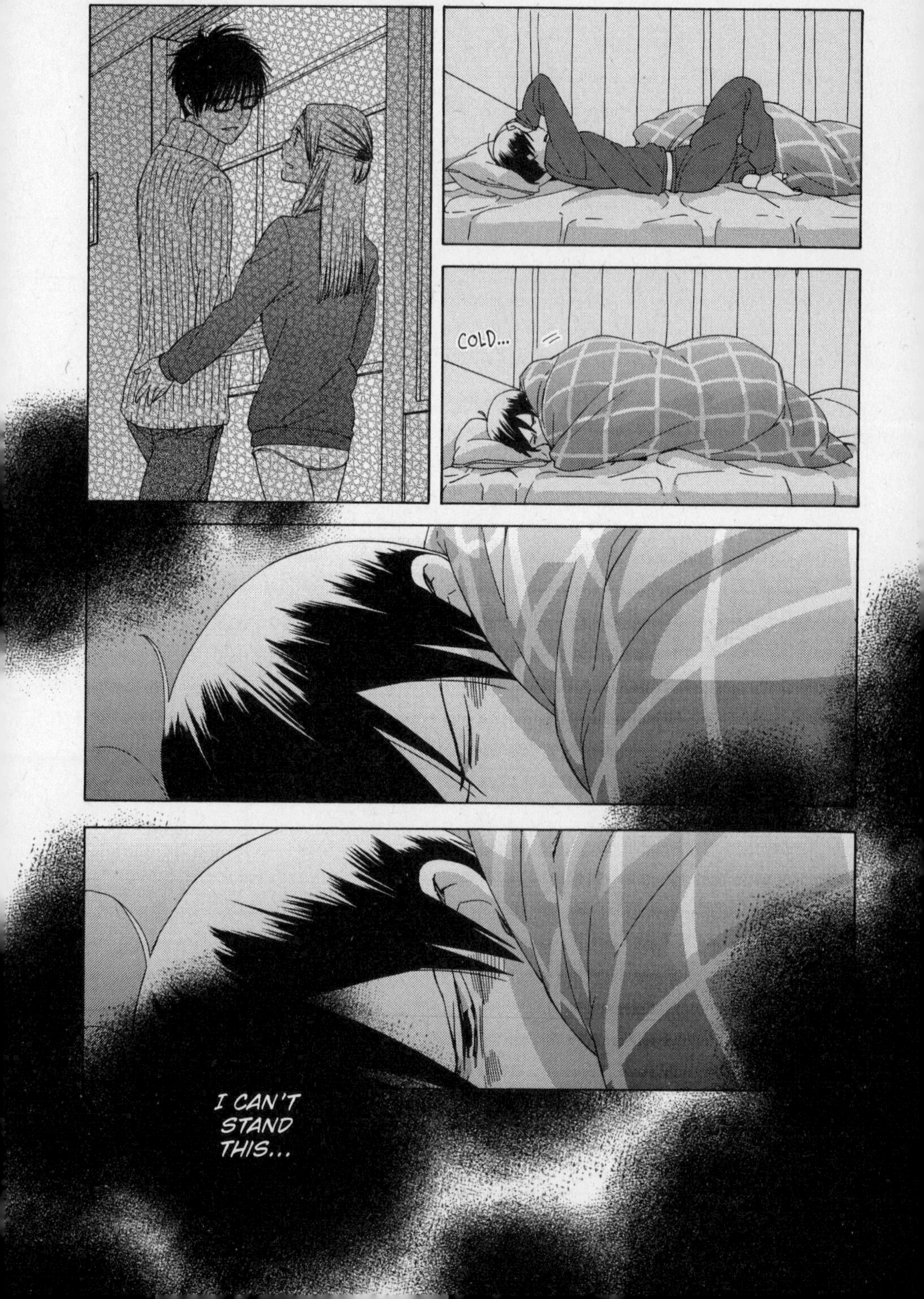
COLD...
I CAN'T STAND THIS...

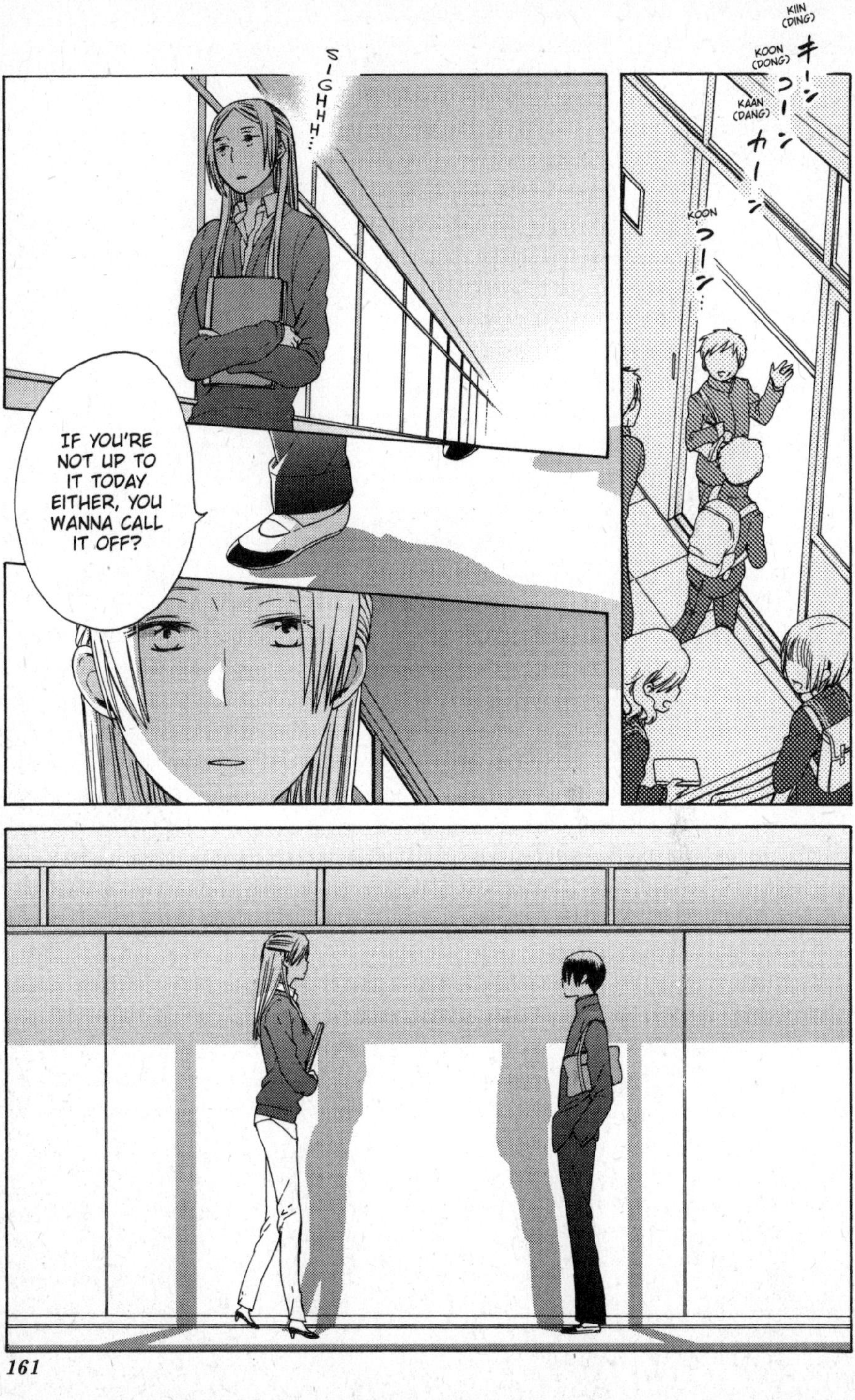
KIIN (DING)
キーン
KOON (DONG)
コーン
KAAN (DANG)
カーン
KOON
コーン…
SIGHHH…
IF YOU'RE NOT UP TO IT TODAY EITHER, YOU WANNA CALL IT OFF?

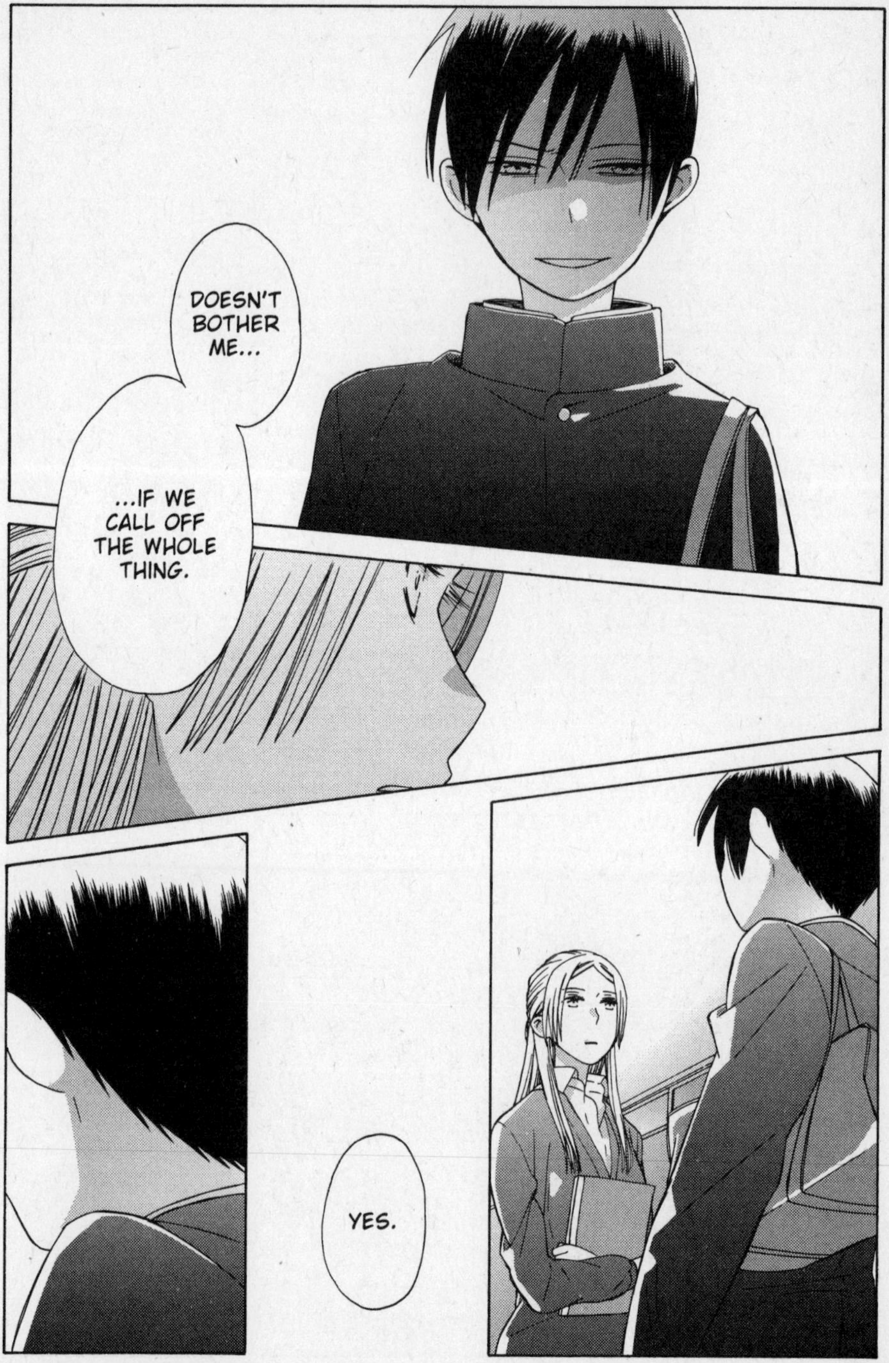
DOESN'T BOTHER ME...
...IF WE CALL OFF THE WHOLE THING.
YES.

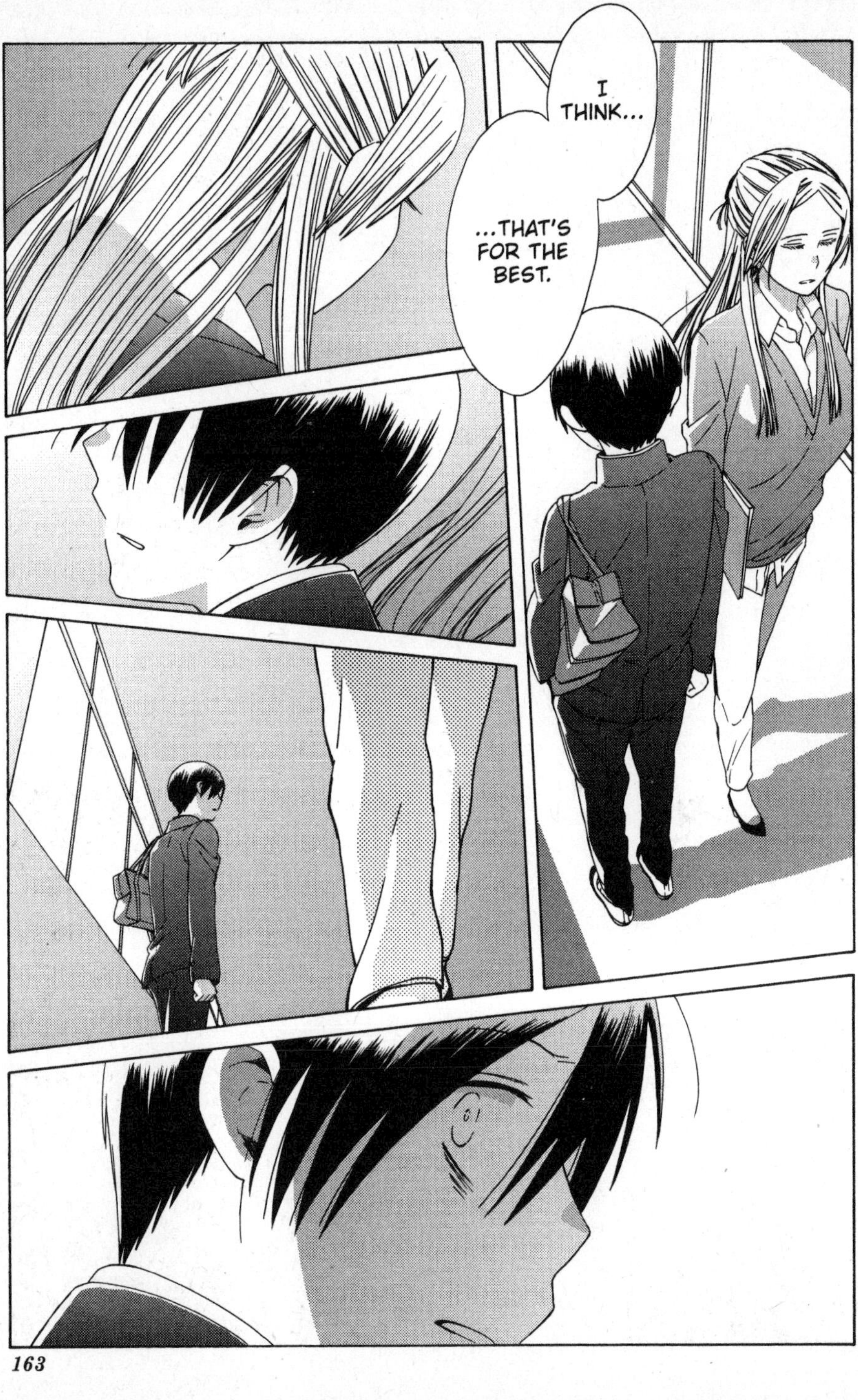
I THINK...
...THAT'S FOR THE BEST.

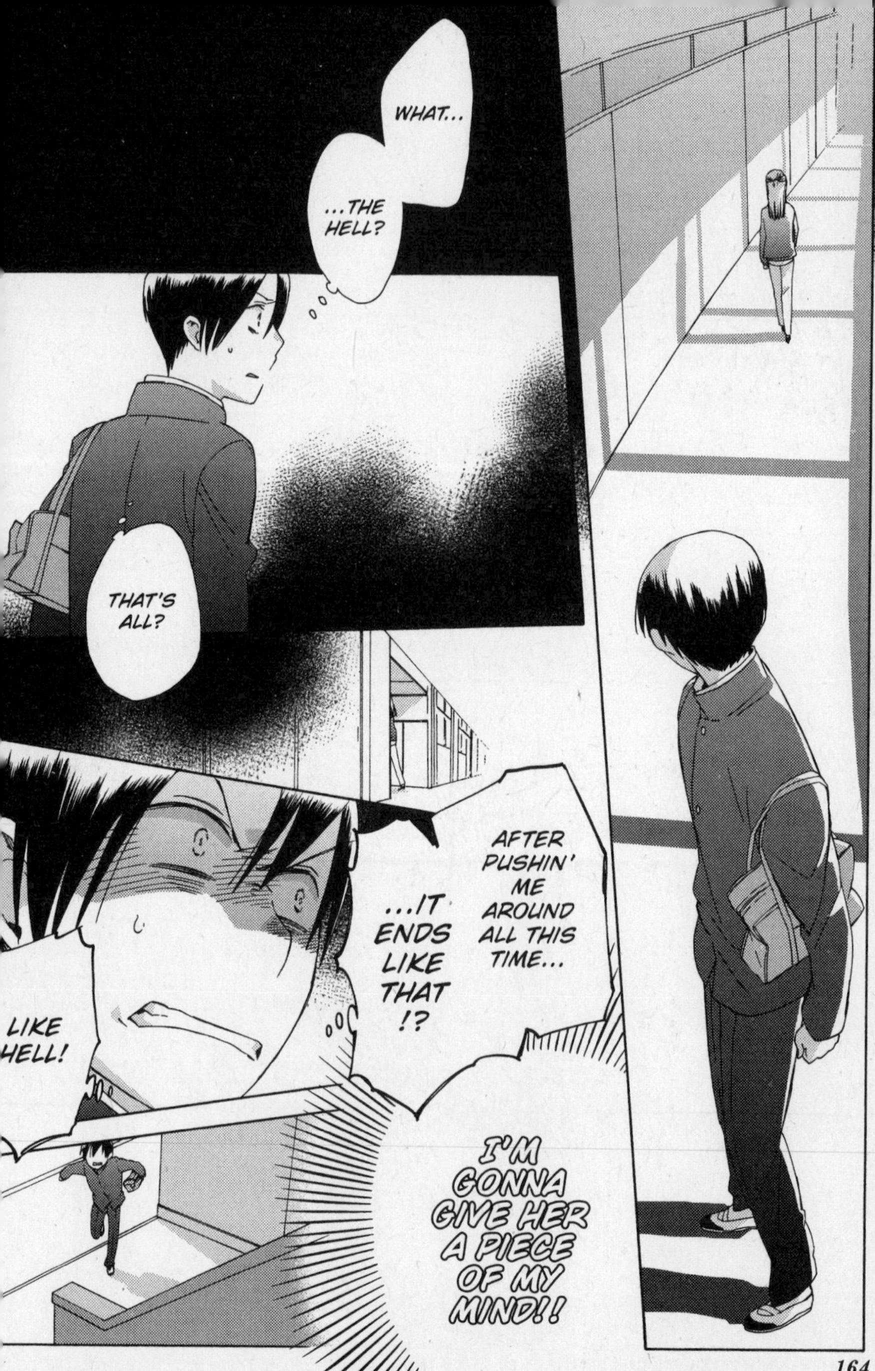
WHAT...
...THE HELL?
THAT'S ALL?
AFTER PUSHIN' ME AROUND ALL THIS TIME...
...IT ENDS LIKE THAT!?
LIKE HELL!
I'M GONNA GIVE HER A PIECE OF MY MIND!!

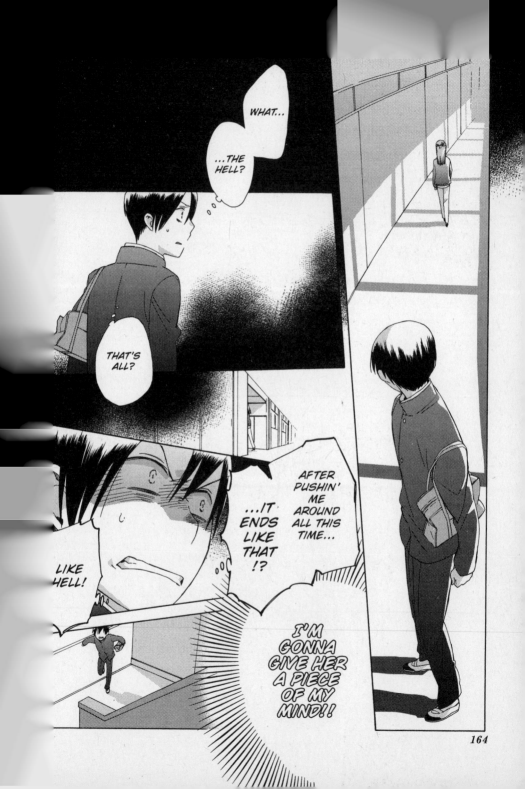

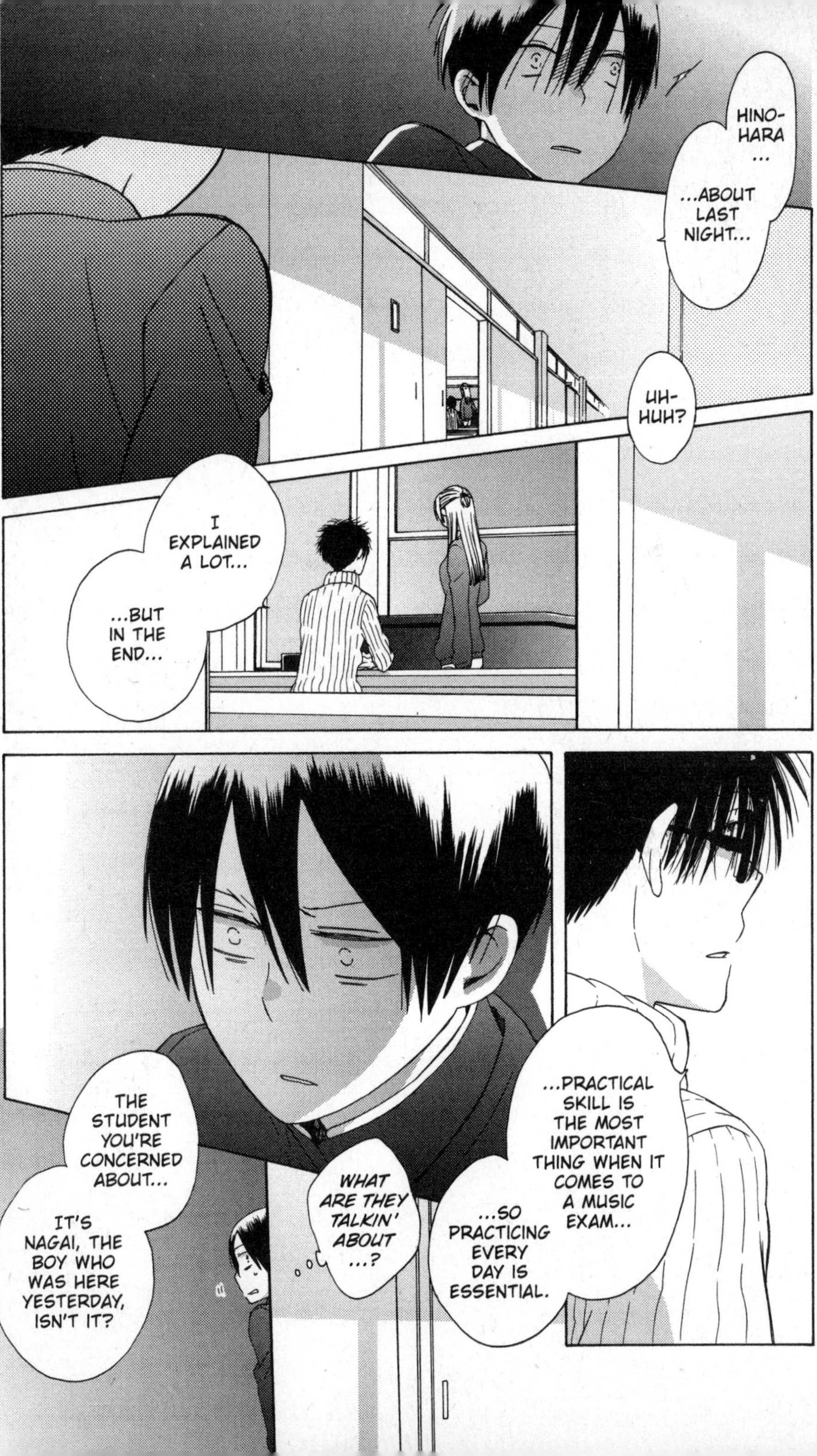
HINO-HARA...
...ABOUT LAST NIGHT...
UH-HUH?
I EXPLAINED A LOT...
...BUT IN THE END...
...PRACTICAL SKILL IS THE MOST IMPORTANT THING WHEN IT COMES TO A MUSIC EXAM...
...SO PRACTICING EVERY DAY IS ESSENTIAL.
THE STUDENT YOU'RE CONCERNED ABOUT...
IT'S NAGAI, THE BOY WHO WAS HERE YESTERDAY, ISN'T IT?
WHAT ARE THEY TALKIN' ABOUT ...?

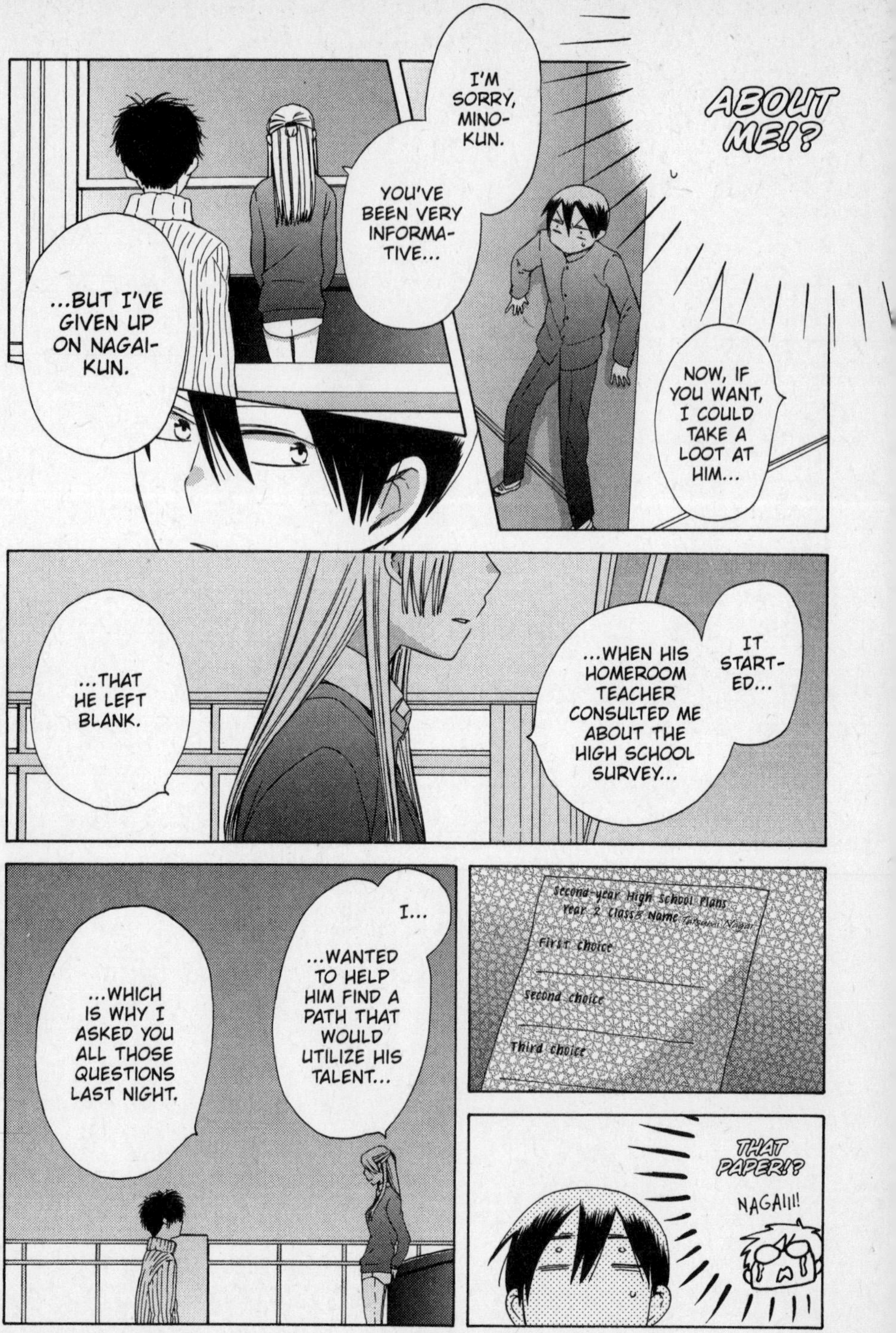
I'M SORRY, MINO-KUN.
YOU'VE BEEN VERY INFORMATIVE...
...BUT I'VE GIVEN UP ON NAGAI-KUN.
ABOUT ME!?
NOW, IF YOU WANT, I COULD TAKE A LOOT AT HIM...
IT STARTED...
...WHEN HIS HOMEROOM TEACHER CONSULTED ME ABOUT THE HIGH SCHOOL SURVEY...
...THAT HE LEFT BLANK.
Second-year High School Plans
Year 2 Class B Name
First choice
Second choice
Third choice
THAT PAPER!?
NAGAI!!
I...
...WANTED TO HELP HIM FIND A PATH THAT WOULD UTILIZE HIS TALENT...
...WHICH IS WHY I ASKED YOU ALL THOSE QUESTIONS LAST NIGHT.

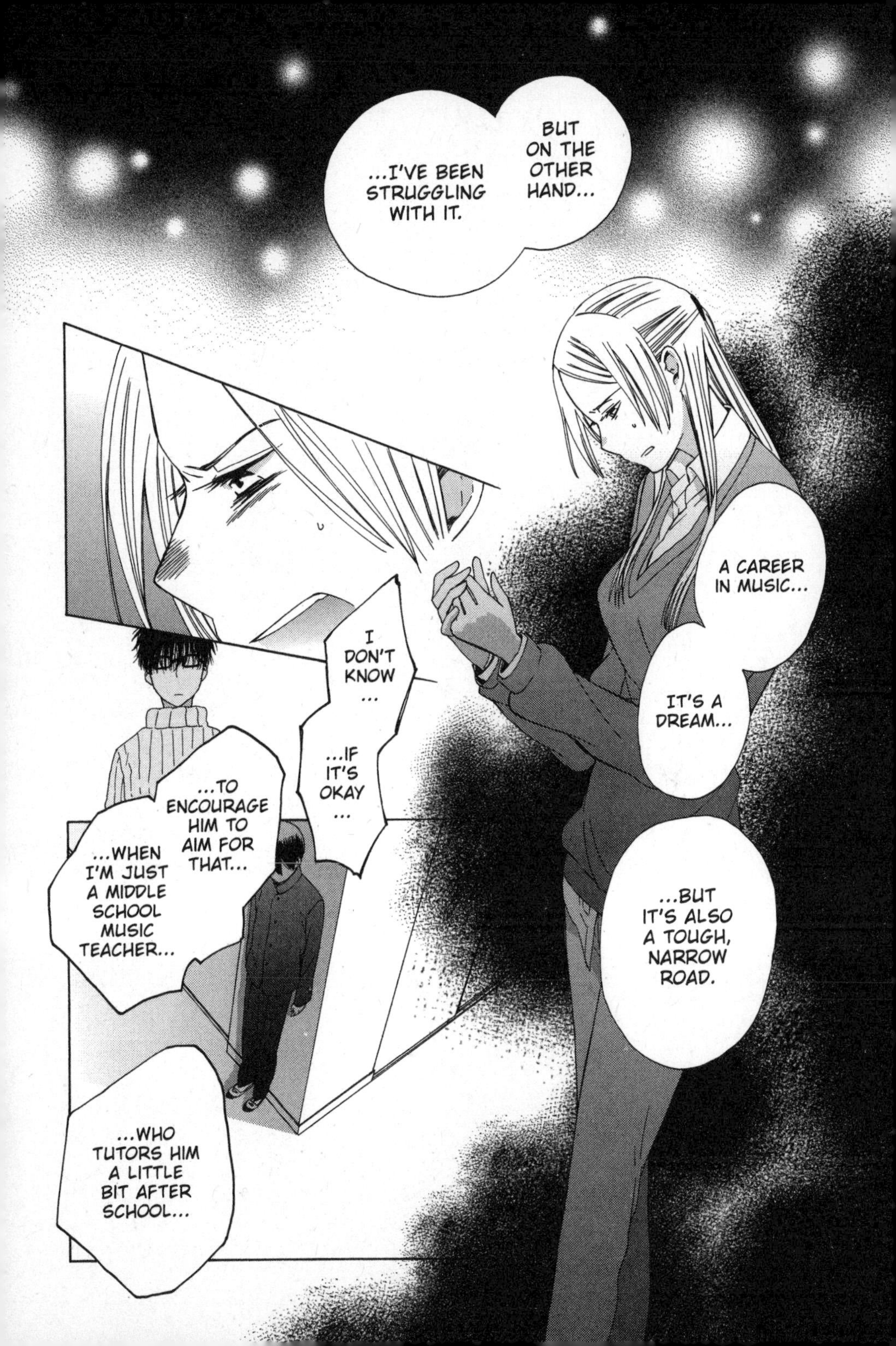

BUT ON THE OTHER HAND...
...I'VE BEEN STRUGGLING WITH IT.
A CAREER IN MUSIC...
IT'S A DREAM...
...BUT IT'S ALSO A TOUGH, NARROW ROAD.
I DON'T KNOW...
...IF IT'S OKAY...
...TO ENCOURAGE HIM TO AIM FOR THAT...
...WHEN I'M JUST A MIDDLE SCHOOL MUSIC TEACHER...
...WHO TUTORS HIM A LITTLE BIT AFTER SCHOOL...

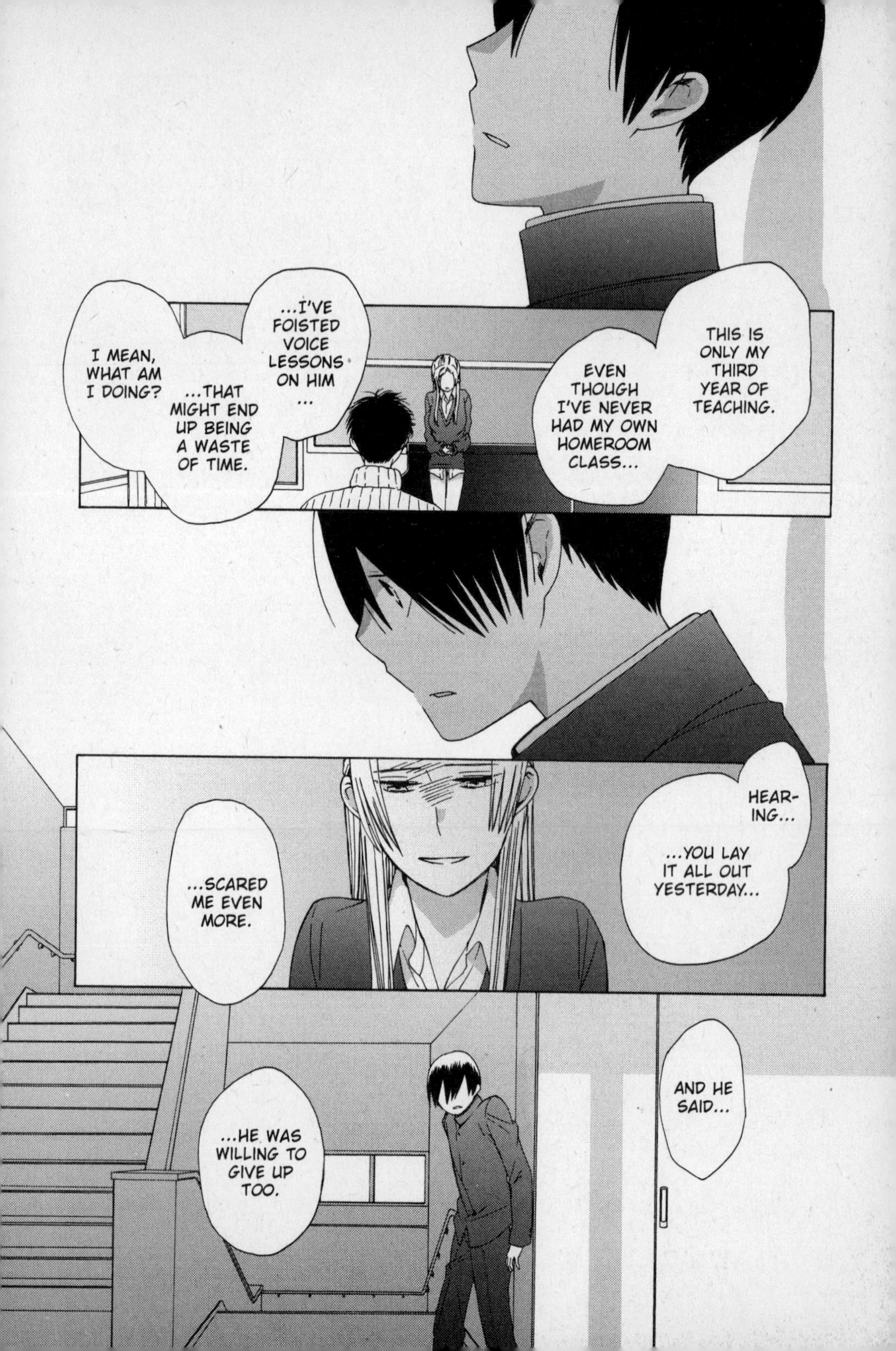
THIS IS ONLY MY THIRD YEAR OF TEACHING.
EVEN THOUGH I'VE NEVER HAD MY OWN HOMEROOM CLASS...
...I'VE FOISTED VOICE LESSONS ON HIM ...
...THAT MIGHT END UP BEING A WASTE OF TIME.
I MEAN, WHAT AM I DOING?
HEARING...
...YOU LAY IT ALL OUT YESTERDAY...
...SCARED ME EVEN MORE.
AND HE SAID...
...HE WAS WILLING TO GIVE UP TOO.

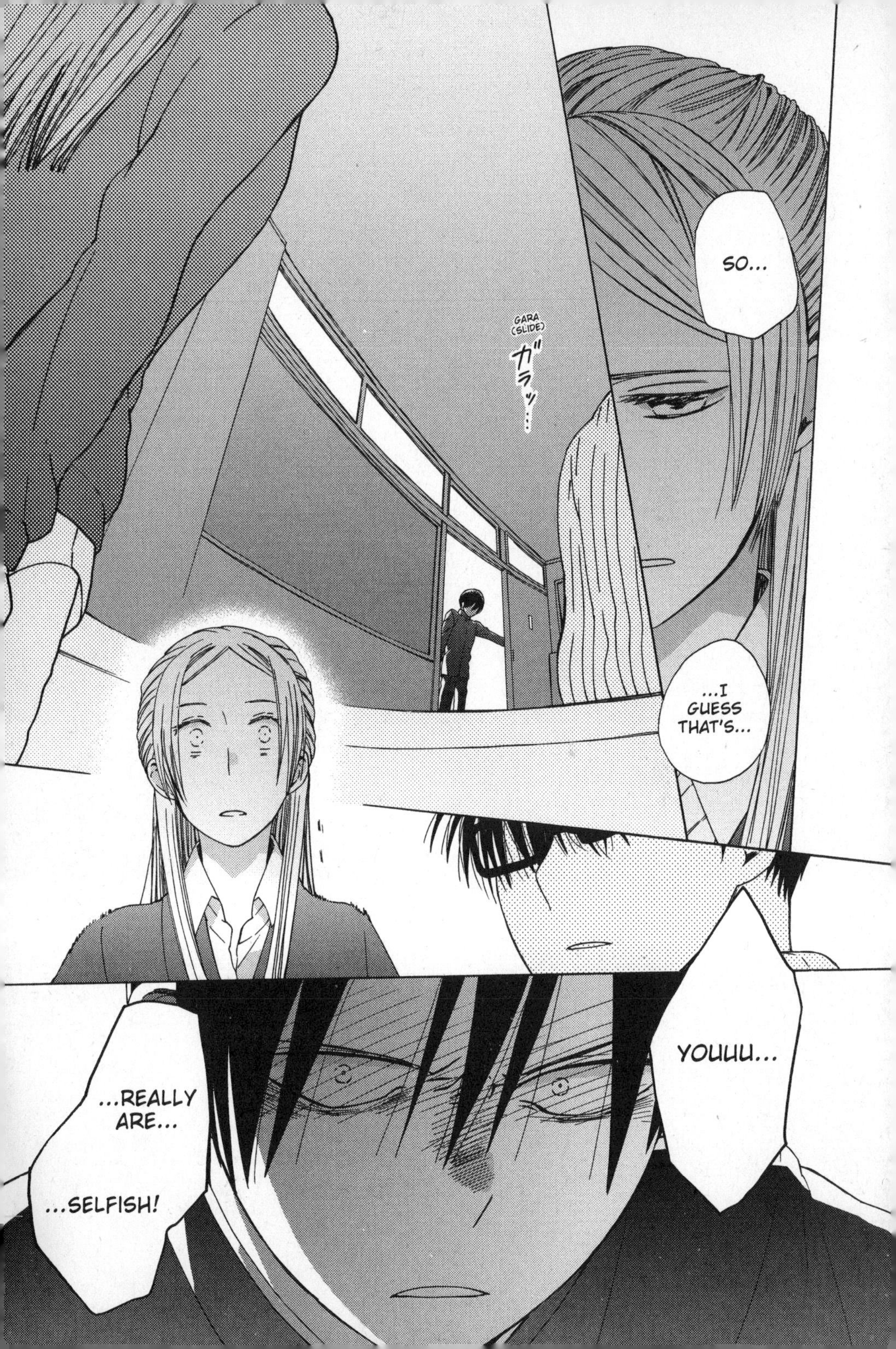
SO...
...I GUESS THAT'S...
GARA (SLIDE)
ガラッ...
YOUUU...
...REALLY ARE...
...SELFISH!

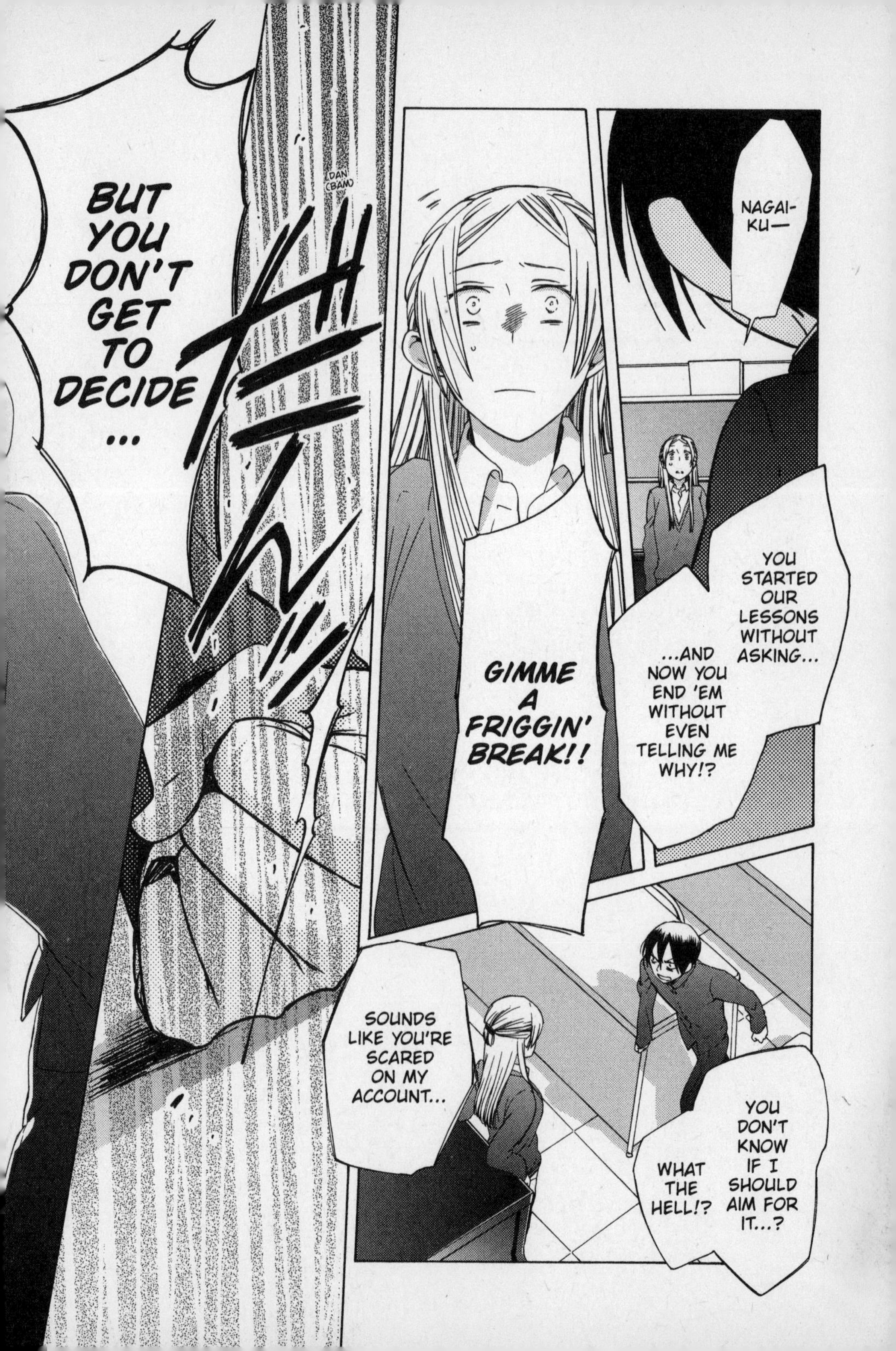
NAGAI-KU—
YOU STARTED OUR LESSONS WITHOUT ASKING...
...AND NOW YOU END 'EM WITHOUT EVEN TELLING ME WHY!?
GIMME A FRIGGIN' BREAK!!
YOU DON'T KNOW IF I SHOULD AIM FOR IT...?
WHAT THE HELL!?
SOUNDS LIKE YOU'RE SCARED ON MY ACCOUNT...
DAN (BAM)
BUT YOU DON'T GET TO DECIDE...

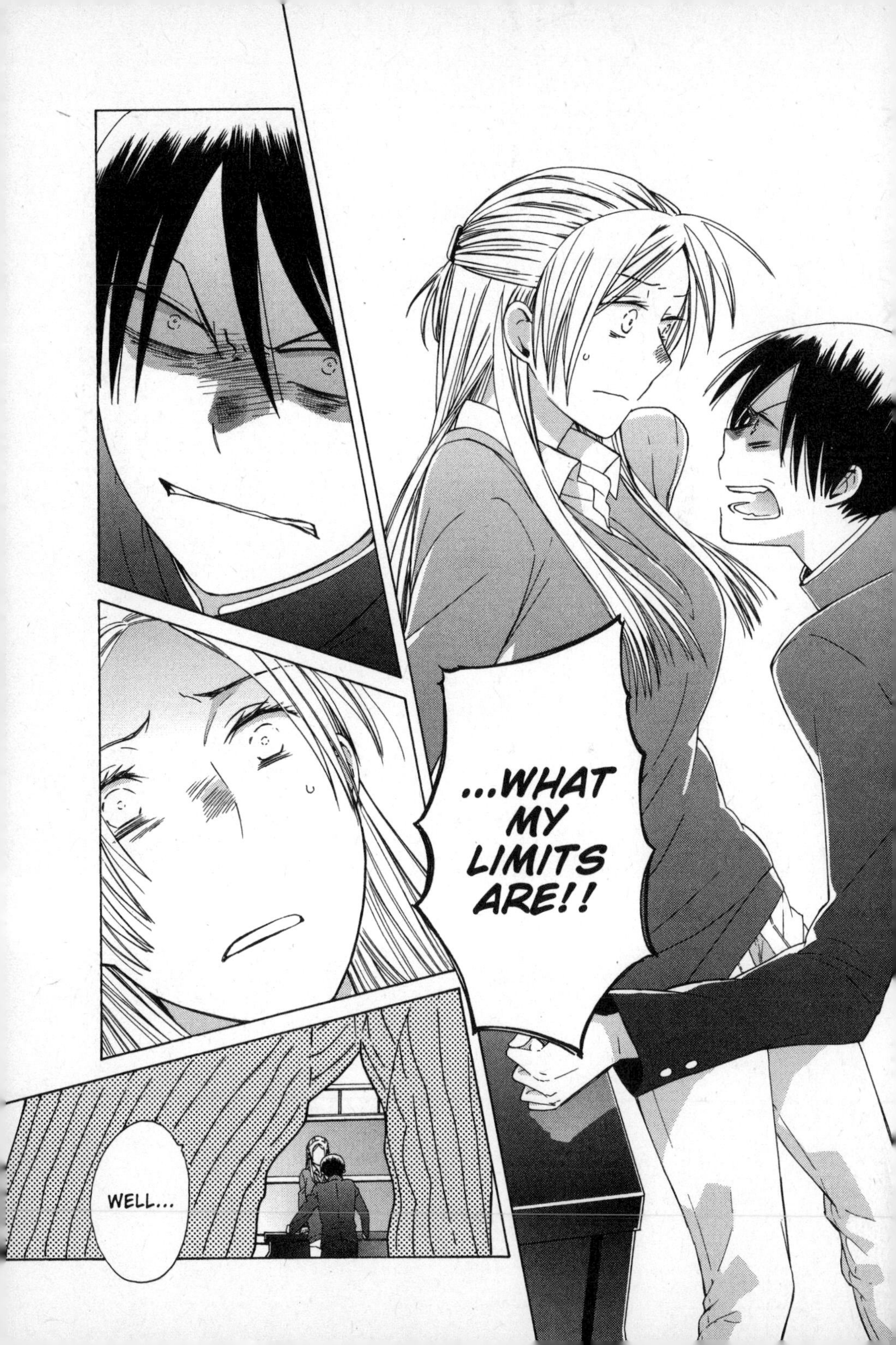
...WHAT MY LIMITS ARE!!
WELL...

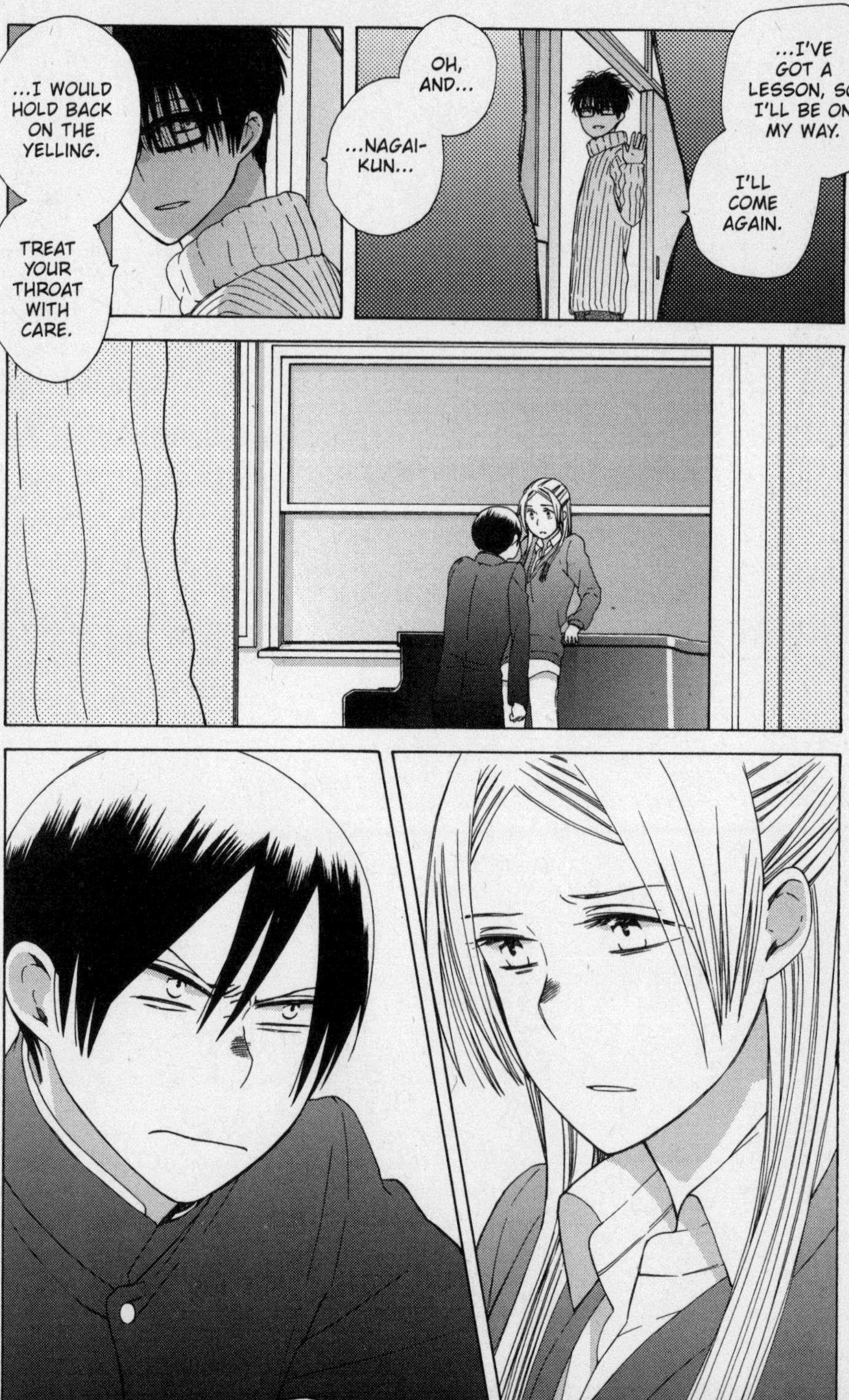
...I'VE GOT A LESSON, SO I'LL BE ON MY WAY.
I'LL COME AGAIN.
OH, AND...
...NAGAI-KUN...
...I WOULD HOLD BACK ON THE YELLING.
TREAT YOUR THROAT WITH CARE.

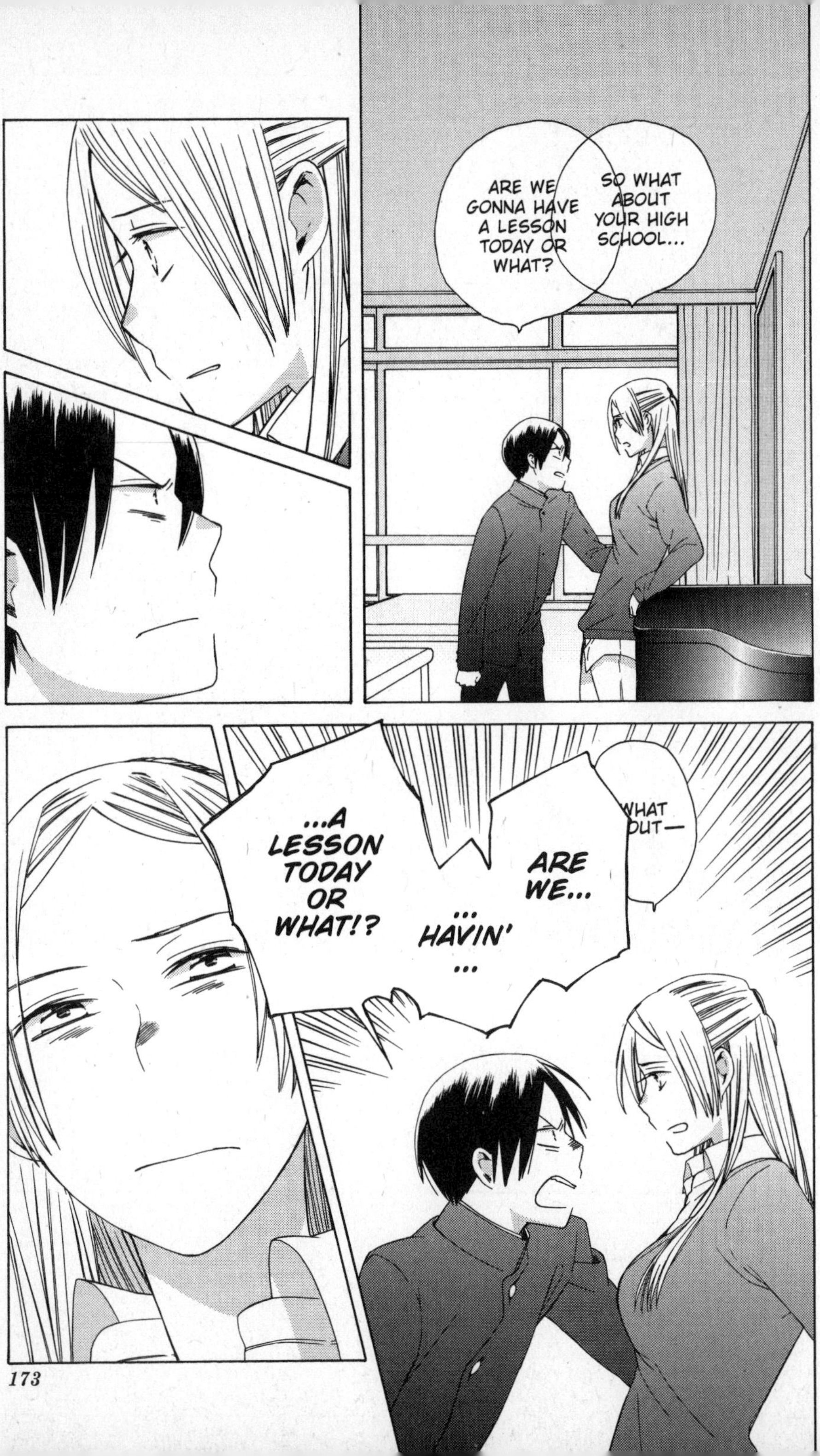
SO WHAT ABOUT YOUR HIGH SCHOOL...
ARE WE GONNA HAVE A LESSON TODAY OR WHAT?
WHAT
OUT—
ARE WE...
...HAVIN'...
...A LESSON TODAY OR WHAT!?

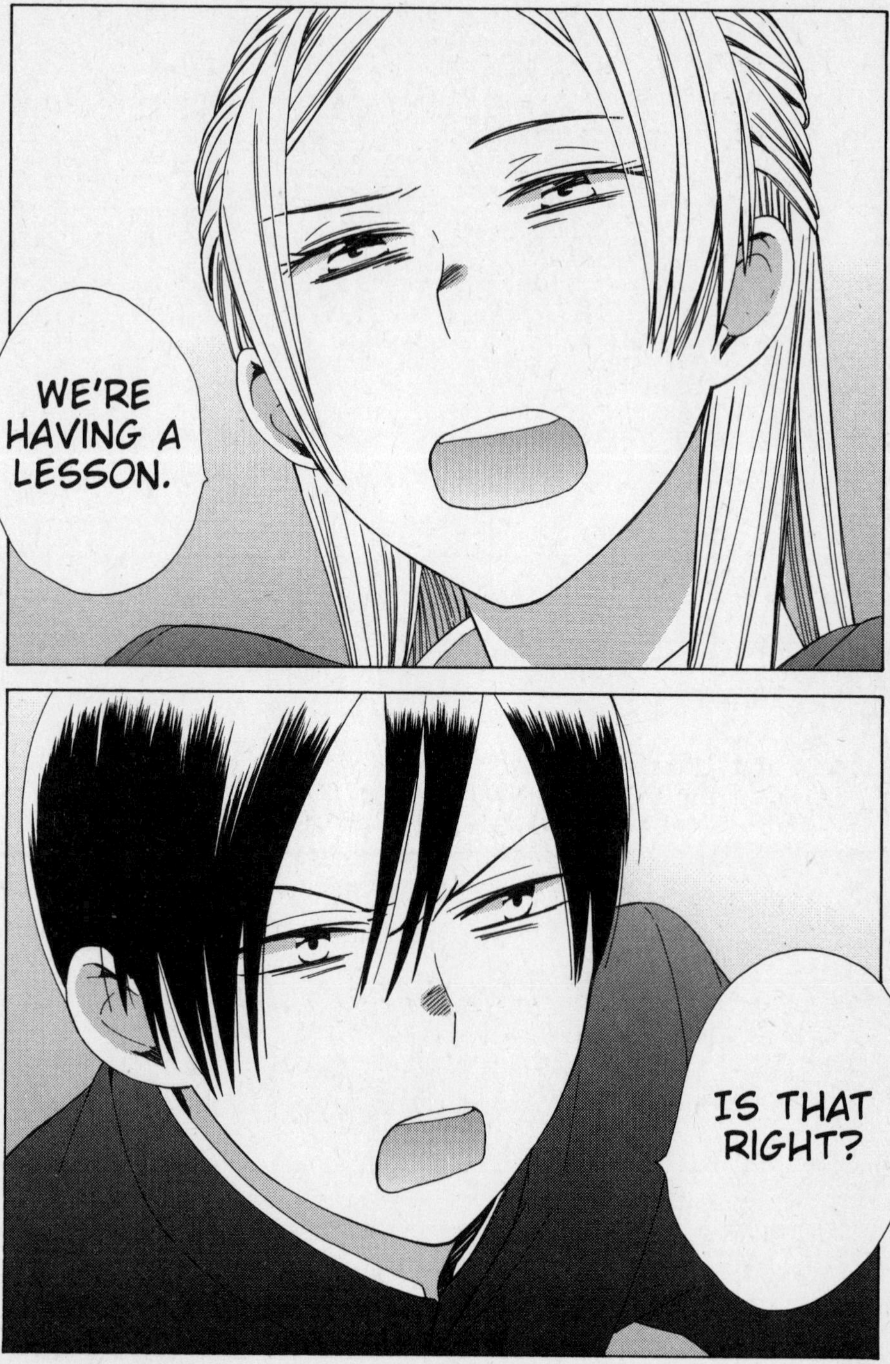
WE'RE HAVING A LESSON.
IS THAT RIGHT?

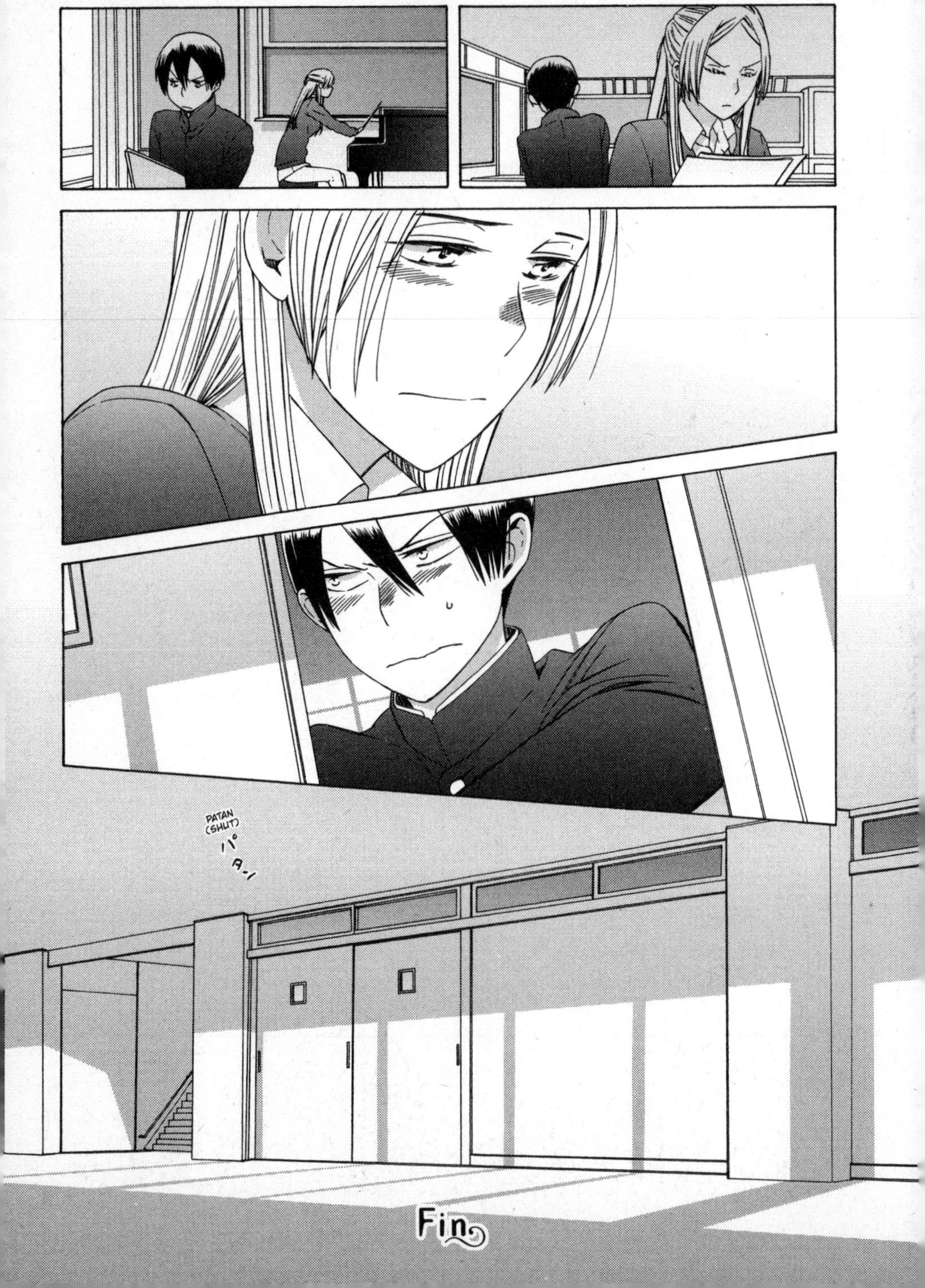
PATAN (SHUT)
パタ…ン
Fin

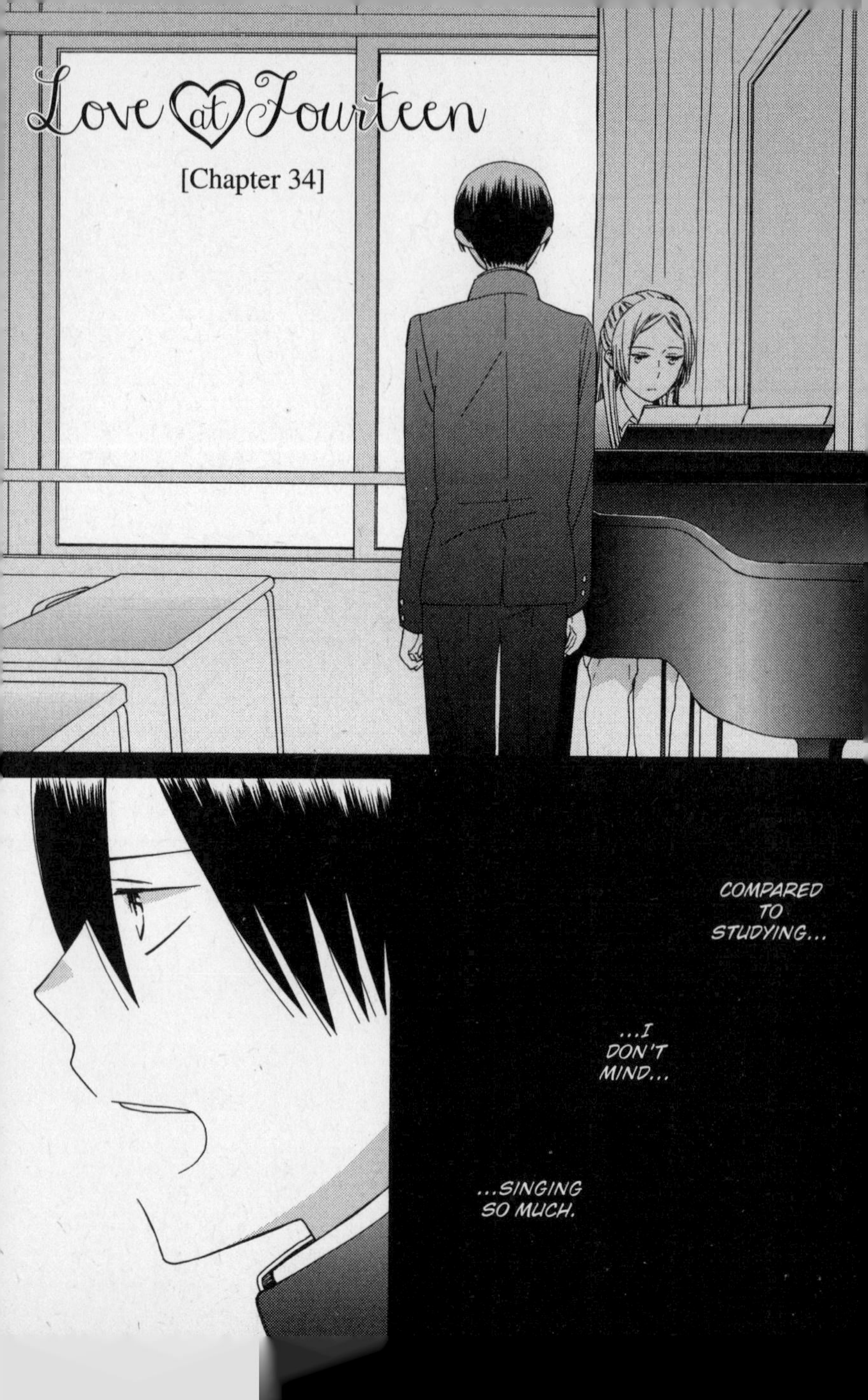
Love at Fourteen
[Chapter 34]
COMPARED TO STUDYING...
...I DON'T MIND...
...SINGING SO MUCH.

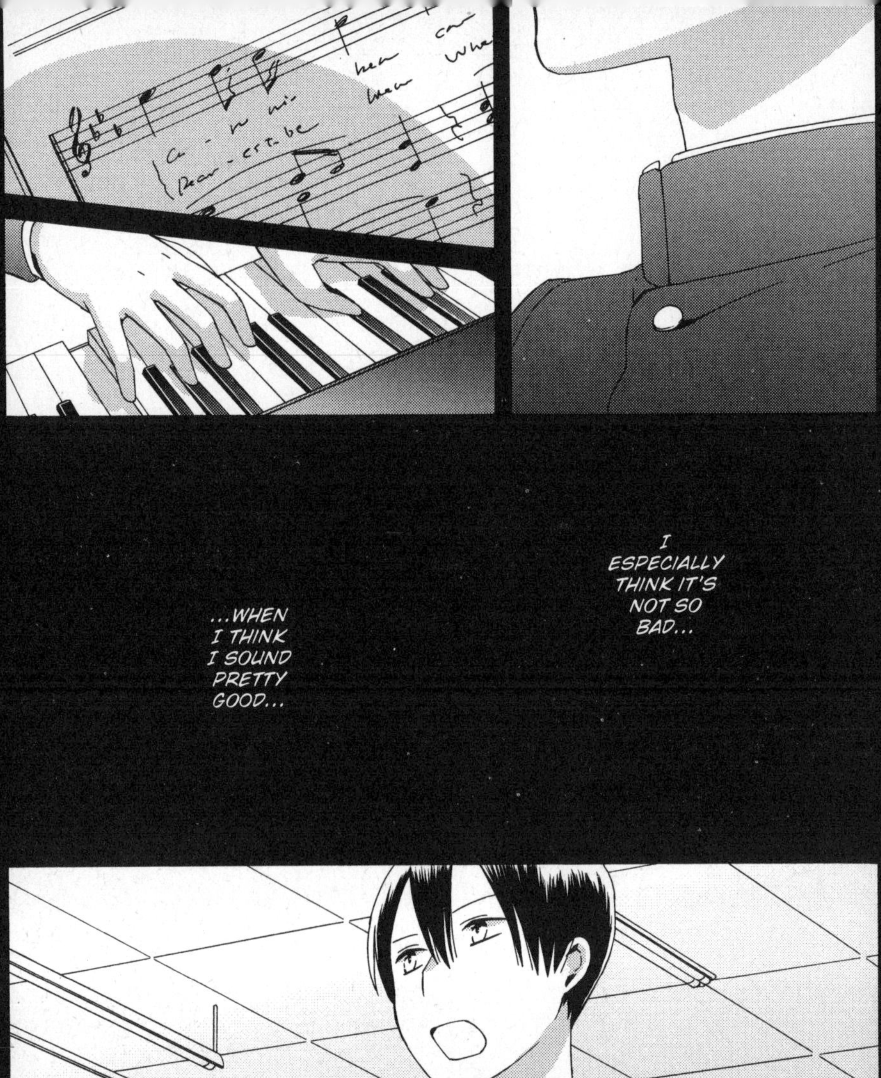
I ESPECIALLY THINK IT'S NOT SO BAD...
...WHEN I THINK I SOUND PRETTY GOOD...

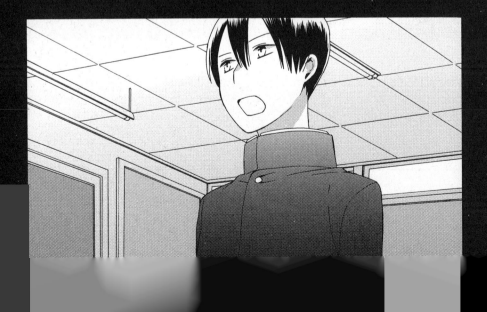

...AND
HER
FACE...

...LOOKS
LIKE
THAT.

Fin

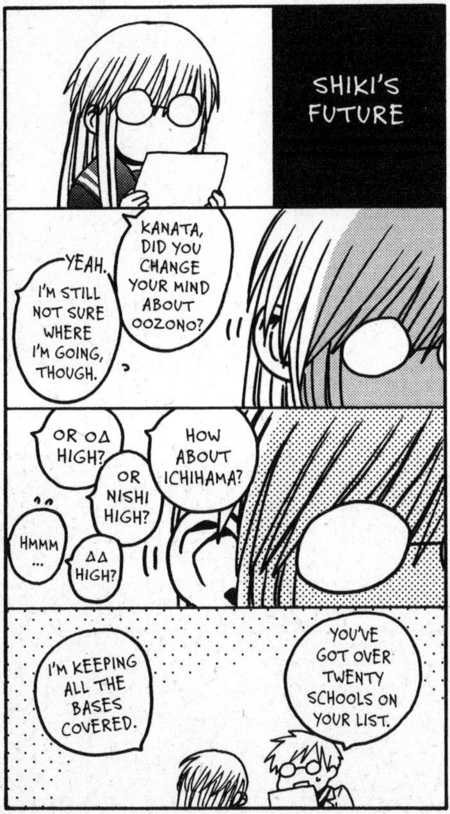
SHIKI'S FUTURE
KANATA, DID YOU CHANGE YOUR MIND ABOUT OOZONO?
YEAH.
I'M STILL NOT SURE WHERE I'M GOING, THOUGH.
HOW ABOUT ICHIHAMA?
OR OΔ HIGH?
OR NISHI HIGH?
ΔΔ HIGH?
HMMM...
YOU'VE GOT OVER TWENTY SCHOOLS ON YOUR LIST.
I'M KEEPING ALL THE BASES COVERED.

Love at Fourteen

Fuka Mizutani

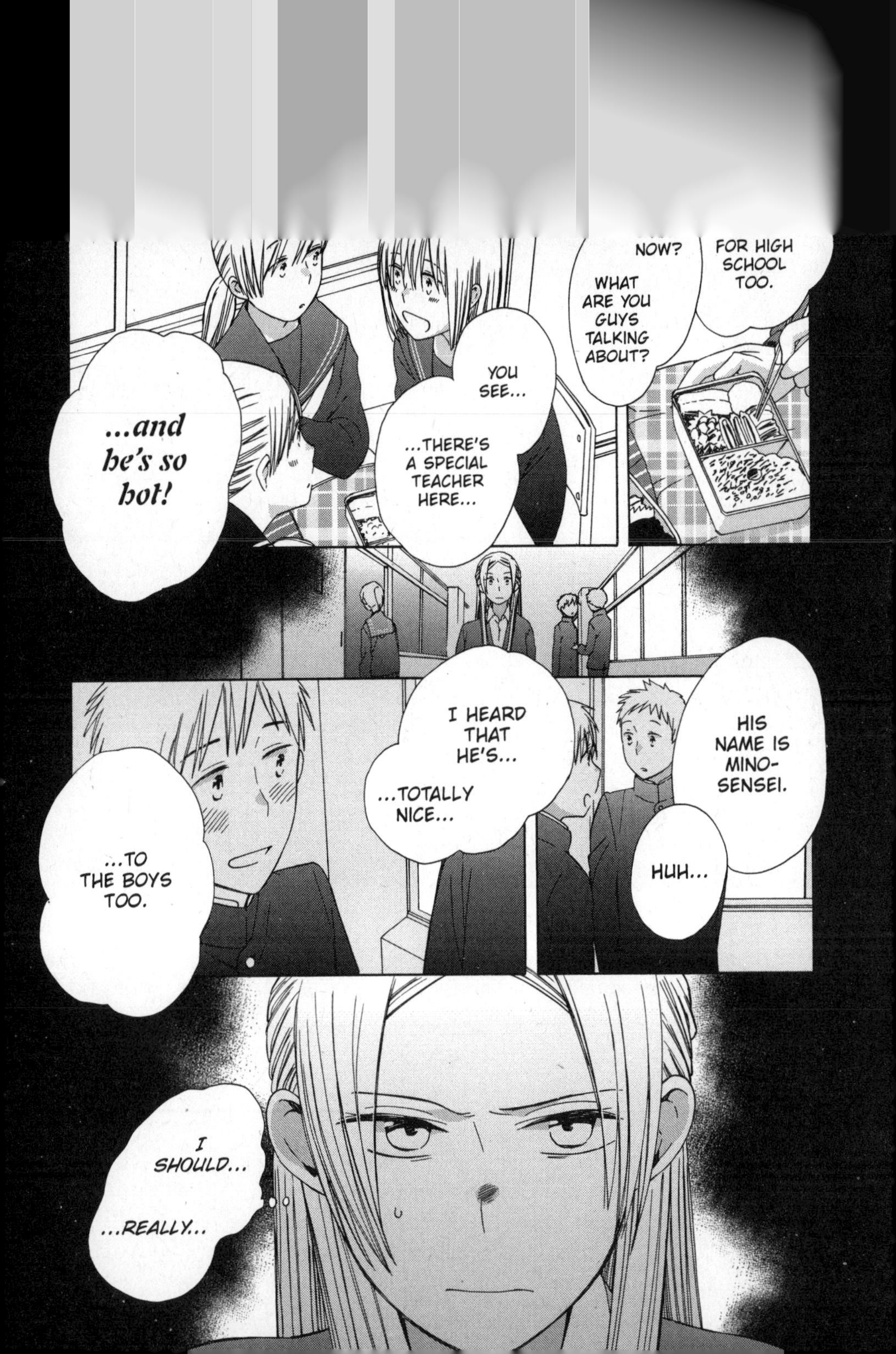
FOR HIGH SCHOOL TOO.
NOW?
WHAT ARE YOU GUYS TALKING ABOUT?
YOU SEE...
...THERE'S A SPECIAL TEACHER HERE...
...and he's so hot!
HIS NAME IS MINO-SENSEI.
HUH...
I HEARD THAT HE'S...
...TOTALLY NICE...
...TO THE BOYS TOO.
I SHOULD...
...REALLY...

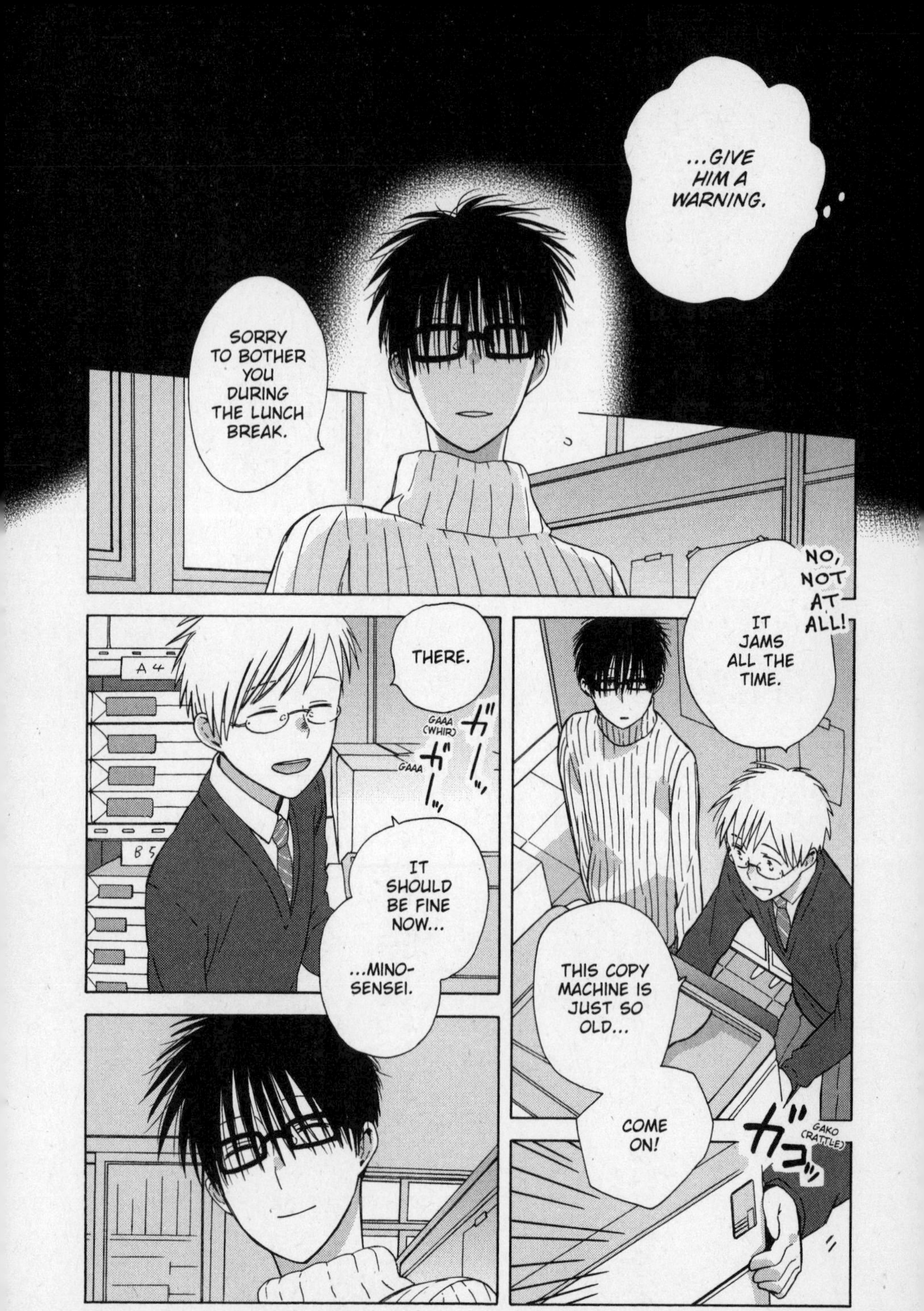
...GIVE HIM A WARNING.
SORRY TO BOTHER YOU DURING THE LUNCH BREAK.
NO, NOT AT ALL!
IT JAMS ALL THE TIME.
THIS COPY MACHINE IS JUST SO OLD...
GAKO (RATTLE)
COME ON!
THERE.
GAAA (WHIR)
GAAA
IT SHOULD BE FINE NOW...
...MINO-SENSEI.

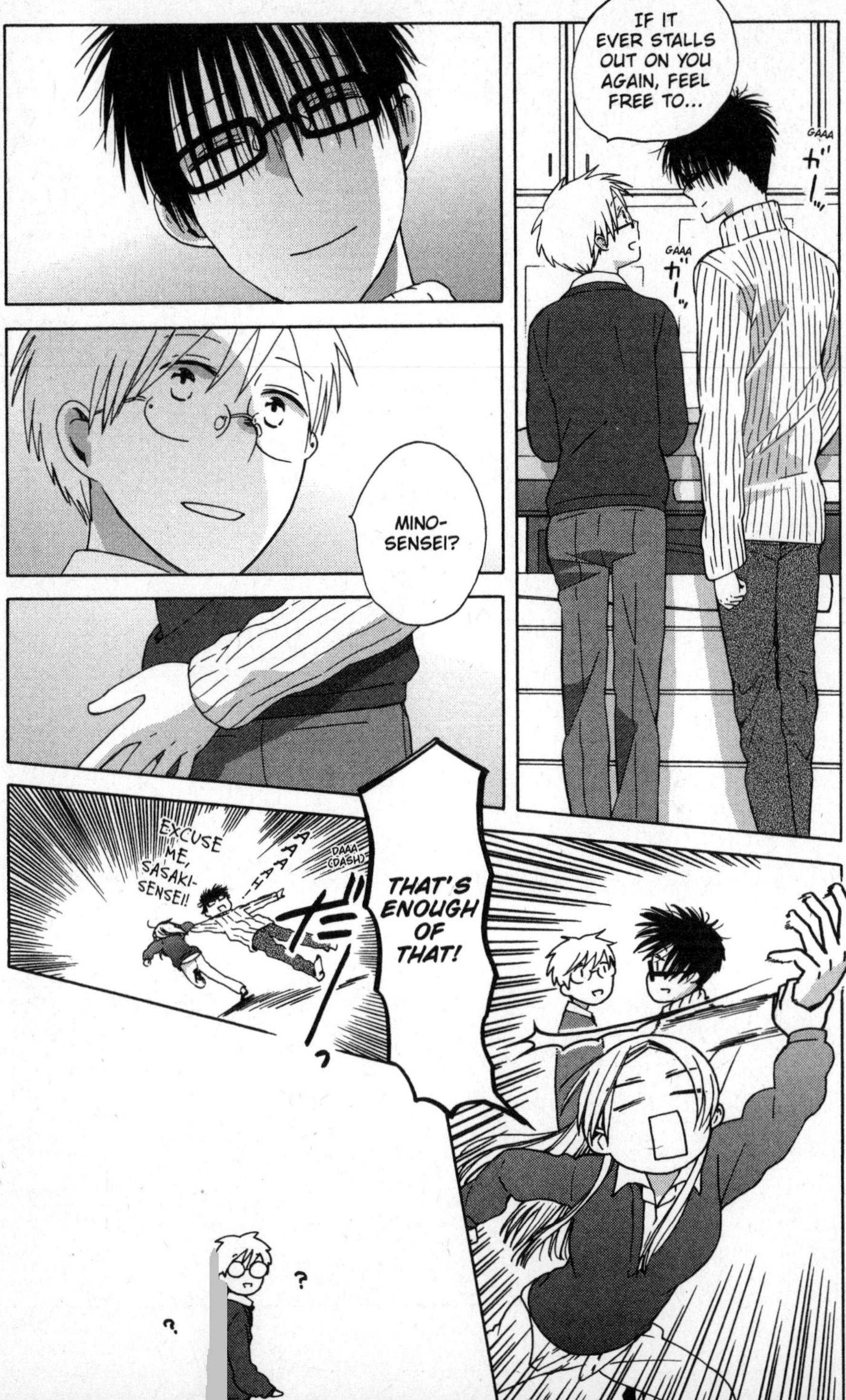
IF IT EVER STALLS OUT ON YOU AGAIN, FEEL FREE TO...
GAAA
GAAA
MINO-SENSEI?
THAT'S ENOUGH OF THAT!
DAAA (DASH)
AAAAH!
EXCUSE ME, SASAKI-SENSEI!

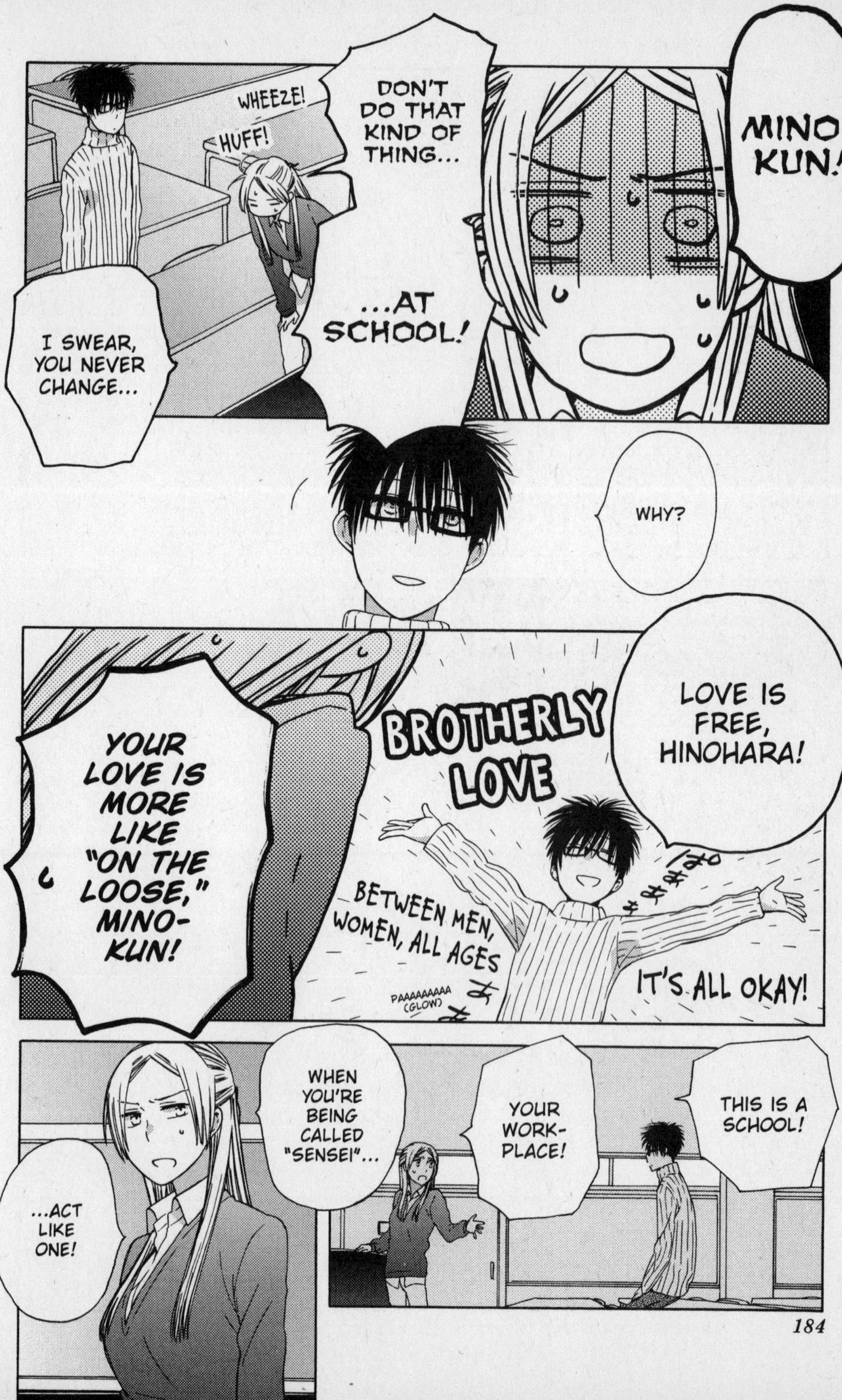
MINO-KUN!
DON'T DO THAT KIND OF THING...
...AT SCHOOL!
WHEEZE!
HUFF!
I SWEAR, YOU NEVER CHANGE...
WHY?
LOVE IS FREE, HINOHARA!
BROTHERLY LOVE
BETWEEN MEN, WOMEN, ALL AGES
IT'S ALL OKAY!
PAAAAAAAAA (GLOW)
YOUR LOVE IS MORE LIKE "ON THE LOOSE," MINO-KUN!
THIS IS A SCHOOL!
YOUR WORK-PLACE!
WHEN YOU'RE BEING CALLED "SENSEI"...
...ACT LIKE ONE!

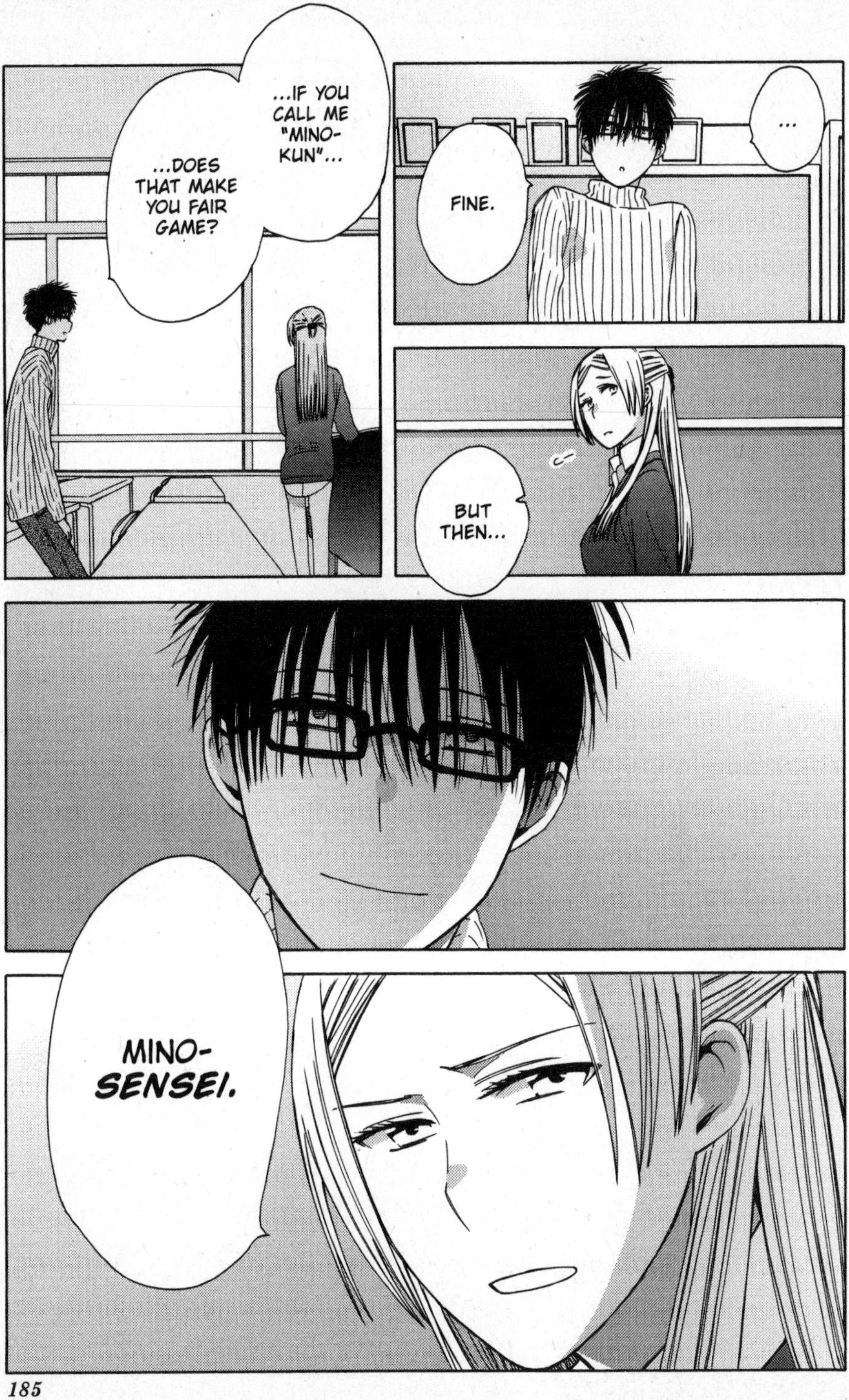
...
FINE.
C-
BUT THEN...
...IF YOU CALL ME "MINO-KUN"...
...DOES THAT MAKE YOU FAIR GAME?
MINO-SENSEI.

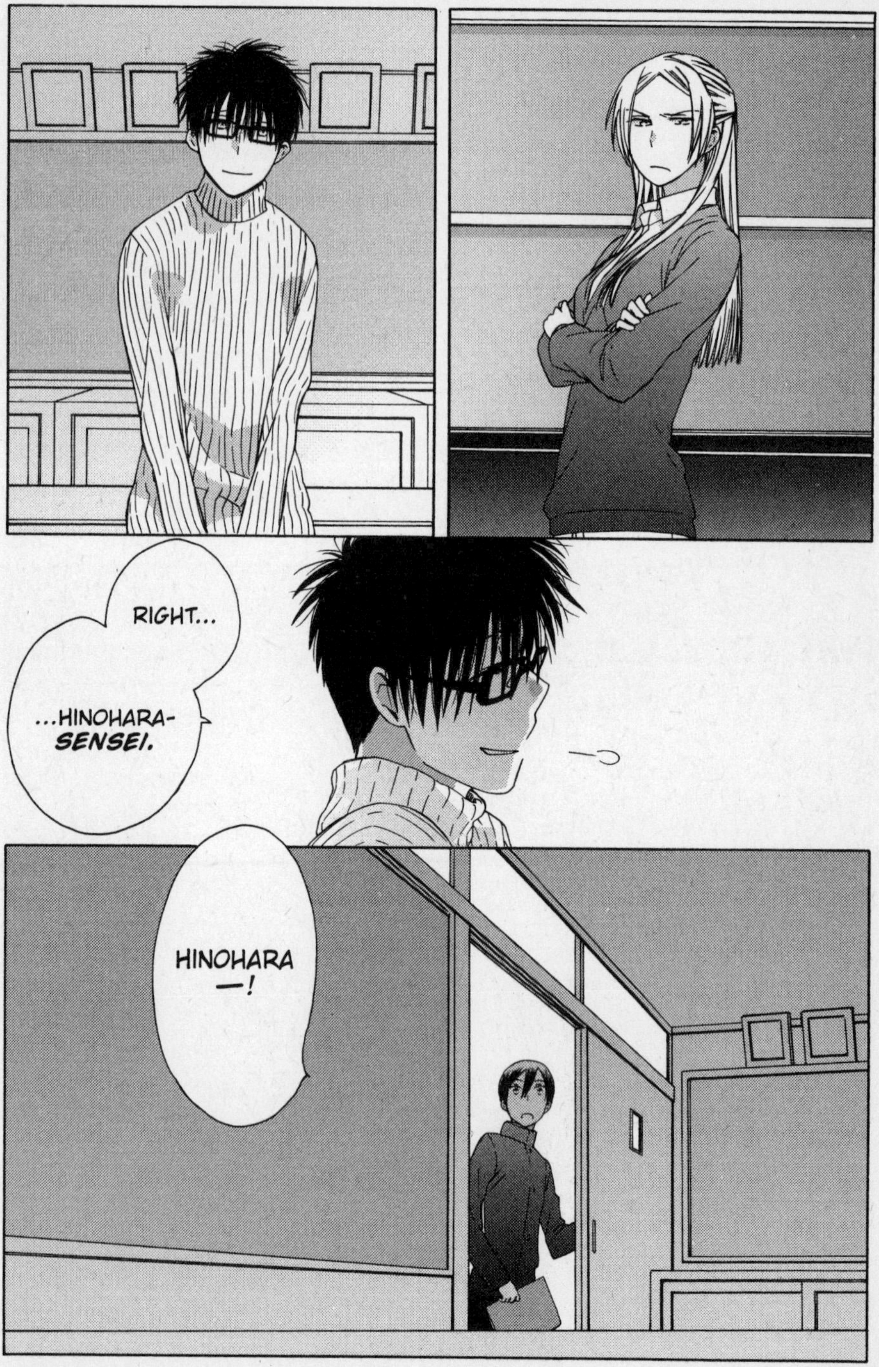
RIGHT...
...HINOHARA-SENSEI.
HINOHARA—!

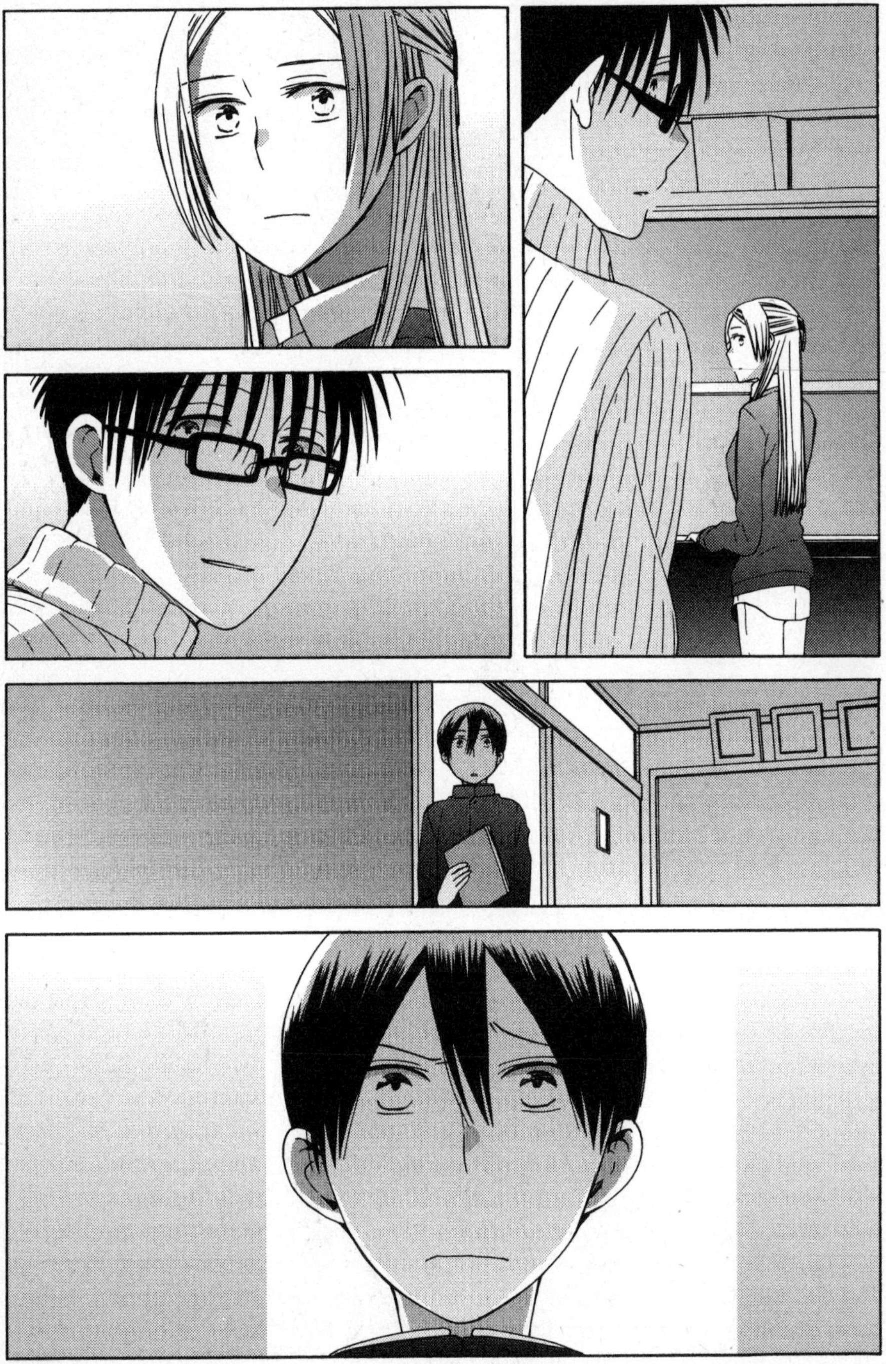

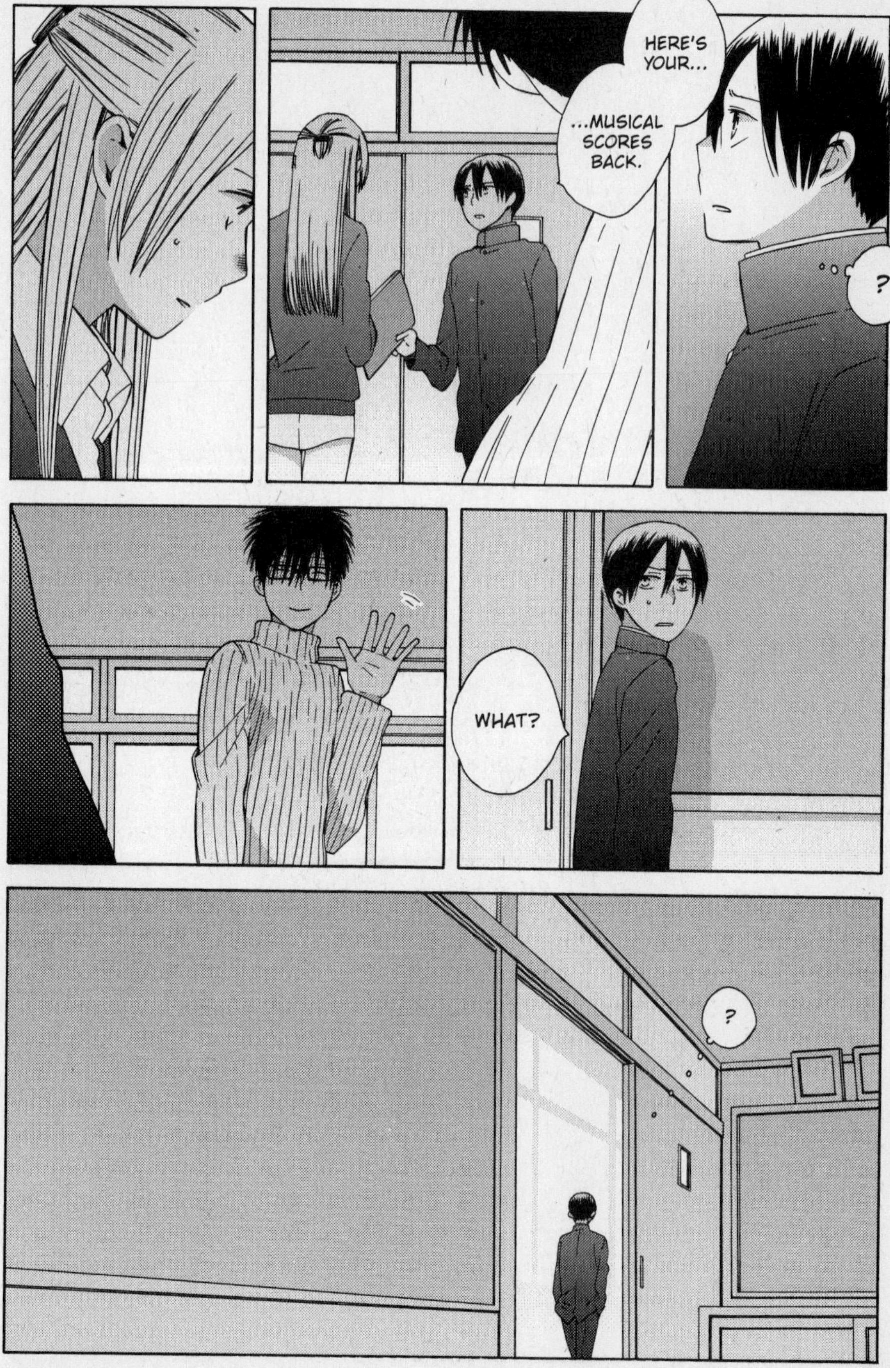
HERE'S YOUR...
...MUSICAL SCORES BACK.
?
WHAT?
?

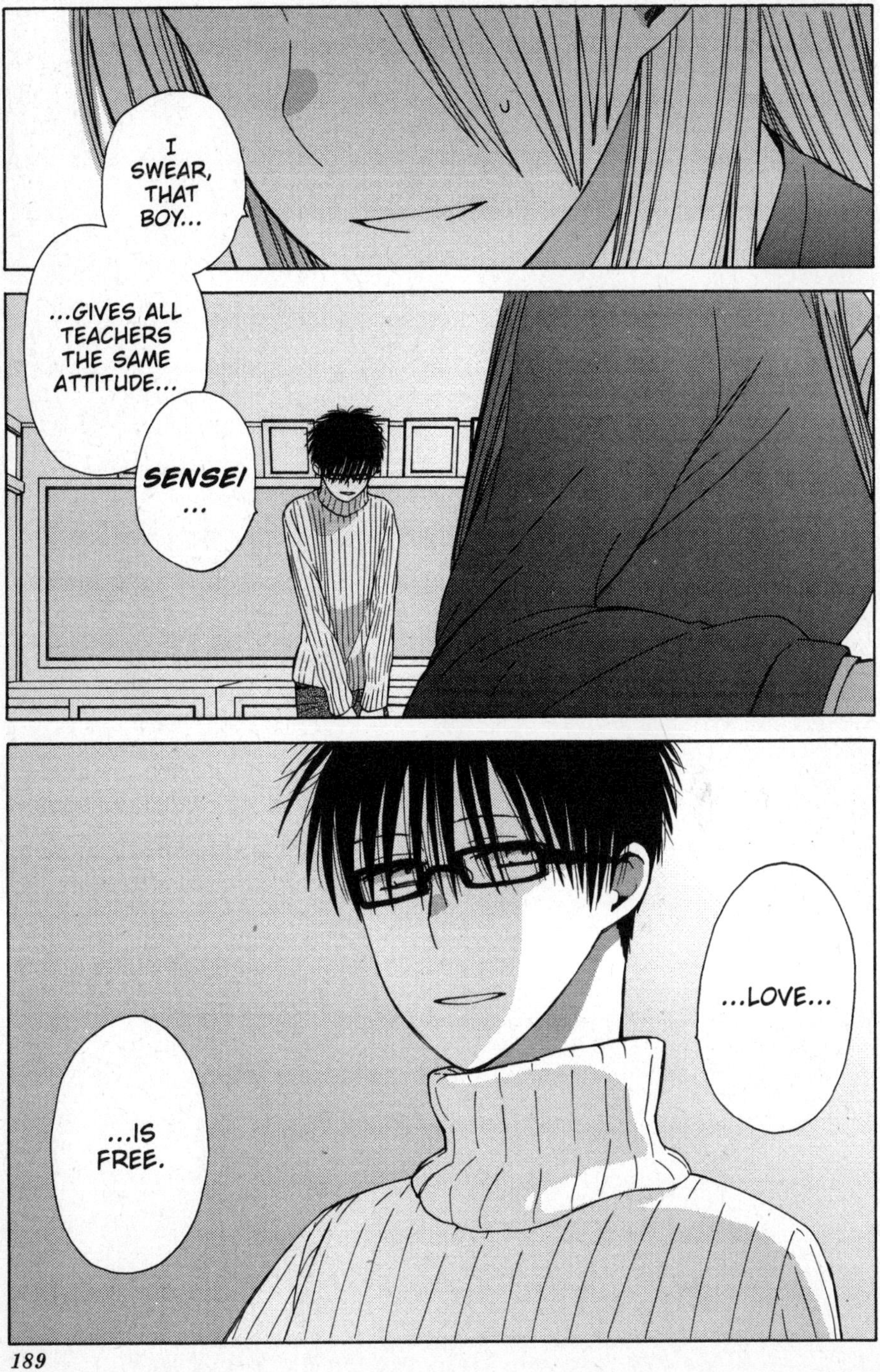
I SWEAR, THAT BOY...
...GIVES ALL TEACHERS THE SAME ATTITUDE...
SENSEI ...
...LOVE...
...IS FREE.

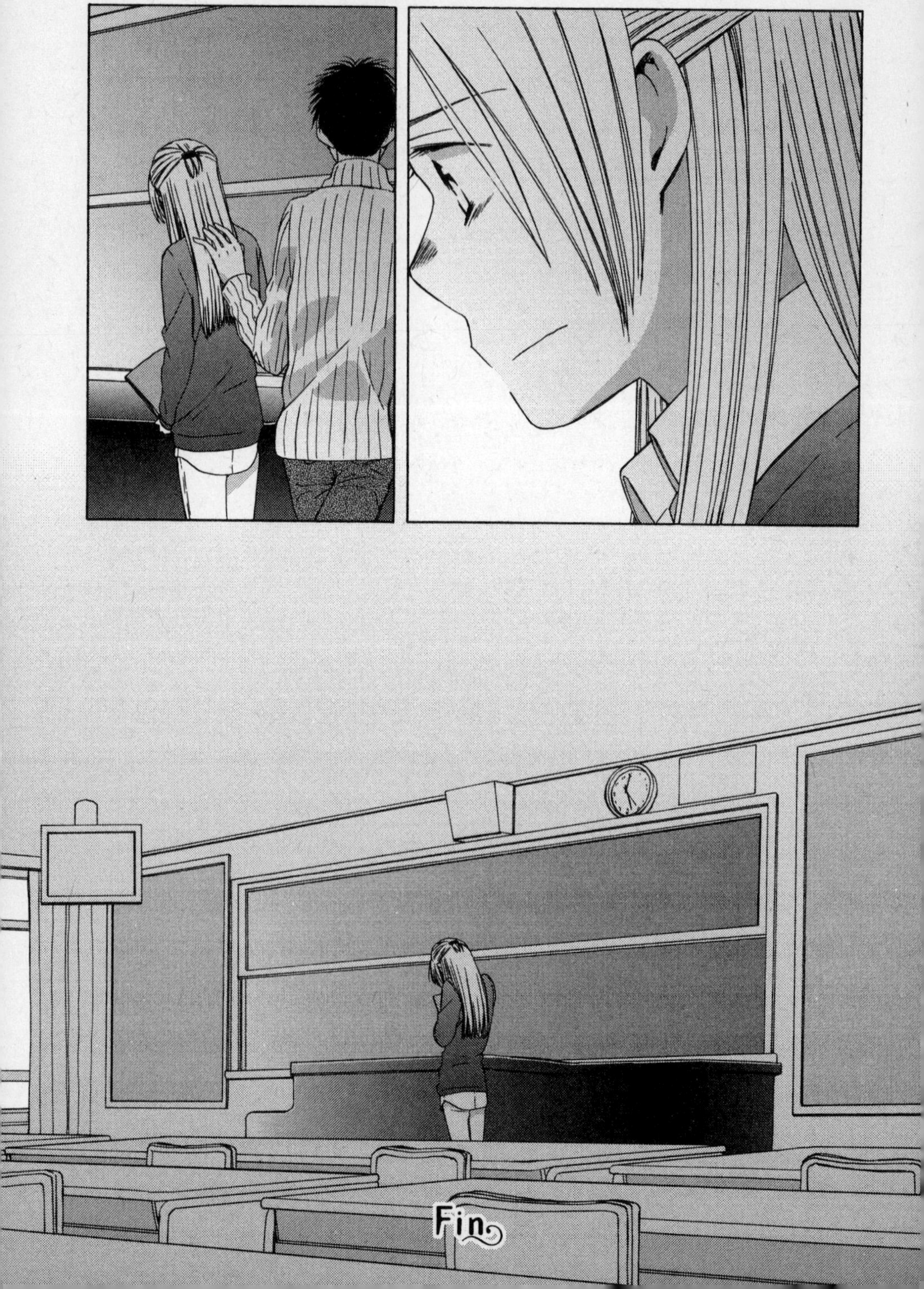
Fin

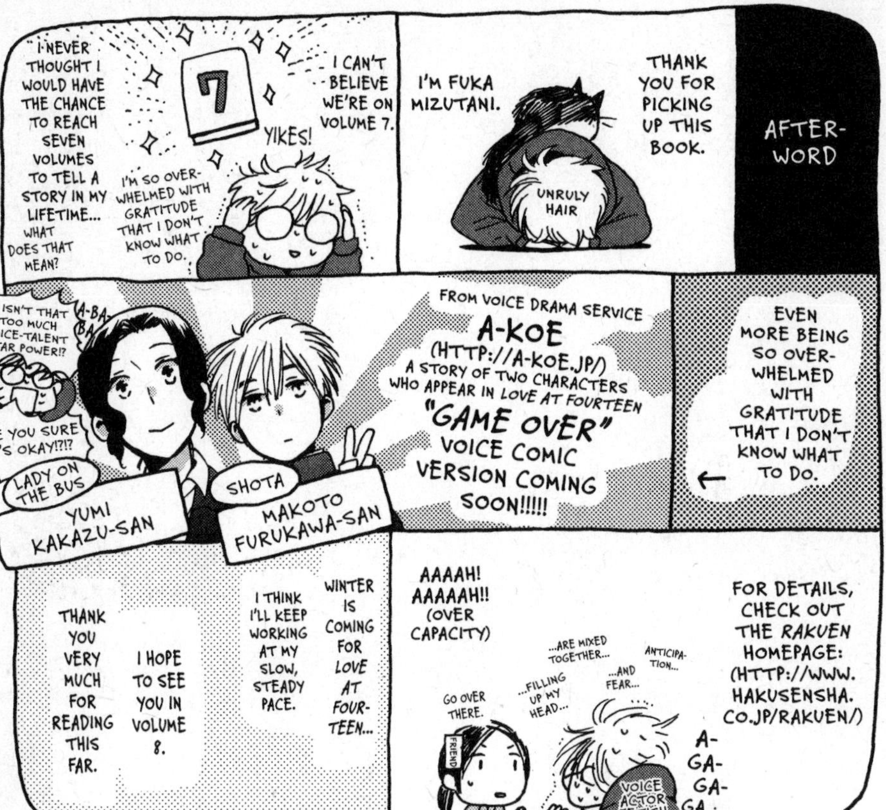
AFTER-WORD
THANK YOU FOR PICKING UP THIS BOOK.
I'M FUKA MIZUTANI.
UNRULY HAIR
I CAN'T BELIEVE WE'RE ON VOLUME 7.
I NEVER THOUGHT I WOULD HAVE THE CHANCE TO REACH SEVEN VOLUMES TO TELL A STORY IN MY LIFETIME...
7
YIKES!
I'M SO OVER-WHELMED WITH GRATITUDE THAT I DON'T KNOW WHAT TO DO.
WHAT DOES THAT MEAN?
EVEN MORE BEING SO OVER-WHELMED WITH GRATITUDE THAT I DON'T KNOW WHAT TO DO.
←
FROM VOICE DRAMA SERVICE
A-KOE
(HTTP://A-KOE.JP/)
A STORY OF TWO CHARACTERS WHO APPEAR IN LOVE AT FOURTEEN
"GAME OVER"
VOICE COMIC VERSION COMING SOON!!!!!
SHOTA
MAKOTO FURUKAWA-SAN
LADY ON THE BUS
YUMI KAKAZU-SAN
A-BA-BA
ISN'T THAT TOO MUCH VOICE-TALENT STAR POWER!?
A-BA-BA-BA-BA-BA
ARE YOU SURE IT'S OKAY!?!?
FOR DETAILS, CHECK OUT THE RAKUEN HOMEPAGE: (HTTP://WWW.HAKUSENSHA.CO.JP/RAKUEN/)
A-GA-GA-GA...
ANTICIPA-TION...
...ARE MIXED TOGETHER...
...AND FEAR...
...FILLING UP MY HEAD...
VOICE ACTOR FETISH
GO OVER THERE.
FRIEND
AAAAH! AAAAAH!! (OVER CAPACITY)
WINTER IS COMING FOR LOVE AT FOUR-TEEN...
I THINK I'LL KEEP WORKING AT MY SLOW, STEADY PACE.
I HOPE TO SEE YOU IN VOLUME 8.
THANK YOU VERY MUCH FOR READING THIS FAR.

Special Thanks

Hakusensha Iida-sama

Kohei Nawata Design

My family

My great friends

Sayo Murata-chan

And all of you who are reading this now

Spring 2017

水谷フーカ
Fuka Mizutani

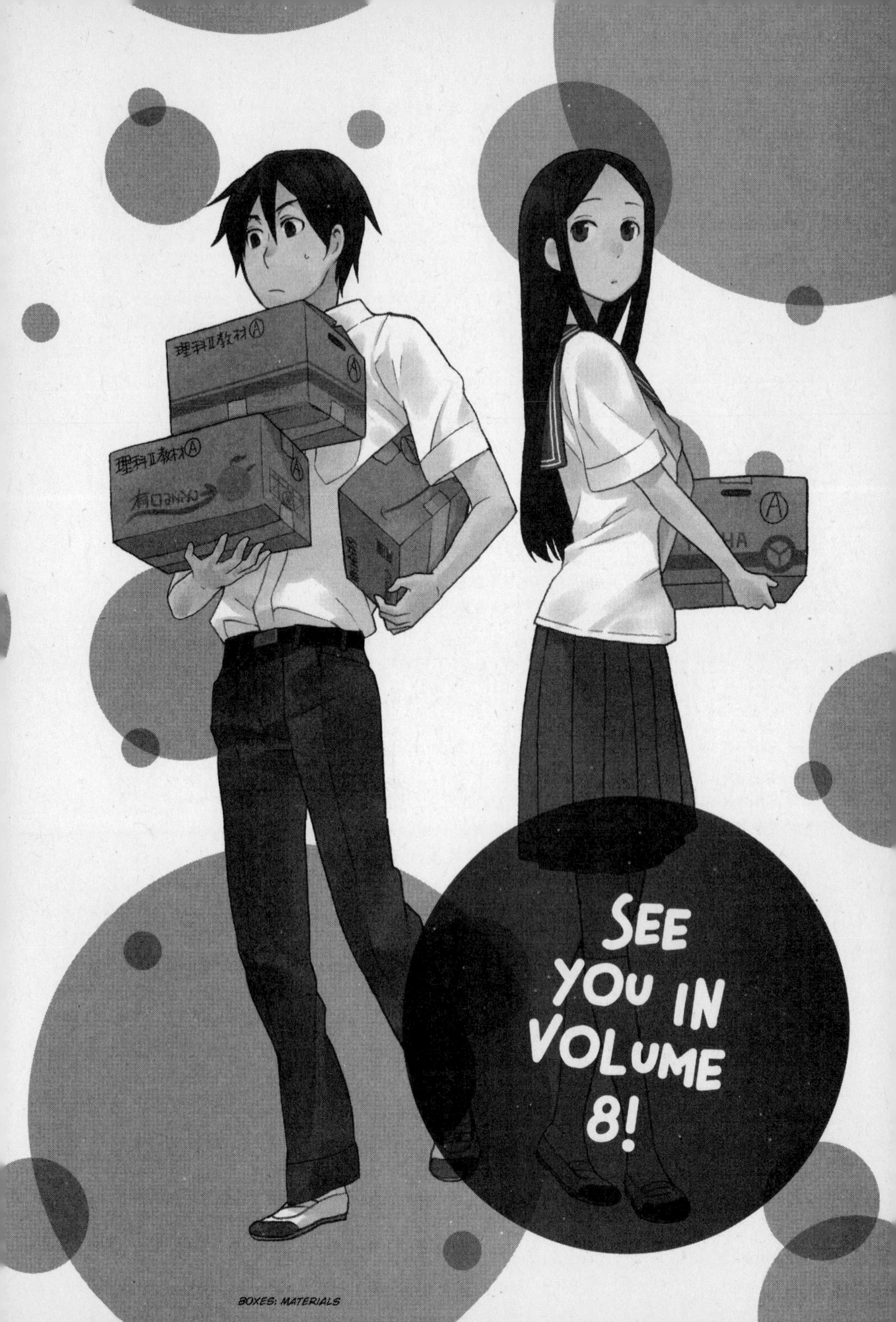
SEE YOU IN VOLUME 8!
BOXES: MATERIALS

TRANSLATION NOTES

COMMON HONORIFICS:
no honorific: Indicates familiarity or closeness; if used without permission or reason, addressing someone in this manner would constitute an insult.
-san: The Japanese equivalent of Mr./Mrs./Miss. If a situation calls for politeness, this is the fail-safe honorific.
-sama: Conveys great respect; may also indicate that the social status of the speaker is lower than that of the addressee.
-kun: Used most often when referring to boys, this indicates affection or familiarity. Occasionally used by older men among their peers, but it may also be used by anyone referring to a person of lower standing.
-chan: An affectionate honorific indicating familiarity used mostly in reference to girls; also used in reference to cute persons or animals of either gender.
-senpai: A suffix used to address upperclassmen or more experienced coworkers.
-sensei: A respectful term for teachers, artists, or high-level professionals.

PAGE 5
The second term: Middle schools and high schools in Japan (each being three years long) generally use a three-term system for the school year, evolving from a two-semester system used back in the 80s.

PAGE 14
Blood type: Using blood type to pin down personalities is a popular (and scientifically dubious) hypothesis in Japan. (A brief rundown: People with blood type-A, the most common kind over there, tend to be uptight workaholics. Type-B: laidback, selfish creatives. Type-AB: A mix of A and B types, exhibiting characteristics of both. Type-O: "O" for optimistic, purportedly make good leaders.)

PAGE 26
Seven Wonders: This genre of urban legends is built around the notion that schools in Japan are hotbeds of eerie supernatural activity. In fact, each school that plays host to paranormal phenomena reputedly has seven separate hauntings or otherwise unexplainable things, such as those in this story (haunted restrooms and extra stairs are common). As is mentioned here, learning all seven "wonders" supposedly causes the enlightened person to be cursed.

PAGE 29
Salt: Placing a small paper origami basket with salt in it in a corner of a room to banish evil and bring good luck is a popular superstition.

PAGE 80
Entering high school: High school isn't mandatory in Japan, nor is it free. Whereas students in the United States generally go to the high school that's closest to them (if public), in Japan, distance to your home is only one factor you would use to determine your high school. It's somewhat similar to going to college, in that students take tests to get into the high school of their choice and, again, have to pay tuition, which is cheaper for public than private. There, too, each high school has a reputation: good, bad, or middle of the road.

PAGE 87
Flight attendant: This is thought of as a prestigious job in Japan, one that is especially suitable for young, attractive, intelligent women.

PAGE 88
T-score: Called *hensachi*, this is the "curve" of students, a score based on a standardized test. A score of 50 is the mean, with every 10 points above that equating one standard deviation above the mean. If Kanata's score is indeed 70, then she's two standards above the mean. In terms of universities, this would make her a shoo-in for everything except perhaps Japan's most prestigious schools, Tokyo University and Kyoto University.

PAGE 128
Seeking employment: Again, high school isn't mandatory, but there, as in the United States, there are not many quality jobs available these days for people without at least a high school diploma.

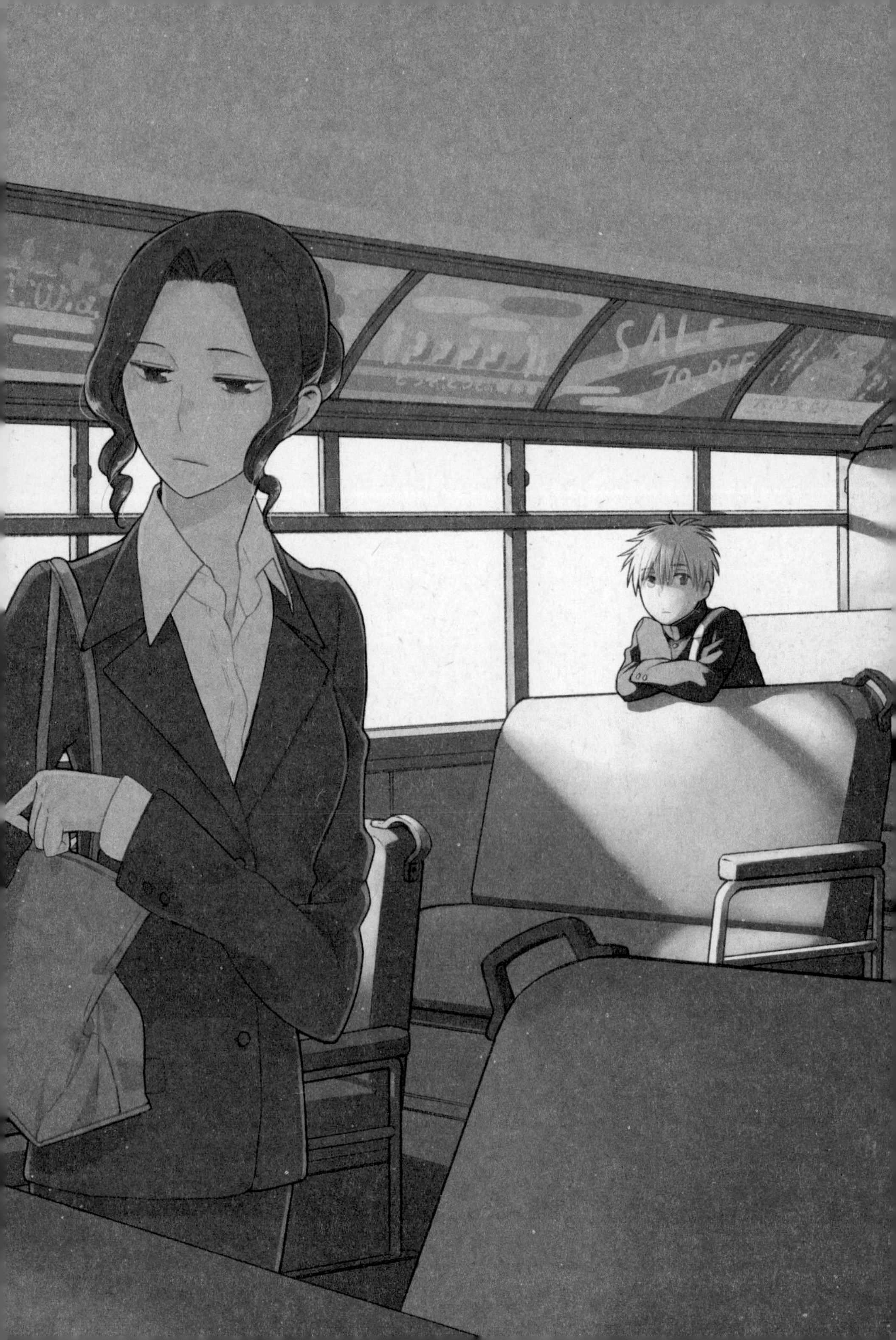
SALE

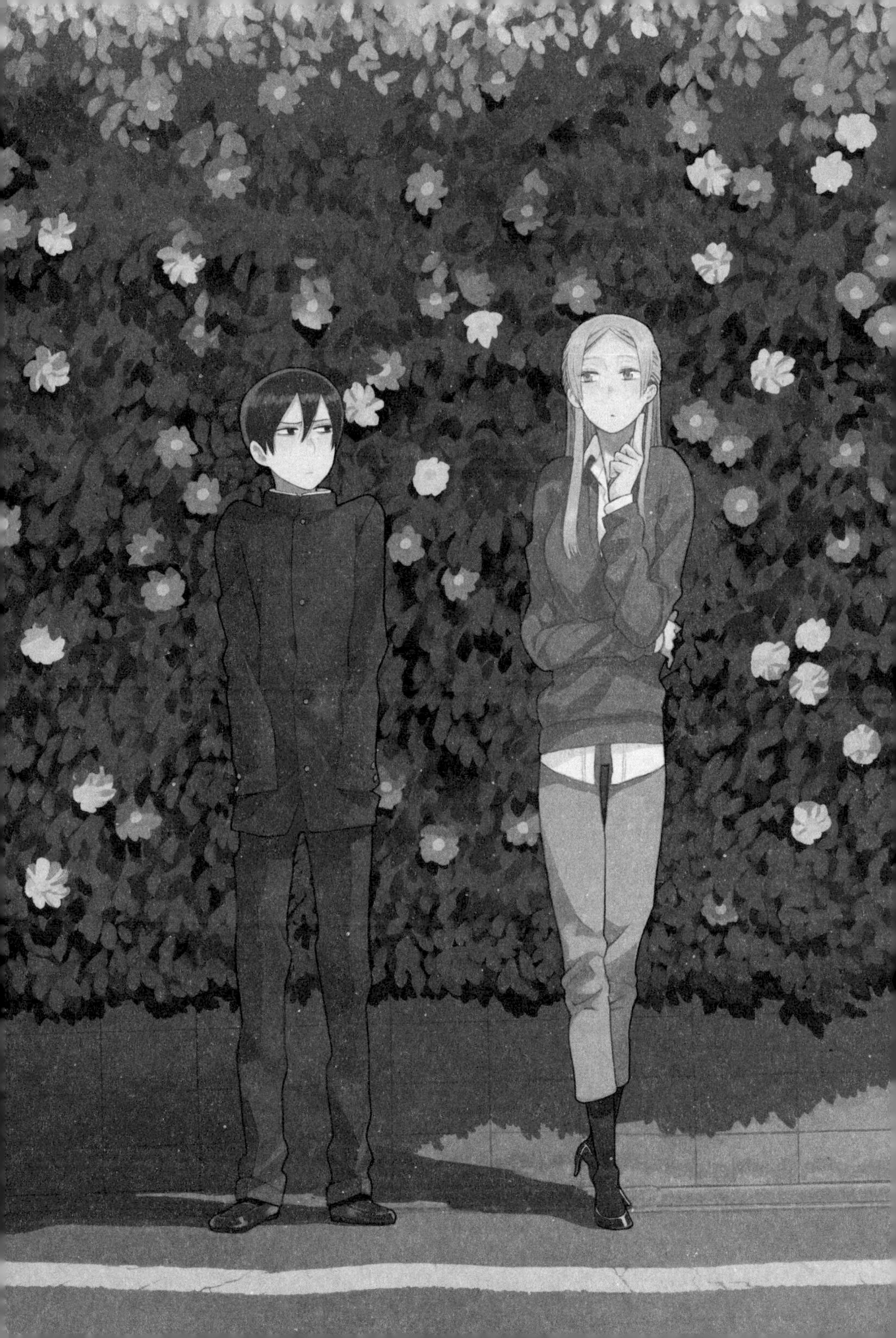

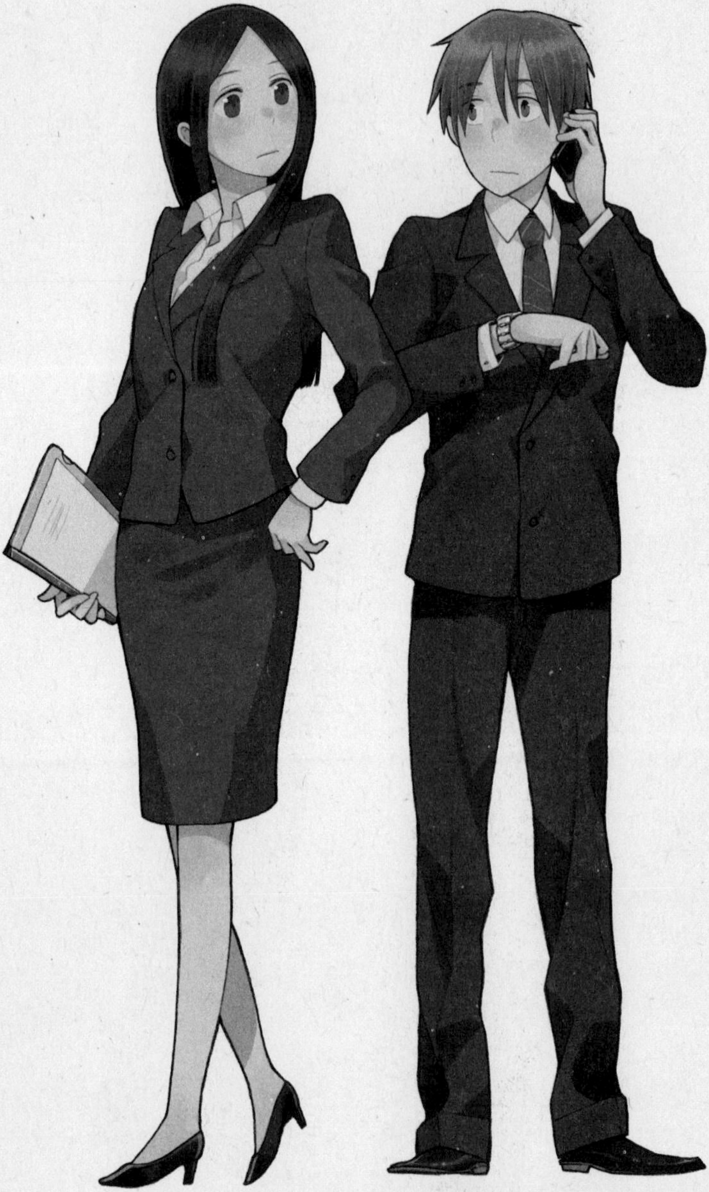

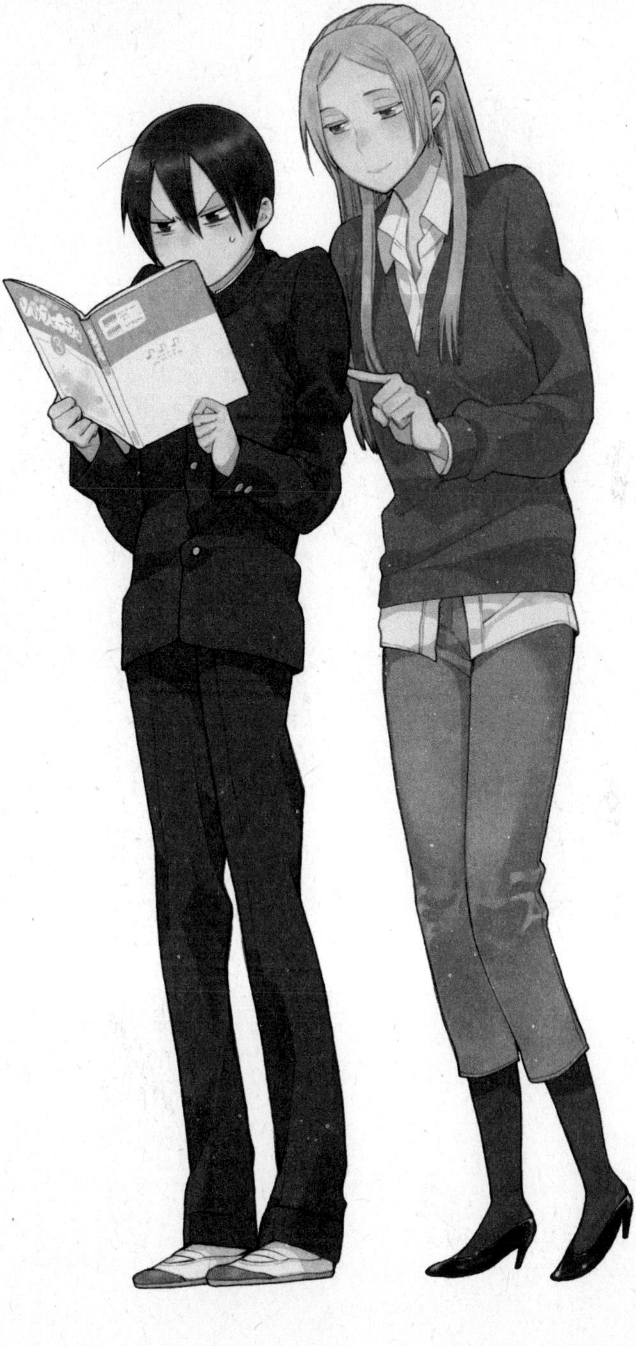

LOVE AT FOURTEEN ⑦

FUKA MIZUTANI

Translation: Sheldon Drzka

Lettering: Lys Blakeslee

This book is a work of fiction. Names, characters, places, and incidents are the product of the author's imagination or are used fictitiously. Any resemblance to actual events, locales, or persons, living or dead, is coincidental.

JUYON-SAI NO KOI by Fuka Mizutani
© Fuka Mizutani 2017
All rights reserved.
First published in Japan in 2017 by HAKUSENSHA, INC., Tokyo.
English language translation rights in U.S.A., Canada and U.K. arranged with
HAKUSENSHA, INC., Tokyo through Tuttle-Mori Agency, Inc., Tokyo.

English translation © 2018 Yen Press, LLC

Yen Press, LLC supports the right to free expression and the value of copyright. The purpose of copyright is to encourage writers and artists to produce the creative works that enrich our culture.

The scanning, uploading, and distribution of this book without permission is a theft of the author's intellectual property. If you would like permission to use material from the book (other than for review purposes), please contact the publisher. Thank you for your support of the author's rights.

Yen Press
1290 Avenue of the Americas
New York, NY 10104

Visit us at yenpress.com
facebook.com/yenpress
twitter.com/yenpress
yenpress.tumblr.com
instagram.com/yenpress

First Yen Press Edition: March 2018

Yen Press is an imprint of Yen Press, LLC.
The Yen Press name and logo are trademarks of Yen Press, LLC.

The publisher is not responsible for websites (or their content) that are not owned by the publisher.

Library of Congress Control Number: 2016297684

ISBNs: 978-1-9753-0008-1 (paperback)
       978-1-9753-2609-8 (ebook)

10 9 8 7 6 5 4 3 2 1

WOR

Printed in the United States of America